Maya Blake's hopes of becoming a writer were born when she picked up her first romance at thirteen. Little did she know her dream would come true! Does she still pinch herself every now and then to make sure it's not a dream? Yes, she does! Feel free to pinch her, too, via Twitter, Facebook or Goodreads! Happy reading!

Clare Connelly was raised in small-town Australia among a family of avid readers. She spent much of her childhood up a tree, Mills & Boon book in hand. Clare is married to her own real-life hero, and they live in a bungalow near the sea with their two children. She is frequently found staring into space—a surefire sign that she's in the world of her characters. She has a penchant for French food and ice-cold champagne, and Mills & Boon novels continue to be her favourite ever books. Writing for Modern is a long-held dream. Clare can be contacted via clareconnelly.com or at her Facebook page.

BOUND BY MY SCANDALOUS PREGNANCY

MAYA BLAKE

REDEMPTION OF THE UNTAMED ITALIAN

CLARE CONNELLY

MILLS & BOON

First Published in Great Britain 2020
by Mills & Boon, an imprint of HarperCollins*Publishers*
1 London Bridge Street, London, SE1 9GF

Bound by My Scandalous Pregnancy © 2020 by Maya Blake

Redemption of the Untamed Italian © 2020 by Clare Connelly

ISBN: 978-0-263-27804-0

MIX
Paper from
responsible sources
FSC® C007454

This book is produced from independently certified FSC™ paper
to ensure responsible forest management.
For more information visit www.harpercollins.co.uk/green.

Printed and bound in Spain
by CPI, Barcelona

BOUND BY MY SCANDALOUS PREGNANCY

MAYA BLAKE

CHAPTER ONE

REINCARNATION. KARMA. SINS coming home to roost.

Once upon a time, in the not-too-distant past, if anyone had asked me if I believed in any of those things I'd have rolled my eyes and told them to get real. That life worked on the amount of effort you put into each day.

On love.

Loyalty.

Hard work.

How wrong I was.

Frozen outside the towering glass and steel offices of one of the most powerful men on the globe, my wrists tingling from the phantom handcuffs that might become real before the hour was out, I wondered which deity I'd wronged to bring me to this end.

Did it even matter that the domino effect of sheer rotten luck mostly had nothing to do with me? Was it worth ranting that the sins of the father shouldn't be visited upon the daughter?

No.

The awful truth was, while the majority of what happened to me in the past few years wasn't my fault, this last, shocking misstep was one hundred percent mine.

Sure, I could prove that a collection of things had culminated in that one gigantic error, but the reality was inescapable. The buck, and the blame, stopped with me.

Time to own it, Sadie.

One more minute, I silently pleaded to whatever higher power held my fate in its cruel grip.

But, adding to every other misfortune unfolding in my life, my plea went unheeded.

The two sharply dressed security guards who'd been

eyeing me with increasing wariness through the imposing glass frontage were heading my way. These days the whole world was on edge. I of all people should know that.

The economy had been partly responsible for decimating the family I once took for granted. The family currently hanging by a very fragile thread.

And dressed in threadbare clothes that were at least five seasons old, my troubled expression reflected in the polished glass, I wouldn't be surprised if I was wrestled to the ground and arrested for trespassing. Or worse.

Disturbingly, that possibility gleamed palatably for a second, attesting to my true state of mind. *Really?* I'd rather be arrested than—

'Excuse me, miss. Can I help you?'

I jumped, my hand flying to my throat to contain the heart beating itself into a frenzy. The burlier of the two guards had stepped through the revolving doors without my noticing and now stood a few feet away. Everything about him promised he could switch from courteous to menacing in a heartbeat.

Definitely time to own it, Sadie.

'I...' I stopped, moved my tongue to wet desert-dry lips. 'I need to see Mr Xenakis. Is he in?'

His eyes narrowed. 'You'll have to ask for him at the reception desk. Do you have an appointment?'

I nearly laughed. How could I make an appointment to confess what I'd done?

'Um, no. But—'

'I think you should leave now, miss.' His tone indicated it wasn't a suggestion.

'Please! It's a matter of life or death.'

He froze. 'Whose life?'

I bit the inside of my lip, afraid I'd overexaggerated things a little. For all I knew, the man I'd wronged wouldn't bat an eyelid at my actions. Truth was, I wouldn't know until I confronted him.

'I… I can't tell you. But it's urgent. And private. If you could just tell me if Mr Xenakis is in?'

For an interminable minute he simply watched me. Then he grasped my elbow. 'Come with me, Miss…?'

I hesitated. Once I gave my name there'd be no going back. But what choice did I have? Either confess and plead my case or wait for the authorities to show up at my door. 'Preston. Sadie Preston.'

With swift efficiency, I was ushered across the stunning atrium of Xenakis Aeronautics, through a series of nondescript doors that led to the bowels of the basement and into a room bearing all the hallmarks of an interrogation chamber.

Hysteria threatened. I suppressed it as the guard muttered a stern, 'Stay here.'

The next twenty minutes were the longest of my life. In direct contrast to the speed with which my life flashed before my eyes after the enormity of what I'd done sank in.

The man who entered the room then was even more imposing, leaving me in no doubt that my request was being taken seriously. And not in a good way.

'Miss Preston?'

At my hesitant nod, the tall, salt-and-pepper-haired man held the door open, his dark eyes assessing me even more thoroughly once I scrambled to my feet.

'I'm Wendell, head of Mr Xenakis's security team. This way,' he said, in a voice that brooked no argument.

Dear God, either Neo Xenakis was super thorough about his interactions with the common man or he was paranoid about his security. Neither boded well.

Another series of incongruous underground hallways brought us to a steel-framed lift. Wendell accessed it with a sleek black key card. Once inside, he pressed another button.

The lift shot up, leaving my stomach and the last dregs of my courage on the basement floor. I wanted to throw myself at the lift doors, claw them open and jump out, consequences be damned. But my feet were paralysed with the unshakeable acceptance that I would only be postponing the inevitable.

Besides, I didn't run from my responsibilities. Not like my father literally had when things got tough. Not like my mother was doing by burying her head in the sand and frivolously gambling away money we didn't have. A habit that had veered scarily towards addiction in the last six months.

I stifled my anxiety as the lift slid to a smooth halt.

One problematic mountain at a time.

This particular one bore all the hallmarks of an Everest climb. One that might only see me to Base Camp before the worst happened.

Not a single member of the sharply dressed staff I'd spotted coming and going downstairs roamed this rarefied space, which boasted the kind of furnishings that graced the expensive designer magazines my mother had avidly subscribed to back when money had been no object for the Prestons. The kind that had always made me wonder if the pictures were staged or if people actually lived like that.

Evidently, they did.

The dove-grey carpeting looked exclusive and expensive, making me cringe as my scuffed, cheap shoes trod over it. Lighter shades of grey silk graced the walls, with stylish lampshades illuminating the space and the twin console tables that stood on either side of the immense double doors.

Made of white polished ash, with handles that looked like gleaming aeroplane wings, everything about them and the glimpse of the expansive conference rooms I could see from where I stood screamed opulence and exclusivity. The type that belonged to owners who didn't take kindly to strangers ruining their day with the sort of news I had to deliver.

Sweat broke out on my palms. Before I could perform the undignified act of rubbing them against the polyester weave of my skirt, Wendell knocked twice.

The voice that beckoned was deep enough to penetrate the solid wood, formidable enough to raise the dread digging its claws into me…and enigmatic enough to send a skitter of…*something else* down my spine.

That unknown quality threatened to swamp all other emotions as Wendell opened the doors. 'You have five minutes,' he informed me, then stepped to one side.

The need to flee resurged. How long would a prison sentence be for this kind of crime, anyway?

Too long. My mother wouldn't survive more upheaval. And with our landlord threatening eviction, the last thing I could afford was more turbulence.

With no choice but to face my fate, I took a shaky step into the office.

And promptly lost every last gasp of air from my lungs at the sight of the man braced against the floor-to-ceiling glass windows, arms crossed and fierce eyes locked on me.

If his surroundings screamed ultraexclusivity and supreme wealth, the man himself was so many leagues above that station, he required his own stratosphere. Even stationary, he vibrated with formidable power—the kind that commanded legions with just one look.

And his body…

The navy suit, clearly bespoke, enhanced the bristling power of his athletic build. Like his impressive six-foot-plus height, his wide tapered shoulders seemed to go on for ever, with the kind of biceps that promised to carry any load rippling beneath the layers of clothes. Above the collar of his pristine white shirt, his square jaw jutted out with unapologetic masculinity, and his pure alpha-ness was not in any way diluted by the dimple in his chin. If anything, that curiously arresting feature only drew deeper attention to the rest of his face. To the haughty cheekbones resting beneath narrowed eyes, his wide forehead and the sensual slash of his lips.

He was…indescribable. Because words like *attractive* or *breathtaking* or even *magnificent* didn't do him nearly enough justice.

And as he continued to appraise me, every last ounce of my courage threatened to evaporate as surely as my breath. Because the way he stared at me, as if he found me as fascinating as I found him, sent a spiralling wave of pure, unadulterated awareness charging through me.

For some inexplicable reason my hair seemed to hold singular appeal for him, making me almost feel as if he was touching the tied back tresses, caressing the strands between his fingers.

The snick of the door shutting made me flinch—a reaction he spotted immediately as his arms dropped and he began to prowl slowly towards me.

Sweet heaven, even the way he moved was spectacular. I'd never truly comprehended the term 'poetry in motion.' Until now.

Focus, Sadie. You're not here to ogle the first billionaire you've ever met.

I opened my mouth to speak. He beat me to it.

'Whoever you are, you seem to have caught Wendell in a good mood. I don't believe he's allowed anyone to walk in off the street and demand to see me in…well, *ever*,' he rasped in a gravel-rolling-in-honey voice, sending another cascade of pure sensation rushing over my skin.

Momentarily thrown by the effect of his voice, I couldn't tell if his tone suggested he'd be having a word with Wendell later about that misstep or if the whole thing simply amused him. He was that enigmatic to read. The mystery stretched my already oversensitive nerves, triggering my babble-when-nervous flaw.

'That was Wendell in a *good* mood? I shudder to think what he's like in a bad mood,' I blurted. Then I cringed harder when the meaning of my words sank in.

Oh, no…

His eyes narrowed even further as he stopped several feet away from me. 'Perhaps you'd like to move whatever this is along?'

Impatience coated his tone even as his eyes raked a closer inspection over my body, pausing on the frayed thinness of my blouse, the slightly baggy cut of my skirt following my recent weight loss, before dropping to my legs. The return journey was just as sizzling. Hell, more so.

That stain of inadequacy, of not being worthy—which had dogged me from the moment my father's abscondment-announcing postcard had landed on the front doormat, in shocking synchronicity with the bailiff's arrival on our doorstep eight years ago—flared like a fever.

I didn't need one of my mother's magazines to tell me that this man didn't meddle with the likes of me…*ever*.

It was in every delicious frame of his impeccable body, every measured exhalation and every flicker of those sooty, spiky eyelashes that most women would pay hundreds to replicate. He would date socialites with faultless pedigree. Heiresses with flawless bone structure who listed royalty as close friends.

Not the callously abandoned daughter of a disgraced middle-grade financier and an almost-addicted gambler, whose only nod to the arts was learning how to execute a half-decent jeté in year-five ballet.

'Or do you feel inclined to use your five minutes in melo-dramatic silence?' he drawled.

The realisation that I'd been gaping at him brought a spike of embarrassment. 'I'm not being melodramatic.'

One brow hiked, and his gaze scanned me from top to toe again before his face slowly hardened.

'You stated that you needed to see me as a matter of life or death, but between the time you set foot in my building and your arrival in my office I've ascertained that every member of my family is safe and accounted for. My em-ployees' well-being will take longer, and a lot of manpower to establish, so if I'm being pranked I'd caution you to turn around and leave right now—'

'This isn't about your present family. It's about your future one.'

He turned to stone. A quite miraculous thing since he was such a big, towering force of a man whose aura threw off electric charges. His ability not to move a muscle would have been fascinating to watch if I hadn't been terrified of the look in his eyes. The one that promised chaos and doom.

'Repeat that, if you please.'

I couldn't. Not if I valued my life.

'I… Perhaps I need to start from the beginning.'

A single clench to his jaw. 'Start *somewhere*. And fast. I'm not a patient man, Miss Preston. And I'm about to be late for an important meeting.'

My rib-banging heart rate shuddered in terror.

My life flashed before my eyes. *Again.*

I pushed away disturbingly bleak images of a life unfulfilled and dreams dashed. Curled my sweaty fists tighter and cleared my throat.

'My name is Sadie Preston…' When that only prompted a higher arch of his brow I hurried on. 'I work…*worked* at the Phoenix Clinic.'

Right until I was summarily fired, three hours ago. But the problem of my unemployment would have to be addressed later. Provided I didn't end up in jail—

My train of thought screeched to a halt as he rocked forward, slid his hands into his trouser pockets and brought muscular thighs into singeing relief. Time pulsed by in silence as the very masculine stance ramped up the heat running through me.

'For your sake, I hope this isn't some sort of misguided attempt to garner employment, because I can assure you—'

'It's not!' My interruption was much more shrill than I'd intended. And I knew immediately that neither it nor my tone had gained me any favours. Hell, his imposing presence seemed to loom even larger in the vast office, his aura terrifying. 'Please…if you would just hear me out?'

'*You're* the one who seems to be tongue-tied, Miss Preston. While *my* precious time bleeds away. So let me make this easy for you. You have one minute to state your business. I advise you to make it worthwhile, for both our sakes.'

Or what?

For a single moment I feared I'd blurted the words, the volatile mix of annoyance and trepidation having finally broken me. But he didn't seem any more incandescent. Simply terribly hacked off at my continued delay in spilling the beans.

'I was fired this morning because…' *pause, deep breath* '…because I accidentally destroyed your…' I squeezed my eyes shut. When I opened them, he was still there, breathtaking and immovable as a marble statue.

Firm, sensually curved lips flattened. 'My what?' he demanded tersely.

Tension vibrated through me as I forced my vocal cords to work. 'I destroyed…your…your stored sperm sample.'

For a horribly tense minute he simply stared at me with utter confusion—as if he couldn't quite comprehend my words—and then that face that defied description tautened into a mask of pure, cold disbelief.

'You. Did. What?'

It wasn't shouted. Or whispered. It was even toned. And absolutely deadly.

I shivered from head to toe, severely doubting my ability ever to speak again as I opened my mouth and words failed to emerge.

Terrifying seconds ticked away as we stood in rigid silence, gazes locked.

'Speak,' he commanded, again without so much as any inflexion in his voice. His lips had gone white with grim fury and he was barely breathing.

I prised my tongue from the roof of my mouth. To do what I'd come here to do. Appeal to his better nature.

Taking a hesitant step towards him, I tried a small smile. 'Mr Xenakis—'

One hand erupted from his pocket in a halting motion. 'Do not attempt to cajole. Do not attempt to prevaricate. I want the facts. Bare and immediate.'

This time his voice had altered. It was a primordial rumble. Like the nape-tingling premonition before a cataclysmic event.

My smile evaporated. 'When I arrived at work this morning...' *late because of my mother and another futile attempt to get through to her* '... I was given a list of samples to dispose of. I... It's not part of my job description, but—'

'What is your *actual* job at the Phoenix Clinic?' The barest hint of an accent had thickened his voice, making him impossibly sexier.

'I'm a receptionist.'

It was the only half-decent paying job I could find that would support my mother and me until I figured out a way to help her out of her dark tunnel of despair and resume the marketing degree I'd suspended so I could care for her.

'And what business does a receptionist have handling patient samples?'

His tone was a chilling blade of reason. He wasn't furious. Not yet, anyway. Right now Neo Xenakis was on a cold, fact-finding mission.

I managed to answer. 'It's not the usual procedure, but we were severely short-staffed today and the list I was given stated that the samples had already been triple-checked.'

'Obviously not. Or you wouldn't be here, would you?' he rasped.

A wave of shame hit me. My error could have been avoided if I hadn't been so frazzled. If I hadn't been worried that my mother and I were about to lose the roof over our heads. If my boss's medical secretary hadn't called in sick, leaving *me* as temporary—and infinitely unlucky—cover.

About to attempt another pleading of my case, I froze when a loud buzz sounded from his desk.

For the longest time he stared at me, as if trying to decipher whether or not everything I'd told him was some sort of hoax.

When the intercom sounded again, he strode to his desk with unbridled impatience. 'Yes?' he grated.

'There's a Spencer Donnelly on the line for you, sir. He says it's urgent.'

My breath caught. He heard it and speared me with narrow-eyed speculation. To his assistant, he said, 'I don't believe I know a Spencer Donnelly. Who is he?'

I stepped forward, earning myself more intense scrutiny. 'That's my boss. My ex-boss, I mean. I think he's calling you to explain.'

And most likely to ensure the blame stayed squarely on my shoulders.

Neo hit the mute button. 'Is he responsible for what happened?' he demanded from me.

'Not…not directly. But he's the head of the clinic—'

'I don't care what his role is. I care about who's directly responsible. Are you saying it was you and you alone?'

My nape heated at the imminent fall of the axe, but seeing as there was nothing more I could do but admit my total culpability, I nodded. 'Yes. It was my fault.'

His nostrils flared as he unmuted the line. 'Take a message,' he informed his assistant, then sauntered back to where I stood.

For another stomach-churning minute he pinned me beneath his gaze. 'Tell me what your intention was in coming here, Miss Preston,' he invited silkily.

His even voice did not soothe me for one second. Whatever his reason for depositing a sperm sample at a fertility clinic, the consequences of my mistake would be brutal.

Alternate heat and cold flashed through my veins. I would have given everything I owned to be able to flee from his presence. But, seeing as fate and circumstance had already taken everything from me, leaving me with very little of value…

'I thought you deserved to hear the truth from me. And also my a-apology,' I said, my throat threatening to close up at the look on his face.

He said nothing, simply waited for several seconds before he elevated that characterful eyebrow, his silent sarcasm announcing that I hadn't actually proffered any apology.

I cursed the heat rushing gleefully into my face at his icy mockery as he saw what he was doing to me. 'I… I'm sorry, Mr Xenakis. I didn't mean to destroy your property. If there was a way to undo it, I would…' I stopped, knowing the words were useless. There was no reversing what I'd done.

'And I'm simply to let you off the hook, am I? Based on you doing the honourable thing by coming here to throw yourself on my mercy?'

What could I say to that? 'I know it's a lot to ask, but I promise I didn't mean to.'

His gaze dropped and I caught the faintest shake of his head as a wave of disbelief flared over his face again. For the longest time he stared at the carpet, his jaw clenching and unclenching as he fought whatever emotion gripped him so tightly.

In that moment, my senses wanted to do the unthinkable and put myself in his shoes—but, no. I couldn't afford to get emotionally carried away.

If, by some cruel twist of fate, there was something wrong with Neo Xenakis's reproductive equipment, wouldn't he have seemed a little…*desolate*, somehow, instead of looking as if he could go toe to toe with Zeus? And win?

Several expressions flitted across his features, too fast to decipher. But when he lifted his gaze to mine once more, chilling premonition swept over me.

Mr Donnelly had known I wouldn't be let off scot-free, which was why he'd insisted I be the first in the line of fire in admitting culpability. The hurried internet search I'd done on the bus ride into the city had left me reeling at the enormity of the adversary I'd unwittingly created with one fatalistic click of the mouse.

Neo Xenakis regarded me with the flat coldness of a cobra about to strike. 'You *didn't mean to*? That applies when you tread on someone's foot. Or accidentally spill your coffee at an inopportune moment. Correct me if I'm wrong, but the Phoenix Clinic has a stringent set of checks in place, does it not?'

I opened my mouth to answer, but he was shaking his head, already rejecting my confirmation.

'Whatever you thought was going to happen with your coming here, I'm afraid it won't be that easy, Miss Preston.'

'What do you mean?'

God, did he want me to beg? Fall on my face and prostrate myself before him?

The weirdest thought entered my head. That however he intended me to pay, it would be welcome. Perhaps even a little…*life-changing*.

When his gaze dropped to my parted lips I entertained the notion, while staring at his mouth, that whatever those reparations were they would be *carnal* in nature. That I would perhaps even…*enjoy* it.

Sweet heaven, Sadie. What's wrong with you?

Dragging my focus from the lush curve of his lips, I met his gaze—only to find the grey depths alight with the same blaze that singed my blood.

Abruptly he turned away, returned to his desk and picked up a sleek-looking tablet. 'Willa, please come in.'

Confusion mingled with those peculiar feelings rioted through me, rendering me speechless as the door opened and a stylishly dressed blonde entered. The woman was more suited to traipse down a runway than give executive assistance. The dismissive glance she threw me before sashaying her way to her boss's desk said she was well aware of her assets.

'Yes, Mr Xenakis.' Unsurprisingly, her voice dripped with sensual interest as she smiled at him.

Curbing my instant dislike for Willa, I listened to them exchange a low-voiced conversation about his upcoming meeting before he rounded his desk.

'Escort Miss Preston to my penthouse. She's to stay there until I'm done with my meeting. If she attempts to leave, inform Wendell.'

My irritation at being discussed as if I wasn't there doubled at the edict he'd just delivered. 'What? You can't... I won't just stay here at your whim!'

The fury he'd kept at bay finally flared into singeing life. 'You've destroyed my property, Miss Preston, making your actions a crime. Attempt to leave and I'll be forced to let the authorities handle it. You have two options. Stay and discuss this further, after my meeting. Or leave and face the consequences.' He strode towards the door, throwing over his shoulder, 'I'll let you inform Willa of your decision.'

Then he was gone.

I veered towards the windows, hoping for a ray of enlightenment. But the typical English weather had greyed in complete alignment with my circumstances.

I couldn't leave. Not unless I wanted to risk worsening my situation.

Neo Xenakis was in shock, still grappling with the news. Would he show mercy when he'd calmed down? Was I better off handing myself over to the authorities and pleading my case with a lawyer through the courts?

With what funds? Even before I lost my job we were barely scraping by. I didn't have the resources to pay a lawyer for even ten minutes of his time!

I was better off waiting. Perhaps talking him round to getting him to return to the clinic to deposit another sample...

Willa's pointed throat-clearing triggered a wince. Turning, I lifted my chin and met her contemptuous stare.

'I'll stay,' I announced, with as much firmness as I could manage, considering my stomach had gone into a thousand-foot free fall.

CHAPTER TWO

RETREAT. REGROUP.

For the dozenth time in what felt like the longest afternoon of my life, I shook my head.

'You don't agree, Mr Xenakis?'

I refocused on the leader of the Brazilian marketing team gathered around the conference table and wondered what I'd missed while my brain was stuck in that endless cycle of life-altering words uttered by the most captivating creature I'd ever seen.

I'm sorry... I've destroyed...everything.

To think I'd been convinced she was pranking me. Or, even more amusing, that she had latched on to an inventive method of getting my attention, since most feminine ploys left me cold these days.

My steep drop in interest in the opposite sex hadn't gone unnoticed in recent years. Socialites who'd smugly decided they were an integral part of my healing process were scratching their heads, wondering why I'd permanently lost their numbers. Heiresses who'd eagerly and blatantly sought an alliance with the newly *un*engaged Xenakis bachelor were left stunned as every avenue of contact was firmly rebuffed.

It hadn't even been worth the time to inform them that the thrill of the chase had stopped being, well...*thrilling.* That the eighteen months I'd spent sowing every wild oat I could had left me ashen mouthed and even more jaded than I'd been when I woke up in that hospital to the cruellest betrayal.

To think I'd imagined *that* was the worst moment of my life.

The stark reality of Sadie Preston's presence in my penthouse—as per Willa's confirmation, minutes ago—attested to that moment having well and truly been usurped.

Was this how my brother Axios had felt when presented with the noose-like proposition he'd faced almost a year ago?

No, Ax's sentence was finite. It would end…or rather should have been ending in a matter of weeks, had his bride of fewer than twenty-four hours not fled from him and vanished without a trace, leaving him bewildered and stuck in limbo.

Christos. *If he's feeling even a fraction of what I'm feeling now…*

But then the bride he'd acquired hadn't been wanted. Whereas what Sadie Preston had taken from me was… *priceless.*

The dreaded cancer diagnosis which had precipitated my sperm donation in anticipation of radiation might have turned out to be a false alarm when I was twenty-five, but the scars marring my skin beneath my clothes were a reminder of why that visit to the Phoenix Clinic had turned out to be a pivotal, life-affirming event for me. A light in the bleak darkness of the blissful ignorance I'd lived in for almost a year, before the blindfold had been ripped from my eyes almost as ruthlessly as the accident that had attempted to rob me of my life.

Anger and pure, unadulterated disbelief flashed like lightning through my system. I shook my head again, aware that I was attracting bewildered stares from the marketing gurus I'd hired to promote the interests of Xenakis Aeronautics in Brazil.

It had taken a draining amount of mental dexterity to get through my other two meetings, and now a quick glance at the presentation slide brought me up to speed with what I'd missed. Or rather, what *they'd* missed.

'This isn't going to work. Besides being unexceptional, you've aimed it at the wrong demographic.'

The team leader nodded enthusiastically. 'Which demographic were you thinking of, Mr Xenakis?'

I stopped myself from rolling my eyes. Was I required to do *all* their work for them? 'You have the data from the beta test. From what I'm seeing, you haven't bothered to consult it. I'm not seeing any application of the feedback we received from millennials with children.'

My chest clenched as another percussive wave of shock pummelled me. Children. Families. *Fatherhood.*

A state I'd never experience now, thanks to the actions of a redhead whose lips had dripped words of remorse but whose attitude vaunted defiance. Those startling green eyes had dared me to *bring it on* even as her bedroom voice wobbled with apology.

That little chin had been raised in silent combat, displaying the silken skin of her throat and a shadow of cleavage. And as for the other treasures hidden beneath her cheap, threadbare clothes…and that hair I wanted to wrap my fist around…

Theos mou. *Get a grip.*

It was searing shock that had stopped me from instructing Wendell to hand her over to the authorities as soon as she'd confessed her crime.

And shock was the reason she was in my penthouse while I bought myself some time to deal with the earth-shattering news. Besides, as much as I trusted my security chief, some things were private. And this matter couldn't get more private.

Sadie Preston had essentially taken every last shred of hope for my future and trashed it. And the worst thing was that I hadn't known how much the nebulous prospect of fatherhood had meant until any chance of it had been destroyed—first with betrayal and lies, and then with a careless press of the delete button on a computer.

My chest growing tighter, I jerked to my feet, the need to do something clawing through me. 'Ladies and gentlemen, I trust we know which direction we're heading for in the campaign now?' At their nods of assent, I headed for the door. 'You have one week to get it right. Don't let me down.'

Don't let me down.

Was I wasting my breath, saying that? Was I doomed to be disappointed in everyone I put my trust in? Be it in personal stakes or in a supposedly exclusive, top-of-the-range clinic?

My mouth soured as I strode for the lift.

The Brazilian contingent only needed a little guidance—they'd come through eventually. If they didn't, they'd simply be...replaced.

While I... Christos, *I would never be a father.*

I braced a hand against the wall, the weight of reality attempting to crush my shoulders.

So what if in the past I'd had my doubts about my potential effectiveness as a father? Xenakis men were many things, but exemplary fathers they were not. My grandfather had buried himself in work up to the point when he'd dropped dead of a heart attack, trying to save his near-bankrupt family. And long before that, my father had been denied his father's favour, resulting in the neglect of his own family.

While we tolerated each other now, for the sake of the family business, I didn't have a single memory of any bonding experience with my father. Boarding school had taken care of my formative years, followed by a gruelling apprenticeship at Xenakis Aeronautics.

I had respect and loyalty, earned from my position.

But affection? Or, hell, *love*?

In light of the bombshell that had flattened my life three hours ago, even the fake-it-till-you-make-it plan I'd so loftily believed would work with any future offspring had been shattered.

The finger I lifted to press the lift button shook with the force of the loss raking my insides. The moment I was inside the cubicle I attempted to breathe through the anguish, to get myself back under control.

Not even when Anneka had shown her true colours that day in the hospital three years ago had such a sense of deep loss affected me. While her betrayal had been similarly life altering, deep down a part of me had been thankful to have been given the opportunity to cut her out of my life before she truly sank her claws into me. Sure, my male pride had smarted for well over a year after she'd made a fool of me—cue excessive wild oat sowing—but ultimately, I'd escaped her trap.

With this there was not a single upside.

Save perhaps making the culprit pay?

The notion had gathered considerable pace by the time I entered my penthouse.

She stood at the glass window, her attention on the view. At some point between leaving the conference room only minutes ago and now, the sun had decided to shine. It threw a halo over her, turning her hair into living flames. Tendrils had slipped their loose knots, and as I watched she absently tucked a strand over her ear, slid her hand over her nape, then her shoulder, to massage it in firm, circular strokes.

The action sent another wave of tension through me, drawing my attention to her translucent skin, to the perfection of her hourglass figure and the stunning legs framed against the glass. Her other hand was splayed against it as if she yearned for the freedom beyond. Sensing my presence, she whirled around, those endless pools of green going wide at the sight of me.

'Oh… I had no idea you'd returned.'

My lips tightened, and that percussive mix of anger and desolation threatened again. 'I believe it's your lack of awareness that has led us to this point.'

She had the audacity to look hurt. The surrealness of it nearly made me shake my head again—but *enough*. I was done with being confounded. The important thing was how to proceed from here.

Doctors. Specialists. Investigate one final time.

Every option left a trail of displeasure, and the prospect of having my dire circumstances prodded was even more unwelcome than the verdict I'd woken to after a three-week coma three years ago: the severity of my skiing accident meant that I couldn't father children naturally. That my only hope of becoming a father rested on a sperm sample donated years ago, when I'd faced another crisis.

A seemingly miraculous turn of events that was now crushed to nothing.

Sadie Preston fidgeted where she stood, even as that pert little nose started to rise.

Christos, had no one ever taught this creature the concept of true contrition? But she wasn't as calm as she attempted to look. Her chest rose and fell in gathering agitation, and her small feet were curling and uncurling within the cheap flat shoes she wore. The action highlighted the smooth definition of her calves, and against my will I dropped my gaze, the better to absorb it.

When that only prompted a sharp need to test their suppleness beneath my fingers, I turned, made a beeline for my drinks cabinet. A dash of Hine in the crystal tumbler clutched in my hand brought a little clarity.

At the delicate throat-clearing behind me, I squeezed my eyes shut for a control-gathering second. Before I turned, she was speaking.

'I know you only need to look at me to remember why I'm here. What I've done. But I've been thinking… If you wouldn't mind giving me a little information, maybe we can put our heads together and come up with a solution.'

Another urge to laugh this away in the hope that it was some extended acid dream hit me. '*"Put our heads together"*? Why would we want to do that? Are you a doctor?'

Rose-red lips compressed, drawing my attention to yet another tempting part of her body.

The body of your nemesis.

'You know I'm not. I'm just trying to help—'

'I think you've done quite enough, don't you? Imagine we are the last two people on earth. Then be assured that I would rather take my chances with whatever apocalypse I face than accept *your* help.'

Her translucent skin lost a shade of colour. 'Do you need to be so cruel?' she muttered.

Absurdly, that plaintive question sent an arrow of guilt through me. *Theos mou.* What the hell was going on? Was it Upside Down Day? I downed half my drink, hoping the alcohol would burn through the fog.

The hope was in vain. So I approached until we stood half a dozen feet apart. 'Fine. Humour me. How would you propose we "put our heads together"?'

'Well, I was thinking that if you wouldn't mind telling me the circumstances behind your needing to use the Phoenix Clinic the first time around—'

'No, I would not. Next scenario.'

She hesitated, the tip of her pink tongue darting out to wet her lower lip. This time the punch in my gut was purely carnal. Ravenous. Demanding. *Lustful.*

For *this* woman? *Christos*, the world had truly turned upside down!

'Okay. If you're in a position to deposit another sample, perhaps I could contribute financially towards the future storage?'

Bitterness and bleakness lanced me in equal spikes. 'You don't look as if you can afford decent attire, let alone the fees of a clinic that charges upward of six figures. Do you have secret access to a gold mine, Sadie Preston? Or clairvoyant insight to the next set of lottery numbers?'

Her eyes flashed. 'Has anyone ever told you it's a mistake to judge a book by its cover?'

'If I am misjudging you, I'll consider rendering you an apology. Am I?'

She managed to hold my gaze for all of three seconds before her eyes dropped. Against her smooth cheeks, her long, unadorned eyelashes fanned in a seductive curl, highlighting her delicate eyelids. The combination of delicate, defiant and alluring made me grip my glass harder. But, more than that, I wanted her to lift her gaze, to show me those hypnotic green pools once again.

When she did, my breath caught.

I was attracted to her.

This woman, who'd brought me news of an apocalyptic kind, had awakened a libido grown so jaded I'd set it on the back burner in favour of pursuing even more success in the challenging boardrooms of Xenakis Aeronautics.

Was it the heightened bleakness of it all triggering this? And why was I wasting time deciphering it when I had no intention of following through on it?

'No, you're not wrong. I can't afford to foot the bill now. But perhaps we can come to an agreement?'

Here it comes. The age-old proposition.

The idea that she would offer herself to me on a platter drew deep disappointment. Enough to make me down the rest of my drink in abject resignation.

'Enlighten me about this agreement.'

'I'm two semesters away from completing a marketing degree. I've been top of my class every year. I can maybe work for your company from when I'm done? Pay you back that way?'

Surprise jolted me, followed by the familiar echo of wanting something because I'd been denied it. Had I *wanted* her on a platter? More specifically in my bed?

Yes!

I ignored the blaring affirmation, concentrated on what she'd said. So she wasn't just a simple receptionist.

The determination stamped across her face almost made

me believe her. *Almost*. For all I knew she was just spinning tales. Just as Anneka had spun lies around our relationship until an unguarded phone conversation had revealed the depths of her deplorable nature and the lengths she'd been prepared to go to ensure she received an unrivalled payday.

'How old are you?'

The mutinous look that crossed her face said she was debating not answering. Perhaps suggesting I mind my own business. But she realised very quickly that the question pertained to the proposal she was making.

'I'm twenty-five,' she offered, with clear reluctance.

'Most twenty-five-year-olds are done with their education.'

'My circumstances are different. I had to interrupt my education for personal reasons.'

Reasons she clearly wasn't about to disclose. I hid my disgruntlement. For now. 'Why a receptionist? Why not a paid internship in your chosen field?'

Impatience crossed her face. 'With respect, my reasons are private. But what I've said can easily be verified with my university professors.'

Enough. This had gone on long enough. 'You walked in off the street to confess a crime. As admirable as you seem to think admitting your culpability should be, I have zero reason to trust you. Not with my personal property and certainly not with my business. Your offer is declined.'

She inhaled sharply, the action drawing my attention to her chest. To her parted lips. *Christos*.

'So that's it? You're going to throw me to the wolves?'

'For what you've done? Yes, Sadie Preston. That's exactly what I'm going to do.'

Despite his doom-filled decree, he didn't move.

In the hours I'd been stuck in his opulent penthouse, one question had persistently swarmed my mind—why did a man whose every breath and expression spelled out his masculine potency and unapologetic virility need to store a sperm sample?

Eventually, curiosity had got the better of me. And the internet had been breathlessly efficient in providing high-resolution digital answers.

'Is this to be a staring contest?' he mused now, in a bone-dry tone tinged with that note I'd mistaken for bleakness earlier when I delivered my news. 'You're attempting to hypnotise me into reversing my verdict, perhaps?'

'What if I am?' I parried. If he was about to throw me to the wolves, what did I have to lose?

One corner of his mouth twitched with stark amusement. But then his face settled into a hard mask. My heart lurched. With every breath I wished I could go back, take my time, pay better attention—even with Mr Donnelly's unpleasant presence hovering over me.

But it was too late.

The damage had been done.

Neo Xenakis took another step closer, bringing that hard-packed body brimming with tensile, barely leashed power into my space. I wanted to step back, flatten myself against the glass wall, but that would exhibit a weakness I couldn't afford to show.

The internet had supplied ample examples of his shark-like business savvy too. This was a man who relished challenge. He'd never step into the arena with a weaker opponent, and the inevitable victory of his trouncing big-ger targets was all the sweeter for it.

Was that why I didn't look away?

Was that why I even dared to clench my jaw and all but urge him to do his worst?

Because I wanted him to conquer me?

White-hot sensation flashed through me, made my nape tingle and my body blaze with the same anticipation I'd felt earlier, even before I knew that he'd entered the room. That misplaced illicit thrill that had ratcheted higher when

I turned around to find him watching me with those hooded eyes containing an indecipherable gleam.

Here it was again, eating me alive when all I needed to do was hold my tongue and continue to demonstrate appropriate contrition.

For how long, though? And then what?

He'd given his verdict. Clemency was off the table. And yet, despite what he'd said about throwing me to the wolves, he seemed in the mood to play with me. Seemed perfectly content to indulge in the staring contest he'd ridiculed moments ago.

'Would it work?' I asked.

Dear God. Be quiet, Sadie. Just shut—

To my eternal shame, my stomach chose that pithy moment to announce its intense hunger.

Neo Xenakis's gaze dropped to my belly at the unladylike growl, then returned to mine with a dark frown. 'When was the last time you ate?'

I shrugged. 'I don't remember. It doesn't matter.'

'It matters if I wish to enjoy my evening drink without your digestive system providing accompanying acoustics.'

Heat burned my face. 'I… I had a coffee this morning.'

His frown deepened. 'That's all you've had all day? It's six in the evening.'

'I know what time it is, Mr Xenakis.'

He raised a brow at my crisp tone. I wasn't about to admit I'd gone into the office with hopes of snagging a stray Danish left over from the early-morning client meeting, only to be confronted by an incandescent Mr Donnelly before I could satisfy my raging hunger. After that, fear and panic had eroded my appetite. Until now, evidently.

Neo Xenakis regarded me with quiet intensity, weighing his decision for a terse moment. Then his lips flattened. 'Far be it from me to send a criminal to the gallows on an empty stomach. Shall I instruct my chef to set another place for dinner, or are you in a hurry to face your crimes?' he drawled.

Bite your tongue, Sadie!

'That depends. Do you intend to torture me for the rest of the evening by recounting just how your wolves are going to tear me apart?'

'You think you know what torture is?' he asked, with a veil of deadly calm that didn't fool me for a second.

I'd inconvenienced him, angered him by necessitating a return trip to the clinic to make a second deposit, when he'd much rather be occupied with other things. Like dating another supermodel.

And he wasn't in a mood to let it go.

'There are only so many times I can say I'm sorry. It's clear you're not going to forgive me or tell me what I can do to make this right. Right now I'm failing to see how joining you for dinner improves my circumstances.'

'It could simply be an act of further character exploration on my part. To tell me which way I should lean in the punishment scales. Unlike you, I don't wish to undertake that task on an empty stomach. But, of course, your options are very much yours to take.'

Oh, how cunning of him. That insidious need to surrender to his will swept over me. I resisted by squaring my shoulders. 'Then I guess that's fine. If that's the only way to progress this…discussion.'

The merest hint of a smile twitched his lips. Then, seeming almost stunned by the action, he scowled.

Not the most enthusiastic response I'd ever had to meal-sharing, but I imagined under the circumstances a beggar couldn't be a chooser.

For another short second he stared at me, as if debating the wisdom of his offer. Then abruptly he crossed the vast, magnificently decorated living room to a dainty-legged console table, picked up a phone and relayed a message in rapid-fire Greek.

Finished, he set his glass down. 'Come.'

The command was quiet, but powerful enough to pro-pel me forward. I told myself I couldn't object because I'd agreed to dine with him. And because I owed Neo Xenakis a few non-confrontational gestures.

Thinking he was leading me to the large, antique-filled dining room I'd spotted earlier during my brief and tenta-tive search for the bathroom, I followed him in surprise into a kitchen fit for the world's most exacting chef.

Every imaginable gadget gleamed in polished splendour atop marble surfaces. On a large centre island, silverware gleamed under strategically suspended ceiling lights. Even the elevated stools looked too expensive for such a mun-dane activity as sitting.

But when he pulled one back and waited with tight ex-pectancy, I swallowed the unnerving sensation that I was tangling with a supremely affluent and powerful man.

To the stout, rouge-faced chef who entered, I gave a quick smile. With a deferential nod, he started to uncover silver dishes.

Glorious smells hit my nostrils, and I stared at the mouth-watering array.

Exquisitely prepared Greek meze dishes were laid out next to an old-fashioned English shepherd's pie. I didn't fool myself into thinking this consideration had been made be-cause I was joining him on such short notice. If the internet was right, Neo Xenakis was a man of extensive tastes and larger-than-life appetites.

Why that reminder triggered another wave of heat through my system I refused to consider as, with a few words, Neo Xenakis dismissed the chef and reached for the bottle of red wine that stood an arm's length away.

Seeing the label, I felt my eyes widen. Once upon a time, before he'd pulled the rug from beneath our feet with his stark betrayal, my father had been as much of a wine enthu-siast as my mother was a magazine fanatic. When I was old enough to take an interest, he had often recited his dream vintage collection. The five-figure-price-tagged Château Cheval Neo cavalierly reached for now had ranked among the top three on my father's wish list.

I watched, slack jawed, as he deftly uncorked the bottle and set it aside to breathe.

Catching my expression, he narrowed his eyes. 'Something wrong?'

I swallowed. 'Nothing that doesn't involve my wondering if you normally share expensive bottles of wine with criminals before sending them to their doom.'

His gaze hooded, he shrugged. 'Satisfying your curiosity isn't on my agenda, so you'll just have to keep wondering. Eat.'

I toyed with refusing the order. But I was starving. And, really, he didn't *have* to feed me. With one quick call he could have Wendell tossing me out. Staying might grant me the opportunity to make another plea for mercy.

I placed two beautifully wrapped vine leaves onto my plate, then added a couple of spoonfuls of Greek salad. About to lift my fork, I paused when his eyes narrowed again, this time on my plate.

'You haven't eaten all day and that's all you're having?'

'Yes.'

He nodded at one of the many platters. 'The *kopanisti* won't keep. Don't let it go to waste.' He picked up serving tongs and caught up a dish of salad, roast peppers and an orange paste laid in between two crisp flatbreads. 'Try it,' he said.

Tentatively, I picked up the large morsel and bit into it. Sensations exploded in my mouth as the orange paste, which turned out to be the most incredible aged feta, combined with everything else immediately became the best thing I'd ever tasted—which in turn triggered a groan of appreciation before I could stop myself.

Perhaps my vivid imagination was playing tricks on me,

but I could have sworn Neo swallowed hard at that moment, and I felt his tension ramping up.

Abruptly, he spooned several more items onto my plate, then reached for the wine bottle. 'Would you like some wine?'

The chance to try the jaw-droppingly expensive vintage, especially considering that my fate hung in the balance, was too much to resist. 'Just a little, please.'

After pouring two glasses, he chose steamed white cod and a spoonful of salad himself, which he polished off with a military efficiency that spoke of fuel intake rather than enjoyment. Then he simply sat, slowly twirling the stem of his wine glass, lifting it occasionally to his lips as he watched me eat.

Self-conscious, and reluctant to broach the ultrasensitive subject of my crime, I stilled my tongue in favour of enjoying the most exquisite meal I'd had in a long time, all the while painfully aware that his gaze hadn't shifted from me.

'Which university?'

I started. 'What?'

'Your marketing degree,' he expounded.

I named it, and again caught the faintest hint of surprise in his eyes as he slotted the information away, his long fingers still twirling his glass.

'Do you like aeroplanes?' he asked abruptly, after another stretch of silence.

'Who doesn't?'

His lips tightened and his gaze dropped to my empty plate, then shifted to the platters of lamb cutlets, grilled meatballs, roasted vegetables and bread.

Sensing he was about to push more food on me, I sat back. 'That was delicious. Thank you.'

He frowned, then lifted the lid off a dish set apart from the main courses. The scent of spun sugar and warm pastry washed over me, almost eliciting another groan. I'd been cursed with a sweet tooth—one that needed constant attention.

'Dessert?' he offered gruffly, pushing the baklava directly in front of me.

The sight of the perfect little squares of delight was too much to resist. At my helpless nod, he placed four pieces on a fresh plate and slid it in front of me, again seemingly content to simply sit back and watch me eat.

Perhaps this was Neo Xenakis's method of torture. To feed me until I burst.

At that mildly hysterical thought, I let my gaze flick up to meet his. Again that spark flared in his eyes, and the charge seized me, causing tingles from my palms to my toes.

'If it wasn't for this wholly unfortunate situation, I'd think you didn't want me to leave,' I mused. Then immediately cursed my runaway tongue.

He froze, his grey eyes turning as turbulent as a lightning storm. His hand tightened around his glass, his fingers turning white.

'I'm sorry. I didn't mean—'

'Perhaps you're right,' he interrupted, his voice low, rough and raw, as if scrabbled from a pit of utter despair. 'Maybe I *don't* want you to leave. Maybe I need you sitting there in front of me as a reminder of what has happened. Of the fact that the nightmare you brought to my doorstep isn't one I can wake up from.'

The utter bleakness in his tone launched a lump into my throat. My fingers tightened in my lap as the need to reach out, to lay my hand on his or cup that rigid jaw, powered through me. I did neither, sensing it wouldn't be welcome.

'Is it really that hopeless? Is there no chance that things can be salvaged?' My question was a desperate one. But the thought that things could really be so dire for a man so incredibly masculine and virile looking seemed unthinkable to me.

'Excuse me?' he rasped icily, his eyes turning almost black with the strength of his emotions.

I pushed my plate away and forced myself to answer before I lost my nerve. 'I… Surely it doesn't surprise you that I'd wonder why a man who looks like you—'

'Looks like me?' he grated.

I wetted suddenly dry lips, suspecting I'd strayed into dangerous territory but unable to locate the road map to take me out of peril.

'You're not blind. You look like the poster-perfect image of virility. Is it beyond the realms of probability that I'd wonder why you'd need to use a facility like the Phoenix Clinic?'

His eyes slowly rose. 'Did you not admonish me for judging *you* based on your outward appearance?'

Even as my face heated, something inside me reacted sharply to the notion that I might have ended this man's line with my mistake. Something that utterly rejected that thought.

'Please answer the question, Mr Xenakis,' I urged, aware of my escalating desperation.

'Why? Are you distressed by the thought that a man who *"looks like me"* might be impotent or infertile?' he drawled.

He was goading me, pure and simple. I should've looked away. Backed down.

'Are you?'

He rose and stepped away from the island. 'Come with me,' he grated.

Something raw and intense pulsed in his tone, warning me that whatever he had in mind would decimate me emotionally.

'And if I refuse? Is this where you threaten—'

He slashed one powerful hand across my argument, his lips flattening into a displeased line. 'A word to the wise, Sadie. If you have any desire for self-preservation left in that body, be wise and stop defying me at every turn. I'm a man who faces adversity head-on. Right now, I'm *this* close to tossing you out the door and letting the authorities deal with your crimes. But, again, the choice is yours. Leave and face the consequences or indulge the man you've so gravely wronged. Which is it to be?' he asked, his eyes pinning me in place.

'I... Fine. I'll do what you want. For now,' I tagged on, simply because that self-preservation he'd mentioned was kicking in wildly, doubling my thundering heartbeat. 'I reserve the right to leave any time I want.'

He left the kitchen without responding.

I followed, striving not to breathe in his intoxicating scent and failing miserably.

Senses jumping, I watched him stroll over to the plush sectional sofa, sit down on it in a deceptively relaxed pose, one long arm lazily stretched out on the top of it. He rested one ankle on his knee, and lifted his wine glass to take a liberal sip.

'If you wish. But why postpone the inevitable? And why annoy me further by forcing me to carve another appointment into my schedule when we can settle this one way or the other tonight?'

Because I needed the headspace to think straight!

But Neo Xenakis would be equally imposing and breathtaking tomorrow—and most likely every day from now until eternity.

So why delay the inevitable indeed?

With legs turned rubbery, and nigh on useless, I approached him.

'Let me give you the broad strokes of the consequences of your actions. I come from a large family. Perhaps not your conventional Greek family, but we adore babies without reservation, regardless of how they were conceived,' he said, his hooded gaze on the contents of his glass. 'Which means that from a relatively young age, certain obligations have been required of me. Obligations I had every intention of fulfilling at some point in the future. Do you understand what that means?'

My nod was jerky at best. 'Something along the lines of keeping the family name going?'

'Exactly so. And I take my duty seriously. So what do you think you owe me for effectively ending my chances of fulfilling my obligations?'

'But…have I really?' I asked, unabashed curiosity getting the better of my tongue.

The turbulent emotion in his eyes receded for a moment, replaced by an equally arresting gleam as his gaze raked my face before resting with quiet ferocity on my mouth.

'I see we're back to that little nugget you can't let go of. Are you asking me if my equipment works, Sadie?' he drawled.

There was a layer of danger to his tone that should have frightened me but instead caused the blood to rush faster through my veins, pushing a flood of colour into my cheeks.

'I can't help thinking…it would help to know if the situation is as dire as all that…'

God. Stop talking.

'And if it isn't?' he rasped. 'Are you hoping that with one simple answer you'll be absolved of what you've done?'

God, we were really discussing his…his…

'No. Maybe. Yes…' I whispered.

'My ability or inability to engage in intercourse is not the issue here,' he said.

'Answer the question anyway,' I blurted, attempting to keep my mind on the important subject at hand and losing the battle in favour of racy thoughts of the exploration of his mouth-watering body first-hand.

Growing stupidly breathless, I scoured his face, his sculpted cheekbones, the hard angles of his jaw, the shadowed enticement of his strong throat and…dear God…the sensual curl of his lower lip, currently curved against his glass as he took another lazy sip.

The way he simply...lounged in his seat, was deceptively calm in a still-waters-run-deep manner. I wanted to dive into those waters, lose myself in them until I was completely sodden.

A different sort of heat pummelled me, low and insistent, charting a path of ravenous need directly between my thighs. Against the lace cups of my bra my nipples tightened, and each breath drew urgent attention to the decadent craving coursing through my body.

'I could tell you—but should I? I owe you nothing. You have no right to answers. But if you truly want to know if I can get it up, I invite you to find out for yourself,' he rasped thickly, his hooded gaze announcing that he knew every single yearning crashing through me.

My tongue thickened in my mouth, and that same acute urge to test where this alternative route would take me rammed unadulterated temptation through my bloodstream.

Sweet heaven. Surely he wasn't really suggesting what I thought he was...? And surely I wasn't truly considering it.

Was I?

CHAPTER THREE

MY BREATH BURST from between my lips, the wild, dizzying leap of my pulse a damning testament to the fact that his words had exhilarated me for one blind nanosecond before reason reasserted itself.

He can't truly mean that. He's just toying with you.

Even if he wasn't, the proposal was absurd.

'Is this a joke?'

'Do I look amused, Sadie?' he returned.

No, he didn't. That raw confession in the kitchen returned, and the looming possible result of my actions—that I'd deprived not just him and his immediate family but the larger Xenakis clan of his future descendants—hit me with powerful force.

Helpless despair wove through me, and my chest tightened as I watched him, attempted to see beneath the taut mask of his face. Was this all because he truly didn't want to be alone to confront the dire position I'd put him in?

If so, was this his answer?

I shook my head. 'I… I'm not sure what this is all about.'

He shrugged. 'You want me to provide spoilers for a story you seem very interested in. I invite you to peek beneath the cover. Or are you all bluster?'

'Just so we're clear, I'm not making any so-called reparation in the form of sex,' I blurted. Simply because my imagination was threatening to take flight again, and the look in his eyes was sending my senses into free fall once more.

I grappled them down—hard.

One mocking eyebrow elevated. 'You jump to conclusions with the same careless abandon that I suspect landed you in this predicament in the first place. Perhaps you should wait until you're invited to my bed before you respond in one way or another.'

His censure smarted, regardless of the fact that I'd agreed to give him a little leeway in the perpetrator-versus-victim scenario.

'I'm not stupid, Mr Xenakis. I can read between the lines. And whatever you think is going to happen here, it isn't,' I stressed, although the caution was equally for me as it was for him.

'Has no one told you to quit while you're ahead?'

Many times. But I never went against my instinct.

'I believe in laying my cards on the table.'

Slowly, his relaxed stance altered. His arm dropped from the sofa, his body leaning closer as he pinned me with his gaze. With the width of the sofa between us, he wasn't crowding me. But he didn't need to. His presence filled every square inch of space, proclaiming his power and glory in ways that were hard to define and impossible to dismiss.

'Do you? Well, hear this. If I wanted you in my bed you would come—and willingly. Not because of the unfortunate circumstances you find yourself in.'

'If that's some sort of dare, I promise I won't be taking it,' I stated firmly, despite that insidious temptation striking deep. Deeper. Making my every breath strain, making my nipples tingle and peak and *yearn*.

God, what was wrong with me?

He shrugged again. Drawing my eager attention to the firm, bronzed expanse of his throat. Striking me with a fervent need to place my hand right there…where his pulse throbbed powerfully beneath his skin.

I averted my gaze, but the lingering look he gave me said he'd caught me staring. I needed to get up. Leave. Put some distance between myself and the turbulent temptation that *oozed* out of him. But doing so would send another weakening message. He'd invited me here. I'd lobbed the ball into his court. So I waited for his move.

The muted sound of a door opening heralded the arrival of a butler, bearing a silver tray with more drinks on it. While I was a little startled, Neo looked unruffled, as if nothing unusual had happened to interrupt his normal after-dinner routine.

He accepted a glass of cognac, then glanced at me. 'Nightcap?'

I shook my head, surprised at his cordial tone. Then I snapped my spine straight. I couldn't afford to lower my guard. He still hadn't spelled out the parameters of my reparation. Nor given me a straight answer to my question…

With a few words Neo dismissed the butler. The moment we were alone, he discarded his untouched drink and turned his piercing gaze on me.

My eyes connected with his as if pulled by invisible magnets. As much as I was reluctant to admit it, the man was a superb specimen. His impossibly broad shoulders demanded attention, and the gladiator-like synergy of sleekness and power combined with an animalistic aura impossible to dismiss.

The look in his eyes intensified, sending the distinct message that now we were getting down to the heart of whatever was on Neo Xenakis's mind.

'Come here, Sadie,' he ordered, confirming my frenzied thoughts.

Get up. Walk out. He can't stop you.

But temptation could. It wrapped its sinuous vines around me, hard and fast, left me breathless and speechless.

This was theory testing. Curiosity satisfying. Nothing else.

My life had taken a left turn this morning. Not that things had been rosy before… My mother and her gambling problem, my landlord's growing threats, my jobless state… My life and plans were a world removed from what I'd imagined for myself back in the idyllic days when I had the illusion of a solid family. When a fulfilling career, perhaps eventually a family, wasn't a laughable, ephemeral prospect.

The dismaying sensation in the pit of my stomach that had arrived along with my father's callously dismissive postcard and stayed all these years later, the sensation that mocked and questioned and poisoned my dreams, claimed I was as worthless as my father had deemed me, was very much present now, questioning my audacity to remain here, reaching for this temptation.

Step back, it said. *This isn't for you.*

But I wasn't ready to step back into my life just yet. I craved more time in this peculiar bubble with Neo Xenakis. Just for a little while longer.

Before I could stop the motion, I swayed towards him.

He didn't reach out. Simply lounged against the velvet seat, the king of his shiny castle, awaiting his due. And, like a moth to a flame, I couldn't resist the danger, the excitement, the *otherness* he offered.

One taste. Then I could end this any time I wanted.

One minute, then I could get back to why I was here, perhaps armed with the confirmation that he wasn't impaired in any obvious physical way.

The thought that I was attempting to slot this beneath the banner of *research* drew a hysterical chortle, quickly smothered beneath the pulses of lust swelling through my system.

Before I knew it, my body hovered next to his, almost horizontal on the sofa as I heeded his command.

'Here I am,' I replied in a voice that sounded nothing like mine.

Storm-tossed eyes traced every inch of my face, lingering longest and fiercest on my mouth.

'Yes. Here you are,' he replied.

His warm, cognac-tinged breath washed over my lips, causing them to tingle wildly.

Desperately, I slicked my tongue over them, then again when his sizzling gaze followed the wet path. His next breath emerged a touch harsher, his sculpted chest straining against his pristine shirt. The tingling flashed to my fingers, where the need to explore that mouth-watering expanse lashed harder and faster.

'The invitation still stands, Sadie,' he breathed.

Stay. Explore. *Indulge.*

I lifted my hand until it hovered mere inches from his skin. Until his heat caressed my palm, its gravitational pull tugging me with unrelenting force.

Was I really doing this? Baiting a predator to avoid my own reality?

Snatching a jagged breath, I hesitated.

Eyes even fiercer, Neo shifted. My hand met the hard wall of his chest, rested on the powerful thundering heartbeat. Lust burst through like a hot ray of sunshine through fog, melting away the last of my reservations. I slid my fingers up superbly well-defined pecs, over the tie he'd loosened during dinner, to glide around his neck.

The thought that I was headed in the wrong direction, going up when I should be heading down, evaporated as I explored him. He'd invited this. And I wanted to make sure my investigation was...*thorough.*

His eyes grew hooded when my fingers speared the hair at his nape. Lustrous strands slid through my fingers, and that small act fired up the tempest coursing through me. Enthralled by the sensation, I repeated the caress.

A gruff sound left his throat. His Adam's apple moved in a strong swallow. Had he moved closer or had I? My gaze fell to his full lower lip, so temptingly close. Promising a heady reprieve from chaos, despair and uncertainty.

One tiny, tiny taste.

I strained another inch closer, watched his eyes turn darker, felt his chest expand with a heavy inhalation.

One second ticked by. Two.

Then, with a rush of breath and a growl of impatience,

he breached the gap between us, fused his lips to mine in white-hot possession.

Indecent. *Heavenly.*

Outrageous and masculine and, oh, so powerful.

Neo took control of the kiss, brazenly swept his tongue along the ultrasensitive flesh of my bottom lip before delving in between to taste me. With a whimper of urgent need, I parted my lips wider, welcoming him with the eagerness of a starving woman granted a feast.

But even while his lips clung to mine, his hands remained where they were, maddeningly removed from my body. The challenge was too much to resist. Crawling closer, I wrapped both hands around his neck, drew him deeper into the kiss. Dared to meet his tongue with mine on the next sweep.

His body jerked and another growl left his throat as our tongues found a unique dance of decadent delight, of thrilling desire that built with each ferocious second.

Dear God, he could kiss. Even when he wasn't putting his complete effort into it, even when he wasn't touching me, I was nearly driven out of my mind.

In another heartbeat that was all I wanted. Neo Xenakis's hands on me.

Then I would stop.

Because this was getting out of control.

As if he'd heard my silent plea, he finally dropped his hands from the back of the sofa. They glided over my shoulders, down my ribcage, in slow, sensuous exploration to my waist. After the merest hesitation, he wrapped his large hands around my hips and pulled me with supreme masculine ease into his lap.

No need for any southern exploration.

The unmistakable evidence of his proud manhood was imprinted, hot and thick, against my bottom.

At my muted gasp he broke the kiss and edged me back, long enough to deliver a smouldering look of arrogant confirmation.

'Now you know,' he breathed.

'Y-yes…'

A look flickered through his eyes—one that seemed to ask and answer a question in the same heartbeat. Then he was tugging me back into his body, one hand spiked in my hair, the other on my hip, pinning me to his lower body. It was as if he wanted nothing but his powerful masculinity to occupy my mind now he'd provided the evidence.

As if I could think of anything else. *Feel* anything else.

With only one lover in my past, and a fleeting one at that, sex was still a mystery to me—a land whose borders I'd barely breached before retreating, first out of disappointment and then through the sheer strain of holding the tattered rags of my life together.

Now, presented with this tantalising feast, every past experience paled to nothing. My instinct warned that a man like Neo would have more experience in his little finger than I would in my whole body. That this brief taste was merely a drop in the ocean of what he could deliver to the right woman.

Except I wasn't the right woman.

I was the woman he'd goaded into taking this risky, mind-altering challenge. A challenge whose fire blazed to heights I'd never encountered before.

You can stop. Now.

But his lips were intoxicating. And the way his tongue and teeth and lips commanded mine was intensifying that persistent, needy throb between my legs…

With another moan I locked my hands around his neck, strained even closer to that magnificent body. And gasped when he abruptly pulled back, his hooded eyes darting from my parted lips to clash with mine.

He let out a heavy, unsteady exhale. 'This isn't how I foresaw this meeting evolving,' he rasped.

'Me neither,' I muttered.

He gave a short, jerky nod before his fierce gaze bored

into mine. 'Then perhaps it's best if we draw a line under it,' he invited.

But the slight clench of his fingers on my hip said that wasn't what he really wanted. And when his hold loosened, when I sensed he was about to disengage, I clenched my gut against the lash of disappointment and loss.

'Is that what you want? For me to leave?'

His jaw clenched and that hot gaze locked on my lips. 'The more important question is, are you ready to let go, Sadie? I ask this because you're clinging to me as if I'm the last piece of driftwood in your ocean.'

My arms unlocked from around his neck, slow with a helpless need to stay connected, moved down his chest. At his deep shudder a powerful sensation gripped me, along with a twinge of uncertainty barely born, before it was smashed beneath the colossal hunger clawing through me.

I'd never felt anything like this. And the voice inside telling me I never would again birthed a terrifying need to seize this unique experience.

Everything around me was slowly crumbling to dust. My mother's spiralling gambling. Looming homelessness. The job I no longer had. My own shattered dreams…

A secret fear plagued me in the dead of night. One I'd never admitted to anyone. That perhaps my father was right. That unconditional love was an illusion—an obligation fulfilled only up to a point. Or worse, that *I* hadn't been worthy of the effort.

The urgent need simply to forget for a little while longer hooked me with mighty talons, refusing to let go.

'Say what's on your mind,' Neo insisted.

The raw demand in his voice. The turbulent look in his eyes. The edgy hunger in his face. All of them echoed the deep clamouring inside me perfectly. Like two halves of a magnificent, earth-shaking whole. And really, in the desolate landscape of my uncertain future, where and when would I get the chance to experience anything close to this?

'Maybe I'm not…not ready to let go. Just yet.'

For the briefest moment he hesitated, as if he intended to refuse this…refuse *me*. More than a little panicked at the thought of being thrust back into my dreary life, I clung to his lapel.

Need smashed through his fleeting resistance.

Decadent headiness filled me, swirling in a sense of triumph I knew it was unwise to savour.

Strong fingers delved back into my hair, impatiently freeing the knot. As if he'd uncovered a wondrous sight, his breath caught as he fingered the long strands. 'Your hair is like a living flame,' he rasped, watching the thick tendrils glide over his skin.

The next instant he'd tugged open the button holding my jacket closed, pulled it off and had me back against the sofa, angling his powerful body over mine. I clung tighter to him, revelling in the erotic thrill of his kiss.

A moan ripped free from him as he settled his hips between mine and I felt the full power of his arousal. '*Theos mou*, you're intoxicating.'

And he was far from lacking in the ultimate manhood stakes.

I wanted to return the compliment, but words failed to form beneath the assault of his touch. His tongue boldly stroked mine, coaxed it into a thrilling dance, and all coherent thought evaporated.

We kissed until we grew breathless, only the need for oxygen driving us apart.

Frenzied seconds ticked away as Neo stared down at me. From unkempt hair to parted lips to strained nipples. There was nowhere to hide my attraction to this man—the last man I should've been doing this with.

Whether he felt the same or not became a non-issue as he resolutely levered himself away from me to shrug off his jacket. His tie followed, both tossed away with complete disregard for expense or care.

Hot hands slid around my hips once more, moulded them for an exploratory second before gliding downward, past my thighs and calves to my feet.

He removed and tossed away my shoes. Eyes locked on mine, he conducted the most maddening caress of one foot before digging an expert thumb into the arch.

A melting sensation pooled into my belly, a lusty moan leaving my lips.

For one fleeting moment, his lips twitched, as if he'd gleaned something about me that pleased him.

By the time he was done with paying the same attention to the other foot, my back was arching off the sofa, my whole body caught in waves of pleasure so unique I couldn't catch my breath.

He caught me in his arms, and sensation, earnest and powerful, overwhelmed me. Neo too, if his almost frenzied need to divest me of my clothing, filling the room with decadent sounds that escalated the passion-infused air, was any indication.

In minutes he'd reduced me to my panties and bra, and his hand was exploring every exposed dip and curve.

He lowered his head. At the thought that he was about to put his lips on my skin for the first time, I blindly reached for him, eager to undress him before I lost the ability to perform the function.

The first few buttons of his shirt came undone, giving me a tantalising glimpse of what lay beneath. But when I reached for the next one, Neo tensed, one hand staying mine.

'No,' he rasped, his voice tight.

Before I could question his response, he dropped his head and laid an open-mouthed kiss on the pulse racing at my throat, then counterpunched by grazing his teeth over the sensitive flesh.

'Oh!'

'You like that?'

'Yes!'

His satisfied growl set off cascades of shivers, rendering my nerve endings even more sensitive as he intensified his caress. One hand slid behind my knee, parting my legs so he could mould his lower body to mine, accentuating his lean hips and the powerful outline of his erection. I swallowed, momentarily apprehensive of his overwhelming maleness.

Pausing, his gaze bored into mine. 'Sadie, do you want this?'

The question was grave, and it also held a warning. He was reaching the end of his tether and he wanted to grant me the opportunity of ending this before insanity spun us completely out of control.

I didn't want it to end. I was on that same edge.

I boldly cupped his bristled jaw. He exhaled harshly, his sensual lips planting a hard kiss in my palm even while his eyes demanded an answer.

'Yes,' I replied.

Whatever regrets came later—and I suspected there would be many—I was too far gone, had given too many pieces of myself to heartache, from my father, worry over my mother, despair over life itself, to deny this unexpected slice of heaven. Even if it came in the form of an intense, larger-than-life man who was losing himself in me because of the colossal wrong I'd done him.

'I want this,' I confirmed, glad my voice held firm.

The words were barely out of my mouth when, with a deft flick, he released my bra. Eyes locked on mine, he dragged the straps down my arms. For a taut second after he flung it away, his eyes remained on mine. Then his gaze dropped to what he'd uncovered. A breath shuddered out of him.

'You're exquisite,' he breathed.

Pleasure arched my back, the act snatching his next breath. His head dropped, sensual lips wrapping around one peak to pull the tight bud into his mouth. I cried out as pleasure ripped through me, my senses scrambling further when his tongue swirled in erotic caresses. More decadent sounds fell from my lips. My fingers slid beneath the collar of his shirt to track urgently over his shoulders, to grip his back, eager to hold him to his task.

Neo's caresses grew bolder as he switched his attention to the twin peak. Arrows of need shot between my thighs, dampening and readying me for the ultimate possession. Possession he seemed determined to tease out as he feasted on my breasts for an age, returning over and over to my mouth to demand torrid kisses.

Just when I thought he'd drag the moment out for an eternity he drew down my panties, flinging them away with the same sexy carelessness he'd given my bra.

'I have to taste you,' he said, in that deep, raw voice, gripping my thigh to part me to his avid gaze.

His stare was so potent, so ravenous, I lost what little breath I had left in my lungs. 'Neo...'

'Shh, no talking, *glikia mou*. Quite enough words have passed between us.'

Denied that outlet, I grasped another. I touched, I explored, I kissed every covered muscle within reach, delighting in the slivers of heated olive skin he allowed me.

Right until his bold lips delivered the ultimate kiss between my thighs.

I fell back, boneless, onto the sofa, and another cry was wrenched from my throat as he wreaked wicked havoc between my thighs. All the while delivering rough praise in English and Greek.

How had I even contemplated denying myself this soul-stirring experience? Even at this stage, I knew it paled in comparison with my brief sexual foray back at uni.

Neo tongued my nerve-filled bud and I screamed, the shameless keening urging him into deeper caresses until it all grew too much. Until I had no choice but to surrender to the blistering release that gripped me tight for several electrifying seconds before tossing me into utter bliss.

For endless minutes I drifted, a raw mass of sensation.

But in excruciating increments I became aware of my surroundings, of my fingers clenched in his hair. Of the wide, plush sofa beneath me and the hot body slowly prowling up mine. Of the foil caught between his fingers as he eased back, unzipped his trousers and pulled them and his boxers down.

His shirt remained on, the tails covering the tops of his thighs. Eyes pinned to mine, he glided the condom on with that mask of hunger stamped on his face.

Unable to help myself, I dropped my gaze to his shaft. And again I experienced momentary panic at his sizeable thickness. But, as if he'd willed it away with the sheer force of his attraction, the worry receded as he reclaimed his place between my legs.

Nevertheless, I couldn't suppress my whimper at the first breach.

He froze, teeth gritted, as his turbulent gaze searched mine. 'Sadie…?'

Fear that he would stop, that this insulating little bubble would burst and I would be flung back into dreary reality, pushed me to blurt out, 'Don't stop. Please.'

For heart-stopping seconds he didn't move. Just stared at me with a mixture of edgy intensity and banked lust. Then, as if he didn't want to leave this bubble either, he thrust deep.

Pleasure rolled over me, dissipating the initial sting of his fullness. 'Yes…'

Relief washed over his face, immediately chased away by wickedly ferocious determination. Another thrust. His groan melded with my moan as he slid to the hilt.

'You shouldn't feel this incredible,' he grunted. 'But, *thee mou*, you do.'

His words triggered a weird kind of triumph—a fleeting but overwhelming pride that I was good enough for something, *worth* this moment of nirvana. I sank deeper into sensation, shuddering at the powerful emotions moving in my chest. Then in pure carnal bliss Neo rolled his hips, driving me further out of my mind.

'More. Please.'

A wicked pause, then he seized my arms, dragged them above my head. The movement drew my body taut, enlivening every inch of me with intense awareness as he splayed his fingers between mine and proceeded to give me far more than I'd ever imagined possible.

With every thrust, every glide of his lips over my skin, I was hurled closer to that intense spark I knew would ignite the most sacred bliss I'd ever known.

I wanted to rush it and slow it down at the same time.

I wanted to hold it in my palm and savour it even while I strained for complete annihilation with every cell in my body.

'Please...' I panted, unsure which path I yearned for more.

With a series of piston-fast, mind-melting strokes, the moment arrived. White-hot, searing, intense. I was catapulted into unadulterated bliss, eagerly surrendering to the power and might of it.

His head buried in my neck, Neo gave a muted shout, his body shuddering for endless moments in the throes of his own release.

After the frenzied pace of his possession time slowed to a crawl, as if the power of our jagged coming together, the intensity of the moment, needed reverse momentum to slow and steady it.

Heartbeats slowed. Pulses quieted. Like a powerful drug taking me under, lethargy stole over me. I closed my eyes and drifted, cloaked in a moment's peace before I had to face what had happened.

The moment arrived all too soon.

First came the loss of the searing palm-to-palm contact that had somehow heightened this experience from base act to something...*more*, followed by the complete withdrawal of body heat when Neo rose lithely from the sofa, triggering an acute self-consciousness of my naked state in contrast to his almost completely clothed form.

Then, with his thick curse uttered in Greek, but nevertheless unmistakable, I was wrenched from my insulated bubble.

The living room lights, which had provided seductive ambience during our furious coupling, suddenly blazed too bright, exposed too much, making me blink a few times before I focused on the man frozen in a half turn from me, a look of stark disbelief and something else that looked like furious self-loathing etched into his face.

'I… Is something wrong?' I cringed at my husky sexhoarse tone.

Neo ploughed his fingers through his hair, turned and stalked down the hallway. Dread dripped torturous ice water down my spine. The frantic darting of my mind was locked in place for several long seconds before I jackknifed upward, my feet landing on the plush carpet as I tried to marshal my thoughts.

It took far too long to find and wrestle my tangled panties on. I was cursing my shaking hands and their inability to straighten my bra straps when brisk strides signalled Neo's return.

My disquiet intensifying, I glanced his way. He ignored me. I told myself to be glad, but my stomach churned harder, the regret I'd anticipated and almost accepted would arrive suspiciously light in place of the hurt and confusion swamping me.

His movements jerky, unlike the smooth, animalistic grace he'd exhibited earlier, he headed for the drinks cabinet, but at the last moment veered away and stopped before the glass wall.

Silence pulsed as he stared out, ferocious tension riding his shoulders.

I dragged my fingers through my hair, shoving it out of

the way in order to secure my bra, and hurriedly punched my fingers through the sleeves of my blouse. I was tugging the sides together when he turned.

If his eyes had been turbulent pools before, they were positively volcanic now. But that fury was aimed more at himself than at me. There seemed to be bewilderment, as if I was a puzzle he'd tried and failed to put together and now loathed himself for attempting.

He stared at me for another unsettling minute, his lips parted, his chest rising and falling as if he detested the very words he was about to utter.

'We have a problem,' he grated.

I was surprised he could speak at all, with his jaw locked so tight and the tendons in his neck standing out.

The feeling of unworthiness returned—harder, harsher. *Not good enough*, the insidious voice whispered. *Never good enough.*

I pushed it and my roiling emotions away for examination later. Much, much later.

'I can tell. Although I'm at a loss as to what it is.'

But even as the firm words tumbled from my lips, the cascade and echo of old hurts was deepening, intensifying.

'If you're about to tell me you regret what happened, please save your breath. We don't need to dissect it now or ever. I'll be out of your hair in a few minutes. You need never set eyes on me again if that's what you—'

'The condom broke.'

The words were delivered like a chilling death knell. I was glad I hadn't attempted to stand, because my legs would have failed me. I was aware that my jaw had sagged, that I probably made an unattractive sight, sitting there half-dressed, with my skirt askew and unzipped and my blouse wrinkled.

He confirmed it with a quick rake of his gaze and a harder clenching of his teeth. 'Get dressed, Sadie.'

I ignored the command for the simple reason that I

couldn't move, couldn't force my brain to stop repeating those three damning words on a loop.

'I… What?' I finally managed.

'Cover yourself,' he repeated tersely.

'Why? My nakedness didn't cause the condom to fail,' I flung back, and then compounded my words with a furious blush as his eyebrows hiked upward in flaying mockery.

I turned my back on him, a much more earth-shaking tremble seizing me as the ramifications landed home. While he'd listed everything I may have deprived him of, Neo hadn't definitely confirmed his inability to father children. So did I face a possible pregnancy on top of everything else?

Dear God…

Motherhood? When my own blueprint of childhood was so flawed?

Somehow, through sheer will to fight this battle on some-where-near-equal footing, I straightened my clothes, slid my feet into my shoes.

There was nothing I could do about my hair, what with the cheap band I'd used nowhere in sight and my refusal to dig around for it under Neo's heavy, brooding stare. So I took a deep breath, and turned around to face the conse-quences of yet another wrong turn.

CHAPTER FOUR

MISTAKE.

Big, colossal mistake.

Disbelief, raw and searing, tunnelled deep, bedded down into my bones with unstoppable force until I had no choice but to acknowledge its presence. To accept that I'd simply compounded one problem with not one but two further mistakes.

For the first time in my life I wanted to find the nearest sand dune. Bury my head in it. But I couldn't.

Because there she stood, a flaming hot testament to the temptation I'd given in to when I should've walked away. Should have heeded my own agency to retreat and regroup instead of arrogantly imagining I could handle this—handle *her*—like a normal business challenge, to be ruthlessly and efficiently dismantled before moving on to the next problem.

The chaos she'd brought upon me wasn't a business problem or even a wider family problem, to be accommodated only so far until it could be slotted under *someone else's problem* when in reality it was deeply, straight-to-the-core *personal*.

It had needed addressing, sure. But only once I'd thought things through. Executed a solution with military precision, as I did with everything in my life.

Not losing myself in the very object of my misery. Not letting go of the reins of my sanity so thoroughly and completely that the world could've burned to the ground and I wouldn't have minded in the slightest if it meant I could continue to enjoy her silken warmth, the intoxicating clutch of her tight heat. To hear those spellbinding gasps and cries fall from her lips as she begged for more.

Acid seared my throat, flooded my mouth, bringing with

it a recollection of the only other time I'd let blind lust get the better of me.

An invitation to some faceless heiress's birthday party in Gstaad I'd almost refused—until a possible business opportunity had been thrown in to sweeten the invitation.

A big deal bagged, followed by a night of hedonistic revelry.

A mistaken conclusion that I'd found a worthy soulmate, even though I'd never truly believed in that sort of flighty fantasy.

When that illusion had seemed to hold true in the clear light of day, for weeks and months, I'd congratulated myself for a wise choice made even in the midst of frivolity and decadence.

A proposal in Neostros, before friends and family, an engagement party to trump them all, and I was all set to buck the Xenakis family trend of backstabbing and buckling underneath the smallest pressure.

Even when suspicions arose…even when I allowed Anneka to talk me into another visit to Gstaad and a reluctant turn on the black ski run ended with me being launched twenty feet into the air and descending via a jagged aspen tree…she hadn't bailed.

Unlike most, who barely remembered their trauma, mine still played out in excruciating detail. I heard her cries as she held my hand and urged me to hold on. And I held on, remaining alert right until the doctors were forced to put me in a medical coma. I embraced even that, knowing she would be waiting for me when I woke.

But those fervent wishes for me to hold on had been born not of love but of callous greed and an unconscionable disregard for loyalty and integrity.

She calculated every move, right up until my eyes opened—literally and figuratively—to the betrayal and falsehoods so deeply ingrained she wore them like a second skin. One she attempted to hide with tears and cajoling until she'd learned that she couldn't fool a Xenakis twice.

I'd made a vow never to be caught in another traitorous web ever again.

Where was that vow an hour ago, Neo?

I stifled a growl at the mocking inner voice. There'd been quite enough growling for one night. One *lifetime*. The cold calculation with which I should have approached this situation finally arrived.

I stared at Sadie Preston. Watched her fidget, like she did in my office.

Then slowly that chin went up, throwing the face I'd framed in my hands and caressed into alluring relief while those green eyes began to spark.

'Are you going to stand there glaring at me all night? Look, I know the news is upsetting—'

Harsh laughter barked out of me, startling her, but there was no help for it. 'You think this is merely *upsetting*? Do you not understand that there's no making this right? No glossing over this?'

'I was just—'

'Attempting to make me feel better? Urging me to look on the bright side? Is *that* what the episode on the sofa was all about?'

Raw colour flared in her cheeks but she dared another step closer, that temper I'd suspected bubbled just beneath the surface rising. 'How dare you belittle it?' she breathed, stunning me with her fierce tone. 'It wasn't just a sordid little episode to me.'

'Wasn't it? If I didn't know better, I'd think you actually *mean* that.'

Another less readable look flashed in her eyes. Lips that had tasted exquisite beneath mine firmed, holding in whatever response she'd intended to utter for several seconds before she shook her head and spoke anyway.

'I know there's nothing I can say or do to alter what's

happened. But I was actually talking about the…the incident with the condom, not what brought me here in the first place.'

Christos, the broken condom. Another intensely unwelcome first in a day of abysmal firsts that needed to be smashed out of existence.

But then you wouldn't have met her.

Skatá! What was wrong with me?

I'd hung on to her when I should have handed her over to the authorities within minutes of her confession. Now was I playing devil's advocate with *myself*?

Never crossing paths with Sadie Preston was a trade-off I could cheerfully accept—and that gritty little knot in my stomach that called it out for a white lie be damned.

So what if my digital little black book hadn't been used for the longest stretch since its inception, and she, with that mystifying allure of defiance and sexiness, would've been a prime addition to it had we met under different circumstances?

Facts were facts. And the simple fact remained: sending her packing should have been my first and only course.

'The accident with the condom is another consequence to deal with. But it should be a fairly straightforward matter. I'll start by assuring you that you have nothing to worry about health-wise.'

She arched one well-shaped eyebrow. 'And I'm to take your word for that? Because you're…*you*?'

The clear censure in her tone grated. 'That's your prerogative. But other than the fact that I abhor liars, a man in my position would be extremely foolish not to take the necessary precautions when it comes to every facet of his life. My last medical check returned a clean bill of health. You're the only woman I've slept with since.'

Her eyes widened a touch, questions glinting in their depths. 'And what about…?'

The inevitable question. I needed to answer and it burned

its way up my throat—a searing reminder of why my association with this woman should have ended many hours ago.

'I'm sorry, but I can't *not* ask, can I?' she muttered.

Her expression morphed into one I'd seen on too many faces of friends and family members. Even those without full knowledge of what had happened in that hospital room deigned to pity me. It was why I'd banned my family from discussing my accident.

'I don't need your pity, Miss Preston. Or whatever that look on your face is supposed to signify. The simple truth is, I cannot father children. The *why* doesn't concern you. It's a proven reality—which makes your offer of a further visit to your previous place of employment null. The only thing I need from you right now is reciprocal reassurance that I'm not at risk after this unfortunate mishap.'

Her expression snapped back to that mixture of fiery irritation, hurt and censure.

She wore her feelings so plainly. She would be an abysmal poker player. So why did I crave to keep staring, keep attempting to read what else she felt within this chaos?

'I tell you this only for reassurance, in light of everything that's happened. Let's call it a courtesy.' She paused, pursed her lips. 'I've had one relationship. It lasted five months, while I was in my second year at uni, and I took every necessary precaution. So you have nothing to fear from me medically either,' she snapped.

A layer of tension released its grip on me, even while questions multiplied in my brain. Questions I batted away because, no, I most definitely did *not* care who that relationship had been with. Or why it had ended. These days not being 'in a relationship' didn't mean a woman was celibate. Did she belong to anyone now?

The urge to know was overpowering enough to force my fists closed, to grit my teeth just so the question wouldn't tumble out.

Thee mou, I was losing it.

Her eyes widened as she stared at me. Evidently, my poker face needed work too. She glanced away, her eyes lighting on the shabby little handbag resting on the entryway console table.

When she headed for it I remained where I stood, not trusting myself to approach her. But staying put didn't mean denying myself one final scrutiny of her body. Now that I'd tasted the passion and beauty beneath her tasteless clothes, my body wasn't in any mood to obey my commands to relegate Sadie Preston to the wasteland where she belonged. Instead, it tracked the supple shape of her calves and ankles, the tempting curve of her backside, the dip of her waist.

Her hair…

My fist clenched tighter. I'd never given much thought to a woman's hair before, except perhaps in the way it framed the overall package. I'd dated blondes, brunettes and everything in between without alighting on any specified preference.

Sadie's hair had trademarked its own siren call. One that had hooked into me, driving me to a new and dizzyingly dangerous edge.

'I suppose you want me to leave?'

I refocused on her face. She'd reclaimed her bag and slung it crossways over her slim torso, dragging my attention to her full breasts. I forced my gaze away from the perfect globes, crossed the living room to the front door to summon the lift.

A draining type of despair, a kind I'd never known before—not even when I stared into the heart of Anneka's cruel betrayal—sapped the dregs of my energy. I held it at bay with sheer willpower.

Barely.

'Neo…'

I pivoted to face her, renewed tension vibrating through to my very bones.

'I don't recall inviting you to use my first name. There's

nothing more to discuss. And, just so you're disabused of any lingering notions of attempting to make this right, let me lay it out for you. There's no way back from what you've done. Short of divine intervention and immaculate conception, you've effectively *ended* me, Sadie Preston. My last hope of ever becoming a father was that sample you destroyed. So I'm confident that you can get it through that stunning red head of yours that if I never see you again it will be too soon. Attempt any form of communication with me for any reason and this stay of execution I'm considering will be off the table and you'll be handed over to the authorities to answer for your crime. Is that understood?'

All colour drained from her face, but that stubborn chin remained high. *Defiant.*

'Perfectly. Goodbye, Mr Xenakis.'

Nine weeks later

'You shouldn't be going to work today, Sadie. You look even worse than you did yesterday. And you were out like a light when I looked in on you before I went to bed. I didn't disturb you because I thought a full night's sleep would do you good, but I can see it didn't.'

I busied myself fetching milk I didn't need from the fridge to make a cup of coffee I didn't intend to drink. All so I could avoid my mother's gaze and the questions lurking therein.

Despite despair and bone-tiredness leaching the strength from my bones, I strove to remain upbeat. 'I can't afford not to go to work. And I'm fine, Mum.' The *I promise* I usually tagged on to the reassurance stuck in my throat. I couldn't promise anything. Because I *wasn't* fine.

I hadn't thought it possible to be this far from fine when I blinked back tears as Neo Xenakis's lift hurled me down to the ground floor after that unforgettable night.

I'd been wrong.

That cloying sense of unworthiness, germinated after my father's desertion and watered by doubts and hopelessness, had trebled overnight, and the enormity of what I'd done both before and after meeting Neo Xenakis had thrown me into a state of raw despair. One that'd grown exponentially with the final notice from our landlord a week ago.

We were on a countdown clock to homelessness.

I hadn't been able to bring myself to tell my mother yet.

But I'd been doing a lot of evading lately.

In between sporadic temping I'd ignored the flulike symptoms leaching my energy, initially attributing my delayed period to the condition. Even after a second period was a no-show, I'd refused to believe that fate would be so brutal. That the unthinkable could truly happen.

Then had come the bracing, inevitable acceptance that I wasn't the victim of lingering flu, or a stomach bug that only attacked in the morning, but that, yes, I *was* capable of conceiving immaculately.

Shock.

Disbelief.

A brief spurt of searing anger at Neo Xenakis and his lies.

Followed by that ever-present tug of despair. That feeling of unworthiness. That cruel little reminder that my own blueprint was flawed.

But even while despair lodged a heavy stone in my chest there also came a quiet, even more bewildering…*elation*. Even though I was twenty-five, working jobs that paid a pittance and on the brink of homelessness with a mother who'd promised me, when I finally broke down and begged her to seek help, to combat her growing gambling addiction but had since regressed—as evidenced by the online betting pages I'd spotted on her phone yesterday.

That crushing list of failings was what had overwhelmed me last night. Made me pretend to be asleep when my mother entered the bedroom we shared.

Elation should be the farthest emotion on my reality spectrum.

A hysterical thought flitted across my mind. Perhaps I should have taken a gamble on myself. I'd be wildly wealthy and down one less problem by now. Because, despite all the odds against it, I'd fallen pregnant with Neo Xenakis's baby after one utterly misguided folly.

A baby…

Sweet heaven…

I can't father children…

The lie had dripped so smoothly, so convincingly from his lips. And I'd *believed* him. Had even hurt for him. When all he'd been doing was cruelly toying with my emotions.

Had he seen my feverish desire to stay anchored, *connected*, for just a little while, and viciously exploited it as some sort of payback? Did the man I'd given myself to, in an act I suspected had involved more than just the physical, bear traits of the father who'd so callously rejected me…?

'Sadie, dear, are you sure you're all right? You've gone as white as a ghost.'

I swallowed the encroaching nausea and a bubble of lurking panic, thankful that my mother hadn't noticed that on top of my pseudo-flu I was also plagued by bouts of vomiting.

'I'm not sick, Mum. Really,' I said, infusing as much warmth into my voice as possible.

'Okay, well…if you're sure. I'm going back to bed. Have a good day at work.'

She left the kitchen after sliding a comforting hand down my back. Absurdly, the gesture made my eyes prickle.

I blinked the tears away, forced myself to revisit the subject that filled me with equal parts anger and dread: relaying the news to Neo.

His last tersely worded warning before tossing me out of his penthouse still lingered, two months on. And I believed he'd meant what he'd said.

Then, of course.

But in light of this life-changing news…

I wouldn't know until I tried. *Again*.

My initial attempts to contact Neo had met a brick wall, with a few snooty receptionists even threatening to block my number if I kept trying to reach their illustrious boss. Apparently Neo had issued word that I was persona non grata.

Initially aggrieved by the realisation, I'd stopped trying to reach him for all of three days, before accepting that this reality wasn't going to go away.

Neo needed to learn of his child's existence sooner rather than later. And answer a few pointed questions in the process…

Since returning to his building and risking arrest or worse was out of the question, I ventured onto social media—only to discover that the Xenakis family were embroiled in the kind of publicity that drove the tabloids wild.

Apparently, in the last few weeks, Neo's older brother Axios had returned from a brief trip abroad with his young wife in tow. A wife whose previous absence had been highly conspicuous, fuelling all kinds of scandalous speculation.

Now, not only had the young Mrs Xenakis returned from her mysterious absence without explanation, she'd apparently given birth while she was away. The reunited family had asked for privacy, but already several shots of a baby boy, Andreos Xenakis, had been leaked to the media. He was a gorgeous baby, who bore all the strong characteristics of possessing the Xenakis DNA.

How was Neo taking the news? And, the more important question, how would he take *my* news?

It was only eight o'clock. My temp job didn't start until ten. That gave me a little time to attempt to reach Neo again.

Distaste at the thought of stalking him online lingered as I powered up my laptop. The first headline I found made my stomach drop.

*Xenakis Aeronautics Soars to New Heights in the
Far East.*

Exhaling shakily, I read the article, calming down when
I saw it focused mostly on Axios Xenakis and his spear-
heading of the airline conglomerate's global expansion.
Neo would be taking over the European arm of the company, starting with relocating to Athens with immediate
effect.

The article was two weeks old. Which meant Neo might
now be even further out of reach.

Suppressing the strong bite of despondency, I scribbled
down the numbers of the Athens office, shut down the laptop and rushed to the bathroom just in time to heave.

A quick shower and a judiciously nibbled slice of dry
toast later, I picked up my bag and headed for the door—
only to pause when my mother called out.

'Oh, Sadie, when you can, do you think you can buy me
some data for my phone? I seem to have run out.'

Desolation deadened my feet. The urge to tell her that I
was barely holding it together emotionally and financially,
never mind providing a conduit for her addiction, tripped
on the edge of my tongue. But I was woefully ill-equipped
for a replay of the inevitable tears and depression that had
dogged Martha Preston's life since her husband's cruel desertion. As much as I wanted to dish out tough love, I could
barely hold myself together, and nor could I afford to lose
another job because I was late.

Vowing to tackle the subject again that evening, I shut
the door behind me.

The morning trundled by in the tedium of filing and answering phones.

After using the first minutes of my late lunch break to
calm my nerves, I dialled the number I'd saved.

One minute later I hung up, my ears ringing after a crisp,
accented voice informed me that while Mr Xenakis was

indeed at his office in Athens, he did not accept unsolicited calls.

No amount of pleading had shifted the receptionist's stance.

In the middle of the busy London park, I gritted my teeth and resisted the urge to scream. Or dissolve into helpless tears. Instead, on a desperate urge, I called up the web page of a budget airline, my heart racing when I saw a same-day return flight to Athens.

It would put further strain on my tight bank balance, and would require even more ruthless financial rationing, but the temp agency had no placement for me tomorrow and I had nothing planned for the weekend besides tormenting myself with the many ways my failed childhood might affect my baby...

Without stopping to debate the wisdom of it, I booked the ticket.

Regardless of his reasons for stating a blatant untruth, I owed Neo the news that he was going to be a father. Just as he'd deserved to know of my mistake at the Phoenix Clinic.

Would he think it was another unforgivable mistake?

Would he walk away even sooner than my father had?

It didn't matter.

No. It matters. It's why you won't stop shaking.

I smothered the voice, shrugging mentally. For good or ill, I was going to beard the formidable lion that was Neo Xenakis in his den one more time.

But this time, I was suitably armed with what to expect.

The seat of the Xenakis airline empire was housed in a sprawling ten-storey building that took up a whole city block in the centre of Athens. Security was twice as tight as in London, but this time I didn't linger outside. The brief, succinct note I'd hastily written in the taxi ride and shoved into an envelope trembled in my hand as I approached the ultramodern reception desk.

Before the efficient-looking receptionist could voice the disdain lurking in her eyes, I held out the envelope. 'It's essential that Mr Xenakis sees this immediately.'

Whatever expression she read on my face halted her answer. Rising, she took the note and walked away.

I retreated to the nearest set of expensive club chairs, arranged to maximise the appreciation of the stunning marble-floored, three-storey atrium that formed the welcoming entry into the world of Xenakis Aeronautics, the words of the note echoing in my head:

Mr Xenakis,
I'm downstairs in your lobby.
   It's in your interest to give me ten minutes of your time.
   I'm certain you'll regret it if you don't.
Sadie

Bold words, which would either grant me an audience or fritter away the mercy he'd shown me by not asking Wendell to break out the handcuffs that day in London.

I looked up to see Wendell heading my way, as if summoned by my thought. My heart dropped, but I refused to look away.

'If you're here to throw me out, you should know that I'll simply turn around and come straight back. Maybe you should tell your boss that?'

His expression didn't change. 'Mr Xenakis will see you now.'

I swallowed my surprise and followed him.

This time, knowing the calibre of the man who waited behind another set of imposing doors, I tightened my gut, sure I could mitigate the effect.

I was wrong.

Being on his home turf had heaped another layer of magnificent appeal upon a man who already held more than his fair share. In the sunlight that filtered through wide, rect-angular windows, his dark hair gleamed. A skin-skimming stubble highlighted his strong jaw, and with that sexy dimple in his chin it was impossible to stop the flare of heat that attacked my body, robbing me of vital breath for precious seconds.

The matching jacket to his tailored grey trousers hung on a hook in the far corner of his office, leaving him in a pristine white shirt that moulded his broad shoulders and powerful biceps.

Terrified I was already losing the fight for composure, I hurried to speak. To get this over with.

'Thank you for seeing me, Mr Xenakis.'

Eyes that had been conducting a slow, thorough scrutiny of me rose to fix on my face. 'Miss Preston.' His voice was grave. 'I'm beginning to think you have some sort of death wish. Or do you simply relish testing my patience?'

'Neither. Believe me, this is the last place I want to be.'

His arrogant head cocked. 'I sense the inevitable *but* coming,' he drawled mockingly. 'Although I have no earthly idea what it could be.'

Despite his words, he narrowed his eyes, as if he fully suspected a scam. Or worse.

Say it. Just say it and leave.

I sucked in a breath that went nowhere near replenishing my lungs or giving me the courage I craved. 'I'm pregnant. The baby is yours. I thought you should know.'

Deathly silence echoed in the vast office. Then he inhaled sharply, the white-hot sound sizzling across the large room.

'*Christos*, you *do* have a death wish,' he breathed in sizzling disbelief, and his face, unlike last time, when there'd been shock and bleak despair, was a picture of complete and utter fury.

'I don't, I assure you. But—'

'Then you've taken complete leave of your senses. Be-

cause that can be the only viable explanation for this—'
He stopped abruptly, his hands clenching and unclenching at his sides.

For one mad moment I wanted to say yes. That only a peculiar strain of madness would explain why I couldn't look away from his face, why I couldn't quite catch my breath in his presence.

'The door is behind you. Use it right now or I won't be held responsible for my actions.'

It was a hushed entreaty, perhaps even a final attempt at civility for a man hanging by a thread.

Considering I'd jumped on a plane with little hope of being granted even this audience, I was surprised I'd got this far. But complete dismissal wasn't what I'd expected.

The urge to linger, to make him believe, if only for the sake of telling my baby someday that I'd tried, fired through me—along with the question that still demanded an answer. The question about his false statement, the consequences of which had certainly taken *me* by surprise.

But Neo's face was turning even more ashen, his chest rising and falling in rapid shudders as he remained frozen in place.

'Why?' The question was ragged, torn from his soul.

'Excuse me?'

He prowled forward several steps, granting me a better look at his face. And there it was. That look of desolation.

'Why would you do this? Did someone put you up to it? As a joke, perhaps?' he asked from between whitened lips. 'Or a bet?'

'We don't move in the same circles, Mr Xenakis. Nor am I friendly with anyone who would deliberately cause someone distress with such a prank.'

'Then tell me *why*?'

There was a tinge of desperation in his question. Of bewilderment.

'Because it's the truth!'

He jerked forward again, his throat moving as his eyes drilled into me. 'No, it's not. As I told you in London, I'm incapable of fathering children. Three years ago the best doctors in the world delivered that staggering news. And do you know what I did?'

Numb, I shook my head, my anger at his lies dissipating in the face of the searing emotion in his eyes.

'I found a set of doctors with better credentials than the original set. Guess what? They arrived at the same conclusion. So now do you see how what you're saying is impossible?'

Why?

Where?

How?

Questions flashed through my brain even while I accepted that this wasn't the time or place.

I licked lips gone dry with growing anxiety. 'I can't speak to your experience. All I can tell you is my truth.'

If anything, his fury grew. 'Does this *truth* involve a lapsed memory on your part?'

I shook my head. 'I'm sorry—you've lost me.'

His jaw turned to steel. 'You wouldn't be the first woman to find herself in this situation and devise a plan to pass another man's child off as—'

'Don't you *dare* finish that sentence!'

'Because it's much closer to this "truth" you seek to ram down my throat?'

'Because it's most definitely guaranteed to get you slapped! And while we're throwing accusations around, what about what you said to me?'

'I beg your pardon?'

'You assured me I had nothing to worry about. You said I couldn't get pregnant! That it was impossible.'

'And I have a file of medical reports to back that up. What do *you* have?' he snarled.

'I have that immaculate conception you wished for, apparently. Because three pregnancy tests last week and a trip to the doctor confirms that I'm carrying a baby. *Your* baby!'

He shook his head, started to speak.

I held up my hand. 'It's fine if you don't want to believe me. I don't care.'

'You *do* care or you wouldn't be here. Or be crying,' he grated.

Belatedly, I registered the dampness on my cheek. Hating myself for that weakness, I dashed my hand across my cheek. Only to feel more tears spilling.

'It must be a side effect of being repeatedly labelled a liar. Or... I don't know... Pregnancy hormones. But, no matter what, this was the right thing to do. And now it's done.'

There—you've said your piece. Now leave.

But my feet refused to move.

His eyes narrowed with laser focus. 'If there truly is a baby, does the news distress you that much?'

'*Yes!* You lulled me into a false sense of security, made me think I had the flu when I'm *pregnant*!'

He went a little pale, his movements jerky as he closed the gap between us. 'And what would you have done if I'd told you two months ago that there *was* this possibility, hmm? Considered your options *without* me in the picture, perhaps?'

'Watch your tone, Mr Xenakis. The last thing you should be doing is lounging on that lofty perch and looking down your nose at me. What happened between us was consensual. What happened with the condom was unfortunate. You do *not* have the right to question my character. Considering the way we parted, do you really think I would be here, right now, if that was my intention?'

He seemed lost for words even as his gaze scoured my face, dissecting my words.

'You said yourself you only verified the pregnancy a week ago. That means you're about two months along. It's not too late for other options. Maybe that's your plan? To leverage those options?'

His insult sank in, sharp as a stiletto blade. 'God, you can't help yourself, can you?' I realised I'd screamed the words only after they came out.

He frowned. 'Calm yourself, Sadie.'

'If you want me to calm down, then stop upsetting me—*Neo*!'

He sucked in a deep breath, then another. Then he whirled around, dragging his fingers through his hair. Swift strides put the width of the room between us and I watched him stare out of the window at the Friday afternoon traffic, tension riding his shoulders.

Walking out through the door should've been easy, but again that stubborn need to have him believe me held me rooted to the spot.

So when he abruptly grated, 'Perhaps we should discuss this further. Take a seat. Please,' I glared at his back for all of half a second before stumbling over to one of the twin plush sofas positioned tastefully at one side of his office.

Unlike his stunning but impersonal London penthouse, there were more signs of Neo Xenakis's personality here. Priceless objets d'art were placed next to pictures of what looked like his family, and there was even a framed child's drawing. On the coffee table, a large book on Mayan history was open to a well-thumbed page, and several more Aztec-themed books were piled to one side.

The notion that in another time or place I'd have liked to get to know this stranger whose baby I carried hit me hard.

I was busy pushing the thought away when I heard his deep, low tones. He stood at his desk, speaking in rapid-fire Greek. Done, he returned to the window and stood there for an age.

When he turned around, every inch of his body brimmed with purpose. 'You mentioned that you saw a doctor?'

'Yes…after I took the pregnancy tests.'

'And?'

'Everything's fine so far.'

'This probably won't come as a surprise to you, but to me the possibility of an offspring is not…unwelcome.'

The depth of yearning in his low, deep voice rocked me to my core, softening a knotted place inside me I hadn't registered until his words loosened it. Truth be told, I hadn't allowed myself to think beyond delivering the news. Because when it came down to it, Neo had plenty of other options beyond having a baby with the woman who'd brought chaos into his life. If he was willing to accept—

'If it's mine, that is. And at this point I'm hard-pressed to be convinced it is.'

The soft place hardened, strangled tight by his words. 'You really believe I'd lie about something like this?'

The yearning receded slowly, forced back by the power of his scepticism. And something else. Something dark and grave that took complete control of him, hardening his face into a rigid, implacable mask.

'I'm a wealthy, influential man. Anyone with a competent internet connection can see for themselves what any association with the Xenakis family represents. Believe it or not, you won't be the first woman to attempt to saddle me with a paternity claim. Even when the likelihood is remote.'

He believed it. He truly believed he was infertile.

Despite the anguish dredging through me, a tiny voice urged reason. Urged me to see this from his point of view. How many headlines had I caught from my mother's gossip magazines that shouted about a celebrity vehemently denying alleged paternity? How many women had attempted to scam rich men by dangling a baby in their faces?

I was wasting my time.

Neo wouldn't believe even if I shouted until I was blue in the face.

I rose. 'Your hang-ups are your problem, not mine. I have a plane to catch, so I guess it's goodbye, Mr Xenakis.'

He moved with impressive speed. Before I could take my next breath, Neo had arrived before me.

'That's it? You came to deliver the news and now you're just going to head to the airport and return home?'

I dredged up a smile. 'Let me guess. This is where you expect me to make some sort of demand? Maybe ask for financial support or a McMansion to live in while I carry your child? Well, sorry to disappoint you. I want nothing from you.'

The faint colour tingeing his sculpted cheekbones told me I'd hit the nail on the head.

'Did you not hear me when I said I want this baby?' he asked.

'No, what I heard was you hedging your bets on the off-chance that I'm telling the truth. When you decide whether you want to believe me, I'm sure Wendell will be able to find me—'

'No,' he interrupted. 'That is most definitely *not* how this is going to work.'

'What's that supposed to—'

We both froze when déjà vu arrived in the hideously embarrassing form of my stomach giving the loudest growl known to humanity.

He muttered what sounded like an incredulous Greek oath under his breath. 'Tell me you haven't been neglecting to eat?' he bit out.

Heat consumed my face. 'I'm in the throes of a spectacular experience called morning sickness. Anything I eat before a certain time rarely stays down.'

He frowned. 'Surely there's a remedy for that?'

I shrugged. 'If there is, they haven't found it yet.'

His frown intensified. 'So the answer is what…? To starve yourself?'

'I don't do it deliberately, you know. My flight here was at an ungodly hour this morning.'

An exasperated puff of air left his lips as he glanced at

his watch. 'It's now past noon. Does this mean you haven't eaten all day?'

'I tried to eat something on the plane.'

His lips twisted in distaste. 'Budget airline food?'

'We can't *all* afford to travel on private jets, Mr Xenakis.'

'Neo,' he drawled. 'Call me Neo.'

'I'm not sure I want to call you anything, to be honest.'

'If the child you carry is truly mine there's one title you won't be able to deny me,' he stated with stone-rough gravity, just as a discreet knock sounded on the door.

He responded in Greek, and a moment later an impeccably dressed middle-aged woman entered, holding a package which she handed to Neo. Without glancing my way, she discreetly retreated.

He studied me for a moment, then reached into the bag. Although I suspected what the contents were, I was still shocked when he took out the oblong package.

'You sent out for a pregnancy test?'

'With the full intention of accepting any offence it might cause you, yes,' he stated simply, his fingers tight around the box. 'Will you take the test?' he asked, his tone containing a peculiar note I couldn't fathom.

There was something going on here. Something beneath the surface that I couldn't quite put my finger on. Again, questions surrounding the reasons why he believed he couldn't father children crowded my brain.

Resolutely, I pushed them away and accepted the status quo. For now. 'Only to prove I'm not a liar.'

I held my hand out for it but he hesitated, his jaw working for several seconds before he said, 'You should know that this is merely a preliminary test to confirm your pregnancy. A test for paternity will be necessary when the time is right.'

My hand dropped, something hot and sharp lancing my chest. 'You really are something else—you know that?'

'*Ne*, I've been told.' His stance didn't change.

'If you think I'm going to harm my baby just so your suspicions can be satisfied, you can think again.'

Emotion, heavy and profound and almost sacred, gleamed in his eyes. 'So you've made up your mind? You intend to keep it?' he rasped, his voice shaken.

'You think I flew three and a half hours on a cramped middle seat, next to a passenger with a rabid aversion to good personal hygiene, to tell you I'm pregnant, only to go back and get rid of it?'

Neo's gaze dropped to the hand I'd unconsciously jerked up to cradle my still-flat stomach.

'You think I don't have other things to do? I have a life to be getting on with. A mother who needs me to take care of—' I shut my mouth, but it was too late.

The moment his eyes narrowed I knew he was about to pounce on my unguarded revelation. 'Your mother needs taking care of? What's wrong with her?' he demanded sharply.

'It's none of your business.'

'I beg to differ. If this baby is mine—'

I swatted the rest of his words away. 'Enough with the *if*s. Here—hand it over. I'll take your precious test.'

Grim-faced, he held out the pregnancy test. I took it, then followed the tall, imposing body that hadn't diminished one iota in the drop-dead-gorgeous stakes in the last two months down a wide private hallway adjoining his office to a sleek, dark door.

The bathroom was another stylish masterpiece—naturally. Gleaming surfaces held exclusive toiletries, polished floors echoed my nervous tread and the wide mirror faithfully reflected my wan features.

I diverted my face from it, hurried into the cubicle and took the test.

A little over three minutes later, I stepped out.

He stood, square and true, five feet from the door, his gaze piercingly intent on the stick in my hand. For a single moment—knowing what this meant even if he doubted me, knowing I was perhaps about to change Neo Xenakis's life—something moved in my chest.

Then he ruined it by holding out an imperious hand for the test.

I handed it over.

His gaze dropped to it and he swallowed hard.

He seemed to rock on his feet—a fascinating feat to watch, especially for a toweringly powerful man like him. He didn't speak, only held the stick as if it was a magic wand that had the potential to deliver his most heartfelt wish.

Afraid I would succumb to softening emotions again, I hurried to speak. 'As you can see, it indicates how many weeks along I am. I can give you the date of my last period too, if you want?'

It was meant to be sarcastic. It fell far short simply because I wanted him to believe me. Wanted to take away his doubt once and for all.

Because I wanted to hurry to the part where, despite the evidence, he'd conclude that fatherhood wasn't for him after all. That this was a mistake. That *I* wasn't worthy to carry his child.

He didn't respond immediately. When he lifted his gaze his eyes were a stormy, dark grey, the pupils almost black. 'This is sufficient for now,' he finally said, his voice gravel rough.

Then he turned and walked away.

CHAPTER FIVE

I COULD BARELY walk beneath the staggering evidence of what I held in my hand.

Confirmation that there was a child, possibly *my* child, shook through me with every step back to my office. The circumstances astounded me. Seemed almost too good to be true—the stuff of big-screen melodramas.

Had the woman who'd brought desolation to my door returned with redemption, despite my threat to her the last time she'd been in my presence? Despite the medical evidence I'd been provided with to the contrary?

What were the chances of lightning striking twice? Was I setting myself up for the same kind of betrayal Anneka had dished out so callously?

My jaw gritted, my stomach churning with the need for one hundred percent certainty.

I sucked in a calming breath, recalling what rash decisions had led me here in the first place. My fingers tightened around the stick. Not that I regretted it…*if* it was truly happening.

A bolt of euphoria threatened to overwhelm my calm. Brutally, I suppressed it. Rationalised it.

As Sadie had pointed out, the kit I'd asked my trustworthy assistant to purchase was the highest quality, giving an estimation of gestation. The test announced Sadie was more than three weeks pregnant.

Surely she knew how powerful I was? Knew that any information provided could be easily verified by my security team? Would she be so foolish as to toss out falsities that could catch her out?

A throat was cleared huskily behind me, making me aware I'd reached my desk, opened the secure thumbprint-accessed drawer that held confidential documents and was in the process of dropping the stick into it. I needed that connection, this visual evidence that maybe, just *maybe*, I'd defied science and the odds.

Again, stunned awe shook through me. A child. *My child.* But just as swiftly, a less effervescent emotion rose. A little desperate, and a lot dismaying.

The thought struck me that I had no true compass as to how to *be* a father. I'd gone straight from boarding school to boardroom, my spare moments spent watching my grandfather struggle to hang on to the company, and subsequently witnessed my father and Ax embroiled in a cold battle for the helm of the company.

I'd used my time on the sidelines efficiently—learned everything I needed to excel in my field.

Those lessons hadn't included how to be a father.

'Now that we've established that there's a pregnancy, are we done here?' she asked.

Done here? Was she joking? 'No, we're not done. Far from it.'

'What's that supposed to mean?'

'It means I intend to be involved in this baby's welfare every step of the way. Beginning now.'

I forestalled the questions brimming in her eyes by making a quick phone call.

The moment I was done, she approached.

Shock born of the earth-shattering news she'd delivered had partly blocked off the stunning effect of her appearance. Now, with the flood dammed and a plan of action swiftly slotting into place in order to secure what she insisted was mine, I couldn't stem my reaction to her.

The white sundress was a cheap and simple design, but on her it looked anything but. The scooped neckline gave a tantalising glimpse of the perfect breasts that seemed to have swelled a size bigger with her pregnancy. And her skin, now her temper had subsided, glowed with an additional translucence that triggered wild tingles in my fingers with a need to trace, to caress... *Christos*, to lay my lips against that pulse before stealing another taste of those rosebud lips, currently caught between her teeth as she watched me.

I bit back a growl as my gaze rose to that final monument to her beauty. Two months on, her hair had grown longer, the ponytail she'd caught the heavy tresses into almost down to the middle of her back.

The hunger to set it free, to lose myself in the exotic scent of it, powered through me.

'Explain what that means. Precisely. Because less than twenty minutes ago you were almost apoplectic about my perceived deception.'

I forced myself to throttle back this insane arousal that fired up only with her.

It wasn't for lack of trying that I'd remained dateless since that night in London. Hell, I might even have cursed Sadie Preston a little for the sudden urge to set my useless little black book on fire because not a single woman listed within sparked the kind of flame she did with a mere look.

'You have to be aware that I intend to take every precaution with you?'

Her wary glance confirmed that notion was becoming clear to her.

'I've told you I only came here to give you the news—which I could've done by phone if you hadn't blacklisted me.'

While the accusation grated a little, I couldn't allow it to dissuade me from forging ahead. 'From this moment forward consider that status reversed. You will have access to me day or night.'

Curiously, her breath caught, and I glimpsed something that looked like excitement in her eyes—which, perversely, triggered a stronger chain reaction within me.

Her trite reply attempted to disguise her reaction. 'Others might find that offer beyond tantalising, but I don't think much communication between us will be necessary after today…'

Unbidden, my lips twisted in genuine amusement, causing her words to trail off.

'I fail to see what's funny.'

Wonder. Apprehension. Raw anticipation. Panic. The cascade of emotions was threatening to send me off balance.

'You're carrying my child, Sadie. A Xenakis.'

Her eyes widened. 'So you believe the baby is yours?'

Betrayal's curse bit hard—a timely reminder to exercise caution. But for now I needed to buy myself time. After the accusations I'd hurled at her, and her reaction, these negotiations needed to be handled carefully while still keeping her under scrutiny. Because I didn't intend for history to repeat itself.

'In utero paternity tests carry unacceptable risks. We will wait until the baby is born.'

'And how do you know that?'

I clenched my gut against the searing reminder of how wrong I'd been before, how blind trust had almost decimated me.

'That doesn't matter. What matters is that we're in agreement that the health of this baby is the priority.'

She frowned. 'I don't need you to tell me that.'

'Then you'll stay a little while longer? Have lunch with me?'

Her eyes widened, then grew suspicious. 'Why?'

'You need to eat, do you not?'

Memory darkened her eyes and swept the most becoming blush across her skin. She was recalling what had happened after our last meal together. When her long lashes drifted down to veil her expression, I forced back the wild need to nudge her chin up, to see the evidence of the chemistry that heated the very air around us.

'Doesn't mean I have to eat with *you*,' she murmured.

For some absurd reason I bit back another smile, and the urge to keep tangling with her spiralled through me.

'I won't sully your meal with my presence, if that is your wish.'

Surprise jerked her gaze back to me. 'You won't?'

'I have a few more business matters to deal with. You can eat while I take care of them.'

The knock on the door at that moment drew her suspicion.

'You've already ordered lunch, haven't you?'

I shrugged. 'On the off-chance that you'd agree to stay, yes.'

'There's nothing "off-chance" about anything you do, but nice try,' she sniped.

As she headed to the sofa and I returned to my desk, my smile turned resolute. She had no idea how accurate her words were. How meticulously I intended to seal her completely into my life.

If this child was mine—and, *Christos*, I would burn the world down if I'd been fooled for a second time—then nothing in all existence would stop me from claiming it.

For two hours I attempted to ignore her disquieting presence, to concentrate on laying the groundwork for what needed to be done. But with every appreciative bite of the meal I'd had my chef prepare for her, with every stretch of her voluptuous body as she shifted on the sofa and every flick of her hair over her shoulder, my body reacted with visceral hunger.

A hunger I cursed with every breath for messing with my concentration and control. For being neither circumspect nor discerning about the kind of woman it wanted.

First Anneka, with her wide-eyed innocence that had hidden a grotesquely flawed character. Now this green-eyed siren, who should be the last woman to pique my interest and yet fired me up with one simple defiant look.

'You're glaring at me,' she stated, while glaring right back.

I ended a call that was going nowhere fast, rose and approached her. With each step I knew the path I was taking was the right one. Swift. Precise.

Permanent?

She would resist my plans, of course. I chose to ignore the kick in my gut signalling that I'd relish tussling with her. This was more than base pleasure. This was laying the foundations to secure my heir's future.

Her stunning green eyes widened a touch, and I was gratified to see her gaze rush over me before she attempted to look away.

'Did you enjoy your lunch?'

She shrugged. 'It was fine, thanks.'

Her gaze grew more wary the closer I got. Did she know how enthralling she looked, with her face tilted up to me like that, the satin-smooth perfection of her neck just begging to be stroked?

For several heartbeats after I stopped, she stared at me. Then she visibly roused herself, picked up her purse and rose.

'I should be going. If I'm lucky, I might catch an earlier flight.'

'You're aware we have a lot more to discuss?'

She paused. 'Like what?'

'Like your employment status, for starters. Have you secured another job since the incident at the clinic?'

Her gaze swept away. 'Not a permanent one. I'm currently temping.'

I forced my jaw not to grit. 'Are you going to tell me what you meant about your mother?'

Her chin lifted at that. 'No. It's still none of your business.'

'The welfare of this child is paramount. Nothing is going to stop me ensuring it doesn't come to harm. I wish you to be absolutely clear about that.'

'And you intend to dig your way through my life to do that?' she challenged.

'I intend to take away whatever worries you so that you can concentrate on remaining healthy.'

The answer disarmed her. As it had been intended to. Her lips parted, triggering a shot of heat to my groin.

'You…can't do that.'

'Can't I? How exactly do you propose to stop me?'

Her eyes sparkled with that telling green that spelled the start of her temper. 'A restraining order, for starters?'

I curbed the curious smile that threatened. 'What's to stop me from returning the favour? Or have you forgotten the small matter of your crime?'

Vexation receded, to be replaced by apprehension. 'I'm getting tired of your veiled threats, Mr Xenakis.'

'I said you may call me Neo.'

One elegant eyebrow quirked. 'Oh, I can use your first name now, can I?'

A touch of regret zinged through me. 'You'll have to excuse me for not being at my best that day. I wasn't aware that a tangible part of my future had been affected until I heard your news. It was hard to deal with. Almost as I hard as it was for you to deliver the news to me, perhaps?'

After a beat, she shook her head. 'It wasn't easy, no. I guess it's fair you'd want to put it behind you.'

Memories of the passionate way that day had ended blazed hot and insistent. 'Not all aspects of it. And, as it turns out, it will be impossible to do so now.'

Again awareness flashed in her luminous eyes, before she shrugged and took a few steps away from me.

'It is what it is. Now, I'd really like to make that flight, so if you don't mind…?'

I let her leave, granting us both a moment's necessary reprieve. But within seconds of her walking out, I was back at my desk. A quick phone call to my assistant with a hand-

ful of immediate action instructions, and I was heading out
through the door.

She was already in the lift, her gaze triumphant as the
steel doors slid shut between us. I called the next one, further unsettled by the whisper of a smile that I felt curve my
lips. I frowned it off.

This was no smiling matter.

When Ax had delivered the news of his unexpected son I
experienced a moment's searing jealousy, even while being
overjoyed at his good fortune. But I also witnessed his despair at missing his son's first few months.

Nothing would come between me and every step of my
child's growth in its mother's womb. Nor a single moment
of its life.

If it's yours.

Seven months. For the chance at fatherhood I believed
had been cruelly snatched away by a computer mistake, I
would endure the torturous wait.

She rounded on me the moment I stepped out of the lift,
the tail of her long hair a swinging, living flame I wanted
to wrap around my fist.

'Really? You've instructed your goons to stop me from
leaving?' she spat out.

'I have done nothing of the sort. Wendell is aware of
my intention to give you a lift to the airport and he merely
wished for you to wait for me. Isn't that so, Wendell?' I
arched a brow at the stoic ex-military man.

'Precisely, sir.'

Sadie rolled her eyes. 'You two make a cracking comedy
duo. Can I leave now?'

'Of course.'

She looked surprised when I held the door for her. How
had the male she'd indulged in that brief relationship with
treated her? Clearly not well enough, if a little chivalry surprised her. What about her mother?

Registering that I knew next to nothing about the woman

who was possibly carrying my child rankled. Enough to make me grow absent-minded as I slid my hand around her waist.

She started, her breath hitching as she shifted away from my touch and stepped dangerously close the kerb.

I caught her arm, stemming momentary panic. 'Easy, *pethi mou.*'

'I… You startled me, that's all.'

'I merely touched you to guide you to the car.'

Her translucent skin flushed again, the captivating sweep of her long lashes brushing her cheeks as she blinked. 'Well, I wasn't expecting it.'

The car drew up. I waved the driver away and opened the door for her. With another flick of her green eyes, she slid in. I followed, tightening my gut against the punch of lust that hit me at the display of one smooth, shapely leg.

The fact that she seemed determined to secrete herself as far away from me as possible when I joined her triggered a bolt of disgruntlement. Was I really that fearsome?

Yes. You all but slapped on the handcuffs both times she attempted to contact you.

Perhaps I *had* been fearsome—whereas Sadie, both times, had been…brave.

Registering the path of my thoughts, the new respect for her actions, I sheared off the notion. It remained to be seen whether her motives were truly altruistic.

And if they weren't?

The sheer depth of my hollow dread unnerved me. Enough for me to step away from it—leave it alone in a way I'd left nothing alone for as long as I could remember. I wasn't ready to tackle *what if*s. Especially the ever-growing one that demanded credentials as to my suitability as a father. Not yet.

What I *could* do was lay further bricks for the lockdown I had in mind.

'Xenakis Aeronautics is expanding into Latin America—

specifically Brazil and Argentina. But my marketing team are struggling to find traction for our newest marketing venture.'

Interest flickered in her gaze. 'What's the problem?' she asked after a handful of seconds.

'We beta-tested our new airline cabin six months ago, to rousing success, but the take-up fell sharply after three months.'

'What does this new cabin deliver? How is it different from other airline cabins?'

Did she realise she'd leaned forward? That her eyes sparkled with interest and intelligence? Clearly this was a subject she liked. Which begged the question of what had happened to stall her studies.

'They're like suites—one step up from first class, but not out of the realms of affordability for the successful individual.'

'I've seen promotional stuff from other airlines. If your cabins are two-person berths only...'

She paused as I shook my head. 'They range from two to six.'

Her eyes widened. 'That's...amazing. But I bet your team's marketing plan was to target billionaires and oligarchs who have more money than they know what do with?'

She'd hit the nail right on the head. 'Something like that.'

Her pert nose wrinkled in a grimace. 'Which begs the question—why would this oligarch fly in a superclass suite on a premium airline when he could charter his own plane? It'll most likely be for the bragging rights, which will lose their lustre after a handful of flights. I'm confident that's why you're experiencing a drop-off. You need to refine the suites. Since they can accommodate up to six, why not attract an entirely different demographic? Besides the luxury and exclusivity of having a suite to yourself on a commercial airline, the unique design also offers privacy.'

'What would be your plan if *you* were in charge?'

She grew even more animated, her eyes sparkling brighter. 'Oh, that's simple. I'd push hard to attract young, successful millennial families. Believe me, there's nothing worse than having an irate child kicking the back of your seat for hours on a long-haul flight. I can't imagine what it's like for harried parents having to apologise to disgruntled passengers. This will be a win-win for everyone. So why not market the suites to those who will welcome peace and quiet together with luxury and exclusivity? I'm assuming your suites are on the upper deck, like the others I've seen?'

I was a little put out that she knew more about my rivals' products than mine. 'Not only that, the Xen Suites come with premium sound insulation.'

She nodded enthusiastically. 'Just think how much that would appeal to the parents with young families who can afford it. And if you have a loyalty programme in place, where passengers can aspire to use of the suites, then it will boost the uptake even further.'

'The Xen Loyalty Programme is one of the best in the industry.'

'But I bet there's a steep points rise from, say, business class to superior class?'

I shrugged noncommittally.

She gave me a wry look. 'On the basis that I'm right, I'd offer incentives for the target demographic to try the suites for a limited period. I'm confident you'll see a sustained growth.'

'Are you, now?'

About to respond, most likely with a tart rejoinder to my droll tone, she glanced out of the window, then performed a double take.

'Why are we here?'

'You wished to return to England, did you not?' I replied.

'I assume that's your private jet?'

'You assume correctly. We have three hours, give or take,

before we land. A little longer after that to deliver you to your home. We can use that time for further discussions.'

Her enthralling green eyes widened. 'You…you're giving me a lift on your plane?'

'I wish to spare you and the baby the discomfort of a return journey in a cramped middle seat next to malodorous passengers.'

Colour tinged her cheeks, drawing my attention to their smoothness, reminding me of other sensational areas of her body. I shifted, willing the blood racing to my groin to slow.

'But—'

'My pilot is waiting on the steps. That means we have a fast-closing window for take-off. So perhaps we can continue your objections aboard?'

Her lips firmed. 'That sort of defeats the object of the exercise, doesn't it?'

'Are you really that attached to your budget airline seat?'

'Fine. You've made your point.'

'Efkharisto.'

'I don't know what that means.'

'It means *thank you.*'

'Oh. Okay.'

Despite having won this hand, I was reluctant to leave the car…to end the moments of accord we'd shared. Reinforcing my guard, I stepped out, telling myself it was only decent manners that made me hold out my hand to her.

She took it, stepped out and immediately released it.

The balmy early evening air drifted a breeze through the hangar, sliding her dress against her hips as she preceded me up the stairs. That hot tug of lust flamed in my groin, reminding me that the months before and after Sadie's eruption into my life had been the longest time I'd gone without a woman.

The notion that if my plan were to succeed I'd have to endure an even longer spell filled me with unwelcome dissatisfaction as I entered the plane after her.

Most people who were lucky enough to be invited onto the Xenakis jet frothed at the mouth at the no-expense-spared opulence of its interior.

One of four in the fleet of Jumbo Jets used for family and business trips, the Airbus was satisfyingly immense. With upper and lower decks, and filled with sleep, entertainment and business facilities, and even a twenty-seater cinema, it catered to every imaginable taste.

Anneka had loved to travel in this lap of luxury, insisting on the use of the jet several times a week during our engagement. Of course, I'd later found out what those trips had entailed...

Sadie's gaze flitted over hand-stitched cashmere throws, bespoke incorporated furniture and Aubusson carpeting with disarming lack of interest, her feet almost dragging as she contemplated the seats she could occupy, then made a beeline for a detached club chair.

About to follow, I paused when my phone buzzed in my pocket. Catching the attendant's eye, I nodded to Sadie. 'Get Miss Preston whatever she wants to eat and drink. Make sure she's comfortable.'

'Of course, sir.'

With more than a tinge of regret, I answered my phone. Then spent the next two hours putting the finishing touches on my plan to ensure an unbreakable alignment with Sadie Preston.

By the time we landed at the private airport twenty minutes from her North London residence, I was satisfied with my decisions. Enough to be confident that I could counter any argument she might have.

Once I'd dealt with the handful of obstacles still standing in my way.

The first came in the form of Martha Preston—a woman bearing a striking resemblance to her daughter, whose red hair Sadie had obviously inherited.

'You must be Mrs Preston,' I said when she appeared at the door. 'My name is—'

'My goodness—you're Neo Xenakis! Please, come in.' She threw the door wide open, much to her daughter's initial astonishment, then immediate annoyance.

'Mum—'

'Is something wrong?' Martha asked, hurrying down the hallway while throwing wide-eyed looks over her shoulder. 'When you said you'd be gone all day I assumed it was to work, not... Wow... Um... Anyway, welcome to our home, Mr Xenakis.'

'Thank you,' I said, unable to suppress my shudder as I looked around.

This squashed, dilapidated structure wasn't a home fit for anyone, never mind the woman who carried my child. I might not have the right emotional advantages to offer this child, but in this I could offer full benefits. My child would not be spending a second in this place. Nor would its mother.

'Can I get you anything? A drink? We have tea. Or coffee. Or—'

'He won't be staying long, Mum. He has things to do. Don't you?' Sadie enquired pointedly.

Martha Preston ignored her daughter, her smile at me widening. *Kalos*, the mother was going to be a breeze to handle.

I stepped into the even more cluttered living room of this house Sadie wouldn't be occupying for much longer, suppressing another smile even while calculating how quickly I could move.

Magazines of every description covered every available shabby surface, and a gaily coloured sofa was the only bright spot in the dank space. A look passed between mother and daughter before they both faced me.

'I'll take a rain check on that coffee, if I may, Mrs Preston. But I do have a request.'

Green eyes similar to her daughter's widened. 'Of course. Anything.'

Sadie frowned. Opened her mouth.

I beat her to it. Because, really, what was the point in dragging out the inevitable?

'I hope you'll forgive my bluntness, but I would be honoured if you'll give me your blessing to marry your daughter.'

Shock gripped me for a second before I rounded on this towering force of a man who'd gone from complete disavowal of his child to a systematic, head-spinning takeover in the last few hours.

'What? Are you out of your mind?'

'Sadie! Where are your manners? I'd like to think I brought you up better than this. I do beg your pardon, Mr Xenakis. And, please, call me Martha.'

My mother all but simpered at Neo, who inclined his head in gracious forgiveness for my bad manners.

I ground my teeth, partly to hold back my shock and partly with fury at his heartless joke. Because he had to be joking! Or, worse, this was payback for the prank he still believed I was playing on him.

'Please don't make excuses for me, Mum. And while you're at it, forget what Mr Xenakis just said. He didn't mean it.' I fired a telling glare at him, communicating my dim view of his actions.

His expression didn't change from one of intractable determination. For some reason, instead of angering me even more, that sent a sliver of a thrill through me. Until common sense prevailed.

'It's Neo, Sadie. You can't very well keep calling me Mr Xenakis when we're man and wife, can you?' he drawled.

'Since that's not going to happen, it's neither here nor there.'

The trace of the civility I was sure he'd cultivated for my

mother's benefit evaporated, allowing me an even clearer glimpse of the flint-hard resolution in his eyes. Cold foreboding gripped my nape, then slithered down my spine.

While I grappled with it, he turned to my mother with suave smoothness. 'This is a shock, I know. Besides, it's late. I don't wish to keep you up, Martha, but I would be pleased if you'd let me pick up our acquaintance again soon?'

I opened my mouth to counter his words.

The look in his eyes stopped me.

'Of course,' my mother replied, and then, for the first time in a long time, the hazy cloak she clung to, so she wouldn't have to face harsh reality, lifted. Her eyes glinted with steel as she stared at Neo. 'As to your admittedly surprising question—I'll speak to my daughter first. Clearly you two need better communication. When I'm satisfied that this is what she wants, you can have my blessing.'

Her answer didn't cow Neo. If anything, reinvigorated tenacity vibrated from him, filling up every spare inch of the living room.

Inclining his head in an almost regal way, he smiled. 'Very well. May I have a private word with your daughter?'

With a few words and what I expected was a hint of blushing, my mother left the room.

Unable to stand so close to him without losing my mind, or dissolving into hysterics, I hurried across the room, before whirling around. 'I don't know what the hell you think you're playing at, but—'

'I warned you I intended to do whatever it takes when it comes to this baby, did I not?' he said, in the even tone he'd used that day in his office two months ago. The one that announced he was chillingly rational. That every word from his lips had been calculated and calibrated to achieve the result he wanted.

A shiver raced down my body, urging me to stay in the present. To give every scrap of attention to this insane moment, lest I was swept away. 'This is… What are you doing?' I finally managed, when my head stopped spinning.

'Taking steps to secure my legacy.'

'Your *legacy*? You don't even fully accept that this baby is yours!'

He shrugged off the accusation. 'I've given it some thought and I've concluded that for the moment we'll proceed as if the child is mine.'

'Oh, wow. Lucky me.'

My sarcasm bounced off him. 'You got on a plane and travelled two and a half thousand miles to convince me. This is me meeting you halfway.'

'No, this is you bulldozing your way into my life with zero regard for what I want.'

He paused, folded his arms across his wide chest. 'Indulge me, then. Tell me some of what those wants are.'

I opened my mouth to tell him the paramount one. That I wanted him to leave. But with this new level of ruthless determination wouldn't I simply be postponing the inevitable?

'Permit me to start. Do you want a stable home for our child?'

'Of course I do.'

He nodded in that arrogant way that stated he'd scored a point for himself.

'What else, Sadie?' he urged softly. Oh, so dangerously.

I shrugged. 'I want what every normal person wants. To keep a roof over my head and to stop worrying about how to make ends meet.'

He looked around the living room, his face carefully neutral. 'I have several roofs. You will be welcome to any you choose.'

My mouth dropped open, but he was still talking. 'Were you serious about finishing your degree?'

'Of course.'

'There will be nothing standing in your way, should you choose to see things my way. As for your mother—'

'She's still none of your business.'

'Very well. When the time comes, and you confirm my suspicions, that too will be dealt with.'

Everything I wanted. Offered on a platter. Just like that. I gasped as the penny dropped. 'My God, this is why you stalled me in your office all afternoon and offered to give me a ride home? So you could chess move your way into my life?'

He didn't bother to deny it. 'I merely took time to ensure my plan was sound.'

'I'm not a damned charity case!'

'No,' he replied with heart-stopping brevity, as something close to awe flashed across his face. 'But according to every imaginable statistic, what is happening is a miracle. The baby you're carrying is a miracle.' Then that staggering determination returned. 'One I don't intend to let slip through my fingers.'

I wasn't sure whether to be angry or horrified at his calculated move.

'Don't overthink it, Sadie. I've simply come up with a plan to remove any stumbling blocks that will prevent what we both want from happening. You have needs. I can satisfy them. It's as simple as that,' he drawled arrogantly.

If he'd discovered a handwritten wish list crafted by me he wouldn't have been off by even a fraction. But what he was suggesting was unthinkable.

Marriage? I shook my head. 'Even if everything you've listed is true, and I want all of it, why would I bind myself to you?'

'Because I can give you everything you want. All you have to do is marry me.'

I laughed then, because all this insanity needed an outlet. Before I spontaneously combusted. When his eyes narrowed ominously, I laughed harder.

'Is this just a trait of all insanely wealthy men, or are

you cursed with the notion that you can throw your weight around like this and get what you want?'

He didn't answer immediately. Instead he sauntered towards me, his gaze locked on my face as he approached.

'You feel the need to resist and rail at what you see as my overbearing move when this is merely accelerating a necessary and efficient process.'

Laughter dried up in my throat. 'But why marriage?'

'No Xenakis child has been born out of wedlock. I don't intend for my child to be the first.'

'Here's an idea. Buck the trend. This is the twenty-first century. Set your own path.'

'No. I will not. Label me a traditionalist if you will, but in this I will not be swayed,' he replied with deep gravity.

'You forget that for you to achieve that you'll need my agreement.'

'And you will give it. I'm sure of it.'

'Are you? How? Let me guess—this is where you threaten me with criminal charges again unless I bend to your will?'

For the longest moment he remained silent, considering it. Then, astonishingly, he shook his head. 'That incident is in the past. It's time to turn the page. That transgression will no longer be held against you. Regardless of where we go from here, we will not speak of it again.'

Shocked relief burst through me. I searched his face for signs that he meant it and saw nothing but solid honesty.

Where we go from here…

Ominous words that rattled me as he stared at me. As with every second, the urge to consider his offer gathered strength.

To buy myself time, I countered, 'If you're standing there waiting for me to give you an answer, you're going to be disappointed.'

Something crossed his face that looked a little like alarm, but it was gone much too soon for me to decipher it.

'While you wrestle with that *yes* you're too stubborn to say, let's discuss other issues. I believe one has already been tackled?'

The head-spinning encroached. Again, removing myself from his immediate orbit, from the intoxicating scent of aftershave and warm skin that made me want to wrap my arms around his trim waist and bury my face in his neck, I crossed to the small pink-striped sofa we'd managed to rescue from the bailiff's clutches and sank into it.

'I wouldn't hold your breath,' I countered.

An arrogant smile twisted his lips. 'I'd like you to put the marketing plan you outlined into a report for me.'

Excitement of a different kind joined the chaos surging through me. 'Why?' I asked, forcing myself not to think of our conversation in the car on the way to the airport. Of my thrill when I solved his marketing problem. The grudging respect in his eyes as he sounded out my solutions. If he wanted a report, did that mean…?

'Because that will form the basis of your employment with Xenakis Aeronautics,' he said.

I was glad I was sitting down, because I was sure the shock would've floored me otherwise. 'What?'

'Your new role. As my intern starting as soon as we have an agreement.'

More puzzle pieces fell into place. 'All those questions in the car on the way to the airport…you were *interviewing* me?'

He nodded.

'And…?'

'And you presented a sound strategy—one worth consideration. The second you sign an employment contract I'll pass it on to my marketing team—of which you'll be a part. If you wish.'

I did wish. With every atom in my body, I wanted to grasp his offer with both hands.

But all this came at a price.

Neo Xenakis, marketing guru extraordinaire, wasn't handing round internships of a lifetime out of the goodness of his heart. He was bartering my wish list for complete access to my child.

But, even knowing that, I couldn't help pride and satisfaction fizzing through me like the headiest champagne. Regardless of what had led us here, to have the president of marketing for a global powerhouse like Xenakis Aeronautics pronouncing my idea sound was an accolade worth celebrating.

'Thanks, that's…um…a generous offer.'

'You're welcome,' he returned, and then for some inexplicable reason his gaze dropped to my mouth.

A moment later, I realised I was smiling. And he seemed…*fascinated*.

CHAPTER SIX

THE MOMENT STRETCHED as we stared at one another, a tight little sensual bubble wrapping itself around us, making it hard to breathe as heat and need and desire filled my body.

This time he was the one who broke contact, his chest expanding on a long breath before he said, 'Which item do you wish to discuss next?'

None, I wanted to say. But, reluctantly buoyed by the promise of utilising my marketing knowledge, I wanted to hear him out. See where he was going with this.

'What do you suspect about my mother?'

He shrugged. 'That she's far too dependent on you—perhaps uses you as an emotional crutch to hide a deeper problem?'

I pressed my lips together, unwilling to betray my mother.

'Whatever those problems are, they'll only grow if ignored,' he said.

With a grimace, I exhaled. 'She gambles online. It's small sums, but—'

'Addiction like that is insidious, Sadie. It needs to be curbed now or it'll become a problem.'

Unable to meet his gaze, I toyed with the hem of my dress.

'Has it already become a problem?' he intuited smoothly.

The answer spilled out before I could stop it. 'Yes. I've spoken to her about it. Asked her to get help.'

His face hardened. 'You might have to be a little more insistent. Ruthless, even.'

'Like you?'

A look flashed in his eyes, but he shrugged. 'If it makes you feel better to think that way, then so be it.'

Temptation swelled higher. I knew I had to tackle my

mother's problem before I lost the only parent I had, but…
'She's my concern. I'll find her the help she needs.'

Neo nodded after a handful of seconds.

I licked my lips, knowing the most important topic still needed to be tackled. 'Let's talk about the baby.'

'Yes,' he replied, his voice deep and heavy, with that yearning that still had the power to rock me.

'How would it even work?'

'Our marriage would simply legitimise my child and formalise any agreement as to childcare when it's dissolved.'

A beginning and an end. So…a temporary marriage. A get-out clause and a possible end to his duties as a father when the appeal wore off?

The sting of abandonment registered, deep and true, those flippant words in my father's letter burning through my brain.

'You're pulling out the stops to get what you want *now*. How do I know you'll even want to be a father when this baby is a reality? That you won't simply abandon him or her?'

The hands he'd shoved in his pockets slowly emerged. Purpose vibrated from him. But there was something else. A fleeting look of *doubt* which evaporated in the next instant as his confidence returned, expanding into the room as he strode forward and sank down in front of me.

This close, the look in his eyes captivated me, made me hold my breath.

'I've experienced what it feels like to believe that fatherhood will never happen for me. The feeling is…indescribable. So perhaps this is one of the things you'll have to take on faith. I *want* this child, Sadie.'

The fervour brimming in his voice…

The implacable stare.

That…yearning.

I believed him. But…

'How long did you see this marriage deal continuing?'

He shrugged. 'For the sake of the child's stability and welfare, its first few years at the very least.'

'Then what?'

'Then we agree to whatever custody plan works in the best interests of our child.'

The response should have satisfied me, but something cold and tight knotted inside me. Neo might be in full negotiation mode, but at least he was laying all his cards on the table.

Unlike my father, who'd stuck around until the going got tough and then bailed, with a cruel little letter addressed to the daughter he'd claimed to love and cherish. His wife hadn't even received that courtesy—only a letter from his lawyer, inviting her to sue for divorce on the grounds of abandonment. It was an option my mother was yet to take, the shock and anguish of the abrupt turn her life had taken still keeping her in a fog of despair all these years later.

Wasn't it better this way? To know what was coming and prepare for it rather than be blindsided by it? Especially when until this morning the possibility that my child was going to start life knowing only one parent had been great? Could I pass up this opportunity on behalf of my child?

Neo leaned forward, bringing his power and his glory and that intoxicating scent into play. With one hand braced next to my thigh, he pinned me in place with his gaze for an interminable moment before he lifted the other hand to rest against my face.

Heat from his palm accelerated my pulse. My unguarded gasp echoed quietly between us, my heart wildly thundering as he slowly glided his thumb over my chin, my lower lip.

My insides were debating whether to flip over or melt when he said, 'It's better that we approach this with civility instead of conflict, Sadie.'

Deep, even-toned words that nevertheless gave me a glimpse of what it would be like to keep fighting him.

Jerking away before I did something stupid, like wrap

my lips around that masculine thumb, I shook my head. 'I need time. To think about this.'

Mutiny briefly glinted in his eyes before he gave an abrupt nod and surged to his full height. After a short pace round the living room, he faced me again.

'I have a family function to attend in Athens tomorrow. A new nephew to meet,' he said, with a hint of something peculiar in his voice.

I couldn't tell whether it was anticipation, yearning or bitterness. Perhaps a combination of the three.

'How old is he?'

'I'm told he's almost four months old.'

Curiosity ate at me. 'How come you've never met him before?'

His jaw clenched for a taut stretch. 'Because no one in my family, including my brother, knew of his existence before a few weeks ago.'

So Axios had been in the dark about his son's existence?

'Why?'

He shrugged. 'The reasons for that will become clear tomorrow, I expect.' His gaze sharpened. 'You have until my return to consider my proposal.'

His words flung me back to the present. 'There was no proposal, as I recall. Only edicts thrown down and expected to be followed.'

'I merely set out the course of action I believe is best. If you have a better proposal I'm willing to hear you out.'

He said that while cloaked in an arrogant self-assurance that nothing I could come up with would beat his. Blatant certainty blazed in the gaze that held mine for a nerve-shredding minute.

Other sensations started to encroach. Ones that had heated me up from the inside when he'd touched my lips just now and made every stretch of skin his gaze lingered on burn with fierce awareness. It was as if he'd reached out and touched me again. Stroked me. Tasted me.

Intensely aware of my breath shortening, of the place between my legs growing damp and needy, I cleared my throat and stood. 'If we're done here…?'

He retraced his steps towards me, moving with lithe, attention-absorbing grace, his darkened eyes scouring my face one more time. From his pocket, he produced a graphite-grey business card, embossed with the iconic dark gold picture of the phoenix etched into every Xenakis plane's tail fin. The card simply read *N. Xenakis* and listed a mobile number.

'My personal cell. Use it whenever you wish.'

His fingers brushed mine as I took it. At my shallow inhalation, his eyes darkened.

It struck me then that there was one subject we hadn't discussed.

Neo was a virile, magnificent specimen of a man. One who wouldn't be short of female companionship, should he wish it. Did he intend this proposed marriage to come with the certain leeway rumoured to happen within marriages of conveniences like this?

Even while my mind screamed that it would be the rational course to take, my chest tightened, everything inside me rebelling at the idea.

So what would your solution be?

I ignored the snide little voice attempting to prod me into admitting the secret yearning that had no place in this transaction. What happened two months ago had been an aberration. One that had produced consequences we needed to prioritise now. There could be no repeat of it.

So why were my feet leaden as I followed him to the door? Why did my gaze avidly catalogue his every feature as he stepped out, turned and murmured, 'I'll be in touch'?

And why, when I tossed and turned and sleep wouldn't come, when I should have been thinking about what was best for my child, my mother, my career, did I keep returning to that ever-growing knot of anxiety over whether Neo would take a lover outside of our marriage…or if there already *was* one?

'Is there something I should know, Sadie?'

I'd expected the question. Frankly, I was surprised my mother had waited till morning to ask. Now she stared at me over her teacup, worry reflected in her eyes.

I took a deep breath. 'I'm pregnant, Mum. I'm sorry I didn't tell you before, but—'

'You wanted to tell the father first?' she inserted gently, with no judgement and no surprise over the news. 'I'm assuming Neo Xenakis is the father?'

'Yes. I told him yesterday.'

Another sip of tea, then with a short nod she accepted my news. 'And that's why he wants to marry you?' she asked, visibly holding her breath.

'Yes.'

A smile bloomed across her face. 'Oh, Sadie, that's so romantic.' Her eyes sparkled, much as they had last night, when she'd opened the door to Neo.

'Please, Mum, don't get carried away. This isn't like one of your magazine love stories.'

'Oh, *pfft*. A man like that wouldn't offer marriage unless he was hell-bent on permanence. But is it what *you* want?'

Weariness dragged at me. 'I don't know.'

Her sparkle dimmed. Nevertheless, she reached across the small kitchen table and laid her hand over mine. 'Whatever you decide, I'll support you, sweetheart.'

My eyes prickled, my heart turning over with the knowledge that I loved my mother too much to remain blind to the dangerous road she was treading with her gambling.

About to broach the subject, I froze when the doorbell rang. With a curiously trepidatious expectancy, I answered the door.

A courier held a large, expensive-looking box in his

hand. 'Delivery for Sadie Preston from Xenakis?' the young man asked, eyebrows raised.

Senses jumping, I signed for it.

In the living room, I set it on the coffee table, a reluctance to open it rippling through me. Because, more than not wanting whatever lay within the square box, I was terrified I would *like* whatever Neo had sent me. An expensive something, judging by the discreet logo signifying the endorsement of English royalty often attached to exclusive items.

When the suspense got too much, I tore it open.

The box was filled to the brim with packets of handmade biscuits, each exquisitely wrapped with a thin silver bow. On top of the first one lay a small white envelope, with a note within that read:

I'm told these help with morning sickness. Be so kind as to try not to forget to eat them.

Rolling my eyes seemed like the perfect counterfoil for the smile that insistently tugged at my lips. The man was insufferable.

And he thinks the baby you claim is his might not be.

My smile evaporated, my heart growing heavy as I plucked out one neatly wrapped packet and opened it. The scent of ginger was oddly pleasant, and not vomit-inducing like most smells these days. Apprehensively, I bit into the biscuit, stemming a moan at the heavenly taste. Experiencing no ill effects, I finished one small pack, and reached for another.

'I see your Greek god means business. I bet he had these flown in on one of his private jets?'

I jumped and turned to see my mum in the doorway, beaming as her eyes lit on the box.

'You know what he does for a living?'

'Of course I know! You'd have to be living under a rock

not to know about the Xenakis dynasty. Rumour is they've surpassed the Onassis family in wealth and stature. Shame what happened to your fella, though.'

I frowned. 'He's not "my fella"—and what are you talking about?'

Like a magician's big reveal, she produced a tabloid magazine from behind her back. 'I went digging the moment I left the living room last night. Aren't you glad I keep all my magazines, instead of chucking them in the bin like you keep pushing me to?'

I didn't answer, because my gaze was locked on the crimson headline.

Neo Xenakis Emerges from Three-Week Coma... Ends Year-Long Engagement.

Ignoring the fine tremor in my hands, I scoured the article, concluding very quickly that while the reporter had one or two facts, the majority of the piece was conjecture. But the bit that read, *By mutual consent, Neo Xenakis and Anneka Vandenberg, the Dutch supermodel, have agreed to go their separate ways* clearly had some truth to it.

The reality that I had very little knowledge about the man I was marrying attacked me again in that moment.

Then the very thought that I was leaning towards acceptance of this temporary arrangement slammed into me hard, making my heart lurch.

I told myself I was remedying the former when I retreated to the bedroom and dialled his number the moment my mother flicked on the TV and grew absorbed in the soap she was watching.

He answered immediately. 'Sadie.'

The deep, sexy growl of my name sent sensation flaring through my body.

Tightening my grip on the phone, as if it would stop the

flow of pure need, I launched straight into it. 'You were engaged before?'

He inhaled sharply, then I heard the sound of footsteps as the background conversation and music faded.

His heavy silence brimmed with displeasure. 'There are aspects of my past that have no bearing on what's happening between you and I,' he said eventually.

Unreasonable hurt lanced me. 'According to *you*. You felt entirely comfortable digging into *my* life. I think quid pro quo earns me the same rights,' I said, despite the sensation that I was treading on dangerous personal ground.

'I furnished myself with details of your past only as far as it pertained to the welfare of my child. But if you must know, yes, the tabloids back then got that piece of information right.'

'What else did they get right? What else do I need to know about you?'

Did you love her? Why did it end?

'You want more personal details, Sadie? Then marry me.'

My breath caught, those two words tapping into a secret well I didn't want to acknowledge. Because within that well dwelt a fierce yearning to belong. But to be worthy of consideration for *myself*, not like in the past, because it suited my father's professional ladder climbing, or because I was carrying Neo's child now.

'Will you marry me, Sadie?' he pressed, his voice low and deep.

'It's nice to be asked. Finally. And thanks for answering my question.'

'No—*efkharisto*,' he breathed heavily.

Yesterday he'd said that meant *thank you*. Surprise held me mute for a second. 'For what?'

'For going the extra mile to tell me about the pregnancy even when I made things…unpleasant.'

'You're welcome. But still…why?'

'Because, as much as my brother is overjoyed at the existence of his son, the time he's missed weighs on him. I wouldn't have wished that for myself.'

'Oh.' I drew in a shaky breath as that unique place inside me threatened to soften.

Silence echoed down the line. When he ended it, his voice was tense. 'Do you have an answer for me, Sadie?'

My heart lurched, then thundered as if I was on the last leg of a marathon. 'That depends…'

'On?' he bit out.

'On whether your status two months ago still holds true. I know this marriage will be in name only, but if I'm going to make someone "the other woman", even for a short while, I'd like to be forewarned.'

The background noise had faded completely, leaving the steady sound of his breathing to consume every inch of my attention.

'You have my word that there is no other woman, and nor will there be as long as this agreement between us stands.'

Even as the knot inside me inexplicably eased, that last addition sent a bolt of disquiet through me. I smashed it down, dwelling on the positives in all of this. My child would be getting the best possible start in life. My mother would receive the help she'd denied she needed. I could concentrate on finishing my degree and finally starting the career I'd yearned for.

But, best of all, the fervour with which Neo wanted his child meant there wouldn't be a repeat of what my father had done to me. No postcard would ever land on my baby's doorstep, with a few words telling him or her that they'd been abandoned in favour of a better life.

So what if every facet of this agreement made me feel surplus to requirements? That, although my child wouldn't suffer the same fate, it felt as if I was reliving the past, and again others' needs had been placed above my own?

I couldn't deny that the benefits outweighed the momentary heartache. I would get over this. As long as I placed some firm rules of my own.

'There will be no sex in this marriage. Do you agree to that?'

A sharp intake of breath. 'What?' he demanded tightly.

'No sex. Or no deal.'

He uttered something long and terse in Greek. Time stretched, tight and tense. Then he growled, 'If that's your wish.'

I squeezed my eyes shut, hoping for a miracle solution that didn't involve committing myself to a far too magnetically captivating man for the foreseeable future.

You've already been given a miracle.

Whatever had happened to make him believe he couldn't father children, our encounter had proved otherwise. We simply needed to make the best of the situation.

'Sadie?' His voice throbbed with authority that said he wouldn't be denied.

With a deep breath, I gave my answer. 'Yes. I'll marry you.'

He exhaled, then said briskly, 'Good. I will be in touch shortly.'

I blinked in surprise at the abrupt end to the call. But what had I expected? Trumpets and confetti?

He's marrying you to secure his child. Get used to that reality.

'Oh, Sadie.' My mother stood in the doorway, unapologetic about eavesdropping or the emotional tears spilling down her cheeks. 'I'm so thrilled for you, darling. You're doing the right thing.'

I wanted to tell her not to get her hopes up. But the words stuck in my throat, as the enormity of what I'd committed to flooded every corner of my being. When she swamped me in a tight hug, I let her effervescence counteract the quiet dismay flaring to life that reeked of what-the-hell-have-I-done?

'He won't let you down. Not like your father did. I'm confident of it.'

Financially? Perhaps not. Emotionally...?

I skittered away from that thought, wondering when my emotional well-being had become a factor. The idea of Neo and me was so out of the realms of possibility it was laughable.

So why didn't I feel like laughing? Why did the solid ground I should be stepping onto suddenly feel like quicksand?

That thought lingered, unanswered, throughout the dizzying set of events that followed.

Neo's almost offhand offer to me of his Mayfair property—*If you want to be more comfortable during the process*—had felt like another silken trap, but with homelessness a grim reality it was a lifeline I hadn't been able to refuse.

The property was a world away from the flat I'd left behind. The four-storey mansion sat on an exclusive street in an exclusive part of Mayfair, complete with a basement swimming pool and a stretch limo. A Rolls Royce Phantom and two supercars gleamed beneath recessed lights in the underground car park.

Within the house itself, every surface held breathtaking works of art and the kind of thoughtful blending of antique and contemporary decor that the wealthy either paid for through the teeth or put together with indulgent passion. Since Neo didn't seem the decorating type, I could only assume a king's ransom had been lavished on this place.

In the five immaculate suites, every last item of luxury had been provided—right down to the whirlpool baths and voice-controlled shower. An executive chef whose specialities included catering to expectant mothers presented herself within an hour of our arrival, then proceeded to whip up samples of exquisite meals for me to try.

And barely twenty-four hours after Neo's superefficient moving team had installed us in his property, the wedding spectacle commenced.

As did my arguments with Neo.

He'd soon found out that *leave it with me* when it came to the wedding wouldn't fly with me.

Three stages of wedding coordinator interviews were cut down to one, a dozen bids from the world-famous couture houses vying for the privilege of creating my wedding dress and trousseau, together with the present and upcoming seasons' day and evening wear, were whittled down from five designers to two.

The moment I'd managed to pick my jaw off the floor when I saw the wedding guest list, and stopped my mother from swooning with delight at the ultra-five-star treatment, I dialled Neo's number.

A heated twenty minutes later, we'd reached a compromise.

The wedding would be small, and the choice of dress mine alone. In turn, he would pick the venue—his private island in Greece—and the date—as soon as possible.

The only thing I didn't quibble over, was even grateful for, was the psychologist who arrived on the doorstep—despite knowing that this was simply another box being ticked by Neo on the journey to getting what he wanted.

The gambling conversation with my mother had been hard and tearful, and her acknowledgement that she had a problem and was still having a hard time dealing with my father's desertion had cracked my heart in two.

'I guess I should look forward now,' she'd said. 'You need me. I have a role as the mother of the bride and then as a grandmother.'

But within minutes of wiping her tears she had reached for her phone and excused herself, and minutes later, when

I'd approached her bedroom, I'd heard the distinct sound of electronic chips tumbling on a gaming site.

Heart heavy, I had retreated.

Neo called out of the blue an hour later. Still a little out of sorts, I answered my phone.

He immediately grew tense. 'Is something the matter?'

I barely managed to stop a weary laugh from escaping. 'The better question is "what isn't?"'

Tight silence greeted me. 'You are not having second thoughts.'

It wasn't a question but more of an edict.

'Am I not?' I taunted, my nerves a little too frayed to play nice. 'I can't promise I won't send the next person who asks me how many undernotes I like scenting my vintage champagne packing.'

'That's all that's worrying you? Or is there something else? The prenup I sent over for your signature, maybe?'

The question was a little too tight, like a dangerously coiled spring, set to explode.

My gaze slid to a copy of the prenuptial agreement a sharply dressed lawyer had hand delivered a few hours before. I frowned at the curious note in Neo's voice.

'What about it? It's already signed, if that's what you're calling about.'

A stunned silence greeted my response. 'You *signed* it?'

'Yes. Why are you surprised?'

'I'm not,' he drawled. And before I could call him out, he rasped, 'Tell me what's wrong.'

I let the subject of his peculiar attitude over the prenup go as I toyed with sharing my worries about my mother with him. The reminder that the baby I was carrying was the only thing Neo was interested in stopped me.

'I'm not changing my mind, if that's what you're worried about.'

He exhaled audibly, making me realise he'd been holding his breath. Had he been prepared to launch another vanquishing skirmish should I have responded differently?

'That's a wise course of action.'

For some reason that response hurt. I smothered the sting. 'Was there something in particular you wanted?'

'Yes. To give you the date for our wedding. It'll happen two weeks from tomorrow. That gives you a week to finalise your affairs before you come to Greece.'

Since the internship was at the head office in Athens, I'd agreed to the move.

'My mother's coming with me. A change of scene will help with her outlook on life.'

'I'm not a monster, Sadie. Regardless of where she chooses to stay, she'll receive the counselling she needs. But you must accept that our agreement includes not overburdening yourself with tasks that are out of your control. I will not allow it.'

I knew he was dishing out the hard truth, and I wanted to hate Neo. But deep down I knew that had circumstances been different, had I been granted other choices, I still would have chosen this. An internship at Xenakis. A chance to live in a different country, experience another culture. All of it.

Except staying within the orbit of this man who turned my equilibrium inside out?

Maybe...

The objections I wanted to hurl at him died in my throat, and exactly two Saturdays later my breath caught, as it had been catching seemingly every other second, as the tenseater luxury helicopter my mother and I were ensconced in circled over a large island in the middle of the Aegean in preparation to land.

The island was mostly flat, bursting with green and pink foliage and large stretches of stunning white beaches. But on the northernmost point a bluff rose sharply over the water, where towering waves crashed against menacing-looking rocks below.

Magnificent, mesmerising, awe-inspiring—but also dangerous in places.

Just like its owner.

Several small houses, most likely staff accommodation, dotted the right side of the island, after which came extensive stables, a large paddock with thoroughbreds being tended to by stable hands.

The aircraft banked, granting a first view of the resplendent villa and grounds in the mid-afternoon sun.

'Oh, my God,' my mother whispered.

The sentiment echoed inside me.

Spread beneath us was the most magnificent sight I'd ever seen. The sprawling whitewashed villa was divided into two giant wings the size of football fields and connected by an immense glass-roofed living area that could easily accommodate a thousand guests. A sparkling swimming pool abutted the living area, and a tiered lawn went on almost for ever, ending at a large gazebo set right on the beach, complete with twin hammocks set to watch the perfect sunset.

I was still drenched in awe when the scene of the wedding ceremony came into view.

Unlike the spectacle of his brother's wedding—the details of which my mother had delighted in showing me via her magazines—Neo had agreed to a close-family-only wedding. The handful of guests were perched on white-flower-decorated seats, laid out on a blinding white carpet on the vast landscaped lawn. The 'altar' was bursting with white and pink Matthiola, specially imported from Italy, and the florists' gushing use of the flower meant to symbolise lasting beauty and a happy life echoed in my mind as the chopper landed.

The walk from the aircraft to where Neo's family members had risen to their feet felt like a trek across a field of landmines, my pulse leaping with apprehension with each step, the sea-tinged breeze lifting my organza and lace wedding dress, reminding me how far away I was from normal reality.

I was marrying a wealthy, powerful man. One who'd proved he could bend the path of destiny itself to his will. One who was assuming greater and greater occupation in my thoughts.

One who bristled with impatience as my steps faltered.

Beside Neo, a man matching his height murmured to him, a kind of hard amusement twitching his lips. Neo sent him a baleful glare before his eyes locked on mine, compelling me with the sheer force of his dynamism.

Despite our many charged conversations, I hadn't seen him since the night of his skewed proposal. His designer stubble was gone, and the lightning-strike effect of his clean-shaven face stalled my feet completely.

Somewhere along this journey I'd fooled myself into thinking I could handle an association with this powerful man. Now, I wasn't so sure. How could I be when his very presence struck me with such alarming emotions?

The man next to him stepped forward, momentarily distracting me.

Axios Xenakis—Neo's older brother.

He approached, eyeing me with the same piercing Xenakis gaze, unashamedly assessing me before the barest hint of a smile lifted the corners of his mouth.

He placed himself next to me and, with a nod at my mother, offered me his arm. 'As much as I'm enjoying seeing my brother twisting in the wind, perhaps you'd be so kind as to have a little mercy?'

'I'm not doing anything…' I murmured.

'Precisely. You are merely hesitating long enough for him to feel the kick of uncertainty. Believe me, I know what *that* feels like.'

His words were directed at me but his gaze flicked to a dark-haired, stunningly beautiful woman cradling an adorable baby in her arms. They shared a heated, almost indecently sensual look that would have made me cringe had my whole attention not been absorbed by the man I'd pledged to marry. The man who looked a whisker away from issuing one of those terse little commands that irritated and burned but also flipped something in my stomach while getting him what he wanted.

What he wanted, clearly, was for me to honour my word.

One hand twitched, and it was as if a layer of that supreme control slipped as he watched me.

Think of Mum. Think of the baby.

Knowing he was eager to secure his child delivered a numb kind of acceptance over me. Helped propel me to where he stood.

He exhaled, and just like that control was restored.

The ceremony went off without a hitch. Probably because Neo had forbidden any.

In what seemed like a breathless, head-spinning minute I was married to one of the most formidable men on earth. And he was turning to me, his fierce gaze locked on my lips.

It was all the warning I got before he leaned down, his lips warm and dangerously seductive as they brushed mine once. Twice. Then moved deeper for a bare second before he raised his head.

His gaze blatantly raked me from head to toe, his nostrils flaring as his gaze lingered on my belly.

'*Dikos mou,*' he murmured beneath his breath.

'What?'

He started, as if realising he'd spoken aloud, then immediately collected himself. When he circled my wrist with one hand and turned me to face the dozen or so guests, I steeled myself against the fresh cascade of awareness dancing over my body—told myself it meant nothing, was simply a continuation of whatever role he was playing. And when he turned to rake his gaze from the swept-back, loosely bound design the stylist had put my hair into, over my face and down my body, before deeply murmuring, 'You look beautiful...' I told myself it was for the benefit of his family.

Barely minutes later, once the wait staff had begun circulating with platters of exquisite canapés and glasses of vintage champagne, Neo had grown aloof. A fine tension vibrated off him, increasing every time I tried to extricate myself from his hold.

When it grew too much I faced him, thankful that we were temporarily alone. 'Is something wrong?'

His expression grew even more remote. 'Should there be?'

I shrugged. 'You're the one who seems agitated.'

For a tight stretch of time, he didn't speak. Then, with piercing focus, he said, 'I commend you for holding up your end of the bargain, Sadie.'

Despite the backhanded compliment, his expression suggested he was waiting for the other shoe to fall.

I raised an eyebrow, eager to find a level footing with him, despite the cascade of emotions churning through me. Barely a month ago I'd been blissfully unaware that I carried a child. Now, I wasn't simply a mother-to-be, I was the wife of a formidable man from an equally formidable family.

'Does that win me some sort of brownie point?' I asked, more to cover the quaking intensifying within me than anything else—because, despite his expression, the fingers holding me prisoner were moving over my wrist, exploding tiny fireworks beneath my skin.

That touch of hardness tinged his smile. 'Sadly not. You had your chance to win more during the prenuptial agreement signing.' His gaze probed as if he were trying to unearth something. 'Perhaps you regret signing it now?'

I frowned. 'Why would I? There was nothing in there unacceptable to me. It seemed skewed in your favour—just as you wanted it, I suspect?'

He shrugged. 'As with any of my contracts, it seeks to

protect what's mine. But you've signed on that dotted line, so there's no going back.'

'I don't get what's going on here. You *wanted* me to throw a fit over the prenup?' I asked, puzzled. 'Why on earth would I do that?'

He tensed, a flash of disconcertion darkening his eyes before he erased it. 'That was one scenario. But, seeing as you signed it, let's not dwell on it. The deed is done.' His gaze dropped to my belly again. 'Now we wait,' he breathed.

CHAPTER SEVEN

HIS WORDS SEEPED deep into my bones, robbed me of breath.

For one tiny minute I'd forgotten that Neo harboured a very large question mark over my baby's paternity. That every term he'd negotiated and every luxury he'd tossed at my feet in his relentless pursuit of possessing the child I carried had come with the unspoken clause that he was hedging his bets. That my word wasn't good enough.

And where I'd have shrugged off the accusation a month ago, these past two weeks had weakened my foundations, wilting me enough that the barbs burrowed through the cracks. And stuck.

Worse, I only had myself to blame—because his endgame, like my father's, hadn't changed.

This time when I tugged my hand away he released me, although his lips tightened for a nanosecond. 'What's the matter?'

Our progression over the lush green grass had brought us to a section of the never-ending garden with luxurious bespoke seats set around beautifully decorated low tables, more in the style of an elegant garden party than a wedding reception.

He stopped at the seats that were set up on a dais and, beckoning one of the sharply dressed waiters carrying platters of food, helped himself to two gold-rimmed plates overflowing with Greek delicacies.

'Why, absolutely nothing,' I answered, plastering on a bright, patently fake smile.

He started to frown. I looked away, only to catch Ax's watchful gaze.

I turned back to Neo. 'Does your brother know why you...why we...?'

'We're married, Sadie. I'm your husband. You're my wife. You'll have to get used to saying it. Try the chicken,' he said, holding out a silver-skewered morsel to me.

The scent of lemon and rosemary wafted towards me enticingly, but I hesitated, refusing to let that bewildered fizzing inside me gain traction. 'You didn't answer my question.'

He dropped the food back onto the plate, his jaw momentarily clenching. 'Why we've exchanged vows today is nobody's business but ours. You have my word that no one will dare to question you on it.'

'Because you've decreed it?'

His eyes hardened. 'Yes.'

'And they obey whatever you say, without question?'

A spine-tingling glint flickered through his eyes. 'I'm in a unique position to demand that obedience, so, yes.'

'And how did you garner such unquestioning loyalty?' I semi-taunted, a little too eager to get beneath his skin the way he so effortlessly got beneath mine.

'By giving them what their grasping little hearts desire, of course. Isn't that the way to command most people's allegiance? Something in return for something more?'

Flint-hard bitterness glazed his words, triggering a burst of alarm.

Something in return for something more.

Wasn't that what my father had orchestrated for himself with his own family? A calculated means to an end?

Neo couldn't have made his endgame clearer. So why was I plagued with the urge to be sure? 'Does that apply to you too?'

The faintest ripple whispered over his jaw. 'We're not talking about me.'

'Aren't we?' I asked.

But when he started to speak, I shook my head to preempt him. To mitigate the ball of hurt that far too closely resembled the pain I'd felt at my father's actions.

'I'm not sure what happened to you to make you believe that's how everyone ticks—'

His eyes grew icily livid as he stared me down. 'I do not require your pity. Not now or ever,' he stated through gritted teeth.

Aware I'd touched on a raw nerve, I breathed in, curled my hands in my lap to stop them from reaching out for him. 'It wasn't pity. It was a need to understand—'

'Again, this isn't a lesson in dissecting my character, Sadie.'

Aware we were now drawing his parents' gaze, I took another breath. 'Fine. When will I start work?'

Scepticism and suspicion glinted in his eyes. 'So eager to get down to business?' he drawled. 'Not even time to entertain the idea of a honeymoon? You are aware that, as Mrs Xenakis, you now have the power to command my pilot to take you anywhere in the world your heart desires?'

I forced a shrug, and the uncanny sense that this was some kind of test intensified the chaos inside me. 'As tempting as that is, what's the point? We both know what this is. What *my* heart desires is to get started on my internship and finish my degree.'

The tic in his jaw returned, a little more insistent this time. 'You don't need reminding, I hope, that taking care of yourself and the baby is your number one priority?'

My fingers tightened. 'No, I don't. And you're beginning to sound like a broken record.'

'If you wish me to lay off, then have some food. It will please me,' he tossed in silkily, offering the succulent chicken again.

But my appetite had disappeared.

'If you're so interested in the chicken, Neo, then you have it. I'm going to powder my nose. And, in case you don't get that, it's a euphemism for *I need some space*.'

The briefest flare of his nostrils was the only sign he was displeased. In that moment I didn't care. I walked away, making a beeline for the wide opening of the living room wing. With the glass doors folded back and tucked out of sight, and late-afternoon sunlight spilling in through the glass ceiling onto the stylish grey and white Cycladic furnishings, the inside was a breathtaking extension of the outside.

Despite the chaos reigning inside me, I couldn't help but be affected by the stunning beauty surrounding me. But it only lasted for a minute—then reality came crashing back.

I blindly turned down one hallway, relieved when a half-open door revealed the sanctuary I was looking for. Shutting myself in, I attempted to regulate my breathing as questions ricocheted in my head.

The postcard my father left me had testified to the fact that selfishness and greed were his mainstays. But what had happened to Neo to fuel *his* actions?

Over the last week I'd given in to curiosity and done more internet searching. Very few details had been forthcoming regarding his broken engagement to Anneka. Even the circumstances of his accident were obfuscated. Although about the tall, Dutch beauty herself there'd been reams and reams, prompting in me even more questions as to why two people who'd outwardly looked like the kind of couple romance novels portrayed had parted ways.

I wanted to tell myself I didn't care. Again, my very emotions mocked me. The need to know, to see beneath the surface of the man I'd married, clawed at me.

Ten minutes dragged by. Knowing I couldn't remain hidden in the bathroom for ever, I splashed cool water over my hands, dabbed a few drops at my throat before exiting—just in time to see Callie Xenakis enter the living room, carrying baby Andreos.

She spotted me and smiled. 'I came in here to escape the heat for a few minutes. Won't you join me?' she invited, her movements graceful as she sank into one sumptuous sofa.

For some reason I hesitated, my gaze darting outside

to where Neo stood with his brother. There were similar intense expressions on their ruggedly handsome faces as they spoke.

Ax said something to Neo, his expression amused. Neo responded sharply, his mouth flattening into a displeased line which only seemed to further amuse his brother.

'Do me a favour and leave those two alone for now? Ax's been wanting payback for a while,' Callie said with a grin.

'Payback for what?'

Her stare was wickedly teasing but also contemplative, as if she was wondering whether she could trust me.

After a couple of seconds, she shrugged. 'I'm sure you've seen the papers. Let's just say my marriage didn't get off to a rosy start. And Neo… Well, he enjoyed a few jokes at his brother's expense. And those two are nothing if not competitive.'

I frowned. 'So your husband's ribbing my… Neo about me?' Somehow I couldn't bring myself to call him *my husband*.

Callie laughed. 'Ax thought he'd have to wait years to get back at his little brother. If ever.'

'I'm not sure there's much humour in any of this.'

Her eyes grew even more speculative, and there was an intelligence shining in the blue depths that made me wish for different circumstance for our meeting. I would have liked to be friends with Callie Xenakis.

'I don't think you need telling that everyone's wondering about you. This wedding came out of the blue.'

I firmed my lips, reminded of Neo's claim that our marriage was nobody's business.

As if she'd read my thoughts, Callie waved an airy hand. 'It's no one's business but yours, of course, but… Well, no one expected this from Neo. Not so fast, anyway,' she murmured, then grimaced, her gaze searching mine before she returned her attention to her son.

Sensing that she'd said more than she'd intended to, I

let the subject go, unaware that my gaze had strayed to Neo until he turned his head sharply, lanced me with those piercing eyes that threw fresh sparks of awareness over my skin. Even when his brother spoke again, Neo kept his gaze on me, the ice receding to leave a steady blaze that set off fresh fireworks.

It took monumental effort to pull my gaze free, to suck air into my lungs and turn back to Callie, who was laying her son on the wide seat, keeping one hand on his plump little belly to stop him wriggling off as she picked up a futuristic-looking remote and pressed a button.

Immediately a section of the ceiling went opaque, granting a little reprieve from the sun's rays.

As I moved towards her, her gaze flickered over my dress. 'That's a stunning dress,' she said, a wistful tone in her voice.

I stared down at my wedding gown. The style was simple, the bodice had a wide neck and capped sleeves that gave glimpses of my skin beneath the lace, and the soft layered skirt parted discreetly at intervals to show my legs when I moved. The whole ensemble felt like the softest, most seductive whisper against my skin.

'I… Thank you.'

She smiled, but a hint of sadness crossed her face before evaporating a moment later.

'Can I ask you a question?' I ventured.

'Of course,' she invited.

'What does *dikos mou* mean?'

Her eyes widened, and when she blushed I cringed inside, wondering if I'd committed a faux pas. 'I'm sorry. I didn't think it was anything rude—'

'Oh, no, it's not. It's just that Ax says it a lot. Where did you hear it?'

I bit my lip, still not certain I wanted to divulge it. 'Neo said it after…after we exchanged rings.'

A mysterious little smile played on her lips. 'It means *mine*,' she said.

'Oh…' My heart lurched in a foolish, dizzy somersault before I could remind myself that Neo's hand had been splayed over my belly when he'd said the words. That he had simply been revelling in his possession.

Nothing else.

Catching Callie's speculative glance, I hurriedly changed the subject to one I hoped would distract her: her baby. It worked like a charm—the gorgeous Andreos was almost too cute in his little shorts, shirt and waistcoat combo.

The reprieve didn't last, and the tingling along my nape alerted me that Neo had entered the room a second before my eyes were compelled to meet his. His incisive gaze raked my face as he stalked towards me, his brother a few steps behind him.

Axios made a beeline for his wife and son, catching up a giggling Andreos and tucking him against his side before he wrapped a possessive arm around his wife's shoulders.

Sliding her arm around her husband's waist, Callie said smilingly over her shoulder, 'Welcome to the family, Sadie. I have a feeling you'll find things interesting.'

Before I could ask what she meant by that, Neo closed the gap between us, one strong, lean hand held out. 'My parents are leaving. Perhaps you'd be so kind as to join me to see them off?' he enquired silkily.

That look before, as he stood next to his brother…

The terse, revealing little conversation before that…

The thought of taking his hand now…

My instincts shrieked at me to *beware*. And yet every argument as to why I shouldn't burned to ashes when his hand crept up another imperious notch.

I raised my hand.

He took it, his fingers meshing with mine in a palm sliding that jolted electricity through my midriff before spreading out in gleeful abandon over my body, hardening my nipples, speeding my heartbeat and delivering a mocking weakness to my knees.

I was fighting—and losing—the battle for my equilibrium when we stepped outside and approached Electra and Theodolus Xenakis.

Neo had inherited Theo's height and Electra's piercing eyes. Together they were a striking couple, who regarded me with shrewd speculation.

'Perhaps you and Neo would join us for dinner after you return from your honeymoon? I'd like to get to know my new daughter-in-law better,' Electra said, the barest hint of a smile diluting the near command to a request.

About to reply that there was no honeymoon, I paused when Neo answered smoothly, 'Thank you, Mama. We'll let you know when we're free.'

The tenor of his voice put paid to any more conversation. Within minutes they'd departed, followed closely by Axios and Callie.

My mother, the last one remaining, hurried to me, her face creased in smiles. 'It's been a wonderful day,' she said, and sighed. Then her smile turned teary. 'I can't believe my little girl is married,' she mused. 'If only your—'

'The helicopter's waiting, Mum,' I said hurriedly, before she could drop my father into the conversation. She'd agreed to enter rehab to deal with her gambling and the after-effects of my father's desertion. 'I'll see you when I get back to Athens.'

As for my father—I'd tried to block him out, the part of me that blamed him for contributing to my dire straits giving way to the bone-deep hurt caused by his abandonment and never healing. Even the mere thought of walking away from *my* baby filled me with horror. That he'd done so without a backward glance…

Aware of Neo's narrowed gaze on my face, I dredged up a wider smile, hugged my mother and watched her board the helicopter a minute later.

Then, in the dying rays of the sun, bar the dozen or so staff efficiently cleaning up, I was alone on a Greek island with the man I'd married.

The profundity of it hit me square in the chest. A quick glance showed he was still watching me. Still assessing me with those all-seeing eyes.

'The helicopter is coming back for us, right?'

His gaze grew hooded, his eyes flicking towards the aircraft that was now a speck on the horizon. 'Yes. But not till tomorrow evening.'

My heart stuttered and flipped. 'What? Why?'

'Because, as much as we both know why this event happened, I'd rather not fuel further speculation by spending what's left of my wedding day behind my desk in Athens with my new wife in tow.'

'I thought you didn't care what anyone thought?'

He turned, his hand returning to my waist as he led me back inside the sprawling villa. 'Everyone here today values discretion. Beyond the boundaries of that circle is another matter. You'll learn the difference in time,' he stated.

The quiet force behind his words seeped into me, drawing a shiver.

'You could've told me this before trapping me here,' I said, trying to summon irritation but only finding a bubble of hot excitement that swelled with each step I took inside the vast living room with Neo by my side. The potent whiff of his aftershave triggered a hunger deep inside.

'I thought you'd appreciate the peace and quiet.'

And those who didn't know better would imagine I was spending the night making love to my dynamic new husband?

The thought ramped up the heat inside me, making me grateful when Neo guided me past the grouping of sofas I'd used earlier to another set, facing endless lush greenery just beyond the sparkling pool, before dropping his hand.

'Sit down, Sadie. You'll better enjoy the sunset from this spot.' His voice was low, deep, if a little on the stiff side.

One of the wait staff approached and spoke to Neo in Greek. Without another word he walked away, his shoulders still tense.

Choosing to enjoy the temporary release from his overwhelming presence, and grateful to be off my feet, I kicked off my heels. I was smoothing down the floaty layers of delicate chiffon when a beam of sunlight caught the gems in the band on my finger. I'd been a little shell-shocked during the ceremony, but now I stared at the perfectly fitting diamond-encrusted platinum ring, a quiet sense of awe overcoming me.

I didn't need to be a jeweller to know the ring was near priceless. And I'd been stunned to see that Neo wore a similar band minus the diamonds. What was that supposed to prove? That he intended to take this role seriously, even though he was merely biding his time until his child was born? Or was it something else?

You have my word there will be no other...

My heart lurched, despite knowing I couldn't, *shouldn't* read anything into that.

I was writhing in confusion when his bold footsteps returned. I dropped my hand into my lap, sliding the weighted reminder of our wedding ceremony between the folds of chiffon just as he entered my eyeline.

He was carrying a large tray on which several platters of food had been arranged. 'You'll be so kind as not to argue with me over this again, won't you?' he enquired drolly, despite the implacable determination in his eyes.

As if he'd flipped a switch, my appetite came roaring back, the succulent scents emanating off the tray making my mouth water. 'Not this time, no.'

With a satisfied nod, he set the tray on my lap.

'I should change...'

His grey gaze swept over me, lingering at certain points

on my body, including my bare feet, and igniting the sparks higher. When his gaze returned to mine the glint had turned stormy, the sensual line of his mouth seeming fuller.

'There's no hurry. Eat first. Then I'll give you the tour.'

I polished off a portion of moussaka, then a salad with the chicken I'd rejected earlier, almost moaning at the flavours exploding on my tongue.

Keep talking. It'll dissipate the heat threatening to eat you alive.

'Earlier, you said you didn't care what anyone thought about our reasons for doing this. But you'll agree that, you being who you are, everyone's going to be curious about the woman you've married suddenly out of the blue?'

He gave a tight-lipped nod, his nostrils flaring slightly. 'They'll wonder if there's more than meets the eye. They'll wonder if you're pregnant. *How* you got pregnant.'

The food turned to sawdust in my mouth. 'You mean—'

'Certain members of my family know I can't produce children, yes.'

I pushed my tray away.

He firmly pushed the plate back in front of me. 'The deal was that you'd eat.'

For the baby's sake.

The words hung in the air between us.

I chewed. Swallowed. 'So they'll wonder if I'm a liar?'

His jaw rippled, tightened, but he shrugged. 'Only time will resolve that situation.'

Or you could believe me...

The words stuck in my throat, along with the next mouthful of food that suddenly refused to go down.

'The obvious workings of biology aside, why is it so hard for you to believe this baby is yours, Neo?' The question emerged before I could stop it.

'Because I'm not a man who accepts things at face value. Not anymore,' he said with cold precision. 'And I caution you against attempting to change that. You'll be wasting both your time and mine.'

That stark warning should have killed any softening towards him. Put me on the path back to unfeeling composure. Instead it mired me deeper in a quiet urgency to know why.

The urge was stemmed when Neo summoned a hovering staff member to clear away the tray. About to rise, I stopped, suppressing a shiver when his fingers brushed my inner arm.

'You haven't seen the sunset yet,' he murmured. 'Besides, I have something for you.'

I was torn between the stunning sunset unfolding outside and curiosity as to what he had for me. Neo won out. Only he was in no hurry. He nodded at the view.

I watched, awed, as the magnificent combination of orange, yellow and grey danced over the sparkling pool and the sea beyond, stretching across the horizon until it felt as if the whole world was bathed in splendid colour.

'It's breathtaking.'

'Yes,' he said simply.

The weight of his gaze remained as the minutes ticked by slowly and the sun dropped into the ocean. When I turned my head he was staring at me, that fierce light blazing in his eyes. My heart banged against my ribs.

To cover the flustering billowing inside, I cleared my throat. 'You mentioned a tour?'

He nodded, but didn't move. Simply reached into his breast pocket, extracted a small velvet box and prised it open. 'I should've given this to you earlier.'

The magnificent ring consisted of a large square diamond, with a red hue I'd never seen before, surrounded by two sloping tiers of smaller pure gems. The band was platinum, a perfect match to my wedding ring.

I was aware my jaw had dropped with stunned surprise, but I couldn't look away from the most beautiful piece of jewellery I'd ever seen.

'Do you like it?' he asked, his voice a little gruff.

I tore my gaze away to meet his, and was immediately trapped by a different sort of captivation. The *scorching* sort. 'Can I say I hate it, just so I don't have to wear it?'

One eyebrow rose. He was clearly surprised by my answer. 'I fail to see the logic,' he drawled.

'Wearing something like that in public is just inviting a mugging. Or worse.'

His lips twitched a tiniest fraction. 'Let me worry about that.' He held out his hand in silent command.

I hesitated. 'Neo…'

'Wear it, Sadie. It will invite less speculation. And it will please me.'

Perhaps it was the beautiful sunset and the food that had mellowed me. Perhaps this particular fight wasn't worth it because there was no downside to wearing one more ring when I'd already accepted another, binding me to this dynamic man who made my insides twist with forbidden yearning when I should have been shoring up my barriers at every turn.

I gave him my hand.

The act of Neo sliding another ring onto my finger felt vastly intimate, much too visceral. So much so, I'd stopped breathing by the time the band was tucked securely next to its counterpart. And was even more lightheaded when he wrapped his fingers possessively around mine and tugged me up.

'You won't need them,' he rasped, when I went to slip my feet back in my shoes.

He led me to the south wing, where every bedroom and salon was a lavish masterpiece of white and silver and more stunning than the last, and where a private cinema, study and wine cellar were filled to the brim with extravagances only obscenely wealthy men like Neo could afford.

The north wing contained fewer rooms, mainly an immense private living room dividing two master suites. Both suites were bordered by a tennis-court-sized terrace which housed a smaller semi-enclosed version of the swimming pool downstairs.

The urge to dip my bare toes into the sparkling water was too irresistible. I gave in, gasping in delight, only to look up to find Neo's gaze locked on my mouth.

He didn't look away.

Slowly, heat built to an inferno between us. Until that breathlessness invaded again, threatening to drive me to the edge of my sanity.

I stepped back from the pool, hoping to restore a level head. Because sex wasn't part of our bargain. It was the mind-altering drug that had led us here in the first place.

'So, does this island have a name?' I asked as he slowly advanced.

'Neostros,' he supplied, without taking his hooded gaze from me.

'You named your island after *yourself*? How…narcissistic.'

He shrugged off my words. 'More like the other way around. My grandfather bought this place long before I was born and he named it. My parents were vacationing here when my mother went into labour. I was born in one of the houses on the other side of the island.'

That glimpse into his early life made me yearn for more.

'Is your grandfather still alive?'

His face closed up, but not before a flash of twisted pain and bitterness marred his expression. 'No. He died of a heart attack as a direct result of attempting to dig his family out of hard times.'

Looking around me, seeing unfettered opulence at every turn, it was hard to believe that any Xenakis had ever experienced a minute's hardship. 'Hard times? How?'

Again his mouth twisted cynically. 'Another unfortunate example of someone wanting something more than they deserved. In this case it was my grandfather's overambitious business partner. He ran the business into the ground, then left my grandfather to pick up the pieces—but not before extending to him a business loan with crippling interest rates. The strain was too much for him. It broke my grandmother first. After she died... Well, it broke him.'

'From what I can tell, you come from a very large family. Didn't anyone step up to help?'

Neo lifted his hand and caught up a curl of my hair that had come loose. For a long moment I thought he wouldn't answer me, that he intended his intimate caress to swell higher between us until we drowned from it.

When his eyes eventually met mine, residual bitterness lingered, but the heat had grown. 'I don't want to talk about my family anymore. As you can see, someone did step up. Ax and I did what needed to be done to get back what we'd lost. But in doing so we were reminded over and over again that greed and avarice will push people into deplorable behaviour to the exclusion of all decency.'

I opened my mouth to refute it. His fingers left my hair to brush over my lips, stopping my words before I could speak them.

'If you seek to convince me otherwise...again, Sadie, I urge you to save your breath.'

He's showing you his true colours. Believe him.

'So you choose to operate from a position of bitterness and cynicism?'

A hard light glinted in his eyes momentarily before his expression grew shrewd, almost calculating. 'Don't you? Tell me what happened with your father.'

The sudden switch sent a cold shock wave through me. 'What?'

'You take pains to avoid discussing him even though he's alive. And I've deduced that he's a major reason for your mother's troubles. Why the secrecy? What did he do to you?'

I firmed my lips, refusing to be drawn into the painful

subject. But he'd answered my questions, even though it had been clear he didn't want to discuss it.

'Up until I was sixteen? Absolutely nothing. He was a decent father and I guess a good enough husband—I never heard my parents argue or even disagree about anything major.'

Neo frowned. 'What changed?'

'I came home from school one day to find my mother sobbing hysterically. When she calmed down enough to be coherent she handed me a postcard my father had sent from Venezuela. Only problem was, he was supposed to be on a business trip to Ireland.'

Strangling pain gripped my chest, stopped the flow of words for a moment. Neo's fingers trailed down my jaw to rest on my shoulder and, as weakening as it was, I took comfort from the warmth of his hand—enough to finish the sorry little tale of how my family had broken apart with a few scrawled lines on a cheery little exotic postcard.

'He basically said he didn't want to be married anymore. Didn't want to be a father, and he was never coming back. He'd already instructed his lawyers to file divorce papers. What he didn't warn us about was the fact that he hadn't kept up with the mortgage payments for over six months. Or that he'd cleared out their joint bank account. I was still absorbing the news when the bailiffs turned up two hours later with a court order and threw us out of our home.'

Neo cursed under his breath. 'Where did you go?'

'My mother had some savings. Enough to rent us a flat for a year. It would probably have gone further if…' I stopped, fresh shame and the raw anguish of laying myself bare halting my words.

His hand curled around my shoulder. 'If your mother's gambling problems hadn't started?'

I nodded. 'I got a part-time job, which lessened the financial burden. But Mum's depression grew, and she couldn't hold down a job. I think you get the picture of how things panned out eventually.'

'Did you ever hear from your father? Did he give a reason?'

Anguish welled high, consuming my insides. 'No. He stuck to his word and cut off all ties.'

Neo's lips flattened and his eyes bored into mine with a knowing look. 'So the facts speak for themselves. Wasn't he a senior-level banker?' he asked, shocking me anew with the depth of his knowledge about my life.

'Yes.'

'So he had the type of job that demanded respectability. He was fiercely competitive and ambitious, in a high-pressure job that often required cut-throat ruthlessness. Having a wife and child and a seemingly stable home served his purpose. Most likely got him up the rungs of his corporate ambition.'

'You're not telling me anything I don't know, Neo. Yes, my mother and I were just accessories he used while it suited him, then threw away when he was done. So?'

A tic rippled in his jaw, even as his thumb drew slow circles on my shoulder. Did he even know he was doing that?

'So face the facts.'

Unable to stand the waves of anguish, and that need to lean into his caress, I tugged myself out of his hold.

'Is that some sort of warning, Neo?' Had he sensed that occasional misjudged softening? Was this his way of mitigating it?

'Sadie—'

'Enough. Whatever it is you're trying to prove, save your breath. I know what type of person my father was. What type of person you are. There's no illusion on my part.'

His face tightened and he opened his mouth—most likely to challenge me.

'It's been a long day, Neo. I'd like to go to bed, if you don't mind.'

The glint in his eyes morphed, attaining that hooded, sensual potency that sparked every nerve ending to life. But with that spark came greater warning. An edging closer to that dangerous precipice of longing and softening. Wondering if that ring on his finger meant more than simple evidence of the transaction he'd brokered.

'It's your wedding night, Sadie. Surely you wish to make it a little more memorable than simply retiring to your bed at a few minutes past sunset?'

The weighted question started my heart thudding to a different beat.

'You've been at pains to remind me that this marriage is for the sake of the child I'm carrying. How I spend my time tonight is really none of your business.'

He inhaled slowly, and that animalistic aura wrapped tighter around me. 'Perhaps I wish to make it my business.'

I was struggling to stop my pulse from leaping wildly at that statement when his fingers returned to my throat, their sensual caress enthralling, like a magician conjuring up the most delicious trick.

But wasn't this an illusion? A dream from which I'd wake to disappointment?

With monumental effort I pulled away. 'We agreed that sex wasn't part of this bargain. It's an agreement I intend to stick to. Goodnight, Neo.'

I hurried away, my footsteps stumbling at the dark promise in the heavy gaze on my back. The gaze that compelled me to slow down, turn around, find out if he really meant it. If this wedding night following a wedding borne of facility could be something else.

CHAPTER EIGHT

White.

She needed to wear white every day for the rest of her life.

She was walking away from me, her ethereal dress floating about her like the purest cloud, and all I could think about was how enthralling she looked in white.

Sure, I was irritated. Unsettled by that conversation about her father. By her accusation that I wanted to hurt her by making her face the truth. I knew firsthand the consequences of burying your head in the sand.

In that moment none of it mattered except the way her hair shone like a living, breathing flame against the delicate white lace.

Maddeningly arousing.

Everything about this woman I'd married was temptation personified, urging the unschooled man closer. But I was well schooled in the sort of temptation she offered. And, as I'd accurately guessed, granting her wishes had in turn given me what I wanted.

Like Anneka and every woman I'd known, all that mattered to her was getting what she wanted in the end. I didn't doubt that if I was minded to strike another bargain she would accede to my wish to see her clad in white morning, noon and night.

Or perhaps even nothing at all?

The erection straining behind my fly cursed me for agreeing to the *no sex* rule. Why had I? Because in that moment, binding her to me in any way at all had been paramount?

My dealings with women after my failed engagement and the betrayal that followed had taught me one thing. Sex was only complicated when the parameters weren't set out explicitly. Sadie had proved herself a good negotiator. So why not negotiate on this too?

The thought of experiencing her again, of having her beneath me, that breathtaking face turned up to receive my kisses and that body between my hands, mine to pleasure and take pleasure in, powered me several steps after her before I caught myself. Stopped to stare down at the unusual weight of the band circling my finger.

The symbolism wasn't as easy to dismiss as I thought. I had a wife. One whom I suddenly felt a desperate need to bed.

No, not a sudden need. The lust I thought I'd dulled after that first time in my office had been building since she'd turned up in Athens. Since that potent realisation that she could be carrying my child.

Call me primitive, but the thought that I'd sowed a seed in her womb, against all the odds my doctors were still examining after new tests undertook last week, filled me with a sense of...*possession* I hadn't been able to shake.

I twisted the band around my finger. Would it be so unthinkable to strike another bargain, stake my true claim?

Yes, it would. Because that was the kind of bargain that came with a steep price. The Anneka-shaped kind that left only bitterness and regret in its wake.

I turned, heading away from the direction she'd taken.

Three hours later I was still pacing my suite, the tablet laid out with marketing reports and projections to be analysed abandoned in favour of fighting temptation. Fighting the invasion of Sadie Preston...no, Sadie *Xenakis*... in my brain.

And failing.

With an impatient grunt, I slid open the French doors, stepped onto the private terrace. The breeze cooled my skin but did nothing to alleviate the pressure in my groin demanding relief.

A full moon was reflected on a smooth, serene sea, a

picture of calm in direct opposition to the sensations roiling inside me.

Not only were Sadie's words echoing in my head, other observations about her kept intruding, grating like tiny pebbles on my otherwise smooth and solid belief system. Her reluctance to leave that dingy little flat. Her resistance to the lavishness and extravagance of the wedding planning, when most brides would have been rapturous at having an unlimited budget.

Most of all, her complete lack of concern that she'd be walking away with less than one percent of my wealth when I ended this marriage. That clause in the prenup had been deliberate. A ruthless little test she'd batted away without so much as a quibble.

And her bemusement when I brought it up... It had been so...*different*.

But was I seeing what I wanted to see? Repeating the same misjudgement I'd shown when I'd dismissed Anneka's obvious signs of infidelity and shameless avarice in favour of claiming the child she'd sworn was mine?

Restless feet propelled me towards the sound of water. To the pool Sadie had dipped her dainty feet in earlier, triggering awareness of yet another part of her body I found enthralling.

Thoughts of her feet evaporated when I was confronted by the more erotic vision rising from the moonlit pool.

Her back was to me, the tips of her fingers trailing through the water, and her gaze on the view as she moved towards the shallow end. She'd obviously been submerged moments before, because her hair was wet and pearlescent drops of water clung to her flawless skin.

Another few steps and the water dropped below her heart-shaped behind, revealed the bottom half of a white bikini moulding her curves and stopping my breath.

Thee mou, but I loved her in white...

The sizzling thought froze in my mind when she turned

fully to face the view, presenting me with her magnificent profile. If she'd looked spectacular before, now she was a bewitching goddess. At just over three months pregnant her shape hadn't altered profoundly, but signs of her state were visible in specific areas.

Her belly held the slightest curve and her breasts, lush and mouth-watering before, were fuller, more ripe. My palms burned with the need to cup them, to taste them.

A growl broke free from my throat before I could stop it.

She whirled around, one hand holding that rope of hair I wanted to wrap around my own wrist.

'Neo! I... I thought you were...'

'Asleep?' Hell, was that growly mess my voice?

She nodded a little jerkily, her gaze running over my body as I approached. Did her gaze linger below my belt? The throb there grew more insistent, propelling me even closer to the edge of the pool.

'Did I disturb you?' she asked.

'I couldn't sleep. And from the looks of it neither could you.'

A pulse leapt at her throat as her gaze travelled over me once more, her lips parting as she saw the unmistakable evidence of my arousal.

'Was I right? Does this night feel too...extraordinary to waste on sleep?'

Her head tilted up, her smooth throat bared to my hungry gaze as she swallowed. 'I don't know about extraordinary, but it's not every day a woman gets married. Or it could be I'm just getting used to this place—'

'It's not that and we both know it,' I interrupted, almost too keen to have her acknowledge what was happening.

She stared up at me, her breathing beautifully erratic, her face worshipped by moonbeams. Her fingers continued to twist that rope of hair. The whole picture of potent wantonness shattered another layer of my control.

I wanted to grab. To devour. To claim with a thoroughness that guaranteed we'd taste blissful insanity.

'Are you going to stay in there all night or are you done, Sadie?'

She shrugged lazily, drawing my attention to those decadent drops of water on her shoulder.

Two steps back and I snagged a warm towel. Held it out. 'Come out, Sadie.'

Exquisite defiance tilted her chin, long enough for me to feel the weight of her mutiny.

'Is that an order? Because, newsflash, I'm not in a mood to obey.'

We stayed like that, her gaze daring me. Then she turned her back, dived back under the water and swam two more lengths. Only then did she get out and approach me. Eyes on mine, she placed one foot on the shallow step. Then another. Her full breasts swayed with her movement, her hips sashaying in hypnotic motions that drove spikes of lust deeper. With every inch of the body she exposed, my hunger trebled.

Wrapping the towel around her was a perfunctory move to enfold her within my arms. The smile tilting her lips screamed her triumph, stated she was in my arms because *she* wanted it.

When she wrapped her slim arms around my neck, I barely stopped myself from growling again. 'You want to know why I'm not in my bed? Why I'm out here, shattering my concentration even further and seeking peace of mind I know I won't find?'

Her gaze dropped from mine to lock on my lips.

'Because I do this to you,' she stated sultrily, rocking herself against my hardness in a way that left no doubt as to my state.

'Because you tempt me more than I've ever been tempted in my life.' I laughed, despite myself. Or perhaps because of the singular thought that it was no use fighting this. That

I didn't even want to. 'Despite my every reserve, I hunger for you.'

She inhaled, sharp and sweet, her pink tongue flicking out to swipe across her lower lip.

I captured it, bit her sensitive flesh in punishment for the cyclone of need it had created in me. When she moaned, I deepened the caress, slanted my lips over hers, claimed that mouth and satisfied a fraction of that hunger, even while it continued to rage out of control.

Tentatively, her tongue darted out to meet mine, and I took possession of it, gliding and tasting in an erotic dance I wanted to repeat all over her naked body. Especially that snug, glorious place between her legs.

Finally, I speared my fingers into the heavy mass of her damp hair to tilt her face higher, drive my kiss deeper. When she opened wider for me I couldn't stop my groan of pure satisfaction.

'Your hair is a work of art, *pethi mou*. Simply exquisite.'

'Neo…'

I backed us up a few steps, until the terrace wall met her back and the soft cushion of her body moulded my front.

'And this mouth. *Christos*, you have the most divine mouth,' I confessed, rediscovering that sensitive spot in her neck where her pulse throbbed before returning to re-claim her mouth. 'I haven't been able to stop thinking about kissing you since that unsatisfactory sampling at the altar.'

My free hand slid down her body, stopping briefly to mould one plump, mouth-watering breast, before travelling lower, to cup her hot feminine centre.

'Haven't stopped thinking about this special place either. Imagining you wrapped tight around me again, taking me inside you.'

She whimpered against my lips. 'I… I shouldn't be doing this,' she murmured, almost to herself.

And I shouldn't crave you this much. And yet here I am…

Through the damp material of the bikini bottom I caressed her, my thumb circling that engorged bead I craved to have between my lips. When the need grew beyond containment I slipped my fingers beneath the stretchy fabric. Touched her where I needed to touch her.

Her knees sagged and she whimpered again. Muttered words against my lips I was too incoherent to absorb.

Which was why it took a moment to realise that the hand curled around my wrist, and the other flat against my chest, were both attempting to push me away.

'Neo…we can't…'

The protest was feeble, the look on her face as I drew back a touch torn between hunger and rebellion.

I fought the voracious need gripping me and started to withdraw my hand.

Her thighs clamped around it, holding me prisoner.

'You say we can't while looking at me with yearning in your eyes. Your body clings to mine while you deny me what I want. What we both want. You think I don't feel how wet you are for me, Sadie?'

Heat rushed into her face. Her thighs parted with an abrupt jerk and she swiftly dropped her hands. 'This… It's just chemistry.'

'There's no such thing as "just chemistry." Especially not when it's this powerful. When it creates this response.'

My gaze dropped tellingly to the tight furling of her nipples, clearly visible against the damp bikini top.

'It means nothing,' she protested. 'Besides, sex is what got us here in the first place!'

The cold compress of her words washed away a layer of blazing arousal. 'And it's a place you don't wish to be? Is that it?'

'Don't put words in my mouth. I may not have been prepared for this baby but I've vowed to give it the best life possible. That doesn't mean I want to mess up my life with sex. So if you're looking for a way to scratch your itch you'll…' She stopped, her throat moving as she swallowed her words.

'I'll what, Sadie?'

She shook her head, sending wet tendrils flying. I caught a strand, tucking it behind one ear. Her pulse jumped beneath my touch.

'You can't say the words, can you?' I taunted, deriving a little devilish satisfaction from it. 'Did you fool yourself into thinking giving me liberties I didn't want would be easy?'

She turned her face to the side, avoiding my gaze. 'I don't know what you're talking about.'

My grating laughter earned me a ferocious glare. I caressed her cheek, unable to resist touching her even now. 'Do you not? Really? Then let me posit a theory. Perhaps this marriage isn't as clinical as you wish it to be? Perhaps this itch you speak of isn't a one-sided thing?'

Watching her gather her frayed composure was a thing of unwanted awe.

'I'm a grown woman, Neo. With independent thoughts and needs I can choose to indulge or deny. While the last few minutes have been pleasant, it's not worth sullying my life for. So, no, the itch will remain a one-sided thing and no amount of temptation will sway me. Goodnight.'

For the second time I watched her walk away from me, leaving even more chaos behind. Acknowledging that I wanted her much more than I'd wanted any other woman in my life, that I might never have her, disarmed me enough to leave me propped up against the wall long after she and her voluptuous curves and her stubborn defiance had disappeared behind her suite doors.

But when the realisation hit that I, Neo Xenakis, was being denied a woman's attention for the first time in my life, I surged away from that wall, determined to rid myself of this…infernal need.

A teeth-gritting, bracing cold shower restored a little sanity. But with sanity came the acknowledgement that perhaps I hadn't bargained as well as I'd thought for what I wanted.

Because what I wanted was…*more*.

And nothing drove home that realisation harder than the first prenatal scan just days later.

When I heard the strong, powerful heartbeat of my child for the first time.

I couldn't look away from the unrestrained stamp of possession on Neo's face and that flash of uncertainty and apprehension as he stared at the monitor. I might have serious doubts as to his motives in other things, but in this I couldn't dismiss the strength of his feelings. But were they positive? Or calculated?

As the doctor took measurements and studiously recorded details, Neo's gaze drifted feverishly over my face, then down my body to latch onto my belly.

'Dikos mou,' he murmured, with even more fervour than he had two days ago.

Mine.

That proclamation moved something in me, and I was glad for the echo of my baby's heartbeat otherwise I was sure he'd have heard my own thundering heart.

Would it be the end of the world to give in to this unrelenting craving?

The thought wasn't easy to dispel, especially now, when he leaned closer, his body bracing mine on the king-sized bed.

Like a flower reaching for the sun, my every cell strained for him, defiantly ignoring my inner protests.

It was almost a relief when the doctor finished the scan and printed off two copies, which Neo immediately took possession of, sliding one into his wallet and handing me the other.

When I reached for it he held on to it for a moment, his eyes pinning mine as his fingers brushed my skin. Something heavy and intense fired up in his eyes—something that should have sent apprehension dancing down my spine but instead left molten heat in my belly, my heartbeat fast enough to match my baby's.

The moment passed.

After Neo's rapid-fire questions provided reassurance that the baby was healthy, the doctor and his technician were dismissed and Neo turned to me.

'How do you feel?' he asked.

'Well enough to start work.'

His mouth compressed and I geared myself for another disagreement.

'The morning sickness has passed?'

I nodded. 'It stopped about a week ago.'

His gaze returned to my belly, stayed for fevered seconds. 'Very well. We'll leave in half an hour.' With brisk strides, he left the room.

I rose, spinning slowly in place, still awed by my surroundings. By the size of the bedroom that would easily fit my previous home twice over. Not to mention the dressing room.

I approached the large, cavernous room decked from floor to ceiling in wood, and tastefully arranged into sections for shoes, handbags, day and evening wear.

Last night, when the helicopter landed in the exclusive neighbourhood of Voula, minutes from the centre of Athens, I'd been too overwhelmed by the hour spent in close proximity to Neo to appreciate the opulence of his tiered mansion.

Unsurprisingly, every square inch dripped with luxury. Cream with grey-veined marble and hues of dark blue and grey was the theme running through each room. Set into its own vast exclusive hillside, it overlooked a miles-long vista, with the Acropolis the jaw-dropping centre of attraction.

The staff of six spoke impeccable English, and after I'd dressed, the housekeeper directed me to Neo's study.

My knock was answered in deep, crisp tones. When I entered his gaze was hooded, loaded with the sort of heavy speculation and calculation that sent another wave of sensation over my skin.

I'd walked away on Saturday night believing that I'd ended that dangerous episode before it had blown up. But with each look, I got the uncanny sensation that we weren't done. That Neo's machinations were merely gathering pace.

Which made walking beside him on the way to his underground garage a monumental task in composure keeping for me. But once we were seated in the black Maserati, the powerful engine speeding us through early-morning traffic, he was all business.

He indicated the stylish briefcase in the footwell next to my feet. 'The briefcase is yours—so is the tablet inside it. I've loaded three marketing reports on it. I want your thoughts on them by midday.'

I grabbed the case, hung on to it as if it would dilute his effect on me.

It didn't even come close.

Our previous interactions had given me a taster of Neo's power, but my introduction to his corporate life provided a mind-bending main course of the sheer formidable force he wielded. For example, the middle-aged woman I'd encountered in his office months ago was one of six assistants poised to answer his every demand.

And his first demand was to have her summon his top marketing executives into his office, where I was introduced as his wife and personal intern—a statement that garnered speculation and brought a warm flush to my face.

But it was his second demand—that I be set up in one corner of his vast office—that drew a protest from me. 'Aren't you worried about whispers of nepotism?'

One eyebrow lifted. 'Not even a little bit,' he tossed away. At my frown he added, 'I don't intend to make this an easy ride for you, Sadie. But by all means, if you're worried about it, then prove them wrong.'

* * *

In the three dizzying weeks that followed it was impossible not to meet that challenge, to smash it to pieces. Because, while Neo was maddeningly rabid in ensuring I was provided with mouth-watering meals at precise intervals during the day, that my prenatal vitamins were taken like clockwork and my every comfort was catered for, business-wise he was a slave-driver—often lounging back in his thronelike seat while firing questions at me from across the room. He tossed every menial marketing task at me, barely letting me catch my breath before the next project landed on my desk.

And when he wasn't doing that, his gaze rested on me with molten, unapologetic interest.

It was on one such occasion, when I was feeling mellowed from a client's high praise of a marketing analysis I'd put together, that I caught his gaze on me as I rose from my desk.

'What are you thinking?' I asked, before I could curb my curiosity.

The question seemed to startle him. Then his long lashes swept over me. 'White.'

'Pardon me?'

'White suits you. You should wear only that from now on.'

An anticipatory shiver fired through me, because he'd just tossed one of his imperious observations at me. And, oh, how I'd relish batting it away.

'Is this where you say "Jump" and hope I'll say, "Yes, sir…how high do you wish, sir?"'

For some absurd reason his lips twitched with amusement. 'I'd say yes, but we both know you'd never do anything that accommodating. Not without something in return, at least.'

A pang of hurt caught me unawares.

His gaze sharpened on my face, then he grew irritated.

'That was meant to be a compliment, Sadie, not a prelude to a fight. You look beautiful in white.'

'Is that why my wardrobe is suddenly full of white stuff?' The predominantly white outfits had appeared suddenly, with no explanation offered.

He shrugged. 'I was told you didn't seem interested in the whole clothes-shopping process back in London. I made the choice for you. If I was wildly inaccurate, then feel free to amend it.'

Mutiny rose and died almost as soon as my fingers drifted over the soft white cotton dress I'd picked for the office today. The boat-necked A-line design draped over my body without clinging, cleverly disguising the small swell of my belly. And, like this dress, every item in my new wardrobe was a perfect fit.

'It's okay, I suppose.'

He inclined his head in an imperious nod, but not before I caught a look of...*relief*?

Before I could be sure, he was rising, messing with my breathing as he sauntered around to perch on the edge of his desk.

'Come here, Sadie,' he commanded, his voice gravel rough.

'Why?'

His eyes shadowed. 'Because it's time to go over the final details before our meeting,' he said easily.

I wasn't fooled. The fierce gleam in his eye announced other intentions.

But, unable to resist that hypnotic voice, I stumbled over to him. He caught my hips between his hands, positioning me between his spread legs, and as he stared down into my face I struggled to catch my breath. And then the most wondrous thing happened.

I felt the sweetest, most delicate tingling in my belly.

'Oh!'

His gaze sharpened. 'What is it?'

'I just felt…'

Raw, thick emotion arrested his face. 'The baby?'

The hushed gravity of his voice, the depth of yearning in his voice, disarmed me.

'According to all indications you *should* be experiencing the first movements of my child inside you,' he rasped.

'I thought I felt something…a flutter yesterday…but it hasn't happened again—' The fluttering came again, making me gasp. 'Oh!'

His gaze dropped to my belly, and his hand slowly lowered to hover over the small bump. 'I would very much like to touch you, Sadie,' he said, his voice gravel rough.

Shakily fighting back hormonal tears, I nodded. He exhaled raggedly, his warm hand remaining on me for long moments, during which the fluttering was repeated twice more, each time drawing from him an awed gasp.

Stormy eyes rose to mine. 'I said you looked beautiful. That wasn't quite accurate. You look radiant.' One hand rose to caress my cheek. 'Your skin glows with exquisite vitality. I've never quite seen anything like it.'

'It's…it's the pregnancy. Not me.'

'Most women would wholeheartedly bask in such a compliment, but not you,' he murmured, his gaze curiously flummoxed. 'Are you so determined to topple my opinion of you?' he rasped, a touch disgruntled.

'Neo—'

'Hush, *pethi mou*. Let us enjoy this moment,' he suggested, his voice hypnotic.

We stood trapped in that intensely soul-stirring bubble until the ringing phone made us both jump. I hastily stepped back from the exposing moment.

Back to a reality where this pregnancy was the sole reason I had a ring on my finger and a place in Neo's office.

Back to a place where the softening emotions that had been expanding over the past few weeks needed to be shoved back into a box marked *delusional*.

When he reached over to answer his phone I escaped, reciting every reason why resisting temptation and Neo was essential to my equilibrium.

When I returned, half an hour later, Neo's laser-beam eyes focused on the frosted treat in my hand. 'What's that?'

I raised an eyebrow. 'It's a cupcake, Neo.'

'I can see that. I meant *that*.' He pointed his arrogant nose at the thin candle perched in the middle of the frosting.

'It's a candle. Which I'm going to light when I get to my desk and then blow out. Because it's my birthday.'

He went pillar still. 'What did you say?'

'I said it's my birthday today.'

His eyes narrowed. 'If this is a ploy of some sort—'

'You think I'd bother to lie about something you can find out in less than ten seconds?'

The fire and brimstone left his eyes immediately, leaving him looking curiously nonplussed.

'Wow. So much for me thinking felicitations might be forthcoming,' I said.

My waspish tone further unnerved him. Then his lips firmed.

'You scurried away before we were done talking. You do realise you're not doing yourself any favours by annoying me, don't you?'

I shrugged. 'I'm here now, and I don't see a fire, so…'

His eyes widened a fraction, then I caught a hint of amusement. Again I had the feeling that the mighty Neo Xenakis liked being challenged.

Striding over, he took the cupcake from me, set it on my desk and took my hand.

'What are you doing? And, more importantly, why are you separating me from my cupcake?'

He frowned, or least gave an impression of it. But it fell far short of his overriding expression—bewilderment. Perhaps even a little shame.

'You asked where the fire was. Our meeting has been rescheduled to now.'

'What? But—'

'You helped the team land the deal that has brought the Portuguese trade minister here. I don't think you'll want to keep him waiting while you devour a dubious-looking confection from a vending machine.'

'It wasn't from a vending machine. It was from your executive restaurant, which is manned by a chef I hear is on the brink of winning his first Michelin star.'

He simply shrugged and kept moving while he extracted his phone from his pocket. Rapid-fire Greek greeted whoever answered the call, after which he held open the door to the conference room with one eyebrow hiked up.

'You know there's a rule against keeping a pregnant woman from what she craves, don't you?'

My words had been meant harshly. Instead they emerged in a sultry undertone, wrapped in a yearning that was only partly for the cupcake he'd forced me to abandon.

And if I had any doubt that my words had triggered the same thought in him, the darkening of his eyes and the slight parting of his sensual mouth told me we'd skated away from the subject of cupcakes to something more potent.

'I will bear the consequences of it this once,' he rasped, his voice an octave lower. Deeper.

Sexier.

My gaze dropped to the sensual line of his lips and I sucked in a breath.

'The minister is waiting, Sadie. As much as I want to answer that look in your eyes, it won't do for me to start making love to my wife in full view of a potential business associate.'

My wife.

It was the first time he'd referred to me as that since the wedding…

The two-hour meeting passed in a rush of effectively

troubleshooting every last one of the minister's objections. While the team acted in perfect cohesion, Neo seemed intent on lobbing further questions for me to answer, giving a satisfied nod when I did.

Perhaps he wanted to give me a chance to prove my worth, to publicly expunge any hint of nepotism once and for all. Whatever the reason, it left me with a warm, buoyant glow that shrivelled the hard knot of unworthiness that had clung to me and drew a wide smile once the minister left, satisfied.

Perhaps my smile was too wide. Too proud. It certainly triggered something in Neo, and his stride was purposeful as he marched me from the conference room.

'I hate to repeat myself, but where's the fire?' I asked.

'I'm giving you the rest of the day off,' he declared.

'I can't take time off *and* finish the work you've asked me to do.'

He merely shrugged as he stepped with me into the lift and pressed the button for the parking garage, where a valet stood next to his car, keys ready.

'Change of plan,' Neo said, once I was seated and he'd slid behind the wheel. 'There's an event I need you to attend with me tonight.'

'Oh? Do you want to tell me about it so I can prepare?'

While the thought of working on my birthday hadn't disheartened me, because working with Neo was a secret thrill I wouldn't pass up, I wasn't sure I wanted to be thrown into the deep end of an unknown situation.

'Preparation won't be necessary,' he said cryptically. 'But dress formally.'

For the rest of the journey back to the villa he fell into silence, his profile not inviting conversation.

Inside, he excused himself, shutting his study door behind him with a definitive click.

I retreated to my dressing room to face the daunting task of picking what to wear. Eventually, I chose a white gown made of the softest tulle layered over satin. The gathered material swept down from one shoulder and cupped my bust before falling away in a long, elegant sweep to my ankles. I complemented it with light, champagne-coloured strappy heels and a matching clutch, and left my earlobes and throat free—simply because the jewellery I owned was too understated for the gown, and because I still had no clear idea of where Neo was taking me.

As if I'd conjured him up, his firm knock arrived.

I opened the door and suppressed a gasp.

His business suit had been swapped for a dinner suit, a dark silk shirt, a darker-hued tie and bespoke shoes polished to within an inch of their life. With his freshly showered hair slicked back, and his face and that cleft in his chin thrown into relief, it was all I could do to not stare open-mouthed at the overwhelmingly dashing figure he cut.

His return scrutiny was electric, his eyes turning a skin-tingling stormy grey as they sizzled over my body. 'You look exquisite,' he pronounced, managing to sound arrogant and awed at the same time.

The combination melted me from the inside out, and my heart was pounding even before he held out his arm in silent invitation.

I slid my hand into the crook of his elbow, concentrated in putting one foot in front of the other as he led me not to the garage but out through the wide living room doors and down another terrace towards the helipad.

He helped me into the sleek aircraft, then strapped himself in.

'Are you going to tell me where we're going?' I asked.

He slanted me a lazy, shiver-inducing glance. 'You'll see for yourself in a few minutes.'

The aircraft lifted off, flew straight towards the horizon for a full minute, then started to descend again. When it banked slightly to the right to land, I saw it.

The Acropolis.

Lit to magnificent perfection, it was a breathtaking sight to behold. 'We're meeting the client *here*?'

Neo simply gave an enigmatic smile, deftly alighted when the aircraft set down, and held out his hand to me. I'd been in Athens long enough to know that tours took place both day and night. But there was no one around— just a handful of dark-suited men, one of whom looked suspiciously like... *Wendell*.

A sharp glance at Neo showed that enigmatic expression still in place.

My heart thundered harder.

At the Parthenon, I wanted to linger, the beauty surrounding me demanding appreciation. But Neo's fingers tightened.

'You can have a private tour later, if you wish. But not now.'

I discovered why minutes later, felt something sacred break away and hand itself over to Neo without my approval or permission. Because there was no event. No client. Just an elaborately laid candle-lit table set for two in the middle of the Temple of Athena Nike.

Emotion, far too delicate and precious for this man who could be in equal parts hard and bitter and magnetic, swelled inside me. 'Neo, why are we here?'

He stepped forward, drew back my chair. 'You helped land a very big deal for Xenakis today. An achievement worth celebrating,' he said.

And as that warm bubble of *worthiness* expanded inside me, he added, 'Plus, it's your birthday.'

My throat clogged, dangerously happy emotions brimming.

'I spoke to your mother's counsellor at the rehab centre. She didn't think it would be wise to grant dispensation for your birthday. *Syngnómi*. I'm sorry.'

'It's fine. I'm just glad she's getting the help she needs.'

Deep down, while I'd have loved to share this moment

with her, I was selfishly glad I had this all to myself. That I had Neo all to myself, as unwise as the thought was.

It took a few minutes for the shock to wear off, to grasp the fact that he'd had the tours shut down, had his executive chef prepare a sublime meal and transported it to this incredible place. All in a handful of hours.

The impact of his actions threatened to drown me in dangerous emotion. The kind that prompted yearnings that would never be fulfilled. The kind that led to restless, need-filled nights.

In a bid to put some distance between myself and those feelings, I glanced at pillars that whispered with history. 'Was Athena Nike not a fertility goddess?'

Neo inclined his head, his gaze brooding. 'Which makes this location apt, does it not?'

A blush crept into my cheeks, and when his gaze lingered boldly, heat spread fast and hard over my body.

Easy conversation flowed between us as we ate. And when the pièce de résistance was wheeled out—an enormous cupcake-shaped birthday cake, with a single candle set into the pink frosting—I fought back tears as Neo took my hand and led me to it.

'You made a wish?' His tone suggested the idea was alien to him.

'I did. Something wrong with that?' I asked when an involuntary muscle clenched in his jaw.

'Wishes are useless. Reality is what matters.'

Bruising hurt launched itself into my chest. 'It's my birthday. I'm one hundred percent sure you're not allowed to rain on my birthday parade.'

He stared at me for a long spell. Then nodded abruptly. '*Ne*, I'm not. What I *can* do is give you your birthday gift.'

From his pocket, he pulled a sleek, oblong box. Before he could open it, I laid my hand over his.

'I don't need a present, Neo. This…' I waved my hand at the setting '…is more than enough.'

He blithely ignored me and flicked the box open.

Inside nestled a gorgeous necklace. Fiery ruby stones battled with sparkling diamonds for radiance. I couldn't help my gasp.

'You might not want a gift, but it's yours nevertheless,' he stated, in that absolute manner I'd come to accept was simply his nature.

'And you want me to take it because it will please you?' I semi-mocked, using his words from before.

He shook his head. 'Because it will look beautiful on you. Because the rubies match your sensational hair and it would be a shame to keep this thing in a box.'

The compliments burrowed deep inside me, disarming me long enough for him to fasten the necklace, step back and boldly admire it.

'You have a thing for my hair, don't you?' I said.

Expecting a mocking comeback, my heart flipped over when raw need tightened his face.

Before I could draw a breath he was capturing my shoulders, dragging me against his body. 'I have a thing for *you*, Sadie. For all of you,' he breathed, right before his head swooped down.

Helpless to deny the hunger which had been building inside me for weeks, I surged onto my toes and met his fiery kiss. Sensation went from one to one hundred in the space of a heartbeat. In a tangle of limbs we grappled to get closer, to kiss deeper, to sate an insatiable need.

When an abstract sense of propriety finally drove us apart, we were both breathing harshly, and Neo's face was a taut mask of arousal. His hands continued to roam over my body, stoking need, until I feared my heart would bang clean out of my ribcage.

Lips parted in stunned surprise, I watched him sink to his knees, frame my hips between his hands, before leaning forward to kiss the swell of my belly. When he rose again, his eyes churned with thunder and lightning, his hands trailing fire when he cupped my nape and angled my face to his.

'I want you, Sadie. Naked. In my bed, beneath me. Think of the sublime pleasure I can give you and give in to me,' he coaxed, his fingers caressing my throat.

My knees sagged, the heady words finding their target and weakening my resolve. I scrambled hard for it. Because when it came right down to it, what Neo was offering was great sex. But still only sex.

I wanted more. Much more than I'd even allowed myself to dream of.

It was that very monumental need that made me shake my head. 'I can't. Not for a quick tumble that will simply complicate things. Besides, this isn't part of our agreement.'

And it's not enough for me.

His face slowly hardened. 'Be careful, Sadie, that you don't box yourself into a corner you'll regret.'

Those cryptic words stayed with me long after we'd returned to the villa. Long after he'd bade me a curt goodnight and left me at the door of my suite.

Undressing, I caught sight of myself in the mirror and gasped, the effect of the spectacular necklace freezing me in place. I couldn't help but appreciate its beauty. Appreciate the compliments Neo had paid me. Dwell on the look in his eyes before he'd kissed me.

I have a thing for you…all of you…

Had I dismissed his words too quickly? Had he been paving the way for…*more*?

A glance at my bedside clock showed it was only just past ten. My birthday wouldn't be over for another two hours.

Perhaps it wasn't too late to make another wish come true.

CHAPTER NINE

I TOSSED THE covers aside and slid out of bed before I lost my nerve.

My knock on his door elicited a sharp, gruff response. My clammy hand turned the handle and, ignoring my screaming senses telling me to turn back, I nudged it open.

He was reclined in the middle of his emperor-sized bed, his top half bare and his lower half covered by a dark green satin sheet. For several heartbeats he stared at me, a tight expression on his face.

'Come to drive a few more points home?' he asked eventually, his voice taut.

Unable to clear the lump of nerves lodged in my throat, I shook my head.

Slowly, torturously, his gaze roved over my body, lingering at my throat, where the necklace still rested, then my breasts, hips, down my legs, before rising to stop where the hem of my silk night slip ended high on my thighs.

He swallowed hard before his gaze clashed with mine, a turbulence percolating there that triggered a similar chain reaction in me.

'Then what *do* you want, Sadie?' His accent had thickened, throbbing with deep, dark desire.

'What you said, back on Neostros, about me giving you liberty you didn't want to take. What did you mean by that?'

That mask twisted with flint-hard warning. 'Whether you end up in my bed or not, I don't plan to stray. Earlier tonight I thought we could, in time, get to a place where the possibility of renegotiating wasn't unthinkable.'

In time...

Once he was certain the baby I carried was his?

I forced myself to focus as he continued.

'But you shut that down, so I'm not sure why you're here. One thing you should know, though. I abhor infidelity of any sort. If that's what you're here to propose—'

'No!' My heart twisted with dark, rabid jealousy. 'That wasn't... That's not why I'm here.'

'Spit it out, my sweet. There's only so much torture I'll take from my wife. Even on her birthday. Especially when she's standing there looking like my every fantasy come to life.'

His gaze dropped again, this time to the fingers I was unconsciously twisting in front of me. Something eased in his eyes and he reared up from his recline.

At the sight of his sculpted chest, my mouth dried. Then almost immediately flooded with a hunger that weakened me from head to toe.

'Come here, Sadie,' he commanded gruffly.

I shook my head. 'You're going to have to come and get me.'

Expecting an arrogant comeback, I was surprised when his jaw clenched and his fingers bunched on the sheets. For an age, he contemplated me, his gaze weighing mine.

If I hadn't known better I'd have imagined Neo was... *nervous.*

Before the thought could deepen, he swung his legs over the side of the bed and rose.

And for the first time I saw Neo naked. Saw him in his full magnificent glory.

Saw the deep, stomach-hollowing scars that dissected his left hip, then zigzagged their way over his pelvis to end dangerously close to his manhood.

My hand shot up to my mouth, a horrid little gasp escaping me before I could stop it.

Dear God, so *that* was why he believed he couldn't have children?

Neo's head jerked back, his eyes darkening at my reaction. Yet he didn't flinch or cower. Hell, he seemed resolute, even a little proud to show off his scars. He prowled forward, naked and unashamed, his impressive manhood at full mast.

'What's the matter, Sadie?' he rasped when he was a handful of feet away. 'Is this too much for you? Are you going to run from me? Again?'

My gaze flew to his. 'No! What would make you think that?'

His eyes shadowed and he paused for several beats. 'The sight of me doesn't horrify you?' he asked, a peculiar note in his voice.

'Of course I'm not horrified. I'm heartsick that you had to endure that. Who wouldn't be?'

His lips twisted bitterly. 'I've discovered from past...encounters...that there are three reactions to my scars. Horror, pity or stoicism.'

'Well, I don't belong in any of those groups, thank you very much.'

Again his gaze probed mine. 'Do you not?'

'No. And if you keep looking at me like that I'll leave right now.'

'Your words salve me a little...but perhaps I require more? A demonstration of why you're in this room in the first place?' he said huskily. 'If you're not here to torture me, *pethi mou*, then why are you here?'

His voice grew more ragged, his chest rising and falling along with the impressive arousal that was somehow growing even prouder by the second.

I dragged my gaze from his intoxicating body. 'I came to tell you that I've changed my mind. That I... I want...'

God, what a time to be struck senseless. But, really, who could blame me? When he looked this magnificent? When it seemed—powerfully and thrillingly—that I had this effect on him?

'I want the fantasy,' I whispered.

'What fantasy? Tell me what you want, Sadie. Explicitly.'

Nerves ate harder, knotting my tongue.

'Perhaps it would be better to show me, hmm?' he encouraged, his voice a barely audible rasp.

Had he said this with even a stitch of clothing on I would have balked. But with the miles of gleaming olive skin on show, his virility just begging to be explored and every atom in my body screaming for contact, the urge was impossible to deny.

My twitching hands flexed, rose. Brushed over one long, thin, jagged scar.

A sharp breath hissed out.

I snatched my hand away. 'I'm s-sorry. I didn't mean to hurt you.'

He gave a sharp shake of his head. 'It doesn't pain me, Sadie. Quite the opposite,' he grated.

My gaze darted to his face. While his expression was tight with barely leashed control, his eyes blazed with an emotion I couldn't quite name.

'I've never permitted anyone to explore me this way,' he added.

'Really?' Why did that please me so much?

'*Ne*. Continue. Please,' he urged.

Encouraged, I trailed my fingers over the raised skin, tracing the map of his trauma, a little in awe that he'd survived what had to have been a horrific experience.

When I neared his groin the sculpted muscles in his abs tensed, but he didn't stop me. Growing bolder, I stepped into his force field, felt the searing heat of his skin blanket me.

'Will you tell me what happened?' I asked.

He regarded me for several heartbeats, then nodded. 'Later. Much later.' Then, grasping my hand, he growled, 'Don't stop.'

The invitation was too heady to resist.

I explored him from chest to thigh, but avoided the powerful thrust of his erection until, with a growl, he swung me into his arms and strode for the bed.

Laying me down, he divested me of the slip and panties but left the necklace on. Then he stayed by the side of the bed, staring down at me with blazing eyes.

'Our first time was rushed. Understandably chaotic. This time I intend to take my time, learn everything you like. Show you what I desire. Are you willing, *pethi mou*?'

I nodded jerkily, aware that my pulse was racing at my throat.

'Good.'

Boldly, he reached forward and cupped one breast, while the other hand covered the damp heat gathering between my legs. His eyes devoured my every expression as I arched into his touch.

'I want to watch you drown in pleasure. I want to see your beautiful green eyes when you come for me.'

He toyed with one peaked nipple, drawing from me a breathless gasp, then swooped down, twirled his tongue around the tight nub, drew it into his mouth for several hot seconds before he raised his head.

'I want to hear your breath hitch like that when you lose your mind for me.'

His thumb found the needy pearl of my core and rubbed with an expertise that arched my back, made desperate moans erupt from my throat.

'Ah, just like that, *moro mou*.'

'Neo, you're making me… I'm…'

'Give yourself over to me, Sadie,' he grated thickly, urgently. 'Give me what I want and I'll reward you.'

'With…what?' I gasped.

An arrogant smile curved his sensual lips. 'With as much of me as you can take. Would you like that?'

'Yes!'

'Then come for me. Now, Sadie,' he demanded throatily, his clever fingers demanding that ultimate response as his due.

With mindless abandon I handed it over, sensation piling high as he flipped the switch that triggered my release. My screams scraped my throat raw, my body twisting in a frenzied bliss I never wanted to end.

All the while Neo rained kisses and praise on my body, his lips and hands prolonging my pleasure until I was spent. Until all I could do was try to catch my breath as he finally climbed onto the bed, parted my thighs and situated himself above me, arms planted on either side of my shoulders.

Even as my heart raced from one climax, need built again, and the sight of Neo, this powerful mountain of a man whose scars only served to make him even more unique, more potent and desirable, and yet so dangerous to my emotional well-being, rendered me speechless.

Eyes frenzied with need scoured me from head to toe. 'Touch me, Sadie,' he rasped.

Too far gone to resist, I cupped his jaw, gloried in the sharp stubble that pricked my skin, delighted when he turned his face deeper into my touch. I explored him with the same thoroughness with which he'd explored me, until his breaths turned ragged and his stomach muscles clenched with the tightness of his control.

Throwing my legs wider, I let my gaze find his. Our visceral connection thickening the desire arching between us, he surged sure and deep, filling me in places that went beyond the physical. Because as Neo began to move, a kind of joy filled my heart. One that prickled my eyes and made me cling tighter, cry out a little louder.

Because while it was wondrous it was also terrifying, this feeling. Because in those moments when sweat slicked from his body to mine, when he fused his lips to mine with a heavy, passionate groan and stepped off the edge with me, as I touched his scar and felt his pain echo in my heart, I knew this would never, ever be about just sex for me.

When it was over, when I was exhausted but sated, my hand traced the whorls of raised scar tissue, my heart squeezing as I thought of what he'd suffered.

'So was it a helicopter crash or a ski accident? The papers couldn't seem to decide on one or the other,' I said.

He stiffened, then gave a bitter chuckle. 'When have they ever bothered about what's the truth and what isn't?' Silence reigned for a handful of seconds before he added tightly, 'It was on a black run in Gstaad. A run I'd skied many times before. But familiarity and expertise don't mean a thing if there's a lack of concentration.'

I frowned. Neo wasn't the type to court danger by being reckless. The ruthless efficiency with which he'd steered events from the moment he'd learned of his child was testament to the fact that he didn't drop the ball. *Ever.*

Unless… 'Something happened?'

Grim-faced, he unconsciously tightened his hand on my hip. Not enough to hurt, but enough to signal that whatever memory I'd roused wasn't pleasant.

'The company had just started a major international push when Anneka and I got together. She was part of the ski season crowd who worshipped the slopes. I didn't mind so much when she chose to party with her friends without me. But when she told me she was pregnant—'

He stopped at my shocked gasp. 'Your fiancée was *pregnant*?'

His face turned even grimmer, his jaw clenching tight before he nodded abruptly. 'But I began to suspect that she was chasing more than prime snow when she was away.'

'She was cheating on you?'

'I sensed she wasn't being truthful about a few things. But she denied it and I…' His jaw clenched tight for a single moment. 'I chose to believe her. She convinced me to let her stay in Gstaad for a few more days before coming back to Athens. On the morning I was supposed to leave, she wanted to ski on the black run. She was an excellent skier, but she was pregnant with my child and I didn't feel right about letting her go alone. So I went with her. It started snowing heavily almost immediately. I lost sight of Anneka for a moment and lost my concentration.'

He stopped.

'I woke up from a coma three weeks later. Just in time to hear her plotting with her lover about how they would pass off their child as mine long enough to get a ring on her finger and all of my wealth. Within minutes I had no child, a duplicitous fiancée and the dreadful news that my injuries had ended any hope of my ever fathering a child naturally.'

As I was grappling with that, his turbulent gaze found mine.

'Do you understand now why hearing you'd destroyed my one last chance prompted my reaction?'

His stark bitterness threw ice-cold dread over me, keeping me numb for a minute before sensation piled in, puzzles slid into place.

With a horrified gasp I moved away from him, pulling the sheet tight around me. I suppressed another sharp cry as pain lanced me and the weighted certainty that another woman's transgressions had been the measuring rod I'd been judged against all along froze me from the inside out.

'So I'm Project Two Point Zero?'

He frowned. 'Excuse me?'

'You thought I was lying when I said I was pregnant. Then you accused me of trying to foist another man's child on you. Then you thought you'd hedge your bets by marrying me, on the off-chance the child was yours. How are those imagined offences of mine any different from what your fiancée did to you?'

He reared up, his face tightening further. 'For one thing, we're married. And for another, you barely touch the possessions I've showered on you. You don't drive, or ask to be driven anywhere. The thought of going to a social event makes you grimace.'

'So my saving grace is that I'm not a fashion whore and nor do I salivate over the dozen supercars you store in your garage? What makes you think I'm not just biding my time, lulling you into a sense of complacency before I strike?'

One insolent eyebrow rose, as if the idea was amusing. 'Are you? And how do you propose to do that?'

'Give me time—I'm sure I can come up with something.'

'You won't,' he parried arrogantly. 'You want to know how you're different?'

I pressed my lips together, the strong need to know almost overwhelming me.

'The only thing that gets you fired up—truly fired up—is your work. Your eyes light up when you're in the boardroom, challenging men and women with years of experience to better market an idea. Anneka got fired up by shopping until she dropped. The reason she was an ex-supermodel by the time she was twenty-five was because she'd gained a reputation for being unprofessional and lazy—partying and skiing were the only things she lived for. Sometimes I'd go two or three weeks without seeing her because she was too busy flying around in my jet to spend time with me.'

I frowned. 'So what on earth did you see in her? And is it even possible to shop and party that much…?' I muttered.

'Believe me, she gave it a good try. And after a few months we barely saw each other. I was about to break it off when she told me she was pregnant.'

The similarities crushed me harder. Neo and I would never have met again had it not been for the baby.

'You know how else you're different from Anneka?' he said.

I hated these comparisons. Hated the other woman's name on his lips. But I'd started this. And, for good or ill, the need to know more about what had shaped this man who made me terrified for my heart's well-being wouldn't abate.

'Enlighten me. Please.'

He ignored my droll tone, his eyes growing even more incisive as he stared at me, as if the list he was enumerating was necessary to him. Essential, even.

Maybe he needed to scrape together my *worthy* characteristics in order to be able to accept me as the mother of his child? And if he failed? If I wasn't enough? Anguish seared deeper, but he was still talking, so I forced myself to listen.

'You signed the prenup without so much as a quibble. Anneka got a team of lawyers to negotiate every clause—especially the one that stated that should I perish while we were married she would receive one hundred percent of my assets, including the funds I'd set aside for charity. Your attention to detail in the boardroom is exceptional. But I'm willing to bet you can't even remember the details of the financial package in the prenup you signed?'

I shook my head. 'The only part I cared about was what happened to our child,' I replied.

His arrogant smile widened. 'So tell me again how you plan to fleece me?'

I shrugged away the taunt, still consumed with wanting to know why he'd bothered to get together with a woman like Anneka if those were her true colours.

But I knew the answer. She was beautiful, vivacious and he'd thought she was carrying his child. It had become clear over the last few weeks that there was nothing Neo wouldn't do for his child. No sacrifice he wouldn't make.

My heart dipped in alarm and, yes, I felt a bite of jealousy at the thought that the all-encompassing feeling would never extend beyond his child. Not after what he'd experienced at the hands of another woman. Not after what I'd done to him even before our first meeting.

I was simply the vessel carrying what he wanted most in the world. How soon after I served my purpose would I be relegated to the background?

That anguishing thought drove my next question. 'So I'm a step or two up from the previous model—no pun intended. But I still have question marks over my head, don't I?'

'Don't we all?' he drawled.

'No, that's not going to fly. You've just listed the ways

I'm different from your ex, but what does that difference mean to you, Neo?' I pressed, an almost fatalistic urge smashing away my precious self-preservation.

'That remains to be seen,' he replied, and that aloofness I'd fooled myself into thinking was gone for ever resurged, saturating every inch of his perfect face.

'You mean until I prove my *worth* to you? Add the ultimate title of true mother to your child to that list? Maybe *then* you'll stop comparing me to her?'

He shrugged.

Stone-like dread settled in my midriff, depriving my lungs of air. Slowly but unrelentingly, perhaps even since that first night on Neostros, I'd allowed this thing to go beyond doing the right thing for my baby. I'd reached out, taken what I wanted for myself despite the lingering suspicion that my actions would come with emotional consequences.

And now, with this account of what had shaped him, he'd bared my own weaknesses to me.

I started to slide out of bed, froze when he reached for me.

'Where do you think you're going?'

'I'm going to shower. Alone.'

Tension rippled through his frame, his eyes narrowing to ferocious slits. 'We can't go back, Sadie. It's better you're aware of that. That you accept it.'

'You're right—we can't go back. But with your feet firmly stuck in clay you're not going to move forward either, are you?'

Again his silence spoke for him.

'Well, guess what? You may be stuck, but I'm not.'

'Explain that, if you please,' he rasped tightly.

'You're lauded for your sharp brain, Neo. Work it out for yourself.'

When I tugged myself free he released me. And that little act of setting me free, when deep down I wanted him to recapture me, drove the hard truth home.

His actions would always skew towards protecting himself. Towards shoring up his foundations with thick layers that guaranteed everyone else would remain on the outside.

Which was rather a sad and agonising state of affairs, because I very much wanted to be on the inside. So much so that when the composure that had held me together crumbled I let it, allowing the hot scald of tears to mingle with the warm shower jets. The hiss of the water muffling my quiet sobs.

But what I didn't know in those stolen, self-pitying moments was that my agony was only just starting.

Work it out for yourself.

I resented the unnerving panic those five words had triggered.

We were married. We'd made an agreement!

But listing her better qualities had opened my eyes to what I'd known for a while…that Sadie was truly different from Anneka. A wife a husband would be proud to possess.

But…what kind of husband? One who valued her for her brain but was too jaded to look into her heart? Perhaps because his own emotions fell short of fulfilling her needs?

Could I really stop her if she deemed me unfit to hold up my end of the bargain? If the doubts I harboured about my effectiveness as a father grew apparent?

I'd negotiated another deal in my favour by reclaiming her in my bed. One that had given me a yearning for a state I'd never considered before.

Contentment.

Theos mou, the woman I'd married was sensational. She tasted like the purest strain of innocent temptation, which would only get richer when she'd fully embraced her sensuality.

I should be pleased.

And yet, her words had only intensified that hollow sensation I'd woken up with the morning after the wedding. The feeling that had expanded ever since.

Not in a glaring, aggressive way, that could easily be identified and fixed, like a marketing flaw that required sharp intellect and an eye for detail. It had started as a ripple on the surface of a pond, effortless but determined. Unstoppable. Expanding against my will and desire to contain it.

And you need this triple-strength protection, why?

I ignored the wheedling voice, alarmed when I couldn't find any immediate comeback as to why I needed protection against Sadie.

Even more disturbing was the louder voice that questioned whether I was equipped to safeguard what I fought so valiantly for once my child was born. Cynicism and bitterness and being a shark in the boardroom were hardly the cornerstones of fulfilling parenthood...

Would the child I was so intent on claiming eventually resent me?

No. I would do better than the indifferent and bitter hand I'd been dealt. Just as I knew Sadie would too—if only to counteract what her own father had done to her.

The hollow sensation intensified—as if now I'd admitted one craving, several more demanded to be addressed.

Something was missing. Perhaps...within me.

Had I bargained with chips that were flawed? Pushed Sadie into marriage without stopping to examine whether I was the type of husband she wanted? A fit father for our child?

Money. Influence. Power. All things I could offer.

All things she'd rejected one by one without batting an eyelash.

Her question lingered long after she'd disappeared into the bathroom, after the hiss of the shower taunted me with the knowledge that tonight might have been the only pleasure I experienced with her.

And then, like that tree I'd known would be my doom in that moment of clarity right before the accident in Gstaad, when I heard the sharp scream from the bathroom, I suspected things would never be the same again.

When, an hour later, I stood by Sadie's bedside in another hospital, my gut twisting into knots as I stared down the barrel of a metaphorical gun, suspicion became certainty.

CHAPTER TEN

LOOKS MUCH WORSE than it is... Everything is fine, Mrs Xenakis. You just need to take it easy.

I repeated the doctor's words to myself as the limo drove us home from the hospital a few hours later.

The ravaging pain shredding my heart had merely been put on hold in light of the scare in the bathroom. It was still waiting in the wings.

And even if I'd fooled myself into thinking it was in any way diminished, the tight, drawn look on Neo's face testified that our conversation in the bedroom had merely been stayed.

That determined little muscle ticking in his jaw said it all. And it had only intensified with the doctor's reassurance that our baby...*our son*...was fine. Thriving, in fact. That the blood I'd spotted in the shower was concerning, but ultimately nothing to stress over as long as I took it easy.

Why that news had triggered Neo's ashen complexion and lockjawed determination only served to expand the stone lodged in my heart.

Had our conversation and the scare merely fast-tracked the inevitable?

We completed the journey home in tight, fraught silence.

When the driver shut off the ignition, Neo strode around to my side, offered his hand in silent command. I took it, stepped out, but when he leaned forward to lift me up I threw out a halting hand.

So soon after everything I'd experienced in his bed, and afterwards, having him so close would be detrimental to my emotional well-being.

The very thing I should've guarded against in the first place.

'I can walk on my own. The doctor said to take it easy. I think that safely includes walking from the car to the villa,' I said, unable to keep the tightness from my voice.

His lips tightened and he stayed close, unbearably surrounding me with his heat as I climbed the stairs to my suite, then perched on the wide, striped divan and watched the staff fuss with a tray of food and soft drinks Neo must have ordered before we left the hospital.

When the housekeeper lingered, Neo dragged an impatient hand through his hair. 'Leave us,' he snapped, authority stamped in his voice that saw his command immediately obeyed. He paced to the door, shut it, then returned, his footsteps heavy and resolute.

I knew what was coming. Unlike that postcard that had torn my world apart, this heartache-shaped wrecking ball I could see coming from a mile away.

'Don't do it. Whatever you're about to say, don't say it, Neo,' I blurted.

He froze beside the bed, then dragged his hands down his face. Even with two-day stubble and shadows haunting his turbulent eyes, he looked sublime.

The man I craved more than was wise for me.

The man I'd fallen in love with as he glared at me from across his office, tossing bullet-sharp questions about marketing and then reproducing a birthday cupcake at short notice in the most stunning setting on earth.

'Do you know what it felt like to see you there on that bathroom floor?' he demanded raggedly, his voice rough to the point of near incoherence.

My pain twisted, morphed, as a new strand was woven into its jagged fabric. 'Every pregnancy carries a risk. The doctor just said that.'

He gave a violent shake of his head. 'It wouldn't have happened if I'd kept my hands to myself! If I hadn't pushed for more!'

'You don't know that.'

'I do. I feel it, Sadie. Right here.' He pounded his closed fist on his midriff, his jaw tight with recrimination.

'You think you're something special?'

He inhaled sharply. 'What?'

'You think we're the only couple who indulge in sex during pregnancy? That you deserve some kind of special punishment for doing something that comes naturally?'

His gaze turned bleak. 'I can't speak for others, but I know what my actions came close to costing me. The way I've been with you, right from the start, herding you into decisions you were reluctant to take—'

'There you go again—seeking the crown of martyrdom. I have a voice, Neo. And, if you recall, you didn't get everything your own way. What makes you think I didn't want it too? That I wasn't in a hurry to fall into bed with you or marry you for my own reasons?'

He shook his head. 'Be that as it may, I set this ball rolling—'

'What? Gave me a roof over my head? A job opportunity that most would give their eye teeth for?'

'You said yourself—those are just things. What you could've lost—'

'But *we* didn't *lose* anything, Neo. Our baby is fine.'

Raw bitterness tightened his face. 'But for how long?'

My heart shredded. 'What?'

'I only negotiated for the short term, Sadie. As unfortunate as the circumstances are, it's a wake-up call. I need to accept that I don't have the tools for the long term.'

My fists bunched as anguish ripped through me. 'I don't buy that either, Neo. But I can't stop you from this path you obviously want to take, so just spare me the suspense and spit it out?'

His jaw worked for the longest time. Then he nodded. 'I'm leaving for Brazil tomorrow. Then travelling in Latin America for the next few weeks.'

'You're leaving.'

It wasn't a question. More absorbing the impact of the wrecking ball.

'Yes.'

'Because I'm *so different* from Anneka?' I taunted sarcastically.

'Yes!' The word was drawn from his soul. Almost as if he was terrified to admit it.

My jaw dropped. 'Neo…'

'You'll be taken care of—'

'I don't want a laundry list of things you're putting in place to ensure I don't lift a finger. I want to know why you promised me better terms and are now reneging.'

'This is for your own good.'

I couldn't help the laughter that spilled out. 'Is it, though? You know what you remind me of, Neo? My father. Always looking for something better! You changed the rules to suit you when you decided you wanted a wife, not just in name, but in your bed. Then you changed them again because you can't handle a little challenge. I've outlived my usefulness to you in one area. So you're shelving me until you get the other things that you want.'

His jaw clenched. 'No—what your father did, he did for himself. What I'm doing is for *you*.'

'Trust me to know my own mind! Believe me when I tell you what's in my heart.'

He lost another layer of colour, but his eyes blazed with quiet fury. 'I've made my decision. But know that besides my absence, nothing changes.'

'That's where you're wrong. *I've* changed. I know my own worth now. I know I want more than this. I won't be bargained with, or put on a shelf to suit you. So if you think your world is going to stay trouble-free because you've laid down the law, think again.'

'What's that supposed to mean?'

I shrugged dismissively, even though it was the last thing I felt like doing. 'I guess we'll find out. Goodbye, Neo.'

He stayed put, his gaze fixed in that way that said he was assessing me for weakness.

And because I wasn't sure how long I could stay put without cracking, I turned away from him, closed my eyes and simply pretended he wasn't there.

I heard the ominous snick of the door a minute later.

Then the tears fell—long and hard and shattering.

It was supposed to work.

The punishing schedule.

The soul-sucking jet lag.

The endless meetings.

Hell, even barking at executives was supposed to make me feel better. To fuel the conviction that I was doing the right thing.

She'd accused me of being like her father. Initially it had provided sustaining anger, and I'd burned in the righteousness of believing myself the exact opposite.

But, as relentless as time's march, the kernel of truth had expanded…like a weird, never-ending concentric circle that echoed its presence in my quiet moments.

First I'd used her to salve the bad news she'd delivered. Then, from the moment she'd announced she was carrying my child, I'd pinned her to me—my last hope of fatherhood and I was determined to have it, regardless of the fact that I lacked the effective tools to be a father. And during the process, I'd hammered out an agreement that bound her to me only until I had what I wanted.

And when I'd decided I wanted more, I'd worked on the problem until she'd fallen into my arms.

Only then had I realised the full impact of *more*. That, while I could give her every material and carnal pleasure she desired, *I* was the one who was too greedy. Too selfish. Because I'd never stopped to think that she would want more too. Or that I was equipped to deal with her demand.

Fate had given me the rudest wake-up call. And, as much

as every moment of breathing turned me inside out, Sadie deserved for me to stay away. She deserved the peace to bear her child without my greedy, demanding presence. Without the wants and needs and longings that clawed at me every hour of every day, sullying her beautiful existence.

So what if the thought of going another minute, another hour, without seeing her face killed me?

You'll simply have to suffer!

My intercom sounded, ripping another curse from my throat.

'I was quite explicit in my desire not to be disturbed.'

Because I deserved at least ten minutes of undiluted torment each hour, even as other minutes provided unending agony.

'Yes, sir, but I thought you should know—'

'Save your breath. Warning him won't do any good.'

I jackknifed up from my position against the dark wall in my office. Took a step forward and steadied myself against the dizzying effect of her.

Two long weeks during which only the security cameras installed at the villa had provided woefully brief glimpses of this goddess who carried my child. During which daily reports of her improved health and blooming pregnancy had sustained my raging hunger for her.

And now she was here.

A vision in white cotton that clung to her bust, her hips and, *Christos*, the magnificent protrusion of her belly. Her hair was twisted into an elaborate crown on top of her head, further proclaiming her celestial status.

It was all I could do not to fall at her feet in sublime worship of her, this woman who held a heart unworthy of her. This woman who'd exploded into my life and claimed a place in it I never wanted back.

God, would I ever get over the impact of Neo Xenakis?

I doubted it.

Or else every single vow I'd taken and every form of punishment I'd devised for myself in a wild bid to stop thinking about him, stop dreaming about him, would have worked.

Instead, each day had brought a bracing kind of hell. A craving that went against all common sense.

I'd driven Callie quite mad with my pathetic stoicism. While I wanted to blame her for appointing herself chief nursemaid, I'd eventually taken pity on her—succumbed when she'd called up the Xenakis jet and arranged an intercontinental flight, along with a doctor, much to the chagrin of her husband.

From Neo's poleaxed expression now, Axios had kept the secret.

The look was morphing, though, the shock wearing off.

His gaze rushed over me and he paled a little before his eyes narrowed. 'What are you doing here?' he bit out.

Despite its tension, the sound of his voice sent tingles down my spine.

I closed the gap between us by another few steps, my heart kicking against my ribs when his eyes dropped to my distended stomach.

'I work for this company, remember? Unless those privileges have been revoked too?'

'You know exactly what I mean. You should be resting. In Athens. Not…not…' He stopped. Frowned.

'Have you forgotten where you are?' I asked. 'You're in Costa Rica…negotiating to buy the country's second-largest airline.'

His frown intensified. 'Thanks for the reminder. My statement still stands.'

'Does it? Perhaps if you'd been at home I wouldn't have needed to cross continents to have a conversation with you.'

His mouth worked and he swallowed noisily. 'Sadie—'

'No.' I took another few steps, then stopped when his aftershave hit me like a brick of sensation. 'You don't get to speak. Not until I've said what's on my mind. And even then, the jury's out as to whether I want to hear what you have to say.'

'This is the third time you've stormed my office since we met.'

'It seems to be the only place where I can get through to you.'

A raw gleam lit his grey eyes before his expression tightened. 'That's not entirely true. But, *parakalo*, whatever you have to say to me, do it while sitting down?'

'And ruin this superb effect I'm having on you?'

His fist tightened with the blatant need to bodily compel me to the sofa. 'What do you want, Sadie?'

'For you to come home. Or give me a divorce.'

He lost another shade of colour. 'What?'

'Two choices. Take one or the other. But I'm not leaving here without an answer.'

'You dare to—'

'Oh, I do. Very much. Because you know what? I've decided there's nothing you can do to me. Sue the mother of your child? I think not. Toss me out of your company? I'll just find another job, because I'm good at what I do. But I don't think you want to lose my professional skills either. Really, all that's standing in our way is *you*.'

His breathing intensified and he looked, shockingly, as if he was on the brink of hyperventilating. 'You think any of this has been easy, Sadie?'

The raw note in his voice caught at that vulnerable spot I'd never been able to protect, ever since our first meeting.

I stepped into his space, uncaring for my own heart, and glared with everything I had. 'You walked away. And stayed away. You tell me.'

'It's been torture!' he yelled. 'I reach for you at night and you're not there. I turn to throw a question at you in the boardroom and find some lame executive staring back at me. You've ruined me for everything! For everyone! You were supposed to bewitch me for a little while. Until I satisfied the craving you triggered. Instead you're all I think about—every second of every day.'

My heart swan-dived right to my toes, then dared to beat its wings faster, to climb and climb and *hope*.

'Keep…keep talking.'

'That night, when you accused me of not moving forward, I couldn't answer your charge because somewhere along the line I'd gone from holding you to a higher standard to recognising that I couldn't meet those standards myself.'

'What are you *talking* about?'

'I've held myself back from giving my all emotionally all my life, Sadie. My grandfather did and look where he ended up. When Anneka told me she was pregnant I immediately offered her my name and my wealth, but nothing else. I knew I didn't love her and, aside from her betrayal and the lesson that delivered, I haven't spared her a thought since I threw her out of my life. But you…'

He stopped, swallowed.

'I spent weeks after our first meeting unable to get you out of my mind. When you turned up in my office in Athens I thought you felt the same. That you'd simply been better at plotting a reconnection.'

'Instead I dropped another bombshell in your life.'

He shook his head, jerked closer until we were breathing the same air. 'Instead you held out your hands and presented me with the most precious gift any man who wishes to be a father could ask for.'

'So you believe our baby is yours?'

'I believed you before we landed back in London that day. A woman who goes to great pains to admit her wrongdoing when she could have run a mile and passed the blame to others is a woman of integrity, in my book. Even when I gave you the chance to pass the blame on to your boss, you didn't.'

'If you knew all that, then why?'

He shrugged, that domineering alpha male rising to the

fore. 'Because I'm a negotiator, Sadie. I played my cards close to my chest to gain the upper hand. I wanted our child, but I wanted you even more. I could've dispatched you back to London, had a security team watch you and swoop in to negotiate terms of custody once the baby was born.'

'But you didn't because you *wanted* me? Past tense?'

'Oh, no, *glikia mou*. Not even close to past tense. It's very present. Very real. So much it scares me.'

Something electric lit up inside me. 'Is that why you're hiding here on the other side of the world? Because you're scared?'

'I'm here because I don't deserve you. As much as I want to negotiate my way back to you, I can't stand the possibility that you'll wake up one day and be disappointed.'

'My God. You've put us through all this suffering because for the first time in your life you're experiencing the very human emotion of self-doubt?'

He frowned. 'Sadie, this isn't a flimsy—'

'You think I wasn't scared to death when I realised I was in love with you? That I haven't wanted to tear my hair out to see if it would bring me a moment's relief from the constant ache of loving you and not knowing whether you love me back?'

His gorgeous lips dropped open in shock. '*Christos*, Sadie. I—'

'I'm a pregnant woman nearing her third trimester, Neo. The next words out of your mouth had better be words I want to hear.'

His arms darted out, caught me to him, as if he was afraid I'd flee when in fact my legs were threatening to stop supporting me.

'Let's get one thing clear. You're never to touch a hair on your head with an aim of tearing it out. Ever. But, more importantly, Sadie…if this madness inside me that yearns only for you, if this heart that beats true only when you're near, means this is love, then I love you. And if it's not, if

I get it wrong somewhere along the way, I know I'll have you there to steer me true. For a chance to be at your side through this life I will leave the negotiations to you, follow your lead. Show me how to love, Sadie, and I will be your apt pupil for the rest of our lives.'

The depth of his promise took the last ounce of strength from my legs. He caught me up, as I knew he would, strode over to the sofa and sank into it.

'Okay, if that's what it takes. Here's your first lesson. You never leave me behind again.'

'I vow it,' he replied, with feeling.

I rearranged myself in his lap, framed his face between my hands. 'You bring any doubts you have to me. We fix and grow and love together. But most of all, Neo, you just open your heart, let me love you and our baby. We'll be the best versions of ourselves we can be for our family and trust the rest to take care of itself. Will you do that?'

A suspicious sheen glistened in his eyes. But he didn't look away, didn't blink it back. He just stared into my eyes and nodded. 'You have yourself a deal, *amorfo mou*.'

'Good. Now, please kiss me. Then please take me home.'

EPILOGUE

'It's time, Neo.'

Heels clicked closer as my wife entered our bedroom and crossed over to where I stood at the window.

'Our guests are wondering if the two of you are planning to join the festivities—especially since you're holding the guest of honour hostage,' she teased.

I was torn between staring at the vision Sadie created in her white Grecian-style dress and the precious bundle I held in my arms.

With her flaming hair piled on top of her head in an elaborate knot, and the skin I'd explored thoroughly just a few hours ago glowing, Sadie won the attention-grabbing stakes. But only by a fraction.

My son—*thee mou*, would I ever stop being awed by the miracle of him?—three months old and in good health, came a very close second.

'Five more minutes?' I cradled his warmth closer, unwilling to share him just yet.

Sadie shook her head, smiling widely as she approached, her swaying hips wreaking havoc with my breathing.

'You said that twenty minutes ago. I know you don't care what anyone else thinks, but I have a good brownie point system going with your family. I don't want to ruin it.'

'Impossible. Every person out there loves you—they wouldn't been invited to Helios's christening otherwise.'

Her beautiful eyes widened. 'You didn't have Wendell vet them, did you?'

I shrugged. 'Maybe...'

She laughed, and the sound burrowed deep, stirring emotions I hadn't imagined I could experience just a handful of months ago.

But then, so many things had changed since that day in Costa Rica. Sadie had introduced me to the phenomenon of unconditional love, her giving heart and fearless love challenging mine to reciprocate. And the result continued to astound me daily. Even the atmosphere of cool indifference with my parents had began to thaw under Sadie's expert guidance.

She insisted the birth of our miracle son was the reason. I disagreed.

'Well, just to let you know, our mothers are *this* close to staging a break-in to claim their grandson,' she said with a stunning smile. 'I estimate you have about a minute.'

'Then I'll make the most of it. Come to me, *agape mou*,' I murmured, greedy for more of this soul-stirring feeling.

'I love it when you call me that,' she said when she reached me, one hand sliding around my waist, her other caressing Helios's black-maned head. 'He's so beautiful— our little miracle.'

The overwhelming love and wonder I felt was echoed in her voice.

'He's as beautiful as his exceptional mama, but *moro mou*, you're our miracle, Sadie. Without you, our lives wouldn't be this full, mine changed for ever for the better,' I said.

Beautiful green eyes blinked back tears, and when she went on tiptoe to kiss me I met her halfway, revelling in the supreme contentment that this gorgeous creature was mine. That she had given me a son despite my doctors still scratching their heads over tests that showed such a feat was impossible.

Their verdict was that Helios might be the only child Sadie and I would have. But who were they to make pronouncements? I already had the miracle of love and fatherhood. Nothing was impossible.

When we broke the kiss Sadie sighed, resting her head

on my shoulder. 'Okay, Neo. Five more minutes. But I get to stay too.'

As if I would let her go.

'*Agapita*, you should know by now that I wouldn't have it any other way.'

* * * * *

REDEMPTION OF THE UNTAMED ITALIAN

CLARE CONNELLY

To you, a reader of romance, a lover of love.
This book—and every book I write—
is because of you.

PROLOGUE

HE WASN'T SURE why, but Cesare paused outside the restaurant a moment, looking through the deep-glass windows at the elegant scene inside. The room was warmly lit, the crowd painfully fashionable.

He stood on the outside looking in and couldn't fail to appreciate the irony. As a child, he'd often been like this: standing outside rooms of wealth and privilege, kept physically distinct, separate from and unwanted by that world. Even as a teenager with a scholarship placement at the best school in England he'd felt outside the norm. He'd been different and everyone had known it. Unlike the sons of ancient, wealthy families who'd formed the student ranks, he'd been only the son of a poor single mother, a woman who'd served as a nanny to that kind of family.

Now, though, as he looked into the restaurant, he knew places like this existed for the likes of him. He would walk in and people would part as a wave, making way for him, admiring him, wanting his attention. He knew because it was what always happened these days.

He scanned the trendy 'it' spot until his eyes landed on his table. He recognised Laurence immediately, the man who was so desperate for Cesare to invest in his hedge fund he was practically at begging point. A dark smile tinted Cesare's lips. When he'd been a young boy thrown into the world of the British aristocracy, and seen as lesser than it in every way, he'd sworn he would make men of this ilk pay. He'd sworn he would be better, bigger, more success-ful always. He swore he would make his fortune and he swore he would make them pay.

His eyes slid unconsciously to Laurence's companion. Not his companion, his cousin, Cesare remembered, his smile turning mocking now. It was an obvious ploy to win Cesare's favour, or perhaps distract him from matters of business. His reputation as a womaniser was well-estab-lished and he was unapologetic for that. He liked women, different women and often. If Laurence thought having her at this dinner meeting would make an ounce of difference to Cesare's investment plans, he didn't understand the kind of fortitude and intention Cesare brought to his business life.

Jemima Woodcroft was every bit as beautiful in the flesh as all the billboards would have you believe, though. The supermodel leaned across to her cousin, speaking close to his ear, and Laurence nodded, laughing. She in turn smiled, and her eyes flashed with something that sparked a light of curiosity inside Cesare.

Something else, too. Desire.

She was just the kind of woman Cesare usually chose to take to bed: beautiful, sophisticated and, if the media re-ports were to be believed, as happy to employ a revolving door with her bed as he was with his. Her hand pulled her hair over one shoulder, and manicured fingers toyed with its length distractedly, so two vivid images leaped into his mind unbidden: her nails running down his body, pale fin-gers against tanned flesh and her hair forming a curtain around her face as she straddled him, looking down at him, her face tortured by passion.

Suddenly, the night was looking up.

He pushed into the restaurant with a sense of anticipation. Like the steady beating of a drum, it filled his chest. The world was at Cesare's feet—he'd worked hard to make sure of that—and he doubted he'd ever grow tired of reaping the rewards.

CHAPTER ONE

'I STILL FIND it hard to see what's in it for me.'

Cesare Durante spoke with a voice that was naturally husky and deep, his accent ever so slightly Italian but also cultured and British. Jemima observed him from beneath shuttered lashes, wishing he hadn't so completely lived up to her expectations. Everything she'd read about the self-made billionaire had told her what he'd be like: intelligent but charming, with the kind of looks that would make almost anyone weak at the knees.

But there was an arrogance about him too, an arrogance that communicated itself with every curve of his lips, every flash of his sharp, perceptive eyes.

When he'd introduced himself even his name had dispelled any idea that there might be a lingering softness buried in his broadly muscled chest. 'Cesare,' he'd said, almost as a command, the pronunciation faithful to the Italian, so it sounded like 'Che-zar-eh'. From his lips it emerged as a rumble, a deep, rolling wave that crashed over Jemima and momentarily robbed her of breath.

'The fund's versatility is the main selling point,' Laurence interjected with a confidence she knew he didn't feel.

If my investors find out I've tanked a third of the fund's value, I'm screwed, Jem. That's like a hundred million quid.

I need to get Durante on side—it's the only way I can keep things afloat. Please help. Please.'

Even as a child she'd have done anything Laurence asked of her, but after her brother's death Laurence and Jemima had been bonded in that unique way grief conspired to bring about. Laurence was the only person who could understand the void in her life and, at the same time, he was the only person who could go halfway to filling it. They were family, they were friends, they were two souls who'd known intense loss and guilt, and she'd do anything he asked of her.

Just as he'd do anything for her. She knew that was why he'd made such irresponsible, reckless investments: to save Almer Hall. He knew the extent of debt her parents were in and that even her income wasn't equal to it. He was working himself into the ground, taking lavish risks, because he knew what the Hall meant to them and she loved him to bits for that.

'Most funds have a range of assets.' Cesare Durante's expression showed displeasure. 'I didn't fly in from Rome for a middling sales pitch. Tell me what else you've got.'

She felt Laurence's tension and her own stomach swirled. She hated seeing him like this, and she understood his anxiety. She knew what this meant to him. More importantly, she knew what would happen if Cesare Durante didn't invest in Laurence's hedge fund—financial ruin, certainly, and likely criminal charges for the reckless way he'd invested other people's money without advising them of his activities. He'd be ruined, absolutely, and by extension so would her parents, because Laurence would no longer be in a position to offer any financial help to them. They'd already lost so much and couldn't cope with another hurdle.

Reaching for her champagne, she held it just a few inches from her lips, her large green eyes regarding Cesare thoughtfully. Her eyes were one of Jemima's most recognisable features. The first international campaign she'd landed had been for a cosmetic giant and promoting mascara had launched her career globally. She trained the full force of those eyes on the Italian now, leaning forward slightly.

'Did you just fly in today?' She kept her tone light intentionally.

Laurence had been clear: *'With you there, it'll feel social. Fun. Keep the heat off me, distract him from how much cash I'm asking him to kick in.'*

Keeping the heat off with Cesare Durante at the table was apparently a physical impossibility. As he slowly turned to face her, her pulse kicked up a gear and her blood begin to boil in her veins. It took all her discipline to maintain a muted expression on her face.

'This evening.' His gaze shifted over her face in that same appraising way, as though he was studying her piece by piece.

It was impossible to be one of the world's most sought-after models without knowing yourself to be beautiful. Jemima accepted that there was something in the physical construction of her face and body that was widely regarded to be attractive, but she was very pragmatic about it. She knew that she couldn't take credit for any of these things—looks and beauty were almost entirely a question of chance, and as such the fact she was objectively beautiful gave her very little satisfaction. It was far easier to be proud of goals you worked hard to achieve rather than windfalls you were handed. She generally didn't think about her looks much at all, except in relation to her work, to trends she might need to emulate or embrace.

But as Cesare swept his thickly lashed eyes over her face and his wide lips—set in a perfectly square jaw—quirked a little, she felt an unwelcome rush of warmth and feminine satisfaction fill her chest. His gaze travelled to her lips, lingering there for so long they began to tingle, and a flash of something with which she had very little personal experience but still recognised burst through her—desire, unmistakable, overtook her body, warming her insides, making her breath burn in her lungs.

'And you?' He matched her body language, leaning forward a little so she was acutely conscious of his frame. There wasn't an ounce of spare flesh on him and yet somehow he seemed *huge*, as if he took up more than his allotment of physical space in the fashionable restaurant. He had to be six and a half feet, but it wasn't his size alone that was formidable. It was though he'd been cast from stone, or sculpted from bronzed marble. His body was broad, his shoulders squared and strong, his waist slim where his shirt met the leather belt, his legs long and confident. He'd discarded his jacket some time after their main course plates had been cleared and the cotton shirt he wore underneath, though undoubtedly the very best quality, and likely hand-stitched specifically for his body, strained just a little at the tops of his arms, so she could see that his biceps were pronounced.

But it was his face that had fascinated her all evening. It too had the appearance of having been deliberately sculpted, but by a hand of exceptional talent. It was a symmetrical face, with an aquiline nose, a firm, chiselled jaw, thick dark lashes above intensely watchful eyes and lips that were wide and deliberate. And when he smiled—which he hadn't done much—two deep dimples scored his cheeks. His hair was thick and dark, cut close to his face, in contrast to a stubbled chin that she imagined would feel quite coarse beneath her fingertips.

Jemima was used to physical beauty. It didn't generally

impress her. She spent much of her time surrounded by models and, if anything, she'd begun to crave interesting, unusual features: skin that was marked with lines or tattoos, faces that told stories and invited questions.

He was purely beautiful, and yet she was fascinated by him, intrigued by him. She sensed something within him that made her want to ask questions, that inflamed her curiosity.

'Jemima lives around the corner.' Laurence spoke for her at the same time he lifted a hand to call a waiter's attention. Neither Cesare nor Jemima looked away. It was as though they were the only people in the room.

'I have a flat,' she supplied after a beat.

One single brow lifted, changing his face altogether, so now she felt scepticism emanating from him. 'You grew up in London?'

'No.' She shook her head. 'My family has an estate outside of Yorkshire. Almer Hall.' She and Laurence shared a brief look at the mention of the family property that meant so much to them, the family property that would be lost if the hedge fund went down the drain.

Cynicism briefly converted to insolent mockery and then his expression was blank of anything except banal, idle curiosity.

'You're aristocracy.' It wasn't a question and yet she felt compelled to answer.

She lifted her shoulders. 'There's a title there somewhere. We don't use it.'

'Why not?'

'It feels a bit outdated.' She sipped her champagne now, relishing the popping of bubbles as they raced down her throat. His watchful gaze was warming her up, so she was glad for the cooling effect of the drink.

'Scotch, Cesare?' Laurence offered. Cesare finally took

his attention from her and Jemima expelled all her breath in a long, quiet whoosh. She blinked, as though waking from a dream, and leaned back in her seat a little.

What would it be like to have those steel-grey eyes turned on her with the full force of his attention? No, she'd had his attention... With the full force of his desire? What would it be like to lean forward and brush her fingertips over his arm, to flirt with him a little, to smile and murmur an invitation in his ear?

Not for the first time, she felt the burden of her virginity with a burning sense of impatience. If she'd had some experience she'd be sorely tempted to act on those impulses. After all, the media had already hanged her for the crime of being a harlot—she might as well enjoy some of the spoils. Yes, if she'd had even a hint of experience she may well have acted on her impulse despite what that might mean for Laurence, despite the fact it could complicate matters for him.

Cesare's voice was deep as he said the name of a whisky she recognised only because it was one that a photographer friend favoured—it was outrageously overpriced. Laurence ordered the same but, before the waiter could be dispatched, Cesare turned back to Jemima; her pulse rushed.

'You are happy with your champagne?'

Her heart shifted in her chest. Despite all the reasons to maintain her distance, desire pushed her forward a little, just a fraction, as though her body was on autopilot, seeking his.

It was madness. As a teen model, she'd come across more than her fair share of designers, photographers, magazine editors and public relations guys, all of whom had thought she'd do whatever it took to advance her career, so by her fifteenth birthday she'd become adept at saying no without causing offence. In fact, she was very good at saying no without even having people realise that she was rejecting them. Sex, drugs, alcohol, orgies. Jemima had a knack for turning people down and still having them think well of her.

But there was danger in Cesare—a darkness that called to her, that made her certain he could be her weakness, and in that moment she wished more than anything that she was the kind of woman the world thought her to be. She wished she was sophisticated and experienced and that she knew exactly what to say to get a man like Cesare to have sex with her.

The thought alone had her standing abruptly, scraping her chair back so both sets of eyes lifted to her.

'You okay?' Laurence queried.

'Perfectly fine.' She pasted a smile to her face as she became aware more people were looking in her direction. Cursing her recognisability, and the fact Laurence had chosen this celebrity hotspot in an attempt to impress his would-be investor, she nodded jerkily. 'I'll be right back.'

She forced herself to walk sedately towards the facilities. Once inside, she lingered with her back against the cold, marble wall and her eyes swept shut.

She'd likely never see Cesare Durante again after this night. She was there for one reason and one reason only: to help Laurence secure him as an investor.

She had to help her cousin—there was too much at stake to risk ruining the evening because she couldn't stop looking at Cesare and imagining what those broad, capable hands would feel like running over her body... Heat flushed her cheeks because she knew they'd feel good. Better than good. But that was beside the point—nothing was going to happen between them. She needed to get a grip.

Sucking in a deep breath, she quickly checked her appearance in the mirror, pausing just long enough to reapply her soft coral lipstick and finger-comb her generous, side-sweeping fringe so it artfully covered one eye. She sucked in a deep, fortifying breath and pulled the door inward, stepping into the wallpapered, dimly lit corridor that led to the amenities. At one end, there was a sideboard with a huge bunch of lilies sitting on top of it. A nostalgic smile briefly curved her lips.

As a child, Almer Hall had always had flowers. Huge arrangements, just like this, grand and fragrant. She paused in front of the vase, her fingertips lifting on autopilot to gently stroke the petals—like silk, dewy and tender. She inhaled the scent and swept her eyes shut, remembering the feeling of visiting her grandparents as a child, running down the marbled hallways. In summer, the fragrance had been almost overwhelming.

There were no flowers now. More than two-thirds of the house was shut down, doors closed, furniture—what remained of it—covered in sheets. The family quarters, whilst cheery, were modest and beginning to look tatty in parts. What she wouldn't do to see the house as it used to be, tables in each room groaning under the weight of arrangements such as this.

Laurence *had* to pull this off. It was the only way they'd be able to save Almer Hall, to stave off the necessity of its sale. She couldn't see it pass into other hands. It would be the final straw for her parents, who had already lost so much.

She pinged her eyes open with a swirling sense of discontent, but when her eyes naturally landed in the mirror above the flowers her gaze connected sharply with a pair of eyes that had been fascinating her all evening, and they were watching her with undisguised speculation. Her breath began to clog in her throat, making her feel light-headed.

'Did you get lost?' A sardonic lift of one brow was accompanied by a smile that set off a sudden round of fireworks in her belly. The desire she'd been trying so hard to fight lurched through her anew.

She shook her head, her throat parched at this man's sudden appearance. Even more so when his eyes lowered, carrying out a visual inspection of her body in the pale-grey silk slip she wore.

Her heart in her throat, she turned to face him, the action bringing them toe to toe.

'You're shorter than I would have thought,' he murmured so that it was Jemima's turn to lift her brows in silent enquiry. 'Most of the models I know are closer to my height.'

'And I suppose you know lots of models?' The words emerged husky and soft, and for some reason she didn't step back from him, even when it would have made sense to put a little distance between them.

'A few,' he confirmed in a way that made her certain he was intentionally under-stating the facts. But then his expression sobered and he was looking at her more intently, concentrating on her features as though committing them to memory. 'You are tiny. Like a little bird.'

Her lop-sided smile was spontaneous. 'I don't think anyone's ever called me that before.'

He continued to stare at her and her smile dropped. She was conscious of everything: the feeling of her breath in her body, the sound of his, the warmth from his chest, the parting of his lips.

'Anyway.' She shifted her eyes towards the door with effort. 'Laurence will be wondering what's keeping me.'

Cesare's expression shifted immediately. 'On the contrary, I think it is fair to say his entire focus is on whether or not I'm going to save his ass from financial ruin.'

At that, Jemima's gaze skittered back to Cesare. No one knew about Laurence's situation. He'd taken great care to hide the parlous state of the fund, particularly given the risky investments he'd been making with other people's capital. She tried not to think about the fact that he'd drawn her into this mess, nor to wonder whether that made her some kind of accessory. No one was supposed to know. Surely this man, this fascinating, handsome hunk of an Italian tycoon, couldn't really have any idea as to the full extent of Laurence's situation?

'You're surprised?' He correctly interpreted the look flitting across her expressive face. Her skin paled, her lips parted, and she stayed resolutely silent—for lack of any certainty about just what to say.

His body shifted, moving ever so slightly closer to hers—by only a matter of degrees, but it was enough. Enough for everything about him to become bigger, stronger and more overpowering and for all the temptations she'd been fighting off to threaten to consume her. 'Do I strike you as a man who would come to a meeting like this—or to any meeting, for that matter—unprepared?'

'No.' The answer was intuitive.

Approval warmed his face and he nodded, just once, not moving his eyes from her face. 'So you're, what—bait?'

She frowned, not understanding.

'Did Laurence think that having you at the table would distract me sufficiently to make me rush into this investment? That I'd put aside common sense and offer to buy into his hedge fund to the tune of half a billion pounds just because the most beautiful woman I've ever seen happened to be fluttering her lashes at me all evening?'

It wasn't really a compliment, yet butterflies beat their wings against the sides of her belly. There was an insult in there, or at the very least the hint of condemnation. A need to defend her cousin stiffened her spine. 'On the contrary,

Laurence simply wanted it to feel like a pleasant evening rather than purely business.'

Cesare's wolf-like smile showed how little he believed that statement. 'This is business.' He growled the words out. 'And I never let anything affect my judgement where business is concerned.' He moved closer, so now his arm brushed against hers, and she had to suck in a sharp breath of air—which was a mistake, because it tasted of him, all hyper-masculine and citrusy.

'Although, you have made that hard to remember at times.'

Another compliment buried in a tone that was somehow derisive. She stared up at him, the pale overhead light catching her hair so it shone like threads of precious gold. 'Have I?'

His expression was droll. 'As I'm sure you're aware.' He lifted a hand, running a finger across her cheek, and she trembled in response. 'It was an excellent gambit.' His thumb padded across her lower lip and desire sparked like flames against her sides. 'I can see why he would think you might win me over.'

'That wasn't his intention.' Her voice came out stiff and cultured, her tone plummy enough to please even her mother.

Cesare's laugh spread through her veins like warmed caramel. 'Yes, it was. Perhaps he didn't inform you of that, but I have no doubt your cousin believed that serving you up on a silver platter would make this deal go through more smoothly.'

'I'm not being served up, to you or anyone,' she demurred without moving backwards, even when she knew she had to. 'I often accompany Laurence on business meetings.' It wasn't particularly convincing.

'Really?' He lowered his hand to her shoulder, his eyes

chasing the gesture, fixating on the exposed flesh there, pale cream with a pearl-like translucence.

'You find that hard to believe?'

'Yes.'

'Why?'

'Because it's hardly your scene, is it?'

'My scene?' Her heart threw an extra beat into its rhythm.

'International supermodel attends dinner meeting regarding finance fund?'

His mockery made her pulse skitter. 'You think the two are mutually exclusive, Mr Durante?'

'Call me Cesare.'

She found she couldn't resist. 'Cesare.' His name in her mouth was erotic. She pronounced it as he had, 'Che-zar-eh', then swallowed, trying to quell the buzzing that was spreading through her. 'It doesn't matter what I call you. It doesn't change the fact that your opinion is pretty offensive.'

'Name three of the companies your cousin has stakes in.'

She blinked.

'Any three. There are twenty-seven in the hedge fund.'

Heat bloomed in her cheeks. 'I'm not interested in the details.'

'No, you're not. And you're not here to talk business.'

'You honestly think I'm here as some kind of inducement to you?'

He shrugged. 'I cannot fathom any other reason for your presence.'

She glared at him, shaking her head. 'Yeah, well, you're wrong...'

'I doubt that.' His eyes bore into hers and then swept her face. 'You know, I've seen your photo dozens of times. You're everywhere—on buses, billboards, television. You are beautiful always, but in person you are much more so.' He frowned, as though he hadn't intended this to be a compliment. 'If Laurence thought I would lose my mind and simply agree to sign on the bottom line, then he played an excellent bargaining chip.' He dropped his head lower so his lips were only inches from hers. 'I suspect one night with you would be worth half a billion pounds.'

Desire was like a tidal wave crashing over her.

'You don't know anything about me,' she murmured, but didn't move away.

His lips twisted cynically. 'I know what the rumours say. I know that you and Clive Angmore had an affair that almost ended his marriage, despite the fact he was in his sixties and you were barely legal.'

Her heart strangled at that familiar accusation. It was surprising how much it hurt coming from Cesare. After all, she'd lived alongside Clive's lies for a long time—she'd thought she'd developed a thicker skin than this. But hearing Cesare shame her for the supposed affair cut her to the quick.

'And you blame me for that?'

'No.' His eyes were thoughtful. 'As I said, you were just a teenager.'

If she'd been surprised by the hurt his accusation had caused then his next statement was a balm she also hadn't expected. 'Surely you're too intelligent to believe everything you read in the paper?'

'Not everything,' he murmured, the words drugging her with their sensual tone. 'But I've also observed that the old adage "where there's smoke, there's fire" is often true.'

She compressed her lips. It bothered her so much that he had clearly bought into all the rumours, was so believing of the image that the press had created of her 'out of control' lifestyle.

'You're wrong, Mr Durante.' She deliberately reverted to the use of his formal name. 'I'm here to support my cousin, and nothing more.' Her voice wobbled a little, but she was pleased with the coldness of her tone. And now, finally, she side-stepped him, gratefully breathing in Durante-free air.

No, not gratefully. Wistfully. She would have been grateful if she'd stayed exactly where she was, because in a matter of seconds she suspected he'd have been kissing her.

Her mind splintered apart at the very idea and a rush of warmth pooled low in her abdomen.

'Stop.' She couldn't say why she obeyed, but her legs remained perfectly still, unmoving, her face tilted towards his. He was watching her carefully, as though he could peel away her layers and see something deep inside.

'I came here tonight with a sense of amusement. I am not a man to be baited by a beautiful woman. And yet...' He lifted his hand to her cheek once more, his eyes roaming her face thoughtfully.

'And yet?' Her voice was croaky.

'I'd be lying if I said I wasn't tempted.' He didn't move but she felt as though his body was touching her, pressing into her, and her stomach twisted into a billion knots.

'I'm not bait,' she insisted. If only he knew that her experience with the opposite sex was completely non-existent.

He brushed aside her words with a flash of his eyes. 'I want you to come home with me tonight.' Before she could say anything in response, he lifted a finger and pressed it to her lips. 'It will have no bearing on my decision with the hedge fund. Business is business.'

He paused, his eyes devouring her inch by inch. 'Pleasure is pleasure.'

His finger against her lips moved to outline her Cupid's bow. 'Come home with me because you feel what I feel. Come home with me because you're as fascinated by this as I am.' He leaned closer so his warm breath buzzed her temple. 'Come home with me because you want me to make love to you all night long, until your body is exhausted and your voice hoarse from crying my name over and over again.'

She sucked in a sharp breath. Words were beyond her.

'Come home with me, Jemima.'

Her knees were weak, her pulse insistent. She swallowed but her throat felt thick; everything was out of whack.

She couldn't seriously be considering this. Cesare Durante was a renowned bachelor, a self-made billionaire who had no time for relationships that lasted more than a few days. She hadn't needed to run his name through an Internet search to know that—it was an established fact. He wasn't offering anything except one night—sex.

He obviously bought into the articles in the press, the ones that made it look as if she spent her life getting hammered at parties and sleeping with any guy that moved. She'd lost track of how many fictional relationships she'd been in, secret marriages she'd walked out of, how many times she'd been pregnant, dumped and broken-hearted. How many times in rehab, fighting with other models, all of it preposterous and laughable—except she didn't often laugh about it. She simply didn't read the stories any more.

Her manager had hired an exceptional public relations guru who only contacted Jemima when a story wouldn't die, something Jemima was required to respond to, but otherwise Jemima let the papers run their fictional pieces while she got on with her real life. And that was about as far removed from the public's perception as it was possible to get. She spent more time with her hands wrangling tulip bulbs than they did any man.

He had the wrong idea about her. He'd be disappointed

if he learned she had precisely zero experience in bed. And she didn't want him to be disappointed in her.

'I can't.' Her reluctance wasn't faked.

'You don't want to?' he murmured, and now his lips brushed hers so her knees felt as though they were going to collapse beneath her. A soft moan escaped without her intention.

But she did. She wanted to go home with him in a way that should have served as a warning. Her hand lifted of its own accord to wrap around his neck, drawing his head lower, her eyes hitched to his. 'I don't even know you,' she pointed out, but the words were so quiet she might as well not have spoken.

'You know it would be good,' he replied simply, and she nodded, because she did. But he had no idea—he couldn't know what he was getting.

This was crazy. It was utterly mad, yet she felt something inside her tip, and all she could think of was how badly she wanted to do this.

It wasn't as though she'd planned to remain a virgin. Saying no had become a habit, one she was glad of. She'd seen more than her fair share of heartbreak and hurt amongst the models she worked with, models who slept with photographers only to discover the photographer was married, or sleeping with half a dozen other models.

But Cesare was different. He wasn't in the fashion industry at all; they'd never have to see each other again. She could sleep with him, lose her virginity, discover a little bit about the whole sex thing and then get on with her life. Truth be told, she was reaching a point where she felt that her virginity required an explanation and it would be nice not to think about that. Yes, it was a burden, and she'd be glad to be rid of it. And at least with Cesare she could be assured of two things: it would be meaningless and it would be good...

There were a thousand reasons not to do this, but none of them as drugging as the reasons to say yes. Even before she'd come face to face with him, she'd been fascinated by the legend of Cesare Durante, curious about the man who, as the stories said, had gone from being the dirt-poor son of an Italian nanny to one of the richest men in the world. He had the Midas touch, and his confidence was its own source of power and attractiveness. But, now that she'd met him, there was so much more to Cesare, so much more that had caught her completely in his thrall, so she found herself nodding slowly, almost without her knowledge.

'It has nothing do with Laurence.'

His smile was lightly mocking and, damn it, even that she found sexier than she should have. 'I would hope not.' He leaned a little closer. 'I can assure you, he will be the furthest thing from your mind when I make you mine.'

A frown formed on her features, disbelief and uncertainty being swallowed up by a fierce rush of desire. *Make you mine.* The words held such a promise of possession and intent that she was already craving him, craving this. Tonight would be the night she lost her virginity and, all of a sudden, she could barely wait.

'I will make you sing, little bird.' He murmured the words against her ear, so goose bumps spread across her body. 'Come home with me.'

Common sense was completely submerged by desire, so she nodded, her hooded eyes finding his a second before his lips crushed hers. 'Yes,' she agreed into his mouth, though the word was barely necessary. Her hands wrapped around his neck, her body arching to press to his, her agreement evident in every cell of her body. Still, she said it again, partly to convince herself this made sense and also to reassure herself this was really happening. 'Yes, Cesare. Yes.'

He lifted his head to stare down into her eyes. 'Words I am going to make you scream soon.' The grey of his eyes flashed with a silent promise. Her nipples tightened against the soft fabric of her dress and, when he stepped back, his attention dropped to the tell-tale sign of arousal so that heat flashed in her face. 'You are going to be begging me to take you, and I am going to enjoy that.'

CHAPTER TWO

CESARE EYED THE beautiful model across the table, a tightness in his body that came from the pleasurable spread of anticipation—the certainty that enjoyment was near at hand.

He threw back a measure of the scotch, relishing the depth of its flavour, the aged quality that was full of spice. Cesare liked a good scotch—the finest. There were many things he could do without, many luxuries he could afford but rarely indulged in, because he'd spent much of his life doing without, sacrificing.

But now he liked nice things, he liked them when he wanted them. Scotch. A great meal with a world-class view. Being able to get in his jet and fly wherever he wanted on a whim. And women. He liked women who were beautiful, interesting, experienced and sophisticated. He liked sex without strings, without complications, sex that could entertain him and satisfy him without requiring him to think about a woman once he'd left her bed.

Jemima Woodcroft was undoubtedly all these things and he relished the chance to get to know her body, to pleasure her and delight in her before relegating her to the back of his mind, as he always did with women with whom he spent a night.

His mind ran at its usual frenetic pace as he analysed

the deal Laurence was desperately laying before him, but he was conscious of every single movement Jemima made, every shift of her body, flutter of her eyelids, purse of her lips.

Despite the disastrous state of Laurence's hedge fund, Cesare could see the value in the offering. There was a lot of chaff, but a few of the investments packaged in with the group were substantial. One in particular stood on the brink of making major market inroads, and there was value in that, value in investing at ground level. It was clear that Laurence didn't understand what cards he held, or he would be shopping around instead of targeting one investor. If Cesare bailed, Laurence would be sunk.

Good. Nothing suited Cesare better than a desperate negotiator. Desperation made people stupid.

Cesare attributed his success in business to three factors. First, he left nothing to chance. He researched his business options aggressively, arming himself with every bit of information he could. Second, he was hungry in a way no amount of wealth could ever remove. Poverty as a child— so spectacularly in contrast to the extreme wealth that had surrounded him at the grand country houses in which his mother had worked—had left Cesare with a feeling that a blazing fire was always right at his heels, chasing him through life in a way that would never ease. True, it had turned him into a workaholic, but he didn't see any problem with that. Finally, he obeyed his instincts as though his life depended on them.

His instincts told him Jemima was going to be a fantastic lover; he was relishing the prospect of taking her to his bed, despite the fact he usually gave aristocrats a wide enough berth that he could land on the moon.

Still, there was something about her, and it had nothing to do with her cousin's predicament.

Cesare's instincts also told him Laurence was beyond desperate. He could smell the panic in the other man, feel it in his every frantic gesture, in the frequent glances he was shooting Jemima's way, as though half-expecting her to intervene, to say something to help him.

Jemima, though, was silent. Cesare couldn't have said how she was feeling, or if she was regretting her earlier agreement. She was one of the few people he'd met in his life that he found difficult to read. Her body language was relaxed enough. She was leaning back in her chair, champagne glass resting loosely between her fingertips—the same glass she'd been sitting on all evening—her eyes following Laurence and then Cesare without making any attempt to join in their conversations.

Knowing what was coming next, he was more than ready to put an end to this portion of the night. 'Fine.' He nodded, regarding Laurence carefully. 'You have my interest.'

'Your interest?'

Cesare had to bite back a smile when he saw how crestfallen the British man was. The only reason he didn't give vent to his amusement was that Jemima was watching him. He could feel her gaze on his face, and was well aware that she wouldn't take kindly to him ridiculing Laurence's expectations. Besides, despite a lifelong hatred for men like Laurence—spoiled, entitled British brats—there was something in Laurence that Cesare could almost have grudgingly come to like.

'You don't expect me to sign away five hundred million pounds on the spot, do you?'

'I just think it's a really rare opportunity,' Laurence muttered, dragging a hand through his hair. 'And you're getting first option.'

Cesare leaned forward. 'Let's not play with one another. I'm getting the only option.'

Laurence's face glowed pink. 'No, I happen to have a couple of very cashed-up investors on the hook.'

Now Jemima's head swivelled towards Laurence and for the first time in at least thirty minutes she slipped up. Cesare saw the consternation that crossed her features and he understood it. Underneath the table, Cesare lightly ran his fingers over her exposed knee, so now her face jerked back to his, her lips parted in that sensual way she had. His cock strained against his trousers. Anticipation drummed against the fabric of his soul.

'Sure you do.' Cesare's grin was tight. 'Then let me know what they bid and, if I decide I'm still interested, I'll better it.'

Backed into a corner, Laurence grimaced. 'You're my first choice. I know your history. Plus, an investment by you brings a hell of a lot of prestige. Everything you touch turns to gold.'

Cesare heard his words and wondered if he'd ever tire of this. Laurence was exactly the kind of preppy school boy who'd been intent on making Cesare's life hell for a time, and now he was begging for his kindness, his money, his grace. His chest felt three sizes bigger. He regarded the other man for several seconds, enjoying this experience way more than he should, and then pushed his chair back.

'I'll be in touch.'

Laurence stood a few seconds later. 'You will?'

Cesare dipped his head. 'Yes.'

'Okay.' Laurence was ambivalent. He turned to Jemima, who was still sitting down, lost in thought. Doubt briefly dimmed Cesare's sense of anticipation because a huge part of his present mood came down to the certainty he would soon be pleasuring this very beautiful woman from head to toe—and everywhere in between.

'Jemima?' he murmured, and she raised her eyes to his in consternation.

Laurence frowned. 'Jem?'

'I've offered your cousin a lift home,' Cesare inserted smoothly.

'Oh, but you don't have to do that.' Laurence frowned.

'It's been agreed.' Cesare's tone held warning, a warning any of his rivals would know to listen to. And Laurence heeded it now, choosing instead to address Jemima.

'Are you sure? It's no trouble for me to drop you off...'

Cesare was surprised to realise he was holding his breath, awaiting her reply. After what felt like several minutes, but was actually just a few seconds, she stood, placing her still half-full champagne flute on the table.

'No, really, it's fine.' She eyed Cesare, something strange in her expression—trepidation or uncertainty, something he couldn't quite make sense of. But then she smiled and her whole face lit up, as though an army of firebugs had filled her blood. She glowed from the inside out, and his gut kicked with an unmistakable rush of sensual heat. 'I'm ready to go.'

In the restaurant, he'd been an impressive specimen, but here in the confines of his luxury car Cesare Durante was like a whole other species. This was madness but she couldn't summon even an inch of hesitation.

It was one of the pitfalls of her job that she was expected to attend events and parties, and it seemed to go hand in hand with her attendance that she was there to hook up. But she never had. Somehow, seeing such overt sexuality on display had inured her to its effects. Curiosity had been subverted by something approaching prudishness and then, as the years had gone by, embarrassment. Embarrassment about her virginity and what people would say if they knew the truth. And here she was, in the car with a man she found unbearably sexy, and some time tonight she'd lose her innocence... She couldn't wait.

A hint of anxiety creased through her for a moment when she thought of Laurence. Was there any chance being with Cesare could negatively impact the likelihood of Cesare investing in Laurence's fund? Surely not? He'd said as much, hadn't he? Business was business, distinct from pleasure.

She shifted her gaze sideways, eyeing him thoughtfully. He was immaculately dressed. His suit, a charcoal grey, contrasted perfectly with his crisp white shirt, and his black shoes were polished to gleaming. His hair was neat, his nails too. His fingers were long and capable-looking, with hair-roughened knuckles.

They didn't speak in the car. It was as though neither of them could find words, or perhaps both were equally afraid that talking would cut through the spell that had weaved some kind of magic around them, binding them together in a shared moment of madness.

London zipped past, all bright lights and ancient buildings, and then the car was running alongside Hyde Park, bringing them into Knightsbridge. It pulled off the road at a large and gracious townhouse. Despite the age of the building, modern modifications had taken place and an underground garage had been installed.

The car slid into it effortlessly, a gate closing behind them. Only then did Cesare turn to her, speculation in his face, as though waiting for her to change her mind.

She didn't want to.

It was insanity, but it was also the thing she wanted most in the world.

At his look of enquiry, she smiled. 'What are we waiting for?'

He expelled a breath and leaned forward, his lips claiming hers quickly, tasting her so she moaned, lifting her hands to the lapels of his shirt and gripping him tightly.

'Not a goddamned thing. Come on.' He growled the instructions into her mouth then pushed his door open, holding it and waiting for her to step out. She'd entered and exited limousines with the world's press waiting to get a shot up her skirt. She knew precisely how to disembark with an air of dignity—but it was a lot trickier to manage when her knees were quivering and warmth was spreading through her in anticipation of what was to come.

Despite the fact this was a residential address, there was a lift on the other side of the basement. He laced his fingers through hers, pulling her towards it, his enthusiasm making her smile even as his face was so serious.

The lift was as elegant as you'd see in any five-star hotel. More so, in fact, because it had only one occupant, so there was no wear and tear, no scruffy carpet. It was immaculate, just like Cesare—highly polished wood-panelling, a darkly tinted mirror and five buttons, indicating it served the whole house.

'Five storeys?'

His eyes pinned her to the spot. 'A basement and a rooftop terrace,' he pointed out. 'So only three.'

'Oh, that's far more modest.'

His expression showed scepticism as the lift doors opened onto the second floor. He held the door open, waiting for her to step out. 'And you live in a flat share, I suppose?' he responded.

'I live in a flat.' She shrugged. 'Nothing like this.' She waved her hand around the room. The lights had come on when they'd stepped out of the lift, subdued and golden, and they filled the space with a warmth its furnishings required. It was…austere. Yes, that was probably the best way to describe it. She looked around and, even as she recognised every piece was the very best, designer and in brand-new condition, there was an incredible lack of personality.

'Do you spend much time here?' she asked, genuinely curious. After all, it didn't exactly look lived in.

'No.'

'Ah.' She was strangely pleased by that. It wasn't even remotely homely.

'This is good?' he prompted. 'Are you worried I'm going to want to see you again after tonight?'

She stilled, her eyes finding his. That thought hadn't even occurred to her. In fact, she hadn't spent any time thinking about what happened later, tomorrow. 'I…'

'Relax, *uccellina.*' He said the word in his native tongue, and she had no idea what it meant. 'This is strictly a one-night thing.'

Her eyes flared wide, her heart lurching at the line he was drawing. She was glad—simple, quick, no complications. That was better for everyone, including Laurence. 'Perfect,' she murmured, her pulse slamming through her veins.

'I wanted you the moment I saw you tonight.' Something like determination glowed ferociously in his eyes and, for no reason she could think of, a frisson of something like a warning shifted down her spine.

'And here I am.' There was fatalism in her words.

He didn't react.

'Why do I think you always get exactly what you want?'

'What do you base that on?' His hand lifted to the flimsy strap of her dress, sliding beneath it, running it down her shoulder slowly, his eyes holding hers.

'Am I wrong?'

His eyes flared. 'No, *uccellina*.' His fingers ran lower, tracing her arm lightly, his gaze not shifting.

It was the second time he'd used that word. 'What does that mean?'

His hand moved to the other strap, gliding it over her flesh so her breath snagged in her throat.

'Little bird.' His words were gravelled. The straps slipped lower until the dress began to fall. She bit down on her lower lip to stop a sigh escaping. The fabric was silk, and it moved like water over her breasts, her nipples puckering at the slight touch. His hands guided the dress lower still, over her hips, until it fell to the floor, leaving her standing in front of him in only a pair of heels and a lace thong.

Her breathing was ragged, her body covered in goose bumps that had nothing to do with the temperature.

'You are beautiful,' he murmured seriously, the words factual rather than said as a compliment. 'But this you already know.'

It was a statement that came close to implying she was vain, and Jemima resented it, but before she could respond he'd stepped closer so that his body was hard against hers and urgency made it difficult to think, much less speak. She could feel every inch of him, every expansive muscle, his arousal pressed to her belly.

Her hands lifted to his chest, pushing against his shirt, his pectoral muscles firm beneath her curious grip. She undid his buttons one by one, starting at his neck and working down, pausing at the waistband of his trousers so she could lift his shirt out completely. The tip of her tongue darted from the corner of her lips as she concentrated on what she was doing, but before she could push the shirt from his body he'd swooped his head down and sought her mouth with his, his lips mashing to hers, the kiss driven by a mutual, desperate passion.

He took another step forward, so her back connected with the glass window, and he rolled his hips, leaving her in little doubt as to how much he wanted her.

Lust was a new feeling for Jemima. Never had she felt so attracted to a man that she wanted to act on it like this. Her brain had ceased to function; she was operating purely on instinct and her instincts were telling her to enjoy this.

'I need to…' What? See him? Touch him? Feel him? Frustrated by her lack of experience, her total inability to put into words what she was feeling and to explain the fever in her blood, she shook her head.

But he understood, of course he did, because the same fever was raging through him. He scooped her up, wrapping her legs around his waist, carrying her easily through the house, kissing her the entire way, and by the time they reached a bedroom and he dropped her onto the mattress she was ready to catch fire completely.

'I want…'

'Yes?' His own voice was roughened by desire. 'What do you want, Jemima?'

There it was again—the mental block, a complete inability to say what she was thinking. She groaned, reaching for him, sitting up and pulling at his sides, but he didn't move. He kicked out of his shoes, watching her, his chest rising and falling with each of his deep breaths as he shrugged out of his shirt.

He had a tattoo that ran just beneath his heart: '*come sono*'. Her Italian was limited to industry terms and social niceties. '"I am me"?' she said aloud, her eyes chasing the cursive ink.

'"As I am".' He stepped out of his trousers and now a kick of fear hit her gut. Not fear of what was to come, but fear at how out of her depth she was. Her pulse lurched wildly through her body and she knew she should say something. But ancient feminine instincts gave her confidence and had her pushing to the end of the bed so that his legs straddled hers, his body so big, his presence overpowering. His fingers curved through her hair, and then her lips sought his flat chest, pressing to the ridges there as she scrambled onto her knees on the edge of the bed so she could trace one of his nipples with her tongue, flicking it curiously before transferring her attention to the next one.

In the back of her mind, she was vaguely aware of how new this was, and yet she didn't feel anything except pleasurable anticipation and relief. She wanted this. She wanted it so badly. Soon, her virginity would be gone, and she'd know the pleasure of a man's body... She couldn't wait.

His chest moved rapidly with each curious little exploration of her tongue. Power trilled in her veins—the knowledge that she was driving him as wild as she was set her pulse skittering.

CHAPTER THREE

OVER DINNER SHE'D admired the strength of his arms but now, without a shirt, she saw for herself that he was muscled in a way that suggested he worked out often. There was a sense of power and control in his every movement. His chest was ridged with muscles and his flesh showed a deep tan, as though he spent a lot of time outdoors.

He reached down, his fingers tangling in the elastic of her thong, sliding the underwear over her legs in a way that was so sensual and tantalising she couldn't bear it. She ached to reach down and remove it herself to speed this up not because she wanted it to end—she already knew she didn't—but because she needed it to begin. She needed him as though he were oxygen.

His mouth on her breast was completely unexpected. His tongue curled around her nipple, perhaps retaliating for her own leisurely exploration. But his was so much more skilled, so much more thorough. It wasn't a fair match at all.

His tongue swirled around the dusky peach areola and then he drew it into his mouth, sucking there until she was moaning, moist heat slicked between her legs. His other hand curved around her breast so his fingers could torment that nipple, alternating between a light, barely there brush of his fingers to a tight squeeze that sent arrows of desire firing against her flesh.

'Please,' she moaned, no longer aware what she was asking for, knowing only that she needed something he alone could provide. He was still wearing boxer shorts but he pressed his arousal to her womanhood and she writhed at the pressure, the unexpected intimacy of that gesture. His body thrust against hers as though they were already making love, and she ached to be. She ached to feel him inside her.

She'd always wondered if it would hurt—losing her virginity—but in this moment she was far too caught up in the hedonism of sensation to anticipate anything other than wild, utter bliss.

Her nails dug into his shoulders and her lips kept searching for his. His kiss was a temporary balm to the wildness in her veins but not enough—there would never be enough. She needed complete surrender—his? Hers? She didn't know.

'I need you,' she groaned, her hands moving down his back, her nails scraping against his flesh and pushing into the waistband of his shorts so she could curve her grip around his buttocks and hold him tight to her sex. She lifted her hips wordlessly, instinctively inviting him to sweep away her invisible barrier, to become one with her.

'I wanted to do this the moment I saw you,' he muttered, moving to stand, pushing at his boxers impatiently. His eyes were fixed to her face with something like impatience—or possibly accusation—something she didn't understand and couldn't fathom. He reached to his side, pulling a condom from the bedside table, watching her as he opened the foil square.

She stared at him, transfixed, as he rolled it over the length of his cock, so big and hard, so fascinating. Her throat was dry, her heart pounding, and for the first time since agreeing to this she felt doubts creep in.

Not doubts about wanting him.

Doubts about the fact he didn't know about her inexperience.

She didn't need to be a mind-reader to recognise that Cesare Durante was a man who was used to sophisticated lovers. She was pretty sure springing her virginity on him would be poor form.

Her cheeks warmed now with the beginnings of embarrassment rather than desire, and she pushed up to stare at him, disbelief that her conscience was getting the better of her making her frown.

'I am going to make you scream my name,' he murmured, oblivious to the direction of her thoughts. 'Over and over and over again.'

She nodded, but when he brought his body over hers she lifted a hand and pressed it to his chest. Their heads were level, his steel-grey eyes boring into hers, and Jemima told herself to have courage—to do the right thing. It wasn't that big a deal, she reasoned. Surely he wouldn't really care?

'I have to tell you something.' She swallowed, her pupils huge in her pale eyes.

'Tell me quickly.' He brought his mouth to her cheek, kissing her there, dragging his tongue down her body to the valley between her breasts and lower, over her flat stomach towards her womanhood. Of their own accord her hands tangled in his hair, pulling at it frantically. When his mouth connected with her feminine core, she startled, pushing up on her elbows, uncertainty losing the battle to pleasure.

His tongue ran along her seam and she twisted on the bed in an instinctive response so that his hands gripped her thighs and moved her legs wider, clamping down on them and holding her right as he wanted her.

His name tumbled from her lips, just as he'd said it would, the Italian word so exotic in her mouth, so moreish and tempting. Pleasure was a wave building within her and she couldn't stay afloat. It sucked her down into a turbulent ocean and she didn't even care that she was drowning. She didn't care that she could barely breathe.

Her fingers tousled his hair, pulling at it frantically as pleasure eroded her awareness of time and place, and finally she exploded, breaking free of the ocean and finding her place amongst the stars. The orgasm claimed her, every cell of her, every fibre of her being. She was celestial matter, she was time and place, she was ancient and new, she was indefinable.

Pleasure was a thousand barbs beneath her skin. She lay back against the bed, her breathing rushed, her sanity in tatters. His body was coming over her, so even as she was shipwrecked on the shore line of their passion she knew she had to find a way to speak and be heard.

'Cesare, wait.' The urgency of her words stalled him. He braced his body over hers and she felt his sheathed arousal at the entrance to her womanhood; she was so hungry for him and more of this that for a brief second she contemplated not speaking. 'You have to know…'

'Yes?' His tip nudged at her entrance and she groaned, pressing her hands to his chest, wanting him with a ferocity that was beyond her comprehension.

'I want you. I really, really want this.' The words were breathless. She looked up at him and said nothing else. She wasn't sure why—she knew telling him of her innocence was the *right* thing to do—but when she opened her mouth she simply couldn't find the words. Instead, she heard the cacophony of news articles about her, the names she'd been called, the marriages she was said to have ruined, and she was struck dumb, silent in the face of the world's assumptions.

He stared down at her, his gaze intent enough to see all

the way into her soul, and then he smiled, a look of such complete confidence and sexy dominance that her heart exploded, taking up all the space that should have been re- served for her lungs, making breathing impossible.

'I want you.' It was the last thing she said before he thrust into her, claiming her and removing her innocence in one hard movement.

Cesare froze, holding his body where it was with the great- est of efforts, his arousal buried inside the beautiful Jemima as shock tore through him. He'd been a teenager the last time he'd slept with a virgin and it had been a disaster. A simple act of sex to Cesare had meant the world to her and, after seeing the way he'd carelessly broken her heart, he'd sworn he'd never again sleep with an innocent woman.

And he hadn't. He'd steered clear of anyone sexually in- experienced because there was a burden in being a wom- an's first.

Her tightness was unmistakable, as was the resistance he hadn't felt until he was already inside her, too late to change what had happened. He pushed up onto his elbows, his breathing ragged, and even as question after question spilled through him her muscles squeezed him, filling his eyes with white light, blinding him with his own insatiable need for release.

'Damn it.' The words were clipped, gruff.

'Don't.' The wobble in her voice had him re-focussing his gaze on her. 'Don't stop. Please.' His eyes chased her features: the tell-tale flush of pink running towards her brow, lips that were swollen from how she'd been biting down on them, pupils that filled her irises almost com- pletely. 'Please.'

He swore softly because he suspected wild horses couldn't have forced him to stop, even as he knew he would have if she'd been in pain. He moved his body more gently, though, slowly allowing her time to adjust to the feeling of his possession, to acclimatise to the sense of having him inside her, watching her carefully for every flicker of response that crossed her face.

Emotions he hadn't expected pounded him—and emotions were something he generally preferred to keep way, way out of his sex life. But, for the first time in a long time, he felt a heavy sense of guilt. Of responsibility—a feeling of having done something wrong.

'Oh, God, Cesare...'

The sound of his name on her perfectly shaped lips dragged him back to the present, to the physical and the pressing, the passion and the perfection of this. Her nails on his back were desperate, as though she could scratch past pleasure and bring herself back to sanity. There was only one way for that—and he needed the release as badly as she did.

He might have teased her and tormented her, drawing out her orgasm, withholding the ultimate pleasure until she was almost incandescent with desire, tormenting her with the strength of her longing. He would have done so if this had been any ordinary night, any ordinary lover.

But that was gamesmanship and he didn't feel like playing games any more.

Her cries became fevered, her body writhing as pleasure threatened to tear her apart, and when she tipped over the edge he followed her, releasing himself without making a sound, already mentally detaching himself from this, from her, even as he tipped himself inside her and felt her muscles spasm wildly around his length.

This had been a mistake—and Cesare Durante didn't make mistakes.

Nor was he a man who tolerated surprises. He stared

down at the woman beneath him, her eyes fluttered shut, her breathing rapid, and he pulled away from her, removing himself, standing without saying a word. He couldn't.

He'd learned a long time ago not to react when he was angry, not to react when his emotions were in play, but in that moment he felt an odd fury, a sense of having been duped into something he would *never* knowingly have consented to. She'd been a virgin, and he hadn't offered anything beyond one night. What the actual hell?

When he'd been nine years old, a teacher had introduced him to a Rubik's Cube for the first time. It had been a simple warm-up exercise for the class, but Cesare hadn't been able to comprehend how inanimate plastic could not be bent to his will. He'd spent hours staring at it, moving each tile, until some time around midnight on that same day he'd brought order to the madness of the cube.

He felt that same desperate sense of misunderstanding now. Jemima Woodcraft—a virgin? Impossible. Except it wasn't. He'd felt the proof of her innocence for himself. He strode towards his en suite bathroom, dispensing with the proof of their love-making in the waste-paper basket, and with the same motion he grabbed a towel and wrapped it low around his waist.

He met the reflection of his eyes in the mirror, his expression grim. She'd come to his bed knowing what that would entail. Which left one question. Why the hell had she chosen to lose her virginity to him?

Calmer, he turned, moving back into his bedroom. She was sitting up, a sheet wrapped around her body, her gaze averted from his in a way that was infuriating and somehow endearing all at once.

'You were a virgin?' He didn't need the confirmation, yet it still seemed important to establish the fact beyond any doubt. Or perhaps he simply wanted to hear her admit it.

He clamped his jaw together and expelled a harsh breath so his nostrils flared. 'Jemima?'

His eyes narrowed, studying the pallor of her face, and frustration bit at his insides. She wouldn't look at him.

'Yes.' The word was soft.

'And you came here tonight to sleep with me?'

Now her face lifted, though she focussed her gaze about an inch above his shoulder. 'Yes.'

At least she wasn't lying to him. 'You didn't think this was something I ought to have known? Something I might have liked to consider?'

Her chin tilted at a defiant angle. 'I tried to tell you.'

Cesare frowned, guilt and disbelief churning in his gut. 'When?'

'Before! Before you—before we—before we were together,' she finished with a shake of her head. 'I tried but I…was embarrassed, I guess.'

'You thought it was better for me to feel your innocence as I obliterated it?'

She winced, her expression showing hurt.

'I don't know.'

For some reason, everything she said somehow made it worse. He felt angry. Disempowered. As though she'd taken what was supposed to be an easy exchange between two consenting lovers and turned it into something so much more complicated.

'You don't think this is something I deserved to know? To decide if I even wanted to be your first lover?'

Her face drained of colour. 'Would it have made a difference?'

He swore in his native tongue, the curse a harsh invective that slammed around the room and seemingly electrocuted her. She jack-knifed from the bed, the towel locked toga-style to her body.

But he didn't stop; he couldn't. 'You're damned right it would have made a difference. I don't *do* virgins, Jemima. What did you think? This would make me want to buy into your cousin's hedge fund? That I'd feel so guilty at having unknowingly become your first lover I'd pay whatever I could to absolve myself of that responsibility?'

She sucked in a sharp breath, her eyes narrowing. 'How dare you? This had *nothing* to do with Laurence.'

'I find that hard to believe.'

The column of her throat shifted as she swallowed. 'Be that as it may, it's the truth. I came here tonight because I wanted to sleep with you, not for any other reason.'

'And if I knew do you think I would still have wanted to sleep with you?'

Her cheeks paled and he told himself the sensation rolling through him was satisfaction.

'I honestly didn't think it would matter.'

'You were a twenty-three-year-old virgin. I brought you here thinking you were like me, that you enjoy sex for sport. If I had known you'd never been with another lover, I would never have touched you.'

She sucked in a breath that was pure indignation. 'Well, rest assured, Cesare, I have no intention of darkening your door ever again.' She glared at him, somehow managing to look elegant and haughty even as she crossed the room in a bed sheet.

But dissatisfaction rode through him. He still didn't have any of the answers he wanted. He followed her into the living room.

'How is this even possible? There are countless articles about your conquests online…'

'Yeah, and the Internet gets it wrong sometimes, you know.'

'But so completely wrong?'

She paused to shoot him a withering look. 'What do you think?'

Her dress had been discarded on the floor. She lifted it over her head and dislodged the sheet as she pulled it down so that he was deprived of another glimpse of her body. It didn't matter. The sight of her was likely burned into his memory anyway.

'There are photographs. And what about Clive Angmore?'

'An acquaintance,' she muttered, running her fingers through her hair as she looked around for her handbag. 'Nothing more.'

'So you were, what? Saving yourself for marriage?'

Her shocked gasp tumbled through the room and his heart twisted sharply in his chest. 'You should know, Jemima, that this makes no difference to me. For whatever reason you came here tonight, and whatever you were expecting it might mean to me, nothing has changed in my mind. This was just sex, nothing more.'

She glared at him, her expression pinched, her face wearing a mask of contempt, but the effect was lessened by eyes that were suspiciously shimmering, moisture dabbing her eyelashes. His gut rolled.

'I don't want anything from you.'

'So what? You intended for me, a man you barely know, to be your first lover? Why?'

'It's not like I had some elaborate plan,' she snapped. 'You asked me to come home with you and in that moment I couldn't think of a single reason not to.'

His eyes narrowed at the deceptive simplicity of her statement. 'I can give you a reason,' he said quietly. 'I had no interest in being your first. I didn't want the gift of your virginity. What we just did was a mistake.'

She blinked and a single tear threatened to fall from

her eyes. He made a noise and turned away from her, his breathing uneven as he went behind the island bar of the kitchen.

He poured a scotch and when he looked up she was standing exactly where he'd left her, as though frozen in time.

Something shifted inside him. He hated that they'd slept together. All the feelings of panic he'd felt almost two decades ago came screeching back to him, but it was more than that. Cesare didn't like being surprised and she'd surprised him completely.

He hated that he'd completely misread her. He hated that she hadn't told him what he was getting into, and he hated looking at her now, knowing that the tear rolling lazily down her cheek was because of him. Most of all, he hated that he was awash with feelings because of her, when Cesare Durante was a man who prided himself on a robotic level of emotional detachment.

This whole night had been a complete mistake. When he spoke, it was with a stony cool.

'I'll have my driver take you home.'

Her eyes lifted to his face, a frown covering her lips. 'What?'

She looked completely lost. He swallowed past the unwelcome sense of compassion. 'My driver. He will take you home.'

She nodded then, and he felt as if she was going to say something. Then, she shook her head. 'Don't bother. I'll grab a cab.'

A thousand things ran through his mind. He should object. Tell her he wouldn't feel right not seeing her home, or knowing that she got there safely, say something to erase the lines of disbelief that had etched themselves on her brow.

It wasn't a question of caring, it was basic civility. 'Either my driver takes you home or I do. The choice is yours.'

She blanched visibly. 'Fine.' Her lips were a gash in her face. 'Call your driver, then. Frankly, I don't want to see you ever again.'

CHAPTER FOUR

Four weeks later

JEMIMA'S STOMACH ROLLED with a stormy kaleidoscope of butterflies. Anxiety burst through her, but even as the lift ascended to the top floor of Durante Incorporated's offices here in Rome and she gnawed on her lower lip, wondering if there was any alternative to this, she knew there wasn't.

She had to do this.

Her eyes, shielded by the over-sized sunglasses she often wore, flicked to the lift control panel. Buttons lit up as the lift crossed the floors until finally it arrived on the twenty-seventh. Jemima was pretty certain she'd left her stomach and every single one of her nerves down in the marbled lobby.

She'd dressed carefully for this meeting. Where she usually liked to fly under the radar, she felt she needed all her Jemima Woodcroft armour at her disposal today. Conversely, she hadn't wanted it to look as though she'd gone to any effort whatsoever. A pair of skinny jeans, a loose-fitting blouse a crisp white in colour, with a bright beaded necklace she'd bought at Camden Market and a pair of stilettos to give her a little extra height—and courage. Her clutch matched her necklace and she kept it tucked under her arm as she approached the central reception bay. Here, it was like another version of the lobby downstairs—all high ceilings, marble floor, bright and sun-filled, beautiful and extravagant. Everywhere she looked breathed 'success'.

'I'm here to see Cesare Durante.' His name flew from her lips and sparked a deluge of memories, the same memories that had been tormenting her night after night since she'd stalked out of his London home and sworn she'd never think of him again.

If only.

She had thought of him without meaning to. It had been hardest of all to keep him at bay when she'd been showering. Naked, her hands had run over her body, touching her flesh as he had, stirring memories and wants so that desire had begun to simmer inside her all the time. Anger was there too, anger at the way he'd reacted and treated her, but the pleasure of what they'd shared refused to be dimmed, regardless of what had come afterwards.

'Do you have an appointment?'

'No.' Jemima removed her sunglasses. 'But he'll want to see me. We're...old friends.'

The receptionist lifted her head belatedly, swiping at her silky black hair, pushing it back from her face. As her eyes landed on Jemima, she showed obvious surprise, and Jemima tamped down on a familiar feeling—part resentment, part amusement. It was easy to tell the moment people recognised her.

'Jemima Woodcroft?'

Jemima's smile was kind. 'Yes.'

'Oh, wow. Okay, I'll just let him know you're here.'

'Thank you.' She dipped her head forward in acknowledgement. A few moments later, moments in which Jemima's fingers fidgeted unstoppably, moments in which she began to imagine that perhaps he wasn't going to see her after all, the receptionist appeared at Jemima's side.

'This way, ma'am.'

Her feet made a clickety-clack noise as she crossed the reception area. When they approached two wide, glass doors, Jemima knew she was seconds away from seeing him again. Her insides were trembling; she employed every technique at her disposal, everything her professional training had taught her, to hide any outward appearance of nervousness. He couldn't know how he affected her, nor what this visit was costing her pride!

The receptionist opened the door and stood holding it. Jemima expelled a soft breath, dug her nails into her palms and pushed into his office.

And immediately wished she hadn't.

It was so, so very him. Dark timber floors, sleek and elegant, unbelievably masculine in its decor, and there was a faint hint of fragrance, something like pine needles and orange peel, that made her tummy loop around and around in circles with the rush of her memories.

Within seconds she'd taken in the details of the room, looking around on autopilot until her eyes landed on him with a heart-stopping thud and she had no scope left to notice anything else.

Oh, God.

A month. Four weeks. Thirty days. In that time she'd travelled to Istanbul for a magazine shoot, to Paris to film a video for an airline, but no matter where she'd fallen asleep, her dreams had been filled with Cesare, and her dreams were so torturously vivid that she'd woken up again and again and reached for him, as though her fingertips would connect with his warm, toned flesh.

She stared at him now as a drowning man might a lifeline. He wore a suit, dark blue with a tinge of grey, that set off the depth of his tan beautifully, teamed with a white shirt and a pair of brown shoes which she'd bet were hand-stitched. At his wrist there was a gold watch, and his dark hair was brushed back from his brow. He looked strong, vital and unbelievably sexy. She stared at him, wishing she'd pushed her glasses back onto her face, wishing she had some kind of shield, some sort of protection against this.

Images came to her unbidden. Memories of his mouth on her breasts, on her sex, of his tongue running over her body, tasting her, tormenting her, driving her completely wild. Her nerve endings began to tingle; she felt as though her feet had lifted up off the ground.

'Miss Woodcroft.' His use of her surname brought her to the present with a thud. She wasn't here to walk down memory lane—all ten yards of it. She was here on business. She was here for Laurence—that was the only reason she had for weakening and seeing him again. Memories of how desperate her cousin had been when they'd spoken on the phone two nights earlier surged through her now, making it easier to push past her anxiety and desire and focus almost exclusively on the purpose of her visit.

'Mr Durante,' she responded in kind, her eyes subconsciously icing over.

'Thank you, Olivia.'

The door clicked shut behind the receptionist, leaving them completely alone. Jemima was conscious of everything. Her breathing and his, the space between them, the rustle of his suit as he crossed the room to a kitchenette. He pressed a button on a machine and a thick, black liquid began to fill a white ceramic cup. 'Coffee?'

She shook her head, then cleared her throat. 'No, thank you. I'm fine.'

His eyes lifted to her face, scanning it thoughtfully, then he removed the cup from the machine and cradled it in his hand. 'Then perhaps you can explain what you're doing here?'

'Straight to it?' she murmured, as much for her own sake as his.

He sipped his coffee without speaking, his silence deeply unnerving.

She swallowed past her nerves, trying not to think of anything except her cousin. Nothing else mattered—he'd made that perfectly clear when he'd dismissed her from his house. 'I came to find out what's going on with the hedge fund.'

Cesare didn't visibly react, and the longer he stayed silent, the more anxious she became. The directness of his stare was completely unsettling. 'Laurence says you've had the contract a fortnight but you haven't been answering his calls.'

Cesare lifted his brows. 'And?'

Her stomach flipped and flopped. 'It's not fair to keep him in suspense like this.' Her voice was crackly. She cleared her throat. 'If you're going to buy into the fund, you should do it. Otherwise tell him definitively so he can explore other options.'

Cesare's smile was wolf-like. 'Such as bankruptcy?'

Jemima felt the warmth fall from her face. It was a cruel thing to say and it showed in her features, hurt emanating from her as she spun away from him, moving towards the large boardroom that was framed by enormous glass windows.

'Either you're interested or not. Jerking him around like this...'

'He is asking for a large sum of money. You don't think some due diligence is required?'

Jemima placed her bag down on top of the table and focussed her gaze on the stunning vista of this ancient city. 'How long is that going to take?'

Silence. She was glad then that she wasn't looking

at him. She felt his disapproval from a distance and she hated it.

'Let me get this straight,' he said finally. 'Laurence doesn't like how long I'm spending on this and so he sends you, knowing our history, in an attempt to motivate me?' He made a snorting noise of contempt. 'And you didn't think you'd try to guilt-trip me into anything?'

She sucked in a harsh breath, on the brink of denying his charge, but he continued before she could speak.

'I can see why he'd think I'd be persuaded, given what happened between us, but surely you've learned your lesson, Jemima? If you play with fire, you get burned, and I am definitely fire where you are concerned.'

She winced and spun around to find him closer now, only a few feet away, watching her with an intensity that made her heart skip a beat. 'He doesn't know I'm here,' she contradicted. 'And he doesn't know anything about that night. About what happened between us.'

She caught a flash of surprise in the depths of Cesare's eyes, but only briefly, and then he was cynical and detached once more.

'Then why are you here?' He prowled towards her, his eyes morphing from steel-grey to the colour of the ocean on a stormy day. Before she could realise his intention, he was right before her, his body so close they were brushing, his face intently watchful.

Her breath caught in her throat, and for a second she found it almost impossible to think, certainly to find any words to offer.

'I just think you should move faster.' She furrowed her brow. 'I'm *asking* you to make up your mind, one way or another. He deserves to know where he stands.'

Cesare's expression didn't shift. 'And you thought that

if you came here to ask me to snap my fingers and invest in his fund I would simply agree?'

She shook her head. This was a mistake. Why had she thought he'd listen to her? Or that he'd have any motivation to help her?

'No. I guess I'm asking you as a decent human to put him out of his misery.' She swallowed. 'I know it's probably not good business sense to tell you how desperate he is but Cesare, truly, I'm worried about him.' She lowered her eyes so he wouldn't see how close she was to tears. 'He's at his wits' end. And he's worked too hard to lose everything now. He *can't* lose everything. Too much depends on it. Please.'

She'd said too much. This was a gamble she was going to lose and the consequences would be disastrous. 'But you don't care, do you?' she whispered, wondering at the deep sense of surprise that permeated her.

'I barely know your cousin. If you're asking if I'm personally moved by your worries for him, then no. I told you that night, I do not mix business with pleasure. If you think that the fact we slept together somehow predisposes me to want to help Laurence, then you completely misunderstand the kind of man I am. He made his bed, and he may very well now have to lie in it.'

Panic scorched her, but she tried not to lose sight of the man Cesare was. No way would he have come to London to meet with Laurence if he hadn't been motivated to move. 'But you *are* interested in investing, right?'

He dipped his head forward in silent agreement.

'So why delay?'

Cesare's eyes sparked in his face. 'I'm not sure that's any business of yours.'

She bit down on her lip. He had a point.

This wasn't going to work. He was immovable. She

should have known as much. All she'd succeeded in doing today was destroying her pride and possibly weakening Laurence's bargaining position in a way that may well prove fatal.

'You're right.' She shook her head. 'I shouldn't have come here. I really thought you might understand. I don't know why I should have expected anything of you, really. It was pretty obvious that night exactly what kind of man you are. I was stupid to expect a shred of compassion from you…'

'Compassion?' He looked at her as though she were mad. 'This is business, black and white, commercially sensible business. Nothing else. If I invested half a billion pounds into failing hedge funds just because a woman I'd slept with asked me to, I would have nothing left to invest.'

The sting of his words whipped her to the core of her soul. It wasn't as though she was under any illusion when it came to his sexual experience but a reminder of the number of women he'd slept with sat like a boulder in her throat. She stared at him for several seconds and then nodded jerkily. 'Perhaps it would be better if you forgot I came, Mr Durante.' She used his surname meaningfully, side-stepping him and moving towards the table where her clutch bag sat discarded.

He watched her stride towards the door with a frown on his face and, though he'd been frustrated by her sudden intrusion, and even more so at the reason for it, he didn't relish the prospect of her disappearing once more.

His lawyers had quarantined the funds for this investment earlier that same day—as chance would have it, he'd been planning to call Laurence that afternoon to finalise the details.

Instead, Jemima had arrived with her fluffy blonde hair

and the fringe that hung across one eye making him itch to reach over and push it away so he could regard her properly. Jemima with her defiant eyes and trembling mouth, her vanilla fragrance and tantalising curves. The four weeks he'd spent telling himself how bitterly he regretted falling for her many charms had evaporated into thin air.

He was glad to see her. He wanted to see more of her. The realisations were instantaneous, brought to life by her imminent departure.

'Wait.'

Her hand had curved around the door. He stayed exactly where he was, a desire to appear in control innate to him, even as there was a rival instinct to stalk across the room and drag her into his arms.

'What?' She barked the word with disbelief. 'What do you want?'

It was an excellent question and, if he'd been a different man, perhaps he would have obfuscated, sought cover in a lie. But Cesare was not a man to lie. 'You, *uccellina*. Just you.'

Her eyes flew wide and her lips parted, colour invaded her cheeks and beneath the fine cotton of her shirt her breasts puckered so he could see the definition of her nipples against the fabric. His groin tightened, desire rushing over him.

All his adult life, he'd been in charge. Not once had he slept with a woman and had it morph into something else, and this wouldn't, either. This was just sex, desire plain and simple, but one night hadn't been enough. Perhaps it was the way they'd come together, the surprise of her innocence or the abrupt way he'd put an end to what they were doing. He hadn't been able to think of her without regret and now, here she was in his office, a second chance with her tantalising and impossible to ignore.

He held up a hand, forestalling anything she might say in response. 'Hear me out.' He paced towards his desk, a frown on his face as he thought through what he wanted and how to get it. 'You are worried about your cousin. Fine. You wish me to alleviate those worries by investing in his business right now, today?'

She bit down on her lower lip and nodded, angst so obvious in her eyes.

He ignored it. This wasn't about sympathy. It wasn't about compassion—she'd been wrong to expect either of those qualities in him. This was business, pure and simple. She was an acquisition, just like a company he might wish to buy. True, the terms were vastly different, but if mutually agreeable the professionalism of the deal would be the same.

He spoke slowly, placing his palms on the edge of his desk as he eyed her across the room. 'In business it is normal to offer something in exchange. If I were to buy into his hedge fund, which may very well prove to be a complete waste of my money,' he said, knowing full well the fund was likely to double in value in the next six months, 'then I would expect something in exchange.'

She was quiet. His eyes ran over her face and a rush of excitement surrounded him. He'd thought of her frustratingly often—how come it hadn't occurred to him that he could leverage her situation to give them what they both wanted?

'Have you thought of me since that night?' he asked, his body still, his eyes trained on her face so that he could catch any hint of response, the slightest reaction. He didn't have to look too hard. Her hand lifted to her hair, pulling it over one shoulder, and her expression shifted to one of disbelief.

'Why does it matter?' And then, a second later, 'Have you thought of me?'

'Yes.' He held her gaze when she might have looked away. 'You weren't what I expected.'

Her throat shifted as she swallowed. 'So I'm some kind of an enigma?'

An enigma? Yes, that was it. How else could he explain the fact his mind had frequently wandered back to that night without his consent? 'You could say that.'

'So?' Her eyelids fluttered as she lifted her gaze to his and an ache to possess her again—properly this time—soared in his chest. Yes, he wanted her, and not like last time. He wanted to savour every kiss, every movement, every feeling and sensation. He wanted to do this properly, at his leisure.

'I have a proposition for you. A way to help Laurence and give you and me what I think we both want.'

But one more night wouldn't be enough. Instinctively he knew the fever she'd evoked would be harder to quell in his blood than a single night would allow for.

'I will invest in the fund today, this afternoon—no more due diligence, no more delays—if you agree to my terms.'

She crossed her slender arms over her chest, the gesture drawing his eyes to the gentle swell of her cleavage, so every fibre of his being tightened and shook with need. 'What terms?'

The certainty that he was close to success shot through him. He knew what victory sounded like and it was close at hand.

'Two weeks.' His eyes flared as he delivered the terms.

Her lips parted as a small sound rushed out of her and colour peaked in her cheeks, pale pink, so that she was like a very soft rose petal. She knew exactly what he was offering, but he wasn't a man who was prone to uncertainty, so he felt the need to spell out exactly what he was offering and exactly what he wanted.

'In my bed.'

And now, he stepped out from behind his desk, moving towards the door where she stood, his stride long, his manner intent.

She stared at him as he approached and he relished this—the promise of what was to come. For, as sure as night followed day, she would agree to his terms.

'But why?' The words were whispered, hollow-sounding.

He lifted a finger and pressed it to her lips, keeping her silent. 'I am not interested in a relationship—not with you or any woman.' The words were said coldly, but it was better that she understood, unequivocally, how he felt. As a young man Cesare had sworn he would make a success of himself and relationships didn't factor into that. Sex, yes. Anything more serious? Hell, no. And never with a woman like Jemima, who was as to the manor born as it was possible to get.

'What I'm offering is a very clearly defined arrangement.' He felt her swallow this time, her lips pursing as she tried to relax her mouth. He fought an urge to slide his finger into the warm cavity, to feel her moistness wrap around him... Soon. He needed her to agree to this and then it would begin.

'Explain it to me,' she whispered, faint of breath.

He took the question as a win. He was close to victory. 'For two weeks you will be by my side. Morning, noon and night, in my bed any time I wish it, charming me, making love to me. You will be, in every way, mine.'

She trembled a little and a husky gasp escaped her lips. 'Why?'

He laughed. 'You really have to ask that?' He pressed his body forward and, when his hard ridges connected to her soft curves, he didn't relent, stepping forward again so she was shuffled back into the door. He pressed her to it, seeing the moment her eyes flared wide as she felt his arousal hard against her body.

'I mean, why would I agree to this?'

He bared his teeth in an approximation of a smile. 'Putting aside the fact you have just told me how desperate your cousin is, and implied you would do *anything* to help him?'

Her cheeks fired pink and her eyes cut through him with something approaching disdain. It was useful—an excellent reminder of who and what this woman was. Aristocratic. Entitled. Spoiled. All the things he'd come to loathe, all of the attitudes and bigotries of which he'd been on the receiving end time and again, before he'd made his fortune and become the kind of man with whom everyone—regardless of their title and wealth—felt a need to flatter and ingratiate themselves. Her disdain was nothing new, and it fired him up now, reminding him why he kept himself well away from women like this.

This was just sex. Sex, business, pleasure, but each separated from the other by the lines he was drawing now.

'I am the only man you have ever slept with,' he said with a lift of his brow and a twist of his lips that was sheer arrogant machismo. 'And there is much you have to learn.'

Her eyes narrowed and she regarded him with an even greater level of disdain and even a glimmer of dislike. 'How do *you* know you're the only man I've ever slept with?' she prompted.

'I was there the other night,' he reminded her, no dint to his confidence. 'Remember?'

Her voice was soft when she spoke, mellow and husky. 'You were my first lover. It doesn't necessarily follow that you remain my only.'

Cesare—who prided himself on being quick on the uptake—took several seconds to comprehend exactly what she meant. But, when he did, he felt an almighty surge of adrenalin and a burst of male egotism that had him acting without thinking.

'You're lying.' The words ripped from him even as his head swooped down and his lips claimed hers. 'You are lying.' He threw the words into her mouth as his hands curled at her hips, lifting her up and bracing her back against the door.

The idea of another man doing this—touching her, kissing her—flicked something inside him and he was waging a war against a primal instinct of possession, an instinct that went beyond sense and logic, an instinct he couldn't fathom, didn't welcome, yet couldn't deny.

He swore into her mouth and kissed her harder, or perhaps it wasn't a kiss so much as a complete subjugation, a need to show her that he could command her desire and please her more than anyone else on earth.

'What does it matter?' she threw at him, breaking free of his kiss before her lips sought his of their own accord.

What did it matter? Hell, he couldn't say, only he knew it *did* matter, and it fired his determination anew—he would wipe any other man from her mind, he would remove them from her body, he would make her his. For the sheer sake of it. For pride.

CHAPTER FIVE

SHE WAS DROWNING and she didn't care. Water filled her lungs, her eyes, her cells, her heart. She was drowning and there was no point trying not to—she would choose this drowning death a thousand times over. His hands on her body were strong and possessive, his lips unrelenting, his arousal persistent against her so she felt her own need explode in a way that was more fierce than any stick of dynamite, any firework, any flame.

She'd lied to him. Pride had driven her to remove that smug, arrogant look from his face. He might have been right—he was the only man she'd ever slept with, and he had filled her dreams for days and nights on end—but he had no right to look at her and expect her to jump when he snapped his fingers.

He deserved to have his arrogance shaken, his confidence taken down a peg. Beautiful, sexy, smug bastard...

His hands pushed at her blouse, and in his haste he tore the buttons, so one popped clear across the room. She barely noticed; she was just so glad the moment his fingers pushed aside the lace of her bra and cupped her naked breast, his touch instantly familiar and desperately perfect. She rolled her hips, her legs wrapped around his waist, her jeans an unbelievable barrier to what she wanted, what she needed.

And he understood, pushing his cock harder against her, so that even through all the fabric that came between them he found the sweet spot of her nerves and moved himself there, inflating her pleasure, pushing her higher and higher into the heavens. His tongue tormented her mouth, his hands controlled her breasts; she was lost to him and this.

She needed him. After four weeks of being made love to by the phantom memories of Cesare Durante, being held, touched and kissed by the real thing was a heavenly balm.

Pleasure rose, a wave upon which she was travelling, her breath torn from her, need insatiable and fierce. She ached for him—nothing else mattered. In that moment, she wasn't thinking of Laurence, the hedge fund or the deal Cesare had proposed, she was simply a being born of sensation and need.

Lights danced behind her eyelids, bright and persistent, flickering until they became one big inferno, making sight impossible. But who needed sight when there were feelings such as this?

'Please.' She rolled her hips again, her release so close, so tantalisingly close.

'No.' He lifted his head, the word whipping her as though he'd sliced her with a blade.

Her breath was still coming in pants, her eyes awash with desire as she stared up at him in utter disbelief. He eased her feet to the floor, his eyes hard in his handsome, symmetrical face. If it weren't for the dark slashes of colour across his cheekbones, she would have said he had been completely unmoved by what had just happened. But she'd *felt* his response; she knew his desire to be as fierce as her own.

Except now he was looking at her with a clinical detachment, a sense of complete unconcern, as if nothing had even happened between them. He was all business, ruthless, concentrated, intense.

'You will become my mistress. For two weeks.' He held his hand up, two fingers raised. 'In exchange,' he added darkly, 'I will show you a kind of pleasure you can only imagine.'

Jemima swallowed, her traitorous body refusing to listen to sense, refusing to care that he was using her desire to blackmail her.

'I'm not for sale.'

His expression showed mocking amusement. 'Everyone is for sale, for the right price.' He skimmed his eyes over her body. 'You want me to save your cousin? Done. You want me to *please* make love to you?' He mimicked her tone and she winced. 'You want me to touch you all night until you can barely think straight? Done. Choose which of these prices is more palatable to you and we will go with that.'

Her fingers tingled with a desire to slap him, but damn it, he was right. She needed this; needed him. Her eyes showed frustration as they locked with his. She couldn't easily choose *why* she would agree. For Laurence? She would do anything for him. Her future was tied closely to his, but more than that, he was like a brother to her. Yet her love for Laurence had no bearing on her decision.

The temptation she felt to agree to Cesare's proposal had one root only—she needed him and she'd do anything, agree to anything, for that pleasure. Even sacrifice her pride? Apparently.

'And at the end of the two weeks?' she whispered, closing her eyes so as not to see his triumphant expression.

'You disappear from my life—sexually illuminated and your cousin financially secure.'

She swallowed, his words pulling her to pieces. 'And it's that easy?'

'Yes.'

'What if it's not?' She blinked her eyes open now, a frown puckering her brow. 'What if two weeks come and go and you don't want me to leave? Or what if I want to stay?'

His expression was as relentless as a vise. 'Not possible. I offer this and no more. It is a deal, an agreement, no less binding than any of the contracts I enter into on a daily basis.'

She nodded, but her heart did something strange in her chest, lurching from side to side. 'I need to think about it.'

His laugh was like the Niagara Falls emptying on her head.

'What? Why is that funny?'

'It is obvious you intend to say yes. Do not lie to me, now.' He lifted a finger to her lips, tracing their outline before pressing the tip into her mouth. She bit down on it with her teeth, not hard, but in a silent warning that had him laughing once more.

'You are unbelievably arrogant,' she muttered.

'Yes.'

God, he was—why the heck hadn't she been able to put him out of her mind? Why had he somehow got under her skin and into her blood like this? 'I don't even like you.'

His look was one of wry amusement. 'Then it's just as well I'm not asking you to like me.' He moved his head closer towards hers, so when he whispered she could hear every syllable of his words. 'Liking one another has nothing to do with what we are. I am asking you to be my mistress, not my girlfriend. It is a simple yes or no question.'

She swallowed. It wasn't simple, it was complex, but only because she wished she felt more strongly opposed to this. She wished she were outraged or violently offended. She was neither.

In point of fact, she was intrigued and excited. Yes, excited. A month ago, Cesare had woken a part of her that she hadn't even realised was dormant. He'd stirred her to life and, no matter what she might think of him personally, she had no doubt he was just the man with whom to explore this sensual side of herself.

Perhaps she could approach this exactly as he suggested: as a business arrangement. Oh, not in the sense that he was bankrolling Laurence. That had to be removed from her mind. This was a decision about whether she wanted to sleep with Cesare, whether she wanted to become his mistress—for a short period of time. It was about what she stood to gain from this—not financially, so much as physically.

Her eyes clashed with his and something locked in place inside her, something vital. She could make her peace with this situation because deep down she knew that it was her choice. He was providing an option, but she was only accepting because she wanted to.

'I have the Feranti e Caro fashion show next week,' she murmured, hearing herself and knowing there was acquiescence in the words.

'Cancel it.'

Angry heat fired in her belly. 'No way. I can't. This is my career and I won't let them down. I don't ever cancel a show once I've agreed to it.'

His lips compressed, his expression impossible to interpret, until finally he nodded. 'Fine. One night.' His eyes flared. 'Otherwise, you are mine.'

She wanted to tell him that people couldn't belong to people, that the idea of ownership was ridiculous and patriarchal, that it offended every level of her feminist heart. But she knew, even as those words flew through her, that a part of her had belonged to him the moment they'd met, and she wasn't sure she'd ever get it back.

Excitement buzzed through her; pleasure and anticipation, as well. It would have been easy to forget why she'd come to him, easy to forget her cousin and what she owed him.

Cesare made that impossible, though. 'I will advise my lawyers to contact Laurence. It will take a few days for the funds to transfer.' His eyes locked to hers, then he spun away, stalking towards his desk. He scrawled something on the back of a business card then crossed to her once more, his manner strictly business.

'Friday—meet me here.'

She dropped her eyes to the card, reading his confident scrawl.

Hotel Sable d'Or, Cannes.

He pressed a finger to her chin, lifting her face towards his, something in his eyes that spoke of promises and needs. 'Don't disappoint me.'

Her lips parted on a sigh—a sigh that was part promise and all hope. 'I won't.'

And then he dropped his head to hers, this kiss slower, more enquiring, as though he were tasting her, teasing her. It still had the same effect: her knees threatened to buckle beneath her and her mind went blank. It was all too brief, though.

'Dream of me.'

She nodded, because she knew she would, just as she had been, and his laugh was soft. 'I will make you forget whoever it was you slept with after me. I will ruin you for any other man, *uccellina.*'

Thud. Thud. Thud. One foot after the other. Faster. Better. His eyes flicked to his watch, checking his pace and then his heart rate, but only for a second. *Don't take your eyes off the goal.* He dipped his head forward, keeping his frame in its most aerodynamic state, and continued to run. Rome passed him in a blur, as it did every night, his body at one with this ancient city, her secrets breathing into his soul, ancient wisdom soothing him in a way he hadn't known he needed until he'd found his way back here.

He liked to run to the outskirts of the city, to the borderline slum in which he'd spent the first five years of his life. To stare at the building—it was still there—with the peeling paint and the boarded-up windows, the wall with faded graffiti as though even vandals preferred not to come into this part of the city. He liked to listen to the sounds, to breathe in the smells and to remember—this was where he had started in life.

And always at the back of his mind, no matter how hard he ran, no matter how much he achieved, no matter what his bank balance was, Cesare carried with him a latent fear, a certainty that if he didn't keep running, keep working, keep amassing his fortune, he would end up right back where he'd begun—broke, alone, sad and so hungry he could feel the walls of his stomach squeezing in on themselves.

He was thirty-five years old: that time in his life was decades ago, yet the memories were trapped inside him in a way that showed they'd never fade. Despite all that he'd earned, Cesare could never forget the little boy he'd been then—oftentimes grubby, weary, a boy people would cross the street to avoid. How ironic that he could now command the attention of world leaders, of kings and queens and, most importantly, of women like Jemima Woodcroft...

She'd been to Cannes many times and to this hotel, though never to the penthouse. This expansive, stunning living area—stretching the entire footprint of the hotel—was beyond her wild imaginings. Decadent in the French rococo style, with ornate pieces of antique furniture, it was sumptuous and romantic.

The word breathed its way through her mind and she quickly muted it. There was nothing romantic about this. He'd thrown her out of his home, more or less, when he'd realised she'd been a virgin, and a month later he'd propositioned her right back into his bed. Romantic? Ha!

She strode through the double-height living room, with

its floor-to-ceiling glass windows framing a view of the moonlit French Riviera in one direction, with boats lit golden and bobbing on the gentle waves, and in the other of this beautiful, billionaire's playground—equally glamorous hotels, and shops that made this part of the world so renowned.

For Jemima, though, the pleasure in Cannes had always been in the gardens.

The city was—and had been for a long time—home to some of the world's wealthiest residents, and the public gardens were a testament to that. Jemima could lose hours alone in the Jardin des Oliviers, wandering the olive grove, finding her way onto the perfectly lush grass and sitting people-watching, a large hat and sunglasses the perfect disguise to avoid being easily spotted here, where people were well-trained in picking out the celebrities in their midst.

It was a warm, sultry evening and the wind that lifted off the Bay of Cannes was fragranced with salt. She breathed it in deeply, trying to calm the furious beating of butterfly wings against her belly.

The money had cleared the day before. Laurence had been like a new man—the stress he'd carried for over a year dissipating completely. *'It's going to be okay, Jem. It's really going to be okay.'*

And maybe he was right. If the hedge fund returned to the black, then it would mean relief was at hand for Almer Hall, and the enormous debts that encumbered the property. Perhaps, after a decade of fretting about the state of the grand old home and the burden of keeping it in the family, things were finally going to get easier.

The sound of a door clicking had Jemima spinning where she stood in time to see Cesare enter. For the first time since they'd met, he wasn't wearing a suit. Instead, he was casually dressed in dark denims and a pale-blue polo shirt, the collar lifted a little in a way she suspected was a result of movement rather than a contrived attempt at fashion.

His eyes swept the room and landed on her almost as though he hadn't expected her to be there. The second he saw her, he began to move, his body striding towards her as if on autopilot. She stood where she was and all she could think was that she must look like a deer in the headlights. She spent her life projecting an image—she was paid well to do exactly that—but there was something about this man that made it hard for her to act as she meant.

'Hello.' The word emerged soft and husky.

He stopped short, as if waking from a dream. 'Jemima.' A muscle jerked in his jaw as he regarded her with eyes that showed an unmistakable hunger. He swept his gaze over her face, and she was glad she'd dressed up, glad she'd worn her usual armour. A face with the minimum of make-up and a body in a killer dress. Brightly coloured with spaghetti straps, long and floaty, it was somehow sexy without being obvious, and she loved it. His eyes roamed her body in a way it didn't occur to her to mind because her gaze was indulging its own feast, devouring him limb by limb until, satiated, she drew her attention back to his face.

'Here I am,' she murmured. 'One mistress, reporting as ordered.'

'Bought and paid for?'

'Not quite.' She heard the cultured tones creep into her voice and saw his eyes flash with something like contempt.

'Did you speak to your cousin?'

She nodded slowly. 'He's very pleased.'

Satisfaction crossed Cesare's face. 'I can imagine.' He lifted a hand then, his eyes boring into hers in a way she found impossible to look away from. 'Five hundred million pounds, and likely the need for more in six months.'

It was so much money. The idea that he'd paid that simply to get her back into bed was a strange realisation to grapple with. On the one hand, it was completely flattering—she had no doubt he could have, and had had, any woman he wanted. But it was also troubling, because it was a fortune to gamble if Laurence didn't know what he was doing.

'I'm sure it will return well for you.' Her voice didn't ring with conviction.

'We'll see.' His hands dropped to her shoulders, to the straps there, pushing at them slowly, his expression droll, his eyes holding a silent challenge. 'You're over-dressed.'

Her heart skidded through her chest; her eyes slowly lifted to his as desire slammed into her. 'Am I?'

'I'd prefer you to spend the next two weeks naked,' he said, a hint of amusement in the words.

The very idea of being naked in this hotel, waiting for him, existing for their coming together, filled her with an all-over rush of heat that engulfed her soul in flames.

'And you'd be naked too, I presume?' she responded acerbically, and was rewarded with a smile. A true smile that shifted his whole expression and made her heart thump harder.

'Certamente.'

She hadn't worn a bra under the dress, so when he pushed the straps farther and it slipped to the ground she stood before him in a lace thong and stiletto heels, her hair tumbling about her shoulders.

Cesare took a couple of steps back, his eyes traversing her body with impunity, lingering on the curve of her breasts, the swell of her hips. Everywhere he looked her skin seemed to tingle, as though it was his fingertips dragging across her slowly, feeling her, touching her.

When he lifted his attention to her face, there was accusation in his expression, a look of resentment that made no sense. But it was gone again so quickly that she wondered if she'd imagined it. His cheekbones were slashed with dark colour, just as they'd been in his office when he'd reined in their explosive passion.

She didn't want him to rein in anything now.

'You're wearing clothes,' she pointed out huskily.

His nod was slow. 'Perhaps you should do something about that.'

Her throat felt thick and dry. She stepped out of the fabric of her dress that was pooled at her feet, then kicked off her heels, conscious that she lost a vital few inches in the process, padding barefoot across the room to where he stood not far from her.

Up close, memories slammed into her, the kind of memories that were carried by scent and hormone, so that with every breath he tantalised her and reminded her of what they'd shared.

It was ridiculous to feel shy, but she did—or rather, unfamiliar, because she'd never undressed a man before. Though she'd been surrounded by enough naked men to barely even notice when a bare chest or bottom wandered past, given her line of work, it felt strangely intimate to curl her fingers into the fabric of his shirt and lift it from his body.

Her fingertips trailed across his sides, muscles bunching beneath her touch, until she reached his underarms and had to stand up onto the tips of her toes to lift the shirt the rest of the way. It brought her body close to his, her breasts against his hair-roughened chest, her nipples tightening in immediate response. They were so sensitive, aching for his touch, for his mouth; all over, she ached for him.

She dropped the shirt to the ground, her breath hoarse as she turned her attention to his trousers. Her fingers fumbled on the button and she bit back a curse, moving more slowly, forcing herself to concentrate.

But her fingers weren't cooperating. With a groan of frustration, she dropped to the zip instead, pushing it lower and then attacking the button. It worked. *Hallelujah.* His jeans opened, but it was all too much. She felt as if her nerves were vibrating out of her body. She walked behind him instead, pushing his trousers down from behind, glad for the reprieve from his ever-watchfulness, glad for a moment to regroup.

She crouched down, pushing his jeans to the floor, and he stepped out of them at the same time he turned around to face her. Her clever plan to rediscover her sanity was a complete failure, because she found herself at eye height with his unmistakable arousal. Her eyes lifted to his, uncertainty in them, and he held his hands out towards her. She hesitated for the briefest moment and then put hers in his so he could pull her up, guiding her body towards his.

Their faces were so close, their lips separated by only an inch or two. He stared down at her and her stomach squeezed with anticipation; she felt a rush of adrenalin and a spike of desire. She needed to kiss him. Her body lifted up, her mouth now just a hair's width from his, hunger consuming her.

'I'm not naked yet.' He growled the words, so it felt as though he'd breathed them against her.

'No,' she agreed. 'You're not.' Her hands slid into the waistband of his boxer shorts, pushing at the cotton, curving over his buttocks as she guided them from his body. He stepped out of the fabric and brought his body hard against hers in one manoeuvre. She gasped at the feel of his hardness against her belly.

'And now, your turn,' he murmured, crouching down as he removed her thong. She put a hand on his shoulder as she moved her feet from the elastic.

'Do you know what I've been thinking about since that afternoon in my office?'

'No,' she squeaked as his hands gripped her thighs, moving them a little wider.

'You. And all the ways I plan on making you explode.' His smile was devilish, arrogant, cocky, but it didn't reach his eyes.

'I have been thinking about you here...' He pressed a finger to her sex, and she shivered, her body convulsing at the lightest touch. 'About touching you here...' He flicked his fingers over the most sensitive cluster of nerves at her opening and she gasped. 'And here.' He pushed a finger inside her wet core and she moaned loudly, the hand she'd curved around his shoulder digging in, her nails scoring his naked flesh without meaning to.

'I have been thinking about tasting you here,' he murmured, his eyes lifting to hers, giving her a chance to object, to say something—anything. But she didn't. She simply stared down at his dark head as he pushed forward and ran his tongue along her seam.

Her body reacted fiercely to the unfamiliar possession, so his hands lifted to her hips to steady her, which helped a little. At first. But, as his exploration grew more intense and pleasure began to overtake her entire body, she couldn't stop trembling. Wave after wave of pleasure was making her shake. She dug both hands into his shoulders and surrendered to it completely.

Pleasure built and then she was tumbling off the edges of the earth, falling deep into its core where the heat finally matched that within her body. Her eyes sprang open and she stared out at the ocean, the bobbing boats, the ancient moon, the dark sea, and she felt the strangest sense of relief, of pleasure. And, inexplicably, of rightness.

CHAPTER SIX

HE WAS GONE when she woke up—and no wonder. Jemima pushed back the covers, sitting bolt upright in the luxurious king-size bed, jolting her head towards the window. It was bright outside; warm, too.

'What the heck?' She turned back to her bedside table and reached for her phone, squinting a little as she read the time. It was almost ten! She hadn't slept this late since—probably for ever.

Heat suffused her cheeks—was it any wonder she'd gone into a form of narcoleptic stasis? The things they'd done... all night. She moaned softly, memories slicing through her, warming her, and when she pushed to standing her body felt different. Sore, but in the most delicious way.

She luxuriated in a shower then pulled on a bikini and a flowing kaftan that had been a gift from a designer friend. When she moved into the kitchen in search of coffee, she saw a card propped against the machine, almost as if he'd known it would be the first thing she headed for in the morning.

Gone to work.
I'll be back tonight.
Rest up—you'll need it.

More heat in her cheeks. She read the card again and again, imbuing his husky accent over the words, and desire flared in her belly. She found a smile had stretched over her lips as she poured her coffee, and it didn't drop throughout the rest of the morning.

It was a stunning summer's day. Warm without being unbearable. By mid-afternoon, she was growing impatient to see Cesare. It was ridiculous—they'd made love all night. How could she want him again already?

She grabbed a towel and headed to the pool, determined to work off some of this energy with a swim.

It didn't help. By late afternoon, she knew she needed to pull out the big guns. She changed into workout gear and hit the hotel gym, running ten kilometres before coming upstairs to shower.

She was cooling her heels in the most frustrating of ways.

As the sun began to dip in the sky, she made a cup of tea and settled herself on the sofa, intending to read a few chapters of her book. Without realising it, her eyes became heavy and then she was asleep, completely exhausted, so the sleep overtook her entire body, making her limbs heavy and her breathing soft.

She slept until a hand on her shoulder roused her.

'Oh.' She felt groggy. 'What time is it?'

'Seven.'

'I fell asleep.'

His smile was reflexive. 'Apparently.' He ran a hand over her hair almost as though he couldn't help himself and then dropped it to his side. 'You were tired.'

'Understatement.'

'And now? Are you hungry?'

She blinked, pushing away the last few threads of sleep,

and nodded once more. 'Starving. I don't think I've eaten today.'

Something like derision briefly flared in his features, then he was reaching for her hands, pulling her up to standing. 'Then let's remedy that.'

He took a step back, loosening the top button on his shirt to reveal the thick column of his throat. It was stupid—just a part of his body, a part of the body that everyone had, and yet the sight of his tanned expanse of flesh, the hint of hair she could see at the vee of his shirt, made her mouth go dry.

'Shall we go out? Or eat in?'

'Eat in,' she said quickly without a moment's thought, and then, embarrassed, hastened to add, 'I can't be bothered doing all the stuff.' She gestured towards her face.

'Stuff?' He was already moving across the hotel to the phone in the kitchen.

'You know—make-up, hair.' She scrunched her nose up and his gaze lingered on her face a few seconds too long before he spoke into the phone in fluent French. Jemima had a passable knowledge of the language, but she couldn't keep up with his rapid-fire dialogue.

He covered the receiver. 'Anything you don't eat?'

She shook her head.

He delivered a few more commands then placed the phone in the cradle.

'So why bother?'

She blinked, not understanding.

'With all the "stuff".' He mimicked her gesture, waving his hand over his face.

'Oh.' She moved towards the kitchen on autopilot—more specifically, towards him. A smile hinted at her lips, except it wasn't really funny. 'Have you ever read those blogs or magazines? You know the ones: "stars without make-up"?'

He lifted a brow. 'What do you think?'

It was so ludicrous to imagine him scouring gossip websites or flicking through a glossy that she laughed.

'Is there really such a thing?' he prompted a moment later, reaching into the fridge and pulling out a bottle of wine. He poured two glasses then slid one across to her.

'Oh, yeah, it's a *huge* thing. I guess it's reassuring to know that even celebrities can look like crap without all the effort.'

His scepticism was apparent.

'Hey.' She lifted the wine glass to her lips. 'Don't look at me like that. I didn't start the idea. I've just been the focus of more than my fair share of articles.'

'You?' More scepticism.

'Oh, yeah. Come on, you've read all the stuff. How else do you explain my three phantom pregnancies?' She gestured towards her flat stomach. 'Bad angles, awful lighting, coming straight from Bikram yoga—whatever. Photographers make more selling unflattering images than they do for the ones where I look like I've just stepped off a shoot.'

'But you're beautiful.'

Ridiculously, given that she was a highly paid model and didn't go in for false modesty, her heart gave a little wobble at his praise.

'Objectively speaking,' he clarified, his tone no-nonsense. 'You are a very beautiful woman. You could go down to the Croisette right now and be the most attractive woman there.'

'Okay, stop!' She laughed at the luxuriant praise. 'I know you're making *that* up. I've got chlorine in my hair and I've been for a run so I'm all sweaty.'

His eyes narrowed speculatively and heat buzzed through her veins, so she was only aware of the sound of her pulse in the silence that surrounded them. The longer he looked, the more she felt, and after a few seconds the smile dropped from her lips.

'This isn't vanity,' she said with a small shrug. 'It's professional.'

'Oh?' He sipped his wine, his eyes holding hers over the rim of his glass.

'I represent some of the most prestigious luxury brands in the world. There are all kinds of clauses in my contracts but, even if there weren't, I take my job seriously. I feel an obligation to those companies—I've signed on to sell their brands and I do that best when I'm "Jemima Woodcroft"— not some beach-loving scruff.' Besides, she couldn't exactly afford to lose any of her endorsement deals. True, Laurence's hedge fund might finally be out of trouble, and soon he'd be able to start helping with the exorbitant costs of Almer Hall, but until then she needed every penny she could scrape together.

He was quiet. Self-conscious at his lack of response, she pulled her hair over one shoulder and aimed for a joke. 'I bet you never have to think about this kind of thing when you go out in public?'

'Generally not,' he drawled. Then, thoughtfully, 'So why do it?'

'Model? That's easy. It's what I'm good at.'

'The only thing you're good at?' he prompted with obvious disbelief.

'Maybe.' She moved away from him towards the windows, changing the subject out of habit, and because she didn't like to think about the life she could have led if things had been different. Boats sparkled like fireflies on the sea. 'It's a beautiful night.'

'Yes.' His voice was dismissive, intolerant for her attempt to find lighter conversational ground. 'What else might you have done?'

Her smile lacked amusement. In the reflection of the window, she watched as he crossed the room, coming to stand right behind her.

'I couldn't say.'

'You must have wanted to do or be something other than perennially attractive?'

The words were perfectly banal, but she felt a sting to them.

'Or perhaps not,' he added as an apparent afterthought. 'I suppose you might have wanted simply to be Lady Jemima and marry some lord or duke?'

She couldn't say why, but his question was hurtful. She felt a sting in her chest at that casually worded supposition.

'No.' Her response was carefully flattened of any emotion, though. Bland and unconcerned. 'I wasn't really into that scene.'

'Your parents didn't wish you to marry some titled rich guy?'

Jemima's eyes swept shut for a second, her face pale, and she was glad he was behind her, glad he couldn't see the brief, betraying hint of pain—pain at what her family had once been and what they were now. Pain at the fact her parents had lost their ability at and interest in parenting Jemima when Cam had died. 'They don't really involve themselves in my life.'

'You weren't saving yourself for him, some lord or whatever?'

Jemima spun around to face Cesare and wished she hadn't when the intensity of his expression almost felled her to her knees. 'Absolutely not.' She swallowed and focussed her gaze beyond his shoulder. 'Do you mind if we change the subject?'

'You don't like to talk about this?'

'Not particularly.'

'Your parents or your work?'

'Neither. Both.' A divot formed between her brows. 'Besides, this isn't a psychology session. You propositioned me for one reason and one reason only, remember?' She deliberately brought what they were back to sex, back to the futility in them knowing more about each other. It felt good to control that, good to keep a part of herself separate from him. He wasn't offering beyond this fortnight; why should she bare her soul to him?

'Right.' He nodded slowly, lifting a palm and rubbing it over his stubbled jaw. 'Closed subjects. I get it.' He pressed a finger under her chin, lifting her to face him. 'Did you have a good day?'

Her lips parted. 'Yeah.' A husky admission. 'You?'

He lifted his broad shoulders. 'I bought an airline.'

She blinked at him, sure she'd misheard. 'What?'

'Not a big one. Seventy-one planes. But it's my first move into the air travel industry.'

'So, yesterday you bought half a billion dollars' worth of a hedge fund and today an airline?'

His smile stole her breath. 'Apparently I've been on a spending spree.'

'Apparently,' she agreed, his proximity super-charging her blood.

She moved back to the kitchen, taking a sip of her wine. It was sweet and quite delicious, but she reached for a tumbler and filled it with water, knowing that she couldn't drink wine on its own without losing her head. 'And did the airline come with a convenient mistress, as well?' she couldn't resist asking. 'Someone to move on to after I leave?'

He turned to face her without speaking and they stared at one another for several beats, the silence somehow raw and tense. Jemima's pulse began to rush through her, and she was aware of every movement of his, every shift, every lift. 'Have you done this before?'

He slowly began to walk towards her, and her breath burned in her lungs, her body tense.

'Done what, *uccellina*?'

'Manoeuvred a woman into your bed.'

'Is that what I did?'

She swallowed and nodded, seeing no point in telling him the truth—that she was exactly where she wanted to be.

'*Blackmailed* would be another word for it,' she drawled, fascinated by the play of emotions in the depths of his eyes. There was no shame, only a hint of triumph.

'No.'

'No?' She frowned. 'You don't agree it's blackmail to tell someone you'll only help the person they love most in the world if they agree to be your mistress for a fortnight?'

Unapologetically, he reached for her, pulling her body to his, and his eyes held something another person might have taken as a warning.

'No, I haven't done this before,' he clarified. 'I do not generally find it necessary to leverage women into sleeping with me.'

A range of emotions burst through her. Surprise, relief, pleasure. 'I suppose you bat them away with a stick.'

His smile was wolf-like. 'I am not lacking for companionship.'

Jealousy was unwelcome and totally unexpected. It cut her chest right open. She stared at him, wondering where the emotion had come from, and why she should even care. She knew what he was like; she'd known even before they'd met that he was someone who went through women like most men went through underwear. She'd known when he'd kissed her that very first time that he was used to crooking his finger and receiving whatever—whoever—the heck he wanted.

'So why'd you blackmail me, then?'

'Why do you think?'

Distractedly, she toyed with the ends of her hair. 'I don't know.'

His hands found the fabric of her shirt and he lifted it. Not slowly this time. It was unceremonious, impatient. 'It's simple.'

She waited silently, watching him, revelling in the feel of the air against her breasts, in his closeness, the heat of possession he could ignite simply by being close to her.

His finger traced a nipple, running around the edges of her flesh, following the line of her dusky areola with lazy intent. His eyes didn't drop, though, and she felt as though he was seeing all the way into her soul.

'You surprised me, and I'm never surprised.'

He moved his body so that she was trapped between him and the bench, so his hardness was against her, and she surrendered to him completely.

'You were a virgin,' he continued simply, moving his attention to her other breast, teasing it with the same feather-light inquisition, the same insufficiency of feel. She wanted him to cup her breasts, to take their weight in his hands; she wanted him to overtake every single one of her senses.

'And you didn't realise.'

'It didn't even enter my head.' His hands curved in the waistband of her yoga pants so he could cup her bottom and hold her against him. She gasped, his arousal so firm at her belly, his touch so commanding, so strong, that she made a primal sort of noise deep in her throat, her needs overpowering her.

'There are dozens of stories about you—your lovers, your lifestyle—but aside from that, you are not a child.

No, you are very sensual woman…your body catches fire when I touch you.'

She shivered as he did just that, moving his hand to her womanhood and brushing his fingers over the sensitive flesh there. She tilted her head back and then his lips found one of her breasts, his tongue flicking her nipple until she was moaning, incoherent with the pleasures he promised.

'How is it possible you hadn't done this?' He moved to her other breast, but this time he rolled her nipple in his mouth before sucking it—harder, more forcefully, exactly how she needed it, the pressure setting off an intense cascade of feelings that had her pushing out of her yoga pants without realising what she was doing, needing him in a way that defied reason or sense.

Her hands moved to his waist, pushing at his belt, and he made a husky noise as he lifted his mouth to claim hers, his own hands working furiously to free himself from the confines of his fabric. He layered protection over his cock, and at the same moment Jemima lifted up onto the kitchen bench, he pulled her onto his length, entering her in one firm thrust so she cried out with the relief of his body's return, her muscles squeezing him tight in welcome, her flesh lifting with tiny goose bumps as he moved deeply, perfectly, completely at one with her and her needs.

Her hands tore through his hair, and she arched her back on an instinctive wave of pleasure, her soul tormented by this in a way she knew she could become addicted to.

His body was so broad, so strong, so completely dominating, and his hands ran over every inch of her, touching her—feeling, worshipping with his touch, until she was like dynamite, lit and ready to explode.

And then, at the moment when she felt as if she would burst, he cupped her bottom and brought her closer to him so he was buried inside her and his kiss was like a command, their bodies melded together. When she tipped over the edge of pleasure into a world that was all sensation, they were so close that she could feel his breath within her soul, she could feel his heart beating against her ribs, and then she felt his own explosion of pleasure, his body racked with the same madness that had commanded hers, his breathing as ragged and urgent, his cries deep and guttural but no less spontaneous.

There was only the sound of their tortured breathing as sanity began to return. Jemima blinked slowly, as though she were waking from a dream when she hadn't expected to be asleep, looking up at him and seeing him through new eyes.

Through eyes that were fogged by desire and satisfaction. By the newness of this. 'Is it always like this?' she asked quietly, hearing the words and wincing at their naivety.

He lifted his head so he could better see her eyes. There was a query in his expression.

'Sex,' she muttered, swallowing her self-consciousness.

His lips lifted in something close to a smile. She studied the lines of his face, the squareness of his jaw, the strength of his nose, the cleft in his chin. It was a face that looked as though it had been sculpted by Michelangelo. It was a face of perfection.

'Like what?' he prompted, his fingers lifting to one of her nipples, twisting it lightly, indolently, with arrogant possession.

Embarrassment grew stronger. 'So…' The word trailed off into nothing. Mortification made it difficult to frame her enquiry. She wanted to know if it was normal to feel as if she needed to rip his clothes from his body whenever she saw him, to fill her with dreams that were positively X-rated, to make her body ache for him in the day when he wasn't near her, and heat with desire at the slightest touch. But what if he didn't feel anything like that for her? What if she alone was mired in an onslaught of unexpected sensual enslavement?

'Sex is thrilling and addictive,' he said, his cock jerking inside her in a way that made her breath snag, because he was growing hard again and her body was tingling with renewed needs. 'But I find this generally fades.' He flicked her nipple with his fingers. 'I have never met a woman I couldn't get out of my system in a night or three.' His eyes probed hers—no, they lanced hers—a look of defiance and determination in his expression. 'This will fade, *uccellina*, and we will both go back to our normal lives soon enough.'

CHAPTER SEVEN

IF ONLY.

Cesare scowled as he scanned the contracts, aware that he was fighting a tic that had him looking at his wristwatch every few minutes.

In the five days since Jemima had arrived at the hotel in Cannes, Cesare had forced himself to stick to his routines. Hell, he hadn't anticipated that would be difficult. He'd flown his helicopter to Rome, arrived at his desk at the usual time, stuck to his meetings and his schedule, because why the hell wouldn't he? He hadn't missed a single day of work since he'd founded Durante Incorporated. It didn't matter that he owned the company and was now one of the richest men in the world. It didn't matter that he employed an army of executives who were undoubtedly more than capable of keeping things going—if not for ever, at least for a few days.

A few days?

The idea spread like wildfire in his veins. A few days with Jemima. No constraints. No having to get up in the morning and leave her sleeping, her beautiful body naked in his bed, her soft murmur of complaint as she felt him roll away from her, as though protesting the necessity of his departure.

As though she wanted him to stay.

What would it be like if he took the rest of the week off? If he woke her up by kissing her breasts, slowly dragging his mouth down her body, his tongue tracing lines across her flesh, tasting her, teasing her, delighting in her responsiveness.

A curse exploded from him as he scraped his chair back and stalked to the window. He stared down at Rome, his chest moving rapidly with the rise and fall of his breathing, something uncomfortable shifting through him as he accepted that this was different from what he'd anticipated, that it was at risk of getting out of hand.

Oh, it was just sex. He knew that. There were myriad reasons it could never—would never—in a billion years be anything else. Not least of all was her aristocratic birth, her air of being to the manor born, which was something he could never tolerate long term. Not having seen what people like her were capable of, or the way they viewed the world.

But more than that, Jemima was dangerous. She was like a drug—something else Cesare had never indulged in. He had legendary self-control; he refused to be tempted by anything that might prove detrimental to his life, his career, his business, his one-eyed focus.

And yet somehow, he'd willingly become hooked on Jemima Woodcroft. It was all the more reason for him to be firm in his routine, to stick to his schedule, not to let her influence him or affect his life in any way. No woman had ever shaken his convictions, no woman had ever so much as tempted him to blow off work and stay in bed for days at a time, as he wanted to with her.

Jemima was a first.

And why?

Va bene, she was beautiful, but that wasn't exactly a novelty—there were many beautiful women in the world, and in any event he wasn't the kind of man to value looks above chemistry and spark. No, it wasn't a looks thing. So what else could it be? Surely her innocence played a part? She'd been a virgin when they'd met and there was a novelty in that, a curiosity, because it made as little sense to him now as it had that night.

A dark emotion burst through him and he pushed away the dark intrusion on his thoughts—the idea of her having bounced from his bed into someone else's, the knowledge that some other man had made love to her after him.

Curiosity was natural. It was hardly a crime for her to have decided to experiment with her awakened sensuality.

And yet Cesare felt a sharp burst of rage that didn't bear examining. It didn't matter. She was his now, and at the end of the agreed upon two weeks he'd let her go and never think of her again.

It seemed impossible to contemplate, in that moment, when Jemima had been all he could think about all day for many days, but he didn't doubt even for a second that he'd succeed.

Because he was Cesare Durante and he hadn't met anyone or anything in his life that he hadn't had the mental fortitude to conquer. Jemima, ultimately, would prove to be no different.

The bobbing of yachts on the water was a mesmerising sight—hypnotic, almost—and Jemima found, as the days wore on, that it hadn't become less so. She sat at the table now, her hands clasped in her lap, staring at the boats as they moved gently with the water's pull, not fighting it, surrendering to the tidal ebbs and flows, the enthusiasm of the water to meet the shore and recede once more to its oceanic depths, and she felt a strange affinity to the water. The currents of this body were stirred by a power beyond their comprehension but simply obeyed an ancient, cosmic call.

Jemima was not an ocean, but her pull towards Cesare was no less marked than if he'd been the moon, drawing her towards him each night. Five nights in Cannes and she had begun to understand a few vital and key aspects of this man's personality.

He was punctual to a fault. She could set her watch by his arrival back at the hotel and by the time he left each morning. Every day it was exactly the same, almost to the minute. From this it was easy to infer that he liked order and control, that he was driven to tame every aspect of his environment.

And, just as Jemima's career had led to her making an art form out of being charming without divulging anything she truly thought or felt, she began to suspect Cesare operated on a similar principle. Oh, he was significantly less charming. He was definitely not a man who cared what people thought and therefore he didn't waste time trying to curry good favour. But there was something firm within him, some kind of wall or blockage, something that stopped her from ever feeling that she truly understood him.

That was a *good* thing. Understanding him, knowing him too well, felt like it would be a slippery slope to danger.

And yet, despite that, she'd arranged all this—a table set on the balcony overlooking the bay, candles dotted around the floor and hanging from the ceiling and a three-course meal already in the kitchen so they wouldn't be disturbed.

Not only that, a lick of nervousness was making her fingers quiver a little, so she poured herself a half glass of the fine champagne she'd added to the order, wondering if it might ease her energetic nerves.

Her eyes flicked to her phone, and at the precise moment she expected him the door pushed inwards and she smiled to herself, glad his punctuality hadn't failed him. Her nerves were already stretched to breaking point. She stood, focussing on controlling her outward response, pretending she was at a shoot, assuming a look of cool calm that she definitely didn't feel.

She saw his eyes as they ran over her body—she'd deliberately chosen this dress, the same one she'd worn to the restaurant the first night they'd met, the dress he'd pulled from her body the first time they'd made love. She felt the hunger in his eyes, the need in his body, and her own body trilled in response.

She was actually looking forward to this. Looking forward to sharing a meal with him—not grabbed from the kitchen when hunger finally drove them out of bed but a proper meal, across a table, with conversation and...

And what?

She understood the need for caution. In the back of her mind, she remembered every sentence he'd uttered that told her how temporary this was, how determined he was to resume his normal life as soon as their allotted two weeks were up.

And yet, they were sleeping together. It might not mean anything, in the sense of romance and a future, but it still felt strange to know his body intimately when she knew so little of his mind, his stories, his history and life.

'What's this?' He removed his tie as he crossed the room, hanging it over the back of the chair before stepping on to the terrace. The sun was low in the sky, casting the world in shades of violet and gold, and they bounced off his face so that she had to bite back a gasp at the sheer magnificence of him.

'A table,' she quipped, her voice a little raspy, waving a hand towards it. 'Somewhere you sit when you eat a meal.'

'You don't like it when I feed you in bed?' There was a growl to his words as he pulled her body. Heat burst inside her veins.

'Oh, I like that very much,' she responded with a smile. 'But I thought we'd try something different tonight.'

He said nothing, but his eyes showed a hint of something—warning, or a wariness, that she instinctively understood.

'This isn't a *date*—relax. I'm not trying to entice you into anything more than the deal we've made.' She sobered, scanning his eyes thoughtfully. 'What's wrong? Is sharing dinner against the mistress rules or something?'

A muscle jerked in his jaw. 'There's a first time for everything.' His smile was barely a lift of his lips. He stepped away from her, reaching for a chair and separating it from the table, holding it so she could be seated. But as she eased herself into it with a grace that was borne of natural instinct rather than professional training, his fingers lingered on her shoulders and he dropped his head so he could whisper in her ear, 'Let's see how long we last.'

A *frisson* of anticipation straightened her spine and her breasts tingled, her nipples tightening in ready response to his huskily voiced promise. But it was a challenge, a throwing down of the gauntlet, and she wanted to prove him wrong, to prove to both of them that they were capable of having a conversation that wasn't punctuated by sensual need.

He took the seat opposite, but didn't shift forward, so he was far enough across the table to regard her with a kind of scrutiny that filled her body with little electric shocks.

'I gather you don't generally date the women you sleep with?'

His nostrils flared as he exhaled. 'You have an unusual interest in my previous lovers.'

The accusation smarted. She shook her head in an instant denial. 'Not at all. I'm just trying to understand how this usually works.'

'Why?'

Her smile was rueful and lacking humour. 'So I know what to expect after you?'

It was both the wrong—and the right—thing to say. His features cracked with something dark and intense, something like absolute, visceral rejection. It was the first time in Jemima's life that she realised she could get some kind of dark pleasure from an emotion like envy. It was over in a heartbeat, his expression cleared of anything, but it had been there, she was certain of it. He didn't like the idea of her being with someone else. It was why he'd made such a big deal about the other lover who—out of pride—she'd invented.

'I'm not a good barometer of normal when it comes to relationships.'

'Why not?' In spite of her best intentions, curiosity flared to life.

'Because I don't have relationships,' he drawled, the words mocking, but she refused to be cowed.

'Why not?'

He reached forward and topped up her champagne flute without touching his own glass.

'I don't have time.'

She frowned. 'You have as much time as anyone else.'

'My work is my life.' He lifted his shoulders, dismissing her line of enquiry.

'Why?'

His eyes flared briefly with surprise, but he tamped the reaction down quickly enough. 'I employ over eighty thousand people around the world. You don't think I have a reason to be busy?'

'Mmm…' She tilted her head to one side, considering this. 'But you must have people who report to you, a chain of command.'

His eyes narrowed. *'Certo.* But I oversee it. Every aspect.'

For no reason she could think of, a shiver ran down her spine. There was such a mark of determination in his voice that it almost felt like a warning.

'Every aspect?'

'This surprises you?'

Her smile was instinctive. 'Actually, it doesn't.' She dipped her head forward a little.

'No?'

'That you're a control freak? Oh, I think that's patently obvious.' She lifted her gaze then, fixing him with a curious stare. 'Look at the way you manoeuvred me into your bed.' It was a joke, said with a smile, but his expression sobered for a moment.

'I presumed you were a part of the deal that night. I honestly thought you'd come with the intention of flirting with me, of seducing me.'

'I didn't.'

His lips flickered, a smile returning to his face. 'No?'

'You know that's not what happened.' She reached for her water and took a sip. 'Laurence wanted that night to feel social. Truth be told, I think he was probably intimidated as all heck at the idea of meeting you and thought I might make that a bit easier.' She bit down on her lip. 'It's not like he threw me to the wolves—or wolf, in this case.'

Amusement sparkled in Cesare's eyes. 'And yet, here you are, in the midst of the wolf's den.'

'I don't think wolves live in dens.'

'They rear their young in them.'

Surprise at his knowledge had her arching her eyebrow. 'How do you know that?'

'I have a place in Alaska. I go there when I need to work without disruption. A few times a year at least. I learned very quickly that if I didn't become an expert in the local wildlife I wouldn't live very long.'

'What's it like?' she asked, momentarily distracted.

'Alaska?'

She nodded. 'Your place there.'

'It's… You would hate it,' he laughed ruefully, the sound doing strange things to her nerve endings.

'Why?'

'Because it's as far from this as you can imagine.' He waved a hand around the balcony, so beautiful, so luxurious, at the boats bobbing in the background, the air of wealth that was everywhere you cared to look in Cannes.

'It's an old log cabin, built some time in the sixties. It's in the middle of nowhere—you have to either hike for twelve hours to reach it, or you can fly in and land on the lake. The forest is too thick to bring even a helicopter down. When I bought the place, there was no kitchen, no bathroom, nothing. Eventually, I added a small room with basic amenities—no hot water, though—and there's now a small solar-powered generator that means I can run a light and a fridge.'

'Wow.'

'You cannot imagine me there?'

'I didn't say that.' The first time she'd met him, hadn't she been reminded a little of a wild animal? Though he dressed himself in bespoke Savile Row suits, he was clearly a man ruled by passions, powerful in a way that was wild and untamed. 'What do you do while you're there?'

'I work, *uccellina*.' The words held a gentle reminder. 'And sometimes I fish.'

'How can you work? Is there cell reception?'

'Some kinds of work require a complete lack of interruption. I do my best strategising out there. It's where I tend to have big-picture realisations.'

'So you can see the forest for the trees?' she prompted, a smile playing around her lips.

'Exactly.' He rewarded her pun with a grin of his own.

'It sounds kind of amazing.'

He laughed, dismissing her conclusion. 'I think you would truly hate it. There are bugs and bears and leeches and there is not a lot to do.'

She bristled at the implication contained in his words. 'And because I'm a model I can't also like the outdoors?'

'Because you are a model, or because you were raised in a particular way.' He said the words with undisguised scorn that had a thousand questions filling her mind. 'Take your pick.'

'What do you know about the way I was raised?'

His expression was darkly speculative. 'I can imagine.'

'I doubt that.'

'Let's see. Your parents were proud of you but somewhat removed from your day-to-day life. You had a nanny, possibly two, who taught you from a young age—languages, reading and etiquette, because old-fashioned manners mattered almost more than anything else to your parents. You were sent away to school at some point, though you never had much pressure put on you to achieve academically because your future was secured irrespective of your grades. You were encouraged to socialise in a certain set, with your parents ensuring you spent your time with "suitable" children. You received an allowance—a generous one—and knew you had a trust fund waiting for you. All of your closest friends were of a similar social standing to you. Am I wrong in any of this, *uccellina*?'

He wasn't. In fact, his rendition of her childhood was so accurate that a shiver danced over her spine. The one thing he'd missed out was the loneliness she'd felt after Cameron had died. Loneliness at having lost a beloved older brother,

her companion and friend, and loneliness at the way her parents had seemed to withdraw from her, pulling back so she was an island in the midst of everyone's grief, completely set aside from the world. Only Laurence had understood—Laurence, who had been close in age to Cameron, who'd considered him one of his closest friends.

Her voice shook a little, the effect of his summary cutting deep. 'And, because of this, you think I can't enjoy the outdoors?'

'You tell me,' he invited.

She breathed in air that was fragranced partly by the salt of the ocean and partly by his masculinity, and her body responded, her heart pounding with the intensity of her pulse.

'I travel a lot for work.' She pushed aside the troubling memories of her childhood, but a frown lingered on her face. 'But always to places like this. I'm in Milan so often, I might as well be a local.'

His expression could almost have been described as triumphant. She continued before he could speak.

'But in each of these cities I make it my mission to find the gardens.'

He leaned forward a little, surprise obvious on his features, and she felt a burst of satisfaction at having confounded his expectations in some small way. 'The gardens?' he repeated, as though perhaps something had been lost in translation.

She made a noise of assent. 'The gardens. And, whenever I can, I slip away and lose myself in their little corners and hidden pockets. I walk amongst the flowers and I smell them and touch them.' She smiled, her tone conspiratorial. 'Sometimes, I even pick them.'

His own eyes lifted a little at the corners.

'Just one or two, and I take them back to my hotel and put them in a little glass on the window ledge so I can look at them for as long as I'm in town. So it's not like they're dying in vain,' she added with another smile, her blood heating when his eyes thudded to the twist of her lips.

'This I didn't realise.'

'I feel far more at home in gardens than I do in the city,' she said with a lift of her shoulders. 'I always have done.'

'Yet you live in London?'

She slid her gaze back to his face, to those eyes that saw too much. 'It's a good base for someone who travels a lot.'

He dipped his head in silent concession, but when their eyes met she felt a rush of adrenalin, a surge of need that almost overpowered her.

'I ordered dinner. It's in the kitchen.' She stood a little abruptly, so she took a moment to calm her flustered nerves. 'I won't be long.'

She'd half-expected him to follow behind, to pursue the line of questioning, given that she hadn't really answered him, but he didn't, and she was glad. Glad for space, glad to have room to breathe, to gather her thoughts.

A tray of seafood had been expertly prepared. Oysters, scampi, scallops, calamari. She lifted the stainless steel lid from the platter and moved back to the balcony, her heart giving a little skip when her eyes landed on Cesare once more. He sat with his legs wide, his frame relaxed in the chair, his eyes fixed on the view over the bay, so she had a few seconds to observe him in that moment of unguarded repose. Except he wasn't unguarded; not really.

There was a tightness and readiness about him that seemed ever-present. As though he never really relaxed. Even his time spent in Alaska was probably spent like this—tightly coiled and ready to pounce.

He turned to her almost immediately so she skidded her eyes away and pasted a smile on her face, placing the platter of seafood in the middle of the table. Before she could take her seat, his hand curved around her wrist, holding her steady. His eyes searched hers thoughtfully, probing, reading, and she held her breath without realising it.

She wondered if he was going to speak, but he didn't. He simply looked, and she felt as though the earth was tipping a little, making it hard to keep her balance.

It was the work of an instant. He dropped her hand, smiled in that way he had that was more a replica of a smile than a genuine look of pleasure, and turned his attention to the food.

'When is your fashion show?'

She blinked, her mind temporarily blank before she recalled the Ferante e Caro runway she was committed to take part in.

'Saturday afternoon.'

He nodded. 'In London?'

'Yeah.'

Silence. She watched as he lifted an oyster from the tray, ate it then placed the shell down. 'So why did you come with Laurence that evening?'

'I told you, he thought it would be—'

He shook his head. 'That's why he asked you. Why did you accept?'

'Because he asked me to,' she said after a slight pause, spearing a piece of calamari with her fork. 'And because he's my cousin.'

His eyes narrowed. 'It's more than that.'

'Oh?'

'You were anxious about the hedge fund.'

She bit down on her lower lip. She was wary—wary of saying too much, of betraying Laurence's trust. And yet she felt herself wanting to open up to Cesare. She trusted him in a way she wasn't sure he deserved. 'Yes.' It was a closed off answer.

She reached for her champagne, sipping it slowly. Then she added, 'He's worked hard. I didn't want to see him lose it all.'

She could practically see the wheels turning. 'But you could have afforded to bail him out.'

'Half a billion pounds' worth?' She refuted that with a grimace. 'Not anything like it.'

'Your parents, then? Your aunt and uncle?'

Briefly, her eyes swept shut, and she saw her parents. She saw them as they were now, so pale and weak, worn out by grief and its relentless toll, weathered by life in a way only those who had walked a path like theirs could understand. And, out of nowhere, she saw them as they'd been then.

Before.

Vibrant and happy, always throwing parties and entertaining, laughing and dancing in the corridors of Almer Hall.

'No.' Her answer, again, was short. 'No one could help him.'

It undoubtedly sparked more questions, but suddenly she was a little worn out herself. This had been a foolish idea.

She was trying to turn a sow's ear into a silk purse, and to what end? This was what it was.

A short relationship—no, not even that. She didn't know the word to describe their agreement, but she inherently understood its limitations and the fact it wasn't a real relationship.

With a heart that was suddenly heavy and a body that was as much Cesare's as ever, she moved around to Cesare's side of the table. 'On second thought, I think we should eat dinner later.'

CHAPTER EIGHT

SHE WAS TRANSFORMED.

Cesare watched as Jemima moved the length of the runway, her body like silk floating in the breeze, so elegant and effortless, her steps more like a ballet, a glide. The appeal of the clothes was dwarfed by her beauty, their design made insignificant by her universal appeal.

Her hair had been braided and looped around her head, and she wore subtle make-up: perfect, immaculate. She was irrefutably stunning, but from where he sat in the front row he ached to reach up and pull her hair loose, to tousle it about her shoulders and smudge her lipstick, as he loved seeing it after their kisses. He wanted to kiss her until her mascara had been blinked loose and her cheeks were pink despite the foundation. He wanted her to be *uccellina* again, not this—Jemima Woodcroft.

She paused at the end of the runway, spinning slowly, her smile different from the other models'—she had the ability to light up a room, and he was certain he wasn't the only man present who felt that her pleasure was all for him.

To confirm this, he looked around, his eyes drifting through the audience. It was predominantly women, but everyone—male or female—was transfixed by Jemima. She was famous around the world but amongst these people—fashion devotees—she was like a goddess and they stared at her accordingly.

His gaze wrenched back to her and now he paid proper attention to the outfit, to the gauzy, transparent nature of the skirt that showed her slender legs and hinted at the pale underwear she had on. The blazer was structured and navy-blue with brass buttons but she wore nothing beneath it, and the hint of her cleavage was displayed by the vee at its neck.

He continued to watch her, an expression on his face that anyone in attendance might have regarded as bland—mildly speculative, at most—even when something was stirring to life inside him, beating hard like a drum against his chest.

She looked beautiful, and she was there for all the world to see. He wasn't used to a sensation of jealousy, nor the tight grip of possession, but he recognised it, just as surely as he recognised the desire to go onto the stage and wrap her in his arms, throw her over his shoulder and carry her back to Cannes. But this was her life—her real life—and he had no place caring how people looked at her, nor wondering if they were mentally stripping her naked.

His mood didn't improve as the night wore on. He was glad when the fashion show wrapped, glad when a thin man dressed all in black and holding a clipboard came up to him, a deferential expression on his face. 'Mr Durante? Jemima's asked for you to come backstage.'

He stood, moving through the crowd, past security and into a crowded dressing area. The noise was deafening. Models, models and more models, all in a state of undress. His eyes scanned the room, looking for only one. She was changed already, into a pair of skinny leather trousers and a silk camisole that showed the outline of her breasts and the slender fragility of her arms and shoulders. Her hair was loose around her face, just as he'd ached to see it.

'Hi.' There was a shyness to her as she saw him approaching and paused mid-way through unclipping an earring.

His first instinct was to tell her how well she'd done,

that she'd been beautiful, that she'd been captivating, but he said none of those things. Surely she already knew them to be true? And saying them felt wrong, given what they were to one another.

'Did you enjoy the show?' she prompted, removing the earring and placing it on the glass shelf behind her.

Had he? He didn't get a chance to answer. Two women came over and wrapped Jemima in their arms, the floral fragrance of their perfume almost overwhelming. 'You ready, babe?'

Jemima's voice stood out, so cultured and elegant. 'I will be soon. Just give me five, okay?'

One of the other models turned to regard Cesare, her eyes inspecting him with slow curiosity.

'Who's this?'

'Just a friend,' Jemima rushed out, her cheeks heating with pink. He wondered at his impulse to contradict her—they weren't even friends. Could he blame her for not knowing exactly how to define their relationship?

'You should bring him along,' the other one purred.

'I might. Five minutes, okay? Tell Larry I'll be out soon.'

'Hurry. I need a Ginsecco.'

They disappeared as quickly as they'd arrived.

'The after-party,' Jemima explained.

'Ginsecco?'

'Prosecco and gin.' She leaned closer, a smile making her face so familiar that his gut squeezed. 'Half of one is enough to make me loopy.'

'Jem?' A male voice this time. Cesare turned around to see a man powering towards her. Not a model—he was too rugged and unkempt for that. 'Bloody hell, it's been an age. You killed it tonight, babe.'

Cesare took a step back, crossing his arms over his chest, so he wasn't even sure if the other man noticed him when he drew Jemima into his arms and pressed a kiss against her lips.

Her eyes flared wide, though, and flew to Cesare, so he had only a second to tamp down on his first instinct—to rip the other man off Jemima forcibly. With his fist. Was it possible that this was the guy she'd slept with after him? He certainly seemed comfortable with her; their body language could pass as that of lovers.

'You're coming, right?'

She nodded. 'Yeah. Just for one drink.' She lifted her finger in the air to gesture the solitary number and the other guy hooked his fingers around hers, pulling her hand to his chest. 'One of these days you're going to let your hair down. I hope I'm there to see it.' He grinned, a grin that was pure lascivious flirtation, and then he kissed her again quickly, walking away. 'See you at the bar.'

Jemima had the decency to look embarrassed as she closed the gap between them. She lifted a hand to Cesare's chest, staring at it rather than him. 'Sorry about Tim. He's a photographer.'

He didn't say anything.

'The party's just around the corner, in Knightsbridge. Do you want to come in our limo?'

'No.' The word was out before he could analyse it. 'I have work to do.'

'Oh.' Her expression was crestfallen. 'I have to go—it's expected of me, contractually—but I generally only stay for one drink. Are you sure you don't want to…?'

'No.'

'Oh.' She looked away, turning towards the door where some other guy was waving to her, gesturing for her to join him. 'Well, I can come to your place after,' she murmured. 'I'll be an hour, hour and a half max.'

Temptation dragged on him, a temptation that made him

wary because he wasn't interested in anything other than Jemima's body, and only for a limited time. He needed to control this, to remember that this was about sex—the pleasure and hedonism of no-strings sex. She wasn't his real world any more than he was hers.

'There's no need.' He lifted a hand, touching her hair as he'd wanted to while he'd watched her move down the runway. 'We had a deal, remember? This is your night off.'

He thought he'd feel better. He'd thought reminding her of their agreement, the terms, of the role she was fulfilling in his life, would make him feel in control again, would make him feel powerful. But the confusion on her features that was eclipsed by hurt as his meaning dawned did the exact opposite. He wished he could swallow the words back up.

There was courage in her look as she met his eyes. 'What if I don't want a night off?'

Damn it. Powerlessness surrounded him. He moved his hand so his thumb ran over her lower lip. Her eyes fluttered closed, her lashes forming two perfect fans on her face. 'It's what we agreed.' He took a step back. 'My jet will be waiting for you tomorrow.' He slipped a card into her palm with the details of the hangar and his assistant's number. 'Just call when you're ready to fly out and my driver will collect you.'

She dropped her gaze to the card for a second and then looked back at him.

'That's what you want?'

What he wanted? It was getting harder to answer that, but there was always his office, his livelihood, his determination to succeed. These were things that would never wane.

He dropped his lips to hers, buzzing them for the briefest moment. 'Goodnight, *uccellina*. Dream of me.'

The hurt was gone from her features. Now there was defiance as she shrugged her shoulders, turning her body from his, moving towards her friends while lifting her head over her shoulder to call, 'Maybe. Maybe not.'

She dreamed of him in that strange way of haunted dreams, where the fragments seemed so real that she couldn't say if she was asleep or awake. She dreamed of his hands on her body, his lips against hers, his arousal inside her. She dreamed of him, and she writhed for him, and she woke up with a need she couldn't quell. It was a warm day in London, the kind of day that made her ache to be back at Almer Hall, where she could dive into the ancient pond, surrounded by mossy pavers and arum lilies, then turn onto her back, staring up at the sky until the sun formed little circles against her eyelids.

She'd done it a lot after Cameron had died. She'd wanted to escape the house, her parents, their grief and their arguments. She'd wanted to escape the whole world. In the pond, with its murky darkness, its ancient shape, she'd found a world all her own. In the water, she'd been weightless, her ears dipped below the surface so she couldn't hear anything except the beating of her own heart.

In the pond, she'd found peace when her whole world had been falling apart. She'd found relief from summer's bite and loss's tight grip—the water had made her whole again.

The sun stretched across her bedroom now, long and blade-like, brighter than a star. She lifted her hand, stretching her fingers in its path, and sighed.

Cesare filled her pores, her mind, her soul, her every thought. He was a fever in her blood.

She pushed the duvet back, showering restlessly and dressing quickly—a pair of denim cut-offs and an oversized shirt that had a habit of falling off one shoulder.

Her need for him was insatiable, but there was no point rushing. He'd be working today, despite the fact it was a

Sunday, and the thought of returning to their Cannes love nest with no Cesare in sight wasn't a particularly palatable one. She might as well spend the day catching up with friends, seeing as she was in London anyway, and fly out in the afternoon.

In fact, she made a point of going about her life, business as usual: tidying her flat, lunching with her closest girlfriends. She didn't tell any of them where she'd been, nor who she'd been with. It was easy enough to say she was on location for a shoot—she travelled so much for work no one really thought to question it.

Despite the fact she kept herself busy, the day passed interminably slowly. As her cab cut through London in the afternoon—she'd refused to call his driver, to appear as though she couldn't manage to get herself to the airport—she admitted to herself that she'd spent the day in a sort of a trance. It was as though her life, her world, was being viewed through a piece of glass smeared in butter. Everything was blurry and impenetrable. She'd been going through the motions but nothing had felt vibrant or right.

It was the dream that had unsettled her. That, and his comment the evening before, which she'd tried not to think about.

'We had a deal, remember? This is your night off.'

All day she'd pushed those words away, refusing to focus on them, but now as she approached the airport they found purchase in her brain and she couldn't quieten them.

'This is your night off.'

She knew what they were, what she'd agreed to, yet his calm reminder of that tightened around her throat like a vise, so she could barely breathe. As though they could so easily be reduced to a simple arrangement, a contract, she as someone who got 'nights off'. The idea of willingly choosing to be away from him… A shudder ran the length of her spine, a sense of foreboding, because very soon she'd no longer be a part of his life. To Cesare, this was just business, and she was a fool to have forgotten that, even for a moment.

It hurt, but the pain was good. She held it to her chest because it was like a shield—so long as she remembered the truth of what they were, so long as she kept in mind the only thing he'd ever want from her was her body, then she could take the best of what this was, enjoying the sensual pleasure without letting her emotions—her heart—get even remotely entangled.

His fingertips traced invisible circles over her shoulder, waking her softly. Her eyes felt heavy and she blinked them several times to clear sleep from their depths. Disorientation followed. It was warm, as it had been the day before, and she remembered the pond at Almer Hall as though she'd actually been there, so vivid was her recollection. Except she hadn't been; she'd been in London, and she'd been alone.

Craving Cesare.

And now she was back in Cannes, her body his once more, his body hers. Heat warmed her cheeks as she recalled the night before. He'd been waiting for her when she'd returned to the hotel. She hadn't made it four steps into the room before he was dragging her to his body, stripping her clothes, lifting her against him and making love to her as though both their lives depended on it.

'What time is it?' Her words were groggy, infused with exhaustion from a night of passionate love-making.

No, not love-making—sex, she corrected internally.

'Early. I'm going for a run.'

She frowned. He ran every morning, but he'd never woken her beforehand.

'Do you have to?' She rolled onto her side so she could

see him better and caught a look of something like disapproval briefly cover his face.

'I run every day.'

Her smile was teasing, her hand lifting to his shoulder. She pushed him onto his back in the same motion she straddled him, bringing her naked torso down over his chest so her nipples brushed his firm muscles, his hair, and she felt a thousand little blades of desire shoot through her. 'Why don't you *not* run today?' She moved her sex over his hard arousal and his eyes flashed closed.

A rush of power filled her. She bit down on her lower lip as she reached past him to the nightstand where he kept a stash of condoms. Her fingers caught one and she ripped the foil square open with her teeth, her eyes hooked to his as she wriggled down his body. Eye level with his arousal, she risked another glance at him, only to find him watching her intently. Uncertainty shifted inside her but mostly there was still that rush of feminine power, and instincts that had been genetically programmed were now rushing to the fore.

When she shaped her lips over his tip, she felt his body clench, his breath drawn in one ragged intake. She ran her tongue down his length, feeling the pulsing of him, delighting in his obvious pleasure and the feel of him in her mouth.

Her exploration was slow, curious. She'd never done this before and she wanted to enjoy it. She took him in her mouth and listened to his breathing, his guttural moans. She felt when his hands lifted to her hair, tangling in its length, and when his body jerked she smiled and kept going, knowing that she was driving him wild and delighting in that.

But then his hands were tracing her arms and he took the condom from her fingertips, pushing her away as he rolled it over his length, and before she could respond he was pulling her higher, grabbing her hips and guiding her onto his length, holding her down on top of him so he filled her completely. Now it was Jemima's turn to moan as he took over, shifting his body to thrust into her, deeper, hungrier, his hands on her hips firm, guiding her as he wanted her and as he knew she needed him.

And then his hands released her, leaving the tempo up to her, so she could lift her body on his length and satisfy her cravings as his hands ran over every inch of her, feeling her flesh, tormenting her, curving around behind her, exploring her buttocks before lifting to her breasts, cupping their soft roundness. His fingers tormented her nipples, as he obviously knew she adored, squeezing their sensitive tips until she was whimpering with the overpowering sense of pleasure that was tearing her apart.

It was beyond sublime. She arched her back and tilted her head, her eyes finding the ceiling as pleasure detonated through her, through every nerve ending.

'This is…' She had no words. But she was sure he must know, sure he must feel it, too—that he must feel like the world had stopped spinning just for them.

'Great sex,' he supplied as he tilted his hips and thrust into her harder, his hands dropping to her waist again, holding her on his length as he climaxed with a guttural roar.

Blood rushed through her veins. Her heart was on overdrive, her breath was burning and she was tingling all over. *Great sex.*

He was right. This was great sex. Just as he had often. With other women. Just as he'd go on having with other women when their time together was over.

It was a sobering thought, dragging her back to earth, so she lifted off him and collapsed onto her back, the reality of this unfolding through her mind.

He shifted and she waited for him to leave the room, to go for his run. So, when he brought his body over hers, their eyes level, it was a surprise she hadn't braced for.

'Don't you have a run to do?'

'It will keep,' he said, kissing her then, slowly, exploring her mouth as though the kiss could tell him secrets, as though the kiss could fill him with understanding.

He trailed his lips over her body, in the valley between her breasts, lingering there so she held her breath, aching for him all over.

'You were beautiful the other night.'

She couldn't think. He shifted lower, his mouth on her stomach, his tongue circling her navel.

'On the runway. Transfixing.'

'Oh,' she moaned, her nerve endings jangling.

'But you already know you're beautiful.'

His words were said with a smile but she felt something beneath them, something she didn't understand. His tongue flicked against her sex and she bucked, her whole body responding to the intimacy of his kiss. His hands curved around her thighs, pushing her legs wider, and she moaned.

'Was that the guy you slept with after me?'

The question came completely out of left field, and all the more so for the way his mouth was driving her body to another climax, his tongue exploring her slowly, sensually, so that coherent thought was almost impossible.

'What…guy…?'

The words were gasped between her teeth and he pulled away, moving his tongue to her inner thigh so she flinched as he kissed her sensitive flesh there, and she ached for him to bring his mouth back to her sex, back to the very core of her being.

'After the show, in the grey shirt.'

'Tim?' He was a hands-on, flirty guy in general, but

they'd only ever been friends. 'No.' It was a groan. Now his hand moved to her flesh, his finger pushing inside her so that she bucked again, lifting her hips in an instinctive welcome to his proximity.

'No?' His finger swirled and she whimpered low in her throat.

'He's…just a friend.'

'So who was he, then?'

'Who?'

'The other guy.'

She dropped her hands to his hair, running them through it, pleasure like a blade pressing against her. 'Please.' The word fell from her lips.

He relented, running his tongue over her womanhood so that pleasure filled her, release close at hand. But his question hovered on the periphery of her mind and a tumbling sense of shame rolled through her.

She'd lied to him. It had been a moment of silly pride, an embarrassment, a desire not to have him think that he'd been the sum total of her sexual experience. In the heat of the moment, she'd thrown it at him to unsettle him, but now she wished she hadn't. She wished she'd owned her inexperience without apology.

'Was he good, Jemima?'

The question made no sense. His tongue slid over her nerve endings; she groaned.

'Did he make you shout his name?'

She shook her head, needing to deny this, to tell him she'd made it up.

'Don't…he…it wasn't…'

And then he was bringing his body higher, his eyes latching to hers, his expression like thunder. 'On second thought, perhaps I don't want to hear about him.'

Cesare entered her then, swift and intent, and she cried

his name into the room, but he kissed her, swallowing the words, his mouth hypnotising.

Their bodies moved in unison, the possession mutual, the insanity all-encompassing, and they exploded as one, satiation enveloping them both, filling them both and tearing them apart all at once. He rolled off her, his breathing loud, and she pushed up to study him, her own pulse still tearing through her. She was out of breath—her fierce desire had pushed it all from her system—but she needed him to hear her, to understand.

She couldn't say why it mattered, but not being honest with him felt completely counter-intuitive. 'I didn't sleep with anyone else.'

He rolled his head towards hers, his expression giving little away.

She found it hard to meet his eyes but she kept speaking, not backing down from the decision she'd made, from what she knew to be the right thing. 'You were so arrogant and self-assured, and I hated the fact you thought you could click your fingers and I'd come running, so I made it up.' Heat bloomed in her cheeks. 'I didn't think you'd care, anyway. I definitely didn't think you'd ever bring it up again.'

His finger lifted her chin so her eyes were forced to meet his.

'I'm the only man you've ever been with?'

The masculine arrogance of that question was obvious and she rolled her eyes in response. 'Yes.'

His grin was her reward. Sexy, arrogant, devilish. 'You are mine,' he said simply, and her heart did a funny little two-step.

'I'm not anyone's,' she countered, and the words felt strange in her mouth, her tongue reluctant to frame them.

'You are mine,' he said again, and this time she didn't bother denying it. 'For now, at least.'

CHAPTER NINE

HE DIDN'T WANT to be in his office.

He pushed up from the desk, pacing to the window, his mind full of Jemima. Full of her confession earlier that day.

'I didn't sleep with anyone else.'

Hell, he felt like he was floating. She was all his. He was the only man she'd been with. It shouldn't have mattered—he hated that it did—and he knew he had to ignore the rush of pleasure that was pounding through him now. Two weeks had somehow whittled down to five nights. Soon he would let her go, watch her walk away and know it to be the end.

He looked around his office, a sombre expression on his face. He travelled often—it wasn't as though he lived in this one single office—yet here in Rome was his headquarters, and it tethered him.

To take time off, to spend that time with Jemima, was foreign and unpalatable and yet his body craved her—*he* craved her. It wasn't about *wanting* her, though, so much as about giving himself every opportunity to get her out of his system. Frankly, he was surprised that hadn't already happened. Usually, two or three nights with the same woman was more than enough. The first flare of passion was met, answered, satiated and disposed of and then his interest waned.

He'd never wanted a woman like this.

He'd never woken up craving someone to the point of distraction. He'd never struggled to keep his mind on his day, his meetings, his work. He controlled his thoughts with ruthless determination, always, but this time it was harder. With Jemima, it was harder.

Damned near impossible, in fact.

He had to work harder, that was all. He compartmentalised all aspects of his life. Grief from the loss of his mother lived inside him, but tucked away in a small space he rarely accessed. So too did childish hurt from being made to feel as a young boy that he hadn't been good enough. Wanting Jemima was simply another box he would have within him, and the same discipline he brought to all aspects of his life would mean he wasn't beholden to it.

Not after this week was up.

It was a resolution that stayed with him all day until he returned to the penthouse, saw her and felt a rush of longing that refused to be shaped. It infiltrated every cell of his body and overtook him entirely.

She was standing in the middle of the kitchen, except it would be more accurately described as a disaster zone. Smoke filled the space, despite the fact the doors to the balcony were thrown wide open, a bag of something like flour had spilled over the bench top, there was a broken bowl at her feet and, when she lifted her gaze to his face, her cheeks were beautifully flushed, her eyes wide.

'Don't say a thing,' she muttered darkly, words that were somewhat belied by the rueful smile on her lips.

His own mouth lifted in response. 'Doing a little re-decorating?'

She poked her tongue out at him and another wave of need assaulted his body.

'For your information, this was a *nice* gesture,' she muttered.

'Burning my hotel down?'

Her head jerked towards his again. '*Your* hotel?'

He stepped farther into the room, shrugged out of his jacket and placed it neatly on the hook by the door. 'You didn't like the decor?' he teased without answering her question.

She rolled her eyes. 'I was making dinner.' She eyed the bench in dismay. 'I don't know where I went wrong. I followed the recipe, but then I knocked the bowl, and while I was cleaning that up I neglected the oven and…' She shook her head. 'Stop smirking like that. I'll have you know I'm actually a halfway decent cook in my own kitchen. I just couldn't find anything and—'

'Decided dropping a bag of flour would help in some way?'

She laughed, tossing her head back so her blonde hair fluffed around her face. He stood very still, watching her, imprinting the view of her like this in his mind. It was somehow contrary to every preconception he had of Jemima Woodcroft.

'The flour had a mind of its own.'

'Ah.' He nodded sagely. 'I have heard of spontaneous grain combustion.'

'Right? It's totally a thing.'

'Naturally.' He grinned, holding a hand out to her. She moved around the bench after a slight hesitation, putting hers in his. She was so petite. He felt like a giant compared to her, so big, broad and oversized.

'I wanted to do something nice.' She grimaced.

The words held alarm. He didn't want 'nice'. That wasn't what this was about. He didn't particularly deserve nice, given that he'd blackmailed her into becoming his mistress.

Worse than that, he'd lied about his level of interest in the hedge fund, intentionally concealing the fact he knew Laurence had inadvertently bought into the next big thing at ground level. 'Nice' didn't seem right.

'Why?'

She hadn't been expecting the question. Her face clouded with uncertainty. 'I don't know. I just thought…something different.'

He looked around the smoke-filled penthouse, quashing down the feelings her admission had aroused. He couldn't remember the last time someone other than a chef had cooked for him. Nor could he recall anyone, other than his mother, doing something 'nice' for him.

'We can't eat here,' he said after a moment. 'We'll go out.'

She looked over her shoulder. 'I guess we'll have to. Just give me a minute to clean.'

'Housekeeping will take care of it.' He squeezed her hand then dropped it, taking a step back, physically putting distance between them as emotionally he did the same. 'Let's go.'

The restaurant, right on the water, was one Jemima was familiar with. She'd come here several times, usually after a film festival event or following a shoot. It was the preferred haunt of models, actresses, billionaires—anyone who was anyone in Cannes came here to eat, drink, dance and be seen. Which meant there was a slew of paparazzi out the front, waiting for their next pay-cheque photo.

She was prepared for it, but still she stiffened for a moment as the lenses clicked and the flashes exploded. Her smile was instinctive, so too her body language. She had been in the industry long enough to know how to walk in such a way as to avoid giving an unflattering angle shot.

Cesare, beside her, barely seemed to notice the photographers' attention.

Except, of course, he *had* noticed, as he did everything, and when they were seated a little while later he regarded her in that way he had, so watchful, so perceptive. 'You don't like being photographed.'

It wasn't a question. His observation sparked surprise inside her. 'I'm a model. It kind of goes with the territory.'

'I mean by paparazzi. You flinched outside.'

'No, I didn't.'

'I felt it. I saw it. No one else would have noticed, but I was right beside you, and I did. You don't like being photographed.'

'I don't like the paparazzi,' she corrected, reaching for her drink and taking a sip. 'I don't like being photographed when I'm doing something as mundane as walking or grocery shopping or going for dinner.' She lifted her shoulders. 'I don't like being chased through the streets when I'm going for a run or discovering my mail's been opened in the hope they'll find something scandalous. Do you know where one of those fake pregnancy stories came from?' she asked curtly, her lips compressed.

He shook his head a little, silently encouraging her to continue. 'I fell over and sprained my wrist. The doctor wanted to make sure there wasn't a break, so he sent me to get it X-rayed. At a place that also did ultrasounds. The invoice was sent to my home address, a nosy pap saw the name and the next thing I knew I was pregnant. With twins.' She rolled her eyes. 'So, yeah, it does make me a little wary, but I also understand it's just a part of my life.'

'I don't think people going through your mail should ever be a part of your life, irrespective of what you do for a living.'

'No,' she agreed, her anger simmering in her body. 'I

hated that. To have your parents read that kind of story...'
As if they hadn't already been through enough!

He was quiet for so long, she presumed he'd moved on.
She turned her attention to the menu, reading it quietly,
thinking ruefully of the badly burned dinner back at the
hotel.

'Do you dislike it enough to change professions?'

She shook her head. 'I'm not sure I *could* change professions. There's nothing else I'm trained for, and I don't
know if there's anything else I'd be good at.'

'Your parents must have had misgivings about your chosen career?'

'I was fifteen,' she said with a terse shake of her head.
'They didn't really have much choice in the matter.' It was
too much. She was betraying herself, her parents, the truth
of her history. She pasted a bright smile on her face. She
didn't want to talk to Cesare about her life. Not because it
was secret but because it was sad and she didn't want to
bring that into their evening.

'Anyway, I'm really fortunate. It's not an easy industry
to survive in and I'm established enough now not to have to
worry about my financial security. I'm pretty much guaranteed to get jobs and earn well.'

'Not that you need to,' he inserted silkily, and again she
detected the faintest hint of mockery in the simple statement.

She kept her lips sealed. He obviously thought she was
some incredibly wealthy heiress, and she couldn't really
blame him for having formed that opinion. Her lineage was
as it was, and Almer Hall was hardly the kind of house one
owned without being wealthy enough to support it.

He could have no way of knowing how the inheritance
tax had depleted her parents' capital—how Cameron's
death had killed her father's career so that for a long time

there was no money coming in and enormous bills piling up. He couldn't have known that the promise of lucrative modelling income was the only way a teenage Jemima could see of ensuring her parents—and she—kept the roof over their heads.

There was no trust fund waiting for her when she turned twenty-five. And despite her years of excellent earning, there was no safety net of savings for a rainy day. Laurence's hedge fund was the only hope she had that things would one day seem a little easier.

'What about you, Cesare?' She turned the conversation back to him as a way of preventing any more questions about her life and work. 'You could retire now and yet you don't.'

He laughed. 'Why would I retire?'

'You could afford to,' she pointed out.

'*Sì.*' He appeared to mull this over. 'But I would grow bored.'

'Surely you'd find a hobby?'

'A waste of time,' he said with clear condemnation.

'Why?'

'You think I should waste my time with—what?— orchid-growing? Golf? When I have the ability to do what I do?'

'I think there's more to life than work,' she said after a moment's consideration. 'Don't you?'

His shake of the head was slow and purposeful. 'That would depend on the individual.'

'And you don't want more than this.'

'Than what?' His watchfulness intensified.

'Than being a workaholic.'

'Is that what I am?'

She lifted a brow. 'You work seven days a week—unless

you're just doing that now to avoid spending your days with me,' she added, a loop of uncertainty rocking her a little.

'No.' He shook his head. 'I haven't changed anything because of you.'

She was sure he didn't mean the words to be hurtful, but for some reason they were. It was simply further evidence of how little this relationship was going to impact him; how little it mattered.

'I work seven days a week, and have for as long as I can remember. I can't see that there's anything wrong with this.'

'You don't think?' She sipped her mineral water thoughtfully.

'You disagree?'

'Well…' Beneath the table, she crossed one leg over the other, unintentionally brushing his calf with the toe of her shoe. 'It doesn't seem like you have much…balance.'

'*Balance* is a fashionable word invented to give people a free pass to slack off.'

She stared at him, gobsmacked.

'Next you'll be suggesting I take up yoga.'

The idea was so ludicrous that she burst out laughing, shaking her head simultaneously. 'Actually,' she said when her laugh had subsided, 'Bikram is incredibly good for you. Relaxing, physically demanding, clarifying.'

'Perhaps you could show me,' he murmured, the words layered with sensual heat, so her insides squirmed and her breath grew shallow.

'Perhaps.' The word rushed out of her as images of his body, naked and contorting into whatever shape she wanted, filled her mind. She swallowed to clear her throat, but his eyes were teasing now and she flushed to the roots of her hair, the transparency of her thoughts something she wished she was better able to conceal from him.

'Don't you ever get lonely?' The question left her lips before she could analyse her reason for asking it.

'No.'

She contemplated that for a moment. 'I would. If I was you.'

'I like to be alone.' His voice had a rich, deep timbre. 'And when I want company, I find some.'

Jealousy tore through her. She blinked down at the table, surprised by the potency of her reaction. 'Of course.'

'I'm far more interested in how a woman like you lived a celibate life.'

Fortunately, a waiter's appearance saved her from answering. They placed their order and, by the time they were alone again, she was armed with another topic of conversation, something much more banal and light, something safely distanced from anything too personal.

It felt good to keep things on easy ground. She liked talking to him, listening to him, and as long as they stayed away from anything to do with other lovers, or their personal lives, she could actually relax and enjoy the evening. It wasn't until they'd finished their coffees and *petits fours* that a sense of uneasiness crept back in.

'I'm serious, *uccellina*,' he murmured, and beneath the table his hand curved over her knee, so little darts of need immediately began to spiral through her. How much she wanted him was overwhelming—it was a physical need that seemed almost unconquerable.

Combined with the glass of wine she had enjoyed with her steak, it made her feel light-headed, buzzy and ready to succumb to her desire right then and there.

'What about?' The words were purred, kitten-like, and she had the satisfaction of seeing his eyes lower, sensual heat passing from him to her. She leaned forward a little, aware of the way her silk dress gaped at the cleavage, feeling his gaze drop there as though he were touching her.

'I am not a gambling man and yet I would have bet my fortune on the fact you had the same kind of sexual experience as I have.'

'You were wrong.'

Bemusement crossed his features. 'Evidently. Why?'

There was no side-stepping this. 'There's no big reason.'

'I don't believe that.'

'Are you calling me a liar?' It was light-hearted, intended to take the conversation in a different direction, but if anything his look of concentration only deepened.

'You like to keep people at a distance,' he said after a moment, the shift in his questioning unexpected, and all the more so for how right he was. 'Whenever I ask you anything about your childhood, your work, your life, you shut me down. Why?'

She was tempted to deny it, but to what end? He was right. 'Does it matter?'

He frowned. 'Not particularly. I'm just curious as to why you would make a habit of closing people off.'

'I don't make a habit of closing *people* off…'

'Just me?'

She bit down on her lower lip, gnawing on it thoughtfully. 'The parameters of this—' she pointed from her chest towards his '—were established at the beginning. Sex.' She dropped her gaze again. 'In exchange for your investment in Laurence's hedge fund.' Her stomach rolled with self-disgust. 'You didn't buy my inner secrets.'

'You don't think half a million pounds earns me a few secrets?' His tone was light, joking, but the words cut deep. It was her own fault for reminding him of the financial nature of this transaction.

Bitterness coated her insides.

'No.' She toyed with her napkin, wishing the conversation hadn't gone in this direction, wishing she didn't suddenly feel like this. 'There are some things even you can't buy.'

Thud. Thud. Thud. His feet; his heart. Cesare ran, and his body pumped; blood, muscles, legs, regrets.

When they'd returned to the penthouse the night before it had been immaculate once more, the smell of smoke dissipated, fresh flowers placed on the bench. They'd gone to bed and he'd made love to Jemima until dawn, delighting in the feel of her body even as something unpleasant was unfurling in his mind. It was a darkness he couldn't outrun, a presentiment of disaster he couldn't explain.

And then there was a darkness he could understand, one he had grappled with his whole life. Cesare Durante didn't like being told 'no'. He didn't like having his expectations confounded, nor did he like having to compromise.

True, this had begun as an exercise in sexual discovery. He'd wanted her physically and he hadn't much cared about anything else. But along the way the mysteries of Jemima had begun to unravel inside him, so that he needed neatly to tie them back together in order to be able to properly forget about her.

He needed to pull her apart, piece by piece, to understand her completely. Only then would he be able to walk away.

He needed her all to himself, and not just at night. They had four nights left of their agreed fortnight, and spending his days at the office no longer felt like a good use of that time. All his life, Cesare had been a person who did things properly, and he saw now that getting Jemima out of his system was going to involve more than sex. The things he didn't know about her made her all the more compelling, and the questions he had about her life filled him in a way only answers could relieve.

Without making a conscious decision, he turned around, moving back to the hotel. And as he went a plan firmed in his mind, a plan that would achieve his goals, a way to make it easier to walk away from Jemima at the end of this fortnight without a backward glance.

Relief flooded him, along with the certainty that this was the right decision, the sensible decision—the way to free himself of her magic once and for all.

CHAPTER TEN

ISOLA GIADA ROSE from the ocean like something from the prehistoric ages. Green all over, except for the strip of white sand that ran as a band around the island, and the turquoise water that lapped at its edges, it was breathtakingly beautiful.

'Just in case the airline, the hotel, the Alaskan hut and the hedge fund weren't enough?' she murmured, her eyes on his as he held a hand out to guide her from the speed boat that had brought them off the eastern coast of Italy.

'I wouldn't have thought someone like you would find that asset list surprising.'

'I think *anyone* would,' she corrected, his assumption about her wealth and background jarring. She dropped his hand as she surveyed the island some more. 'It's all yours?'

'Yes.'

'What else is there, beside this?'

She pointed a little way along the beach where a stunning building seemed to lift from the sand itself, all white walls and glass. It was architectural and compelling while somehow also being organic and respectful of the environment.

'There are some small houses across the island—for staff, when I need them. On occasion, I have come here for weeks at a time, and generally have a housekeeper and the like to run things.'

'Naturally,' she murmured, his financial situation something she couldn't comprehend. She knew he was self-made, but it was almost impossible to fathom how anyone could build that kind of empire from nothing. 'Have you owned it long?'

Something shifted in his expression. 'Eleven years.'

Curiosity moved inside her. 'Did you build the house?'

'No.'

She gnawed on her lower lip thoughtfully. 'Why do I get the feeling there's a history here you're not sharing?'

He eyed her slowly, raking his gaze from the tip of her head to her toes, and at the same time a light breeze lifted off the ocean, so her loose dress pulled against her flesh, and she shivered for no reason she could think of.

'Because there is.' He held out his hand, and she put hers in it, just as she had the night before when he'd seen the disaster in the kitchen and drawn her from the midst of the mayhem.

'And you're not going to tell me?'

'That depends.' He lifted her hand to his lips, pressing a kiss to her inner wrist. A frisson of anticipation trembled across her spine.

'On what?'

'On what you're prepared to offer in exchange.'

Her heart skipped a beat. 'I don't get it.'

'Nothing is free, *uccellina*.'

He called her that often—little bird—but hearing it here, liberated in the Mediterranean, kissed by the sea air and the sunshine, did something strange to it, so that the moniker pierced the fabric of her being and became a part of her, as much as her eyes and her lips, her heart and her lungs. *Uccellina.*

He dropped his head closer, so his lips were just an inch from hers. 'I will answer any of your questions, if you answer all of mine.' His eyes were asking a billion questions of her and she felt stripped naked, raw beneath his scrutiny. And though it sparked a sort of anxiety inside her, there was also relief—a heady sense of calm that could only come with letting go.

Letting go of her barriers, letting go of their boundaries. Just for a moment, here in this slice of paradise far from the real world.

'Deal.' Her smile turned her eyes from emerald green to a sort of turquoise as vibrant as the ocean. They began to walk towards the house.

'Do you come here often?'

'Often enough.'

'I thought you were going to answer my questions.'

He stopped walking, tilting his face to hers, his eyes slightly mocking. 'By my count, you have left many of mine unanswered.'

'Oh. So I owe you?' she prompted, moving towards him with unconscious grace.

'Definitely.'

She grinned, pushing up onto the tips of her toes to lay a kiss against his lips.

'What do you want to know, then?'

'What do you think?' He held her tight, his body not relinquishing hers, and she felt it again—a loosening inside her, the usual restraint she held on herself sliding just a little. Enough.

The one question he'd asked repeatedly came to her—the pressing interest in how she had been a virgin the night they'd met.

'It's not like everyone thinks,' she said softly, making no attempt to move away from him. On the contrary—she liked being close to him like this; it made it easier to think and speak.

He was quiet, waiting for her to continue.

'Modelling.' She cleared her throat. 'It's exhausting and competitive and by the time I've finished a job the last thing I feel like doing is going out. Half the time, it's written into my contracts that I'll attend an after-party, like the other night—it helps with promotion, and apparently it's good for my image.' She couldn't help layering cynicism on the last few words. 'But I was young when I first started working,' she said wistfully. 'And far from home, and everything was…too much. Too loud and fast, and people were over-familiar, and I was…terrified, if I'm honest.'

She winced, hating how juvenile she sounded. 'I found that the louder it got, the busier, more hectic, the more successful I became and the more surrounded I was by other models and managers and photographers and social media managers and everyone, it just seemed to make me feel lonelier.'

'Your parents didn't travel with you?'

She compressed her lips. 'No.'

She was surprised he didn't push her for information— her response had been seething with words unspoken. But he let it go, and she was grateful for that.

'So you rejected the lifestyle completely and chose to live as a nun?'

She laughed softly, lifting a hand to his chest, her fingers splayed wide across his broad muscles, her nails painted a soft pink, her eyes transfixed by the sight for some reason. 'Pushing people away was a survival instinct and I never really stopped doing it.' She risked a glance at him and wished she hadn't when her heart skidded almost painfully against her ribs.

'And yet your image…' The words trailed off into nothingness. There was a look of uncomprehension on his handsome features, his lips tugged downwards, a frown on his face. 'If I didn't know beyond a shadow of a doubt that you were innocent, I would never have imagined the stories could be so wrong.' His hands lifted, as if of their own accord, to twist around some of her hair.

A troubled look crossed her features. 'I was sixteen when those stories began to run.' She dipped her face and then took a step away, turning to focus her gaze on the glistening ocean. It was stunning—like a mountain of turquoises had been dropped to float on top of the water's surface.

'It was said that you had a long-running affair with him—Clive Angmore.'

She nodded, the pain of that heavy inside of her. 'He was married.'

'But not faithful.'

She swallowed, nodding a little. 'No, he wasn't. His reputation bled into mine. I was *sixteen* when we met.' She shook her head with disapproval now. 'I'd been modelling for a year, but I was still so sheltered. I didn't realise what it meant when he started spending time with me, coming to my shows.'

Her eyes blinked shut at the memories—memories she tried not to think about. 'When he kissed me, it caught me completely off-guard. I'd never been kissed by anyone before and suddenly he was...' She lifted her fingers, brushing them over her lips as though she could erase the memory. She couldn't—it was a part of her, a part of her being, and that experience had built a layer of her armour, shielding her from future hurts.

'He was?' Cesare's voice held a tight restraint.

'He was on me.' Her throat was dry. 'He was heavy and strong—you know. He was older, but really fit. Anyway, I pushed him away, eventually, and he was furious—he was under the impression that I'd consented to being manhandled by him by virtue of the fact we'd eaten dinner together a few times.' Indignation made her voice wobble and she kept her gaze averted so she didn't see the way his hands were forming fists at his side, knuckles white in contrast to cheeks that were slashed with colour.

'I just thought he was taking an interest in my career.' She groaned, because she'd been so incredibly naive back then. 'I was lonely and he was nice. I thought he was…a friend.'

She heard Cesare's harsh exhalation, but didn't look at him. She couldn't. Her feelings were all stirred up inside her. 'I learned my lesson. People aren't just nice. Not without wanting something in exchange.'

Silence followed her pronouncement and, when she angled her face back to his, there was tension visible in his frame. A muscle jerked in his jaw. His eyes showed a hardness that sent a shiver down her spine.

'Anyway, by then the rumour mill was in full swing and no one seemed particularly interested in the truth.'

'So you stayed a part of that world, the same but different, always a little set apart from your friends.'

She nodded. 'It's not my real world,' she said simply. 'It's my job. It's work.'

'But you must have been curious?'

'About sex?'

'Sì.'

'I wasn't.' And then her eyes flitted to his. 'Until I met you, I'd never known anyone who made my world catch fire.'

She looked away again, the admission somehow making her feel vulnerable.

When he didn't speak, she moved to fill the silence. 'It's your turn.'

'For what?'

'To answer a question.'

'Fair enough. Ask away.' His voice was deep.

Her mind exploded with possibilities. There was so much about him she didn't know, and even though she'd sworn early on in this relationship that it would be safer *not* to know all his secrets, it was overwhelmingly vital now that she understood him.

'I don't know where to start,' she said simply, honestly.

When she blinked up at him, a smile had crossed his face. 'Come. Let me show you the house.'

At her sound of indignation, he laughed.

'I'll answer your questions—relax. We have four days. There is no rush.'

Only it felt as if there was. In the seclusion of the island time seemed both to stand still and move at warp speed, so two nights passed almost in the blink of an eye, every moment sublime. Swimming in the ocean, lying on the sunlit deck, a whole day spent in bed exploring one another, learning, needing, rewarding. She'd fallen asleep some time in the evening and woken up in the middle of the night, starving and full of desire all over again.

On the evening of the third night—their second last— they walked along the beach as the sun dipped into the ocean. It had been a perfect day. They'd explored the island, walking for miles until they'd arrived at a waterfall. They'd taken the steep rocky path to its bottom and swum in the creek at its base.

Jemima still didn't feel that she knew Cesare's secrets, but she knew *him*, all of him—his passion, his drive, his determination, his hunger. She understood him.

'It's so beautiful here.' She eyed the ocean. Despite the unendingness of it, she knew she would never tire of this view.

'Yes.'

'You're not tempted to live here permanently?'

'Sometimes.' But it was obvious from his tone that he was joking.

She mulled that over. 'Where *do* you live?'

He angled his head to face her, a grin on his face. 'I'm a citizen of the world.'

She couldn't help but return his smile. 'What does that even mean?'

'It means I fill my passport up every year.' He lifted his shoulders. 'I travel, a lot.'

'Sure, but you must have a home?'

'They're all my homes.'

She frowned. 'I don't think it works like that.'

His laugh was gruff and he stopped walking, pulling her into his arms and kissing her as though he simply couldn't help himself. 'Why not?'

But the kiss robbed her of breath and the ability to think, momentarily, so she had to concentrate to get her brain back into gear.

'Well, a home's a home. I think by its very definition it has to be where you spend the lion's share of your time. It's where you feel most comfortable, the place you crave when you want to just exist.'

Something flitted in the depths of his eyes, but then he kissed her once more and turned away, taking her hand in his and continuing their walk. 'Where's *your* home, then?'

'Almer Hall,' she responded without missing a beat. And because she knew and understood him on a soul-deep level, she sensed the tension that tightened his body even when she didn't comprehend the reason for it.

'You spend a lot of time there?'

'No.' Her smile was wistful. 'I have to live in London,

but I go back to Almer Hall when I can…' She bit down on her lip, aware she'd been about to say more than she wanted.

'But?' he prompted, his voice gravelly.

She looked up at him and something in the region of her heart panged. The sun was low behind his head, the sky a stunning shade of pink with streaks of purple cutting through from the horizon, but nothing was as breathtaking as Cesare Durante, and the full force of attention he was giving Jemima.

'It makes me sad too.' She shifted her head so she was looking straight ahead. It was easier to speak without looking directly at Cesare.

'Why should you feel sad?'

'That's a long story.' She tried to imbue her voice with light-heartedness and failed.

'And you don't want to tell it?'

She never really spoke about Cameron—not to anyone other than Laurence, anyway. It was hard. So hard to think of what they'd lost, of the life he should have been living. And yet, in that moment, on this secluded island, she *did* want to talk about him. To remember him and mourn him openly.

'I had a brother,' she said slowly, the words dragging across her heart.

Cesare didn't speak, and she was glad. She needed a moment to rally her thoughts and find her way to the words. 'Cameron. He was seven years older than me, so I grew up worshipping him, and he treated me like a pet.' Her smile was laced with that particular brand of happiness that reflected loss and remorse.

'He was kind to me and liked to make me laugh. I adored him, and for my parents…well…he was the second coming. The heir to the title, to Almer Hall, the first-born son of the first-born son of a first-born son.' She shook her head. 'You get the picture.'

'Yes.' The word was tight, forced from his lips.

'He died.' Tears filled her eyes; she didn't bother to push them away. 'I was six, and I didn't understand. One day he was there, and then he wasn't, and no one talked about it. My parents didn't know how to cope. They buried him without a funeral—it was just them and a priest at the family crypt. It was like he'd never existed. I couldn't understand it. It took me a long time to come to grips with what had happened.'

When she shifted her gaze to Cesare, he was watching her intently.

'He committed suicide. He was thirteen years old and he decided to end his life.' The words were raw, cut to shreds by the knives in her throat. 'He didn't leave a note or anything, but I caught up with some of his friends a long time afterwards. He was gay,' she said thickly. 'And he had no idea how my parents would react. He struggled for a long time, apparently, and just couldn't see a way past it.'

She swept her eyes shut and saw Cameron's beautiful, happy face. 'He was still a kid. Problems seem a lot bigger when you're young, and there was a lot of pressure on him. He grew up hearing about his legacy, his responsibility, the future of our family.' Jemima couldn't keep the disapproval from her voice. 'Such stupid notions in this day and age.'

Cesare stopped walking and Jemima did likewise, but she kept her face trained on the rocks in the distance.

'I wish I'd been older. I wish he'd trusted me enough to talk to me. I wish he'd known what an enormous hole he'd leave behind. I wish he knew how much I needed him, how much our parents loved him.'

Tears fell unchecked down her cheeks now.

'I'm sorry,' Cesare muttered, and because the words

didn't seem sufficient, he pulled her into his arms, holding her tight to his body, his chin resting on top of her head. She stayed there, bundled against him, and breathed deeply, his masculine fragrance spreading along the rivers of her veins into every cell of her body. And despite the fact she'd carried this grief for almost two decades, it seemed to shift a little inside her now.

'I guess it's why I'm so close to Laurence,' she whispered. Cesare's hand, which had been stroking her back, stilled for a moment before continuing its reassuring journey. 'After Cam died, I was so alone. Mum and dad really went completely off the radar. It broke them. They blamed themselves; I see that now. I know they wish they'd done more, somehow made him see that they would love and accept him always.'

She swept her eyes shut. 'It was hard for them and they pushed me away. I guess I reminded them of him or something. I don't know. They were just destroyed by it. I spent a lot of time with my aunt after that, with Laurence. He was there for me when no one else was.' Her lips twisted into a melancholy grimace.

She pulled back a little so she could see his face properly. 'I came to dinner that night because he asked me to, and I'd do anything he needed.' And then a frown crossed her face and she lifted a finger to his lips to forestall a comment she anticipated he might make. 'But he never asked me to go home with you. That was all me.'

Something dark haunted his eyes. 'I'm truly sorry for what you went through.'

She nodded because there was nothing she could do but accept his words.

'I am surprised your parents were so liberal with you, after losing a child,' he murmured thoughtfully, as by silent consent they began to walk back towards the house.

'To allow you to become a model, without someone to go with you…'

'They checked out,' she said simply, and then found herself confiding the full story, even when it was something of which she *never* spoke, besides with Laurence. 'And we needed the money.' Her voice was thick with emotion. 'After Cam, Dad just…he couldn't function. He stopped working, so the repayments on Almer Hall got completely out of hand—the inheritance tax was pretty crippling even before—and we were in danger of losing the place. Mum and Dad parcelled off some of the land, but it barely made a dent.'

Cesare was looking directly ahead. 'And you use your modelling payments to keep them afloat?'

'I try to,' she confirmed. 'But it's exorbitant. They let the debt get way out of hand so there's millions of pounds in interest payments owing now. Honestly, there are times when I wish we would just sell it, but even if we did there'd still be money owing.'

He eyed her for a long time before nodding. 'And it's your home.'

'Yeah.' She blinked up at him and something twisted in her heart. 'It's my home.'

CHAPTER ELEVEN

'YOU GREW UP in the UK, didn't you?'

Beside her, Cesare pushed up onto his elbow, his eyes tracing her naked body with an insouciant possession that only served to fan the flames of her desire. They hadn't made it to the bedroom.

After their walk, they'd swum as the moon had breathed silver light across the ocean, their bodies seeking one another out in the inky water so that, by the time they'd returned to the house, they'd barely made it through the door before they'd been kissing, limbs entangled, hands moving quickly to disrobe each other of their underwear—not easy when they'd been saturated from the swim.

Lying now on the carpeted floor of the living room, Jemima felt heavy with desire, exhausted by the last few days but desperate not to sleep, not to express that she was tired.

They hadn't discussed it, but they both knew what the morning would bring: their last day and night together.

'From when I was five.' He lifted a finger, tracing the outline of her nipple, drawing delicate circles over her pale pink flesh before he dropped his mouth to flick the same nipple with his tongue. Her body jerked in response and she shot him a look that was intended to serve as a warning but which instead spoke of hunger and flame.

'But you don't consider yourself to be British?'

He pulled a face. 'Definitely not.'

'But you lived there. Went to school there.'

'And left again as soon as I could.'

'Why?' His fingertips trailed down her body so lightly that she moaned and tried to lift up, to press against him and encourage him to touch her more, harder, to satisfy her all over again. His tight smile showed he understood, and it also showed the restraint he was using in not doing exactly that.

'I hated England with a passion.'

Her eyes jerked to his. 'Gee, thanks.'

His eyes sparked with hers, though with no apology in them. 'It's possible I resented being made to move there and that my resentment coloured everything that happened afterwards.'

'Why did you move?'

'My mother got a job.' It was a simple statement of fact and yet she felt a pull of curiosity, a feeling that he was only telling her part of the story.

'What does she do?'

'Did,' he corrected. 'She died, a long time ago. She was a nanny.'

Jemima reached for his hand, capturing it on her tummy and lifting it to her lips, pressing a kiss against his finger-tips and holding it there as she pushed up onto her own side so she could see him properly, her body a mirror image of his.

'And she got a job working for someone in England?'

'Mmm.' He nodded crisply, his eyes glittering with a coldness that chilled her to the core. 'Gerald Montgomery White.' He said the name with abject disapproval.

She waited, watching him, curiosity expanding in her chest.

'You didn't like that?'

He was quiet for a long time, so she wondered if he was planning to ignore her, but then he expelled a long, gruff sigh. 'Not particularly.' He dropped his hand to her hip, tracing invisible circles there, his eyes transfixed by the gesture. 'She was a nanny, but they treated her like a slave. All her time was taken up by those children. And they were spoiled rotten, with a fog of entitlement trailing in their wake. I hated them.'

She grimaced. 'I've known people like that.'

'I'll bet you have,' he drawled.

'You thought *I* was like that,' she said, her eyes widening as comprehension dawned. 'When we first met! You were all things at dinner that night about where I grew up. You honestly thought I was one of those bratty kids, didn't you?'

His eyes probed hers and he nodded. 'Yes.'

She punched his arm, mock-playfully. 'Thanks a lot.'

'You had nannies growing up?'

'Yes.' Her expression softened as she thought of Cara. 'But she was like another mother to Cam and me.' And then, her heart shifted. 'She was fired, after Cam…' She shook her head to clear the memory, not wanting to go down that path. 'When did she pass away?'

'Almost twenty years ago,' he said. 'They didn't come to her funeral.'

'You wanted to keep it small?'

He shook his head. 'No. They were told of the date. None of them came. None of the children she raised—the children she raised while I was sent away to school.' His jaw tightened, his gaze awash with resentment. She lifted a hand to his chest, feeling the steady, deep beating of his heart with a rush of her own heartbeats. 'It was as though she didn't matter, like her life meant nothing.' His frown was deep, his expression so rich with feeling she found it hard to interpret his emotions.

She chose her words with care. 'That must have made it feel like she chose other children over you, and for nothing. I can imagine why you'd feel angry.'

His eyes slammed into hers, shock evident in their depths, as though he hadn't expected her to understand how he felt.

'Yes. It diminished her life. She deserved better.'

She nodded. 'You must have been hurt.'

'I was furious,' he muttered. 'I was sixteen years old and I'd spent six months preparing to lose my mother—she had cancer, terminal. But nothing prepares you for quite what that sense of being alone will feel like. It was the hardest day of my life, standing in the cemetery as her casket was lowered into the ground. That was the day I swore I would make the kind of money they took for granted.'

His features assumed a mask that was fearsome and compelling.

'I bought this island from a man named Ranulph Montgomery White—one of the boys she first looked after when we moved to England. He was a particularly nasty piece of work and seemed to delight in trying to make me miserable. I hated him and he hated me. So when this island came on the market...'

His smile was wolf-like.

'He'd developed a gambling addiction and needed the money. I drove the price down until it was a steal, and he was so desperate by then that he was practically begging me to go through with it. It's one of the most satisfying things I've ever done—sitting opposite a man who'd been a cruel, selfish bastard of a boy, who'd treated me and my mother as though we were nothing, and making him beg me to buy the place from him.'

Despite the chill that spread through her body, she couldn't help but feel a grudging sense of admiration at what he'd achieved, even if his motivations left a little to be desired.

'When I was sixteen, and I lost my mother, I swore I'd make her sacrifices count. And I have.'

'She would have been proud of you.' And then, with a flicker of a smile, 'Not for the maniacal revenge stuff, but for the incredible empire you've built. You are formidable and impressive.' She lifted a hand to his cheek, holding his face steady. 'She would have been proud of you, but I'm sure she was anyway.'

His eyes clung to hers, as though he couldn't pull them away, and she felt the same, her gaze locked to his.

'I've never known anyone like you,' she whispered, wondering at the heaviness that accompanied that admission.

'No?'

'Your determination is…remarkable.'

'You've said that already.' He brushed his lips over hers.

'Then I guess that makes you doubly remarkable.'

She felt his smile against her lips.

'I can't imagine how you did all this.'

'I worked hard.'

'Still…to build this from nothing…'

He lifted his head so she could see the strength in his gaze. 'When I want something, I get it. Not because I am lucky or charmed, but because I move the pieces around until I'm guaranteed to win.'

His words took half her breath away; his kiss finished the job.

It was past midnight. Not far past, somewhere in the small hours of the morning. Cesare presumed Jemima was sleeping. Her breathing was even, her body still. He lay on his back, his head tilted towards her, his eyes resting on her frame out of habit, so when she shifted, rolling slowly to face him, he was surprised.

'You were asleep.'

'Dozing,' she corrected, lifting her fingertip to his lips and tracing the outline slowly, her eyes following the gesture.

'Ah. Same thing?'

'No.' She shook her head, and there was something in her gaze that spoke of trouble and worry. 'I was thinking.'

'Ah. About?'

'The night we met.' She dropped her finger to his chest, spreading her palm over his pectoral muscles, a faraway look in her eyes. 'If you thought I was just a snob, like the kind of kid your mother looked after, why did you kiss me?'

He frowned. The question was valid—it was one he'd asked himself often enough. 'I wanted you.'

She pulled a face. 'Sure. But you're not someone who reacts to his every whim. You're disciplined and determined and a workaholic. No way would you have taken me home with you on a whim.'

His frown deepened, because her assessment was accurate and it filled him with a sense of impatience. 'You were there, and I presumed quite willing to offer yourself to me to make things go more smoothly with your cousin.'

He saw the fierce look of rejection fire in her gaze and wanted to ease it.

'I was wrong.'

Her expression shifted, but her eyes dipped down, away from his gaze, so he couldn't fathom what she was thinking. 'Yes. This was never about Laurence.'

He found himself wishing that were the truth, wishing she hadn't been motivated in part by a loyalty to her cousin.

'Not that night, no.'

'Not any of it.' Her eyes bounced back to his.

'This fortnight,' he reminded her, 'came about because of your need for me to invest in his hedge fund.'

She frantically massaged her lip from side to side. 'It's why I went to see you, but not why I agreed to this.' Her throat shifted as she swallowed. 'I need you to know that before—before tomorrow and before I…we… Before this ends.' She dropped her hand and her face was tight, her features taut. 'I don't want you to look back on this and re-write what we were.'

Something stone-like rolled through his gut. Visceral disagreement. He wasn't going to look back on his time with Jemima. He never thought of past lovers. It wasn't in his genetic coding. And Jemima would fall into that same category once this was over.

He made the promise to himself, but it lacked true conviction. There was a part of him that loathed the fact their agreed time was coming to an end. A fortnight had seemed over-generous, initially—when had he ever wanted a woman for so long?—but he struggled now to imagine her body being denied to him. And her laugh. Her smile. Her kindness.

He closed his thoughts down with the sheer force of his willpower.

It was irrelevant. They had a deal and he intended to uphold his end of it.

'I won't.'

'I'm not here for Laurence.' She pierced him with her bright green gaze then, and he found it hard not to pull her to him, not to kiss her so that she smiled and sighed against him, her body soft and pliant.

'Then why did you agree to this?'

'Honestly?'

'That's what we said, isn't it?'

Her nod was just a slow lift of her head. 'I wanted you. I hadn't been able to stop thinking about you.'

His eyes swept shut for a moment, and he hated how delirious her admission made him feel. It was the exact opposite of what he wanted. He hadn't come into this expecting to *feel* anything. It was sex—lots of sex, great sex—with a woman who meant nothing to him. More than that, she was exactly the kind of woman he wouldn't usually touch with a ten-foot pole—her aristocratic roots were a permanent mark against her.

But she was nothing like he'd expected, nothing like her reputation suggested and nothing like he presumed her upbringing would have made her. She was just Jemima. Sweet, kind and utterly compelling.

'Yes, I was desperate for you to buy into the hedge fund. And I'm so glad you did. I couldn't bear to see Laurence fail and hopefully, if the market goes well, he'll be able to help with Almer Hall soon, to take some of the pressure off me.' Her smile reached deep inside him and yanked at his heart. 'But I never would have agreed to sleep with you again, no matter the price, if it wasn't what I really wanted.'

There was danger in her promise, danger because it suggested she was offering something he had intentionally avoided all his life. Acceptance. Affection.

He was glad their time together was almost over, glad their clean break was at hand. Glad he could go back to the way things had been before this.

Except, he wasn't.

He thought of that future, he thought of not seeing her again, and something like a blade pressed against his chest, making breathing something of which he was painfully aware.

He turned his face away from her for a moment, a frown etched across his features as he studied the view from the window. There wasn't much to see—just the dark ocean with a single, shimmering triangle of moonlight right at its centre.

'So if I cancelled my investment now you wouldn't mind?'

He felt the movement of the bed as she shifted a little. 'Of course I would. But not because I've been here for a fortnight, and this relationship was predicated on that, and you'd be breaking your word or whatever. I'd mind because you made a promise to Laurence and he's counting on you. I'd mind because it would be a terrible thing to do.'

He turned back to face her and spoke softly, wanting to erase the little line of worry that had formed around her eyes. 'Relax. I have no intention of doing any such thing. But you are naive if you don't see how connected my investment is with your decision to become my mistress.'

'I...didn't say they weren't connected.'

'I propositioned you because I desired you, and because I knew that desire to be mutual. But you agreed because you couldn't not.' Her face paled beneath his scrutiny. 'I told you, I'm good at this. I manoeuvre all the pieces until I get what I want. It's not luck. It's not chance. It's how I work.'

It was dark in the room, only the brief glint of moonlight to provide any illumination, but he saw the hint of tears on her lashes. 'You're wrong,' she whispered. 'That's not why I'm here.'

Rejection fired through him, but he softened his tone, speaking calmly, gently, with only the slightest undercurrent of iron. 'Yes, it is. And that's okay. We all have our price—at least yours was charged in the service of something noble.'

His words were still ringing in his own ears in the morning; he hated to think of how she must feel, of how she was remembering what he'd said. They hadn't spoken again since. She'd turned her back on him and silence had fallen, so it had been impossible to push those words from his mind, impossible to forget how he'd felt and why he'd said that.

But as night gave way to dawn, and she continued to sleep beside him, he pushed carefully out of bed. It was their last day together, their last night, and the thought gave him no pleasure.

He wasn't ready to let her go.

It was the one thing he was certain of. The night before, he'd told himself it would be a relief to end this, but that had been a lie.

She was a distraction he didn't want, but her ability to commandeer his thoughts wouldn't disappear when she did.

He had set out to get her out of his head once and for all, but he hadn't achieved that—yet.

He needed more time. More nights and days to let his fascination burn out. He needed to forget her and move on, and then he could go back to being his old self.

Cesare strode from his room, barefoot and naked, pausing to grab a towel from behind the door as he went, which he slung low on his hips as he made his way to his office.

There, he set to work, moving the pieces into position, finding the information he needed, doing everything he could to ensure he would, as before, get the same answer from Jemima that he needed.

Bending people to his will was Cesare's gift, and he intended to utilise it again this morning. The machinations were beneath him, of that he had little doubt, but—more than ever before—the ends would justify the means. He was sure of it.

CHAPTER TWELVE

SHE SLEPT LATE, which was little wonder, given how long she'd stared at the wall of his bedroom the night before, her mind sagging under the weight of his words, his statement filling her with a sense of disbelief she couldn't shake.

We all have our price—at least yours was charged in the service of something noble.

It wasn't true.

Anxiety for Laurence had brought her to Cesare, but nothing that had happened between them was because of her cousin, or his financial predicament. She wasn't mercenary and her body sure as hell wasn't for sale. This had been about temptation, lust nnd desire.

Her stomach squeezed and her heart did the same, twisting inside her, so she made a little gasping noise and pushed back the duvet, looking around for her phone. It was charging, across the room. She strode towards it and checked the time—after ten. She took her time going downstairs, showering and dressing in a pair of white linen shorts and a silk halter-neck top that she'd modelled in Paris earlier in the summer.

Barefoot, she made her way through the house, unintentionally quiet, as though she didn't want to see Cesare. As though she wouldn't know what to say to him when she did.

It was another stunning day. Bright blue sky, turquoise

water, sand that she knew from experience would be soft and spongy beneath her feet. She pressed a button on the coffee machine, her eyes fixed to the view, her body awash with feelings she couldn't process.

This would be her last day with Cesare. She'd prepared for that. From the beginning, she'd known this would end, and she'd made her peace with it. But even after the night before, after what he'd boiled their relationship down to, the accusation that she was so mercenary, she felt an agonising ache when she thought of leaving him.

The coffee machine was silent but efficient. She reached for the cup and pulled it from the machine, lifting the fragranced drink to her nose first, breathing in the comforting aroma before taking a sip, her eyes fluttering shut.

But the second she closed them she saw Cesare. All facets of him, every side that she'd seen over the past two weeks and on their first night together, and her tummy rolled with uncertainty. Doubts and disbelief crowded through her.

This couldn't really be the end, could it?

She tried to imagine her life back in London. Going away on assignment, taking part in that world which now seemed even more superficial than usual, travelling home to Almer Hall and feeling her parents' loneliness, their grief, and knowing that she carried something within her that would eclipse it.

Life without Cesare.

She couldn't think that thought through any further. Cesare entered the kitchen at that moment, his footsteps breaking through Jemima's concentration, and she turned her head to the side, not quite able to meet his eyes.

'Morning.'

His silence had her moving her body to look at him properly, and there was an expression on his face she didn't recognise. He was serious, his features held in a mask of indifference, but his eyes—eyes that she could now read like a book—spoke of something bigger. Something important.

'You're awake.'

She nodded, even though it was more a statement than a question.

'Good. We need to talk.'

She curved her hands around her coffee cup to stop them from shaking and waited, her bottom propped against the kitchen bench. He came to stand opposite her, his frame deceptively relaxed.

'I don't want this to be our last day together.'

She wasn't sure she'd heard him properly.

'What?'

She didn't trust herself to say more than that. Just a small noise, urging him to continue.

He crossed his arms over his chest. 'I don't know how long this will last. I don't have the answers I thought I did. You've surprised me. But I know I don't want this to end.'

Relief began to shift inside her. 'I don't, either.'

'I know.'

His arrogance would have been galling if it wasn't so completely his trademark.

A smile lifted her lips.

'I can't take any more time off work. For this to work, we'd need to be based in Rome. If you wished to take on assignments, you could use my jet for as long as we continue this arrangement.'

Alarm bells began to tremor, just a little. She lifted her eyes to his, confusion marching across her face. 'What arrangement?'

'You being my mistress.'

And just like that, as if a pin had been slipped into a

balloon, her happiness burst. She stared at him, non-comprehending. 'Your mistress?' she croaked after a moment.

He nodded, reaching for her, and she was so shocked that she didn't resist at first. She let him draw her gently towards him, her coffee between them, his body so familiar to her, so perfectly matched; he was everything she wanted.

'It would be more of this, more of what we've shared these last two weeks, until we're ready to move on.'

It was as though she were being pushed towards a cliff in a little buggy over which she had no control. His words were so calm, so ordered, and he spoke with the total authority of a man who had made a plan and expected it to be adhered to. But the last part of his calmly delivered directive rocked her to the core of her being.

Ready to move on.

Her insides began to fill with heat, as though lava were being poured through her body, and she shook her head urgently, pulling away from him, sipping her coffee then placing the cup down so she could dig her hands into the pockets of her shorts.

'We can put a time limit on it again, if that helps,' he murmured, standing exactly where he was, watching her with eyes that saw too much. 'A month?'

Her eyes swept shut as disbelief spun through her. 'A month,' she repeated, nodding a little, even though she had no intention of going along with it. Disbelief was running rampant through her.

A month.

It wasn't enough. It would never be enough. Her lungs seemed to be squeezing shut; she couldn't get enough air. She bit down on her lip and tried to stay focussed; she tried not to let herself give in to the tears that were threatening to fill her eyes.

'I can help you with Almer Hall.'

Her eyes burst open and tore to him. He was watching her, completely still, his body unmoving.

'What?'

'I want to help you,' he said, but it was as though the words were being torn from him against his will.

'Help me how?'

'There are four mortgages against the title.' Now he moved, walking towards her, his eyes holding the slightest recrimination. 'You've been chipping away at them, but not in a way that will make any real dent.'

A sense of defeat made her defensive. 'How do you even know that? It's private.'

'I have ties at your bank.'

'Jesus.' She shook her head in disbelief. 'And they, what—handed over confidential financial information?'

'This information is not confidential—just difficult to obtain unless you know what you're doing. And I do know what I'm doing, Jemima. I want to help you with Almer Hall.'

And then, comprehension dawned. A wave of nausea crested inside her as she tumbled over that cliff, the little buggy she was in not equal to the pressure being exerted on it any longer.

Grateful for the wall at her back, she used it for support, staring at him for several long seconds. Had she misunderstood?

We all have our price—at least yours was charged in the service of something noble.

That was what he truly thought of her. She blinked, and for a second she felt a rush of hatred for him. Hatred that was all the more intense for the fact she didn't hate him at all and her heart knew that. Her heart knew why this hurt her so badly, why after everything she'd been through, why a woman who had—as he'd said—become adept at pushing people away, should feel his insult at the very centre of her being.

'You're saying you'll help me. But only if I accept this… proposition?'

His eyes flared with something she didn't comprehend.

'I'm offering to give you everything you could ever want,' he said simply, neatly avoiding having to answer the accusation she'd laid at his feet.

But he was so wrong! Wrong in every way.

'No.' A whisper. 'You only think you are.'

His finger pressed to her chin, lifting her face to his, his eyes probing hers. His question was raw, though, his words dragged from deep within him. 'Are you saying you want this to be the end? That you would wish to stick to the original terms of our agreement?'

She could fight the tears no longer. They filled her eyes, and she shook her head, knowing her voice would tremble if she tried to speak.

Relief crossed his features, followed closely by triumph. 'And nor do I. This is the solution.' He took her silence for tacit approval. 'Come to Rome with me for one month. You will have everything provided, but most of all I will clear Almer Hall of all debts. One month as my mistress and you can spend the rest of your life knowing your family's home is safe, that your parents can live without worry.'

A sob filled her lungs. She swallowed it away. 'Just like you said?'

'What do you mean?'

'Everyone has their price?'

For the smallest sliver of time, she saw remorse glimmer in the depths of his eyes, but then it was gone, arrogance replacing it. 'It was not intended as an insult.'

She made a snorting noise then, shaking her head. 'You don't think?'

'I wasn't speaking specifically about you—this could apply to anyone.'

'I don't believe that.'

'Believe it or not, it's the way the world works. I'm not saying Almer Hall is the only reason you'll agree to this, but I know that it makes it easier for you to say yes to what I'm offering.'

'You're wrong,' she insisted. 'The terms you've laid out make it harder. If you'd asked me to stay with you longer purely because you don't want me to go, because you can't bear to wake up tomorrow without me in your bed and in your life, then I would have said yes a thousand times over. But to agree to be your mistress on the same mercenary terms as before—after everything we've shared—how can you think me capable of that?'

His eyes shifted with something dark.

'Why do you want me to stay?' she demanded, unable to believe the worst of him, even with all the evidence at her feet.

A muscle jerked in his jaw, as though he were clenching his teeth.

'Tell me.'

He was silent.

'Say it. I need to understand what's brought you to this point. I need to know what you feel.'

'What I feel?' Finally he spoke, the words bursting from him, showing his frustration and impatience. 'I don't know. I've never done this before. I presumed two weeks with you would be enough, and it hasn't been. I know I'll get over this—that I'll get over you—but I need more time. I need more of you.'

'Wow.' She swept her eyes shut for a second. 'I've never heard myself talked about as though I were a narcotic before.'

He grimaced. 'I only meant—'

'That you're not over me. That you want me in your life until it suits you for me to leave, and not a moment beyond that. And what about me, Cesare?'

'I told you, you'd have everything you could ever want.'

'What if all I want is you?'

He looked confused, as though such an idea had never occurred to him.

'You'd have me. Every night, just like you have this last couple of weeks.'

'No.' She shook her head with urgency. 'That's not what I mean.'

'Well, what *do* you mean? What do you want? I will give you anything if you'll agree to this.'

His words pulled at something inside her, something that forced her to dig deep and really see what she'd perhaps known all along. His offer should have been tempting, on some level. More of Cesare? Even one more month, knowing the end would come, was still *something*. But she knew each day would be agony, that to accept his terms with the knowledge he intended to end it would be a form of barbarous torture.

She straightened, moving away from the wall, pacing towards the windows that framed the spectacular view of the ocean.

'Meaning what, exactly?' Her voice was hoarse, her tender heart trying to come to grips with the realisations that were exploding through her.

'Almer Hall will be unencumbered. All you have to do is say the word.'

'And you'll call my bank and pay millions more pounds, just so I'll make love to you until you decide you don't want me?' She whirled around, grabbing onto her fury with both hands, glad to have it, infinitely glad to feel it, needing its barren echo to rattle her into sense. 'And if I want more? Credit cards? Dresses? Diamonds?'

His eyes widened for a moment and then he shrugged, his expression so loaded with determination that her heart swelled in pain for him. How little did he value himself to think such luxuries would ever be necessary?

'If you wish.'

'No, damn it!' She waved her hand through the air emphatically and his eyes followed the gesture, watching her in the way he had that was so intense it was like a caress.

'Damn it.' She groaned again. 'Do you really think I want *any* of that?'

'You have told me how much Almer Hall means to you,' he said quietly.

'I know!' Fury eclipsed everything else. She spun away from him, staring at the ocean, its endless rolling towards the shore something from which she would ordinarily have taken reassurance. But she didn't. Not then. She couldn't.

'And that you would use that knowledge to blackmail... after everything...'

'It's not blackmail,' he denied. 'This is me giving you what you want, and us both getting what I think we need: more time together.'

'And if I let you do this, you'd be proved right in what you said last night, and I will never let you think me capable of that.'

She wasn't looking at him, so didn't see the surprise that crossed his features.

'This wasn't about the hedge fund for me, Cesare. I meant that. I simply wanted to be with you, and I still do.'

His exhalation of breath spoke of relief, but she whirled around to look at him then, grief in every line of her body.

'But you'll never give me what I really want, and spending another night with you, knowing what your limits are, knowing what you think of me…' Her voice cracked and she had to pause to take a breath and calm her breaking heart. 'It's not possible. It would be hell on earth.'

But he wasn't ready to let this go. 'I've just told you I will give you anything.'

'Not this.'

'What? What do you want?' He moved towards her, and she flinched, not out of fear of him so much as a fear of how readily she could weaken and give in, just to have more time with him. That alone was a reason to stand firm, to hold her ground, because it would destroy her to spend more time with him under these conditions.

'I want more.'

'Sì, uccellina.'

His eyes scanned her face and her heart turned over because she truly believed that, in that moment, he would have acceded to whatever demand of him she wished to make. So long as it was within his financial means, at least.

She lifted a hand to her chest, her features showing heartbreak. 'I want this to be real.' She felt his chest tighten. Her voice was hoarse with unshed tears. 'I want to wake up beside you without the phantom ticking of a time bomb as the end draws nearer. I want to wake up beside you every morning for the rest of our lives.' She swallowed, shocked at how important it felt to say this, even as she saw disbelief etch itself across his face. 'I want you to love me like I love you,' she whispered, and even then she hoped. She hoped when there was no reason to because that was the transformative power love held.

She stared at him, her breath held, her eyes huge, and she waited.

And finally he said what she'd known he would. That didn't stop it from hurting, though.

'It's not possible.'

'Why not?' she challenged, her eyes determined even as they filled with tears.

He stayed perfectly still, except for nostrils which flared as he exhaled through them, slowly, as if he was trying to calm his temper. 'I am offering you something very clear. The same thing I've offered all along. Sex. Fun. Full stop.'

'No.' She denied this. 'You really think that's what we've been doing?'

At least he had the decency not to rush into agreement. 'There are limits to this. Limits to the time we will spend together, limits to what I can offer you. There are boundaries and rules, and that's good for both of us.'

'Not for me,' she returned insistently. 'I don't want boundaries with you. I want to tear them down and revel in all of you, all the time.' She lifted up onto the tips of her toes, so her lips were only an inch or so from his. 'Tell me you don't feel the same way.'

He didn't move, and her heart slammed into her ribs and desperate hope overtook her every nerve ending.

'When my mother died, I swore I would earn my fortune. I swore I would devote my life to that, to making something of myself. It is the only thing I have ever wanted, Jemima. Relationships aren't a part of who I am. I made this decision a long time ago, and nothing—no one—will change my mind.' He lifted his hands to cup her face then, holding her right where she was, so his eyes could devour every detail of her features. 'You are not like any woman I have ever known, and if I was ever going to put that rule aside it would be for you.' He padded his thumb over her lip. 'But it's not what I want.'

'*I'm* not what you want,' she corrected.

'I do,' he corrected. 'I want you, just not in that way.' She sucked in a harsh breath that spoke of her pain, but he continued regardless. 'I want what we have now. I want it for a little while longer, and then I want us to look one another in the eyes, to smile and to say goodbye and thank you, knowing we will never see each other again, but that these memories will always be with us. Can't you see how right that is? How good?'

Her chest ached. 'Leaving you will never feel right. Now, or in a month—never. I'm in love with you, Cesare. There's no sense, no reason, no sensible, calm, rational end-point to this for me. I love you. I want to spend my life with you. I want to, I don't know, have a family with you.' The words weren't planned, but as soon as she said them they felt completely true in her soul. 'I want to grow old with you at my side. I just want you.'

His expression was laced with shock. 'This has *never* been on my radar.'

She swept her eyes shut. 'I didn't know it was on mine until a moment ago. But I do know it, Cesare. In every bone in my body, I know how I feel, and I know that I love you and that I can't stay with you another moment if there's no hope that you might love me back.'

'There's not.' The words cracked around her. 'Listen to me.' His voice was gentler then, an attempt to soften the sticks of dynamite he'd thrown into the room. 'You don't love me. It's completely understandable that you do, but that's just your inexperience showing. You love sex.' His lips twisted in something like amusement and her fingertips ached to slap him.

'How dare you?' She shook her head. 'Don't diminish what I feel. I know the difference between lust and love.'

'Do you? How?'

Her temper spiked. 'Lust is what I felt for you that night in London, when you kissed me in the restaurant, when you took my virginity. Lust is what I felt when you made my body yours, when you filled me with desire for the first time. Love is what I felt when you showed me what's in here.' She pushed at his chest. 'When you talked about your mother and your childhood and your business and your life. Love is what I felt when you asked me about *my* life, when you saw beyond the fact I'm Jemima Woodcroft and wanted to know what made me tick. Love is what I felt, night after night, as you held me in your arms and kissed me with a gentleness that came from deep within your soul.'

His features were like ice. 'Jemima...' She waited for him to speak, but he said nothing. He simply stared at her for so long that her lungs hurt, because she was holding her breath and waiting, needing him to say something that would make all this better.

'I think you love me, too,' she whispered, and she felt as though she were stepping so far out on a limb that it was creaking audibly. 'You keep saying I'm different from any woman you've ever known. You spent half a billion pounds to get me into bed and you want me to stay another month. How do you know that will be enough? How do you know we won't be having this same conversation in a month's time?'

'Because I have decided what I want, and I'll stick to it this time.'

She shook her head, sorrow for him rippling through her soul. 'You can't just switch your feelings off like that, Cesare. You want me in your life, and you know you do.' She couldn't let this go. She needed him to see that they were both in love. 'You spent half a billion pounds because you couldn't risk that I'd say no to you.'

His eyes swirled with darkness and he took a step back from her, his face angular, his look somehow distant. 'I had already ordered my lawyers to buy into the hedge fund. Getting you in bed was just the cherry on top.'

His words made no sense. She shook her head, disputing them. 'No, you hadn't. You told me you wouldn't, remember? Unless I came away with you.'

'I lied.' His eyes glowed when they met hers. 'I lied to get what I wanted—you. I leveraged what I could, knowing that you would do anything for your cousin.'

She gaped, none of it making sense.

'This is the man you think you love. This is what I'm capable of.'

She lifted her fingers to her lips, shaking her head. 'But why?'

'Because I couldn't risk that you wouldn't agree. Not because I love you, but because I wanted you, and I succeed at all costs, always.'

She ignored his admission and the wounds it inflicted. 'I mean, why did you buy such a huge share of the hedge fund? I know it wasn't altruism. And if it wasn't for me, then what was it?'

He shifted his eyes above her head for a moment then pinned her with a steely glance. 'Your cousin is sitting on a gold mine and he doesn't yet realise it. The five hundred million pounds I spent will be worth a billion by the end of the year, easily.'

Her knees felt weak. 'What?' It was hoarse. Soft. So soft it was almost inaudible, but he heard because he replied.

'When it comes to business, if not people, I do my research. I knew what he had that night in the restaurant. You were always just a silver lining to that deal. I don't let business and pleasure get mixed up.'

She closed her eyes, wanting to blot out the world, but he was relentless.

'See? You do not love me, right? How could you?'

Her heart splintered for him because she saw the truth so clearly now—the little boy who'd grown into a man who believed all he had to offer was money. Who believed that maybe his mother would have loved him more if she could have seen the wealth he'd amassed. A man who ended things with women before they could walk out on him.

'In spite of this, I love you. In spite of the fact I am hurt, and feel betrayed and used and cheap, I still love you.' She bit down on her lip, the truth of her words etching into her. Saying it was so liberating, so freeing.

'And yet you knew I would never love you back.'

'No,' she whispered, her eyes haunted.

'Yes. I have told you exactly what kind of man I am, what I'm capable of, and you ignored that.'

'You're wrong. I know what you've said about yourself, but I see you as you really are. I see someone you don't even know is there.' She lifted her chin defiantly, her body tense with pride even when her heart was in shreds.

But he shook his head, denying that. 'You only think you do.'

'Cesare…' She sighed softly. 'You've spent a lifetime trying to outrun your roots. You think that if you work harder, make more money, fill your bank account, your asset list or whatever, that you'll finally feel okay? That you'll feel whole?'

She stared him down and saw the shift in his expression, the hardening in his eyes, and she knew he wasn't going to listen to her, that no matter what she said he was determined to stay the course.

'Why did you get your tattoo?' she pushed. '*Come sono*—"as I am".' His surprise was obvious. 'You are as you are and I love you as you are.' She waved a hand around the magnificent beach house. 'None of this matters to me. There's an inherent value in *you*, just you, and I see it even if you don't.'

A muscle jerked in his jaw. 'You're wrong about me.'

'No, I'm not. You're a good man—'

'I mean you're wrong to think I'm broken in some way, or that I don't feel whole. I live my life the way I choose. I do what I want.'

'And that's not me.'

He swept his eyes shut.

'I don't mean for a month,' she added quickly. 'I mean for ever.'

He fixed her with a cool gaze, as though this were easy for him. 'No, Jemima. I could lie to you right now and pretend, just to get more time with you, but I won't do that. This is what I'm offering—the decision is yours.'

She nodded, anguish making her face pale.

'It's not a decision,' she whispered. 'I have to go. I can't stay.'

Neither of them moved or spoke for several seconds, and then she said again more urgently, because she felt as though she were suffocating, 'I have to go, Cesare, please.'

But he shook his head, disbelief etched in his features. 'No.'

Her laugh was dry, lacking any humour. 'You just said it was my decision.'

'Stay a week,' he implored, his voice thick. 'Same terms. All your debts disappear.'

She sobbed. 'Don't.' She lifted a finger to his lips. 'You aren't this man.'

He stared into her eyes.

'You aren't this man, and I'm not that woman,' she insisted. 'You're so much better than this.'

CHAPTER THIRTEEN

HE WAS CONSCIOUS of the date from the moment he opened his eyes. Four weeks to the day after Jemima had walked out of his life, he woke to the realisation this should have been the day they ended it. If she'd agreed to his proposition, then they'd have been together this whole time.

Instead, he'd acceded to her wishes, knowing it was the right thing to do even when every fibre of his being had wanted to insist she finish the fortnight, just as she'd promised; that she give him one more night. Instead, he'd flown her by helicopter to the mainland and had his jet fuelled up to take her back to England. He hadn't travelled with her. It would have felt like prolonging the inevitable.

Besides, she'd barely been able to look at him at the end.

So much for love.

Was it love that could make you push someone away like this?

He stared out at the lake, still as anything, with a mystical layer of fog hovering just above the water on this cool early autumn morning, a scowl on his face as he relived every moment of that last day. Her face pinched and uncertain, her eyes so filled with hurt and disappointment, and worst of all, his inability to say or do anything to fix it.

For the first time in his adult life, Cesare Durante had been without adequate words. He'd wanted to reassure her even when he knew he couldn't—because what could he offer her? Not love.

And that was all she'd wanted. She'd been very clear.

With a sound of frustration, he pushed up from the deck chair, moving into the old log cabin. The morning was cool, but he wore low-riding jeans. No top. He liked the cold. He was glad of it. Glad of the rush it gave his blood, as well as the feeling of being alive, alive in a way he seemed to crave these days.

He made a coffee, thick and black, and poured it into one of the enamel cups his Alaskan cabin had come furnished with.

He drank it quickly, then turned his gaze back to the lake.

He needed to run. To run faster than he had the day before. He hadn't been able to outrun his thoughts then, but maybe today? Pausing only to pull on a crisp white shirt and a pair of joggers, he shouldered out of the door and set off around the lake.

He couldn't outrun her. She was a fog in his brain, filling his mind, taking over his every thought. Except it wasn't her. It wasn't Jemima so much as the fact he knew how wrong he'd been, and he hated that. He hated knowing he'd been at fault, and worse that he'd hurt her. He'd lied to her to get her to agree to be his mistress. He'd blackmailed her with her cousin's future and wellbeing. Then he'd tried to blackmail her all over again, just for good measure.

His behaviour had been deplorable.

He growled and ran faster...*thud, thud, thud.* A twig cracked beneath his foot. He kept running, his head bent low. He ran and he ran and he didn't look where he was going so that he was almost on top of the grizzly bear when he saw it.

He froze, his pulse firing up a notch, his instincts kicking in. Adrenalin sent a metallic taste into his mouth and his eyes flew wide. The bear was eating a fish, ripping it in half, but as Cesare stood there the grizzly turned its formidable head, its dark-brown eyes turning to study him.

He was metres away from a beast that was more than capable of ripping him to shreds. He should run. Retreat. Do something. Anything.

Save himself.

He didn't. He stared at the bear, his expression grim, and not particularly sure he cared what the hell happened to his pathetic excuse for a life. He stared at the bear and saw himself, saw himself clearly. He saw the path he was on, the life he was willingly choosing, and he almost willed the bear to come at him.

Because there was surely no point to life if you lived it as he did?

The thought was brief and fleeting and completely startling. He stared at the bear, the bear stared back and then, remarkably, it shrugged its shoulders, turned and began to thump heavily away in the opposite direction.

Cesare stood perfectly still, watching the bear go, no longer willing to be his quarry. He stared at the bear's retreat and a new sense of purpose filled him.

'Come on, Jem. You're all dressed up. You can't bail now.'

Jemima eyed Laurence without reacting. He was right. In the suite of this fine London hotel, in a vintage gown she'd fallen in love with years ago, she knew she couldn't let Laurence down. Even when all she wanted to do was curl up on the huge bed and stare at the wall.

Just as she'd been doing for five weeks.

Five weeks?

It felt like five years.

When Cam had died, someone had told her that time healed all wounds, and she'd clung to that as a child. She'd truly believed that she might feel less pain as time went on. And in some ways, she had. She thought of her brother every day, she wondered what his life would have been like if he'd lived, but she didn't cry like she used to. Now, she thought of him with a smile, remembering all the ways he'd made her laugh.

Would it be like that with Cesare? Would she one day be able to disentangle this pervasive sense of hurt from all the lovely memories she had? Would she be able to cherry-pick her way through their time together and see only the parts she wished to recall?

'He's not going to be here,' Laurence chided gently. 'I spoke to his secretary a week ago and she was adamant he couldn't make it. You're not going to run into him at the party.'

Jemima's eyes shifted to Laurence's. She'd been selective in what she'd told him about her time with Cesare. 'A fling,' was how she'd described it. 'Just a fun way to pass some time.' It had taken every scrap of energy she had to present a brave face to Laurence, but she was glad she'd done it.

She didn't want him bearing even a hint of guilt over this—he deserved none, but she knew he'd feel it regardless.

'I don't care if he is,' she lied haltingly.

'Sure you don't.' Laurence's laugh was sympathetic. 'Come on. Come for an hour. Drink some champagne. Dance. Be happy, please.'

Her heart turned over in her chest. 'Am I really so bad?'

'You're miserable,' he said earnestly, so handsome in his tuxedo. He lifted a hand and brushed her cheek. 'This is our triumph. I want you there with me. It wouldn't feel right without you.'

She smiled, but her chest was hollow because the celebration was, for Jemima at least, tainted by the knowledge she was privy to.

Cesare had, of course, been right. Two weeks after she'd

returned from Isola Giada, Laurence had called, out of breath with excitement, to say one of the Silicon Valley tech companies in which he'd invested twelve months earlier had just gone viral—its worth had trebled.

She had no idea how Cesare had foreseen that, but he had. He'd known that night at dinner, and he'd known four weeks later when she'd gone to him and begged him to follow through with the purchase.

He'd used her, and the worst of it was he'd told her as much. Not in so many words, but again and again he'd talked about his desire to win, to succeed at all costs, and she hadn't seen that as a warning—she hadn't heeded it at all.

Even knowing that, she couldn't shake her grief. Because it didn't change a damn thing.

She loved him.

One deed didn't define a person.

Besides, she felt an overarching sadness for him. A sadness that he wouldn't see how much he had to offer. He should have asked her out on a date and she'd have said yes.

Except he hadn't wanted to date her. He hadn't wanted anything other than sex, she reminded herself firmly.

'One hour,' Laurence promised, putting a hand on Jemima's back and gently propelling her to the door.

She swallowed, wishing she could tell him she really would prefer to stay on her own, as she had been for five long weeks.

But Laurence was right. This would be good for her, and at some point she had to stop being a hermit and get back into the swing of things.

'He definitely won't be there?'

Laurence stopped walking, his expression showing more sympathy, so she tried to paste a bright smile to her face.

'What did that bastard do to you?'

'Nothing,' she muttered, shaking her head. She'd styled

her hair into a chignon, but her fringe fell over one eye. 'It would just be kind of awkward, that's all.'

'He won't be there.' Laurence's tone showed he wasn't buying her act.

She needed to try harder. 'Okay. Let's go.'

Pausing to check her lipstick in the mirror and grab her clutch, she slipped her arm into the crook of Laurence's. They were on one of the top floors of the hotel, and the ballroom was several floors down. The lift hurtled them there with elegant efficiency, and as soon as the doors opened the noise was deafening. A band was playing crooning jazz songs, and at least two hundred guests were packed into the beautiful, historical room.

Jemima stopped walking, her heart in her throat.

'What is it?' He was so solicitous, she felt like a complete cow for how self-absorbed she'd been. Even his triumph had become about her.

'Laurence, I'm really so proud of you. Look at what you've done.' She gestured towards the ballroom. 'You said you were onto a winner and you were right.' She smiled at him, then lifted up to press a kiss against his cheek.

He grinned, lopsided and so handsome, reminding her for a second of Cam with his cheeky eyes. 'Thanks, Jem.'

The party was filled with investors, some of Europe's wealthiest business people milling about in couture, chatting loudly. But Jemima was internationally known, and her entrance caused a different kind of stir. She was conscious of the eyes that followed her around. She was used to that kind of attention, but she hadn't banked on how difficult it would be to keep up the veneer of happiness, knowing that she was being watched. Fortunately, she found a friend of Laurence's she knew quite well and latched onto him, keeping the conversation light and superficial, so her mind was barely engaged.

When he asked her to dance, she agreed, if only because it would take a few more minutes out of the hour she'd promised Laurence, and she desperately wanted it to be over.

She was weary beyond bearing.

He watched her until he couldn't bear it. He watched her dance, smile, her eyes lifting to whoever the hell was holding her so close to his goddamned body, and he gripped his hands into fists at his side, his expression like thunder so that no one dared approach him. He watched her and he felt as though he was going to punch someone or something.

Fury lashed at his spine, but he knew he didn't have any right to feel like this. He'd told her there was no hope for them. He'd sent her away rather than admit there was any possibility they could be more to one another.

This was his choice. All of it.

He watched her dance and felt as though he was being lit on fire.

With a growl, he stalked from the ballroom, pressing his back to the darkly painted wall opposite, his eyes trained on the door.

He would stand here and he would wait. God help him if she emerged with the other man. What if they were seeing each other? Sleeping together?

His fist pumped. Insanity seemed to burst inside him.

He could picture her body, but never with any one else. It wasn't possible.

Time dragged. He contemplated going back into the party, but he knew it wasn't wise. If she was still dancing with the guy—hell, kissing him—then he wasn't sure he could contain his reaction.

And so he waited, the burgundy carpet of the hotel somehow irritating even though it was an inanimate object.

He waited, and every time the doors opened he leaned

forward, away from the wall. The first time it was a couple, too busy making out to notice he was there. The next time it was an elderly man, hobbling with the aid of a cane towards the lifts. Then, another couple, and following that a mother with a small child.

When the door next opened, he didn't hold any hope, which made it all the more shocking to see her.

He stood straight, his eyes drinking her in. She was alone. His body rejoiced. But she was miserable. His insides rolled. She looked…

Broken.

The word breathed through him accusingly. He stayed exactly where he was, watching as she walked past, her head dipped forward, her forehead crinkled, her eyebrows knitted together, her expression so completely distracted. She sashayed as though she were on a catwalk, but he knew her well enough to know it wasn't intentional. She wasn't even conscious that she did that—it was an ingrained elegance she carried with her all the time.

God, he knew that about her, and everything else.

Why hadn't he realised what was happening? How come he hadn't realised that every night they'd spent together had embedded a part of her inside him?

She'd realised. She'd known. And she'd tried to make him understand that, but he'd been so damned determined.

She stopped walking and he held his breath. She stopped walking and stood perfectly still, her head bent, and then she shook it slowly from side to side before starting to walk once more.

His chest lurched.

She approached the lift, pressed her finger to the button and then stepped back. Only once the doors opened and she disappeared inside did he move. His stride was long and urgency propelled him to move quickly. Nonetheless, he only just made it, sliding his fingers into the steel doors as they were almost completely closed. They sprang open, and Jemima lifted her gaze slowly, and then made a groaning noise, shaking her head and stepping backward, as if he was the last person she'd expected to see.

His breath was ragged, torn from him. He stared at her for several long seconds and she stared back. And then she shook her head, as though she could send him away, or maybe pretend he didn't exist. Keeping his eyes on her, he swiped his key against the dashboard and pressed the button for the top floor. She stayed right where she was, staring at him, her features tight, her eyes heavy on his face.

The lift lurched to life. She lifted her hands and curled them around the railing, as though she might fall.

'Is it you?'

His gut churned.

'I don't… You're not… You weren't going to be here.'

Her words rang with accusation. He bit back a curse. He hadn't planned to come. He hadn't, for a second, thought she would know that, nor that she'd make her plans around it.

Had she chosen to attend the celebration because she thought he wouldn't be there?

Could he blame her?

'Change of plans.'

'Oh.' She nodded, frowning, and jerked her head towards the control panel. 'Can you press number twelve, please?'

He thought about refusing. He thought about lifting her against him and holding her until the lift stopped at his floor, carrying her into his room, placing her down on the floor in front of him and talking to her until she understood.

But he'd done enough damage here. This was about fixing things, not making them worse.

He jabbed his finger into the button, and the lift stopped almost immediately, the doors pinging open.

She pushed up from the back of the lift. 'Excuse me.' He stepped out of the lift to make way for her, keeping his hand against the doors for her.

She moved past without looking at him, her back ramrod-straight, her shoulders squared, and he felt a lurch of self-disgust. She was hurting because of him. He watched her for several seconds with a growing sense of consternation and then he began to move after her. She didn't realise until she reached her hotel door, perhaps sensing he was still there, a safe distance behind her.

She whirled around, and now when she spoke her voice was infused with an almost primal frustration. 'What are you doing, Cesare? Why are you here?'

She was hurting, and it was because of him. He closed the distance between them, but didn't touch her. He couldn't. He had no right. 'I came to see you.' The admission was gruff.

'No.' She spat the word at him emphatically. 'Absolutely not.'

'Just to talk,' he said gently, even as panic was spreading through him. 'For a moment.'

'No.' A whisper now, hollowed out.

'Please.' His voice rang with urgency, and her head jerked a little, disbelief in her features. She was going to say no, and God, what would he do then?

He'd come here knowing she might tell him to go to hell, and he had his answer prepared: he was already there.

But Jemima wasn't like that. She didn't have it in her. She was entirely decent and kind, and far fairer than he deserved.

'Two minutes,' she said firmly, pushing the door open and giving him a wide berth. 'And then you get the heck away from me.'

CHAPTER FOURTEEN

'I'M NOT KIDDING, Cesare. Two minutes. Stop standing there and tell me what you want.'

She was shaking like a leaf. She just hoped he couldn't tell. There was a part of her that was terrified she'd hallucinated him. She'd been thinking of him as she'd left the party. Dancing in another man's arms had made her ache for him in a way that had blindsided her.

And then, all of a sudden, he was in the lift with her, surrounding her with his masculine scent, filling her tummy with butterflies and her veins with flame, and all she'd wanted to do was hurl herself at him and tell him she'd do whatever he wanted if it meant she got a little more time with him. Thank God she hadn't. Thank God she remembered what the last five weeks had been like—no way could she do anything that would set her back.

She crossed her arms over her chest, glaring at him with all the emotional energy she felt, deep in her body.

'How are you?'

She rolled her eyes. 'Fine. Is that it?'

'No.' He moved closer, and she started turning away from him, stalking deeper into her hotel room. She flicked the kettle on and stayed near it, bracing herself in the small kitchen.

'I wanted to see you.'

Something inside her snapped. Her self-control, her temper, something.

'It's been *five weeks*,' she almost shouted.

'I'm aware of that.' His Adam's apple bobbed as he swallowed.

'So what do you want?' She grabbed for a tea cup, slamming it down noisily on the marble bench. 'Let me guess. If I have sex with you tonight you'll give me—what?—a diamond necklace? An Italian villa? What exactly is my price these days?'

He visibly winced, and that empowered her. She liked it. 'Or do you want two nights? Three? It'd cost more for that, you know. At least an aeroplane.' She tore the top off a tea-bag envelope, shooting him a furious glance as she upended the bag into the mug.

'You have every right to be angry,' he said quietly, and his calmness was like fuel being doused over her fire.

'Damn straight I do! I don't want you to be here! I didn't want to see you again! For five weeks I have felt... I've been...' She shook her head—there were no words that would do justice to how she'd felt. 'And now you're here, looking at me like—I don't even know—and I just... I can't do this. Do you have any idea what this is like? What these five weeks have been like?' She swallowed, her throat thick and dry. 'Please, just leave me alone.' Tears streamed down her cheeks. She reached for the kettle, filling the mug and gratefully lifting it towards her lips.

'And I will,' he promised, moving to the other side of the kitchen bench. She was glad there was some distance between them. She needed that in order to be able to think.

'Please just go.'

'I have one minute left.'

Strength rallied in her core, so she glared at him. 'So use it.'

'I don't know what it's been like for you, but I can tell you what it's been like for me.'

She didn't want to hear, though. She shook her head, sipping her boiling-hot tea, her body barely able to contain her blood, it was rushing so hard and fast.

'I went to Alaska. To work. To think. To make sure I didn't weaken and contact you. There's no phone service there, and you were a million miles away from me. I went to forget you, and instead Alaska became an echo chamber of my thoughts and wants. You were everywhere I looked—in my dreams, my head, my blood, my body—and I needed, simply, to hold you.'

She ground her teeth together, refusing to be placated by his words. 'Like I said, one last night? What's my price?'

He flinched. 'You have no price. You can't be bought. Money had nothing to do with us, with what we were. You knew that all along, and perhaps I did too, on some level, but it comforted me to see a commercial aspect to our arrangement. Commerce I am familiar with and good at. If we were simply a different kind of business deal, I could understand how to get you out of my head. I thought I'd be able to work to the terms we'd agreed, just like any other deal. But I was so wrong.'

Against her will, without her permission, his words seeped under her skin a little. She shook her head, physically rejecting the sentiment. 'No way.'

'No?'

'You can't come here after five weeks, after that last day, and say this and think it makes a damn bit of difference.'

He jerked his head in a silent nod and jagged his fingers in his hair in a gesture that was sheer panic. Good. He should panic!

She sipped her tea. 'Thirty seconds.'

'*Christo*, I'm trying.'

'I'm not messing around, Cesare. You haven't said anything that makes me want to hear more.'

'I was mad with wanting you after that first night. When you came to my office, I saw an opportunity. That's what I'm good at. I see weakness, I exploit it. Your love for your cousin was something I perceived as a weakness, because I'd never really known love like it. I've never known loyalty like it. I couldn't understand what you felt, what motivated you, and so I couldn't see, then, how wrong I was to use it to leverage you into my life.'

'Into your bed,' she corrected succinctly, refusing to feel sympathy for him. 'I was never in your life, really.'

'You were my whole life!' The words were animalistic, thrown at her as though everything he was came down to this moment, to her understanding.

But it had been five weeks, and her hurt went too deep to be eased over.

'That's a load of crap. If I was your life, or any part of it, you would never have let me go.'

He opened his mouth to speak, but she shook her head. 'Time's up. It's my turn. You keep all parts of your life in neat little rows. You tried to do that with me, and when you couldn't you let me go, because you would rather not be with me than risk giving me more of you. You have no idea what these five weeks have been like for me, Cesare, or you wouldn't dare show your face to me. I have been in agony. Every moment has been a torment. I have longed for you with every breath in my body. I have woken up in the middle of the night and reached for you. I have seen you everywhere I go. For two weeks I didn't leave my flat. I have been miserable. *Miserable!*' She roared the last word.

The tirade left her feeling exhausted. She glared at him, though, needing to get through this, and then once she was alone she'd give into the full force of the tears that were threatening to engulf her. 'Please leave.'

'I went to Alaska,' he spoke slowly, as though she hadn't said anything. 'And I caught fish and I ran. I ran as though I could escape you, and I never could, because you're in here.' He pressed his fingers to his chest. 'You followed me everywhere I went, and one day I was running, thinking of you, wondering what you were doing—were you thinking of me? Missing me? Did you still love me? Or had that love turned to hate? And I came upon a grizzly bear. At least eight feet tall, dark brown, easily strong enough to snap me in half.'

Her silence was stony even as her heart was compressing painfully in her chest.

'He was no more than a few feet away and, as he turned to look at me, and I knew I was no match for him—no man could be—I thought that maybe if he were to catch me I would at least be out of my misery. At least I could no longer miss you in a way that was driving me completely insane.'

Another gasp.

'You were right, Jemima. You were so right about me. At sixteen, I swore I would make a success of myself. The memory of how poor my mother and I were has stalked me all my life, and I have done everything I could to outstrip it, to ensure I don't get dragged back into that life. For twenty years I have worked almost every day. I have become singularly determined and utterly stupid, all at once. How could I realise the greatest fortune of my life was standing right before me, begging me to see what we were?'

She squeezed her eyes shut, his words rushing through her.

'I have *never* propositioned a woman for sex. I have *never* blackmailed a woman into my bed. And I have spent the last five weeks wondering why the hell I demeaned myself by behaving in such an outrageous way. And, the truth is, I knew from our first meeting that I couldn't live without you. I didn't know how to win you over with any certainty, and failure wasn't an option, so I did what I could.'

He rounded the kitchen bench, lifting his hands to cup her cheeks. 'I didn't know what it was. I didn't know why I felt this way, I didn't know why a beautiful little bird of a woman had begun to monopolise my every thought and dream. *Christo, uccellina*, I get it now—I get it. Please fly back into my world.'

She shook her head, because she didn't know what she wanted or what she could offer. She just felt completely blindsided.

'I will work, every day, to earn back your trust. I will listen to you next time you try to tell me how I feel. I will do whatever you require of me, but please, do not make me leave now.'

She lifted her face to his, staring at him with a frown on her face. 'I only ever wanted one thing from you.' She spoke quietly, softly. 'I wanted to love you. It was simple, really.'

'No one's ever loved me,' he said. 'So, to me, it wasn't simple. It was terrifying.'

'Why?' She shook her head, still fighting him, fighting this, even when her heart and body wanted her to surrender to what he was offering.

'I have had a long time to think about that, too.' He moved to her again, and she didn't step away. 'My mother almost lost her job because of me. As a child, one day I got into a fight with one of the children she cared for and, when I was disciplined and he was not, I went to the tennis court and I chipped up the grass, right in the middle.' He winced. 'I was sent away to boarding school—my mother's boss pulled some strings and got me a scholarship. I was only a little boy still and the bottom fell out of my world.'

Jemima sucked in a deep breath of air.

'I was made very aware of the fact that I was there by the good grace of the school. If my grades slipped, even a little, I was out. I didn't feel I was welcome at the house my mother worked at—I had no home, and no one. And so I devoted myself to my studies. I worked harder than anyone else at school, and have done all my life. And then I poured that into business. It's driven by a need to succeed, *certamente*, but more than that it's a fear I have, deep down, that if I don't do everything right, everything's going to fall apart.'

He cupped her cheeks. 'No one has ever wanted me for *me*, Jemima. It has been my grades and then my wealth— what I can offer. You are the first person to see me as valuable for who I am, and do you know how terrifying that is? You offered me so much—your beautiful, kind heart—and yet what if I don't deserve it? What if you realise that and I lose you? I don't know how to keep you.'

She sobbed then, a sob for her own sadness, but mostly for his, for the little boy he'd been who'd ceased to recognise his own value. 'Do you love me?'

He lifted his head, a frown on his face. 'Isn't it obvious?'

She smiled, because it was, yet she needed him to say it. 'Not to me.'

'I love you, *sì*. I have loved you, I think, for as long as I have known you.'

'Then keep loving me and you will never lose me.' She lifted up onto her tiptoes so she could brush her lips against his cheeks. 'And don't ever, ever hurt me like that again.'

He grabbed her shoulders, holding her away from him a little so he could look at her properly.

'I won't.' It was so simple, so *him*, and she believed him.

She closed her eyes for a moment, letting the truth of this wash over her.

'I love you,' he said simply. 'And I am terrified that one day you will decide you don't love me. But if the alternative is that I go and wave myself around in front of grizzly bears, then I would rather take this risk, throw myself at your feet and beg you to love me for as long as that good heart of yours can bear.'

'I will love you for ever,' she promised, wrapping her arms around his waist. 'Because that's exactly what you deserve.'

Their kiss swallowed most of his groan.

'You'll marry me?'

She laughed, because it was so like him to ask in such a manner, but she nodded anyway, smiling up at him. 'As soon as humanly possible.'

His eyes flared. 'Done.'

'On one condition.'

He stilled, wariness in him, and she ached to wipe that away. But she knew only a lifetime of being loved and accepted would do that. She smiled, so he knew she was joking, and he relaxed.

'Name it.'

'No way will my husband be able to work the hours you do. I expect you to take weekends off, at least.'

He grinned. 'I'm going to spend at least the first year of our marriage working from home. And even then, only sparingly. I have executives, you know, and a very wise woman once suggested I should delegate a little more freely.'

'She sounds inspired.' Jemima batted her lashes.

'She is perfect, in every way.'

'And she's all yours, for always.'

* * *

'I have a wedding present for you.'

Jemima stifled a yawn against the back of her hand. It was late. Somewhere around two in the morning. Their wedding, in the gardens of Almer Hall, had been everything she could have wanted. Small, no more than thirty people, in a marquee in the garden surrounded by candles and flowers, it had been low-key and exquisite all at once.

He'd flown them via helicopter back to London, and they were now in his townhouse where she'd come that first night—which felt so very long ago now.

'I don't need anything.'

'I know.'

'Then don't give it to me,' she teased, moving across the carpeted room and brushing a kiss against his lips.

He smiled down at her then strode towards the dressing table. He'd taken off his tuxedo jacket and waistcoat and rolled the sleeves of his white shirt up to reveal perfectly tanned forearms that made her mouth go dry with wanting.

'It's something I bought a while ago, as a point of fact. We can call it a gift, rather than a wedding present, if that helps.'

'It doesn't.'

'Well, I cannot return it.' He shrugged and pulled a small white envelope from the drawer.

It was so tiny, perhaps a card or a photo. Nothing of intrinsic value. Curiosity sparked, she extended a hand and he placed the envelope into her fingertips. She slid her finger under the triangular back and pulled out a single sheet of folded paper.

It was the deed for Almer Hall.

'I don't understand.'

He came to stand beside her and pointed to a line at the bottom. *Unencumbered.*

A shiver ran along her spine. She lifted her gaze to his face, incredulity on her features. 'Cesare…' Her voice held warning.

But he pressed a finger to her lips, silencing her, and dropped his hand to another line on the deed. Her eyes followed the gesture and it was then that she read the date— the very same day she'd left the island.

'You did this after we fought?' she whispered, emotions rioting beneath her skin.

'I did it before I propositioned you,' he said. 'I had no intention of leaving your family property debt-ridden once I knew the extent of your worries. I wanted you to stay with me, but I was always going to do this. No matter what.'

Tears filled her eyes. He shook his head gently. 'No more tears, Jemima. This is good news. Your parents don't have to worry. You don't have to worry.'

'I know.' She still couldn't make sense of this. 'So you did this *before* you spoke to me?'

'I think even I knew I was going too far,' he grunted.

'Well, I guess that's something.' She looked at the paper again. 'You didn't have to do this.'

He frowned. 'Yes, I did. You needed help, and I could give it.'

Her heart turned over in her chest.

'Anyway, we are family, and one day our children will want to see their family home.'

'Look at you, taking to the aristocratic lifestyle,' she teased.

'Never!' He laughed, pulling her to his body, and she couldn't help think how well they fit together. His lips claimed hers and she sighed, surrendering to his kiss most willingly. But when his hands found the waistband of her simple going-away outfit, she pulled away from him.

'Hang on,' she murmured. 'I happen to have a wedding present for you, too.'

'Oh?' He lifted his brows enquiringly.

'But it's not ready yet. It's on back order. It won't be delivered for around seven months or so.'

'What is it?'

'I don't know for sure,' she said, tilting her head to one side.

'My beautiful Mrs Durante, you are making no sense.'

'Aren't I?'

'Something you've ordered, but you don't know what it is?'

'Oh, I didn't order it.' She batted her lashes. 'I think it was more your doing than mine.'

'I don't...'

And then, as comprehension dawned, his hands rushed to cover her stomach. 'You're not...do you mean...?'

She dipped her head forward, pressing her brow to his flat chest. 'Yep.' And then she jerked her face towards his, trying to read his expression. 'Is that... Are you...happy?'

He stared at her, bemused. 'Am I happy?'

She waited, her breath held, her body perfectly still.

'In one night, I have gained as my wife the woman I am head over heels in love with, and now you tell me I am going to become a father? *Sì*, I am happy. I am happier than I ever thought I would be, and it is all because of you. Everything good in this world is because of you, *uccellina*.'

* * * * *

MILLS & BOON

Coming next month

THE SCANDAL BEHIND THE ITALIAN'S WEDDING
Millie Adams

"Why did you do it, Minerva?"

"I am sorry. I really didn't do it to cause you trouble. But I'm being threatened, and so is Isabella, and in order to protect us both I needed to come up with an alternative paternity story."

"An alternative paternity story?"

She winced. "Yes. Her father is after her."

He eyed her with great skepticism. "I didn't think you knew who her father was."

She didn't know whether to be shocked, offended or pleased that he thought her capable of having an anonymous interlude.

For heaven's sake, she'd only ever been kissed one time in her life. A regrettable evening out with Katie in Rome where she'd tried to enjoy the pulsing music in the club, but had instead felt overheated and on the verge of a seizure.

She'd danced with a man in a shiny shirt—and she even knew his name because she wouldn't even dance with a man without an introduction—and he'd kissed her on the dance floor. It had been wet and he'd tasted of liquor and she'd feigned a headache after and taken a cab back to the hostel they'd been staying in.

The idea of hooking up with someone, in a circumstance like that, made her want to peel her own skin off.

"Of course I know who he is. Unfortunately… The full implications of who he is did not become clear until later."

"What does that mean?"

She could tell him the truth now, but something stopped her. Maybe it was admitting Isabella wasn't her daughter, which always caught her in the chest and made her feel small. Like she'd stolen her and like what they had was potentially fragile, temporary and shaky.

Or maybe it was trust. Dante was a good man. Going off the fact he had rescued her from a fall, and helped her up when her knee was skinned, and bailed her out after her terrible humiliation in high school.

But to trust him with the truth was something she simply wasn't brave enough to do.

Her life, Isabella's life, was at risk, and she'd lied on live stream in front of the world.

Her bravery was tapped out.

"Her father is part of an organized crime family. Obviously something unknown to me at the time of her...you know. And he's after her. He's after us."

"Are you telling me that you're in actual danger?"

"Yes. And really, the only hope I have is convincing him that he isn't actually the father."

"And you think that will work?"

"It's the only choice I have. I need your protection."

He regarded her with dark, fathomless eyes, and yet again, she felt like he was peering at her as though she were a girl, and not a woman at all. A naughty child, in point of fact. Then something in his expression shifted.

It shamed her a little that this was so like when he'd come to her rescue at the party. That she was manipulating his pity for her. Her own pathetic nature being what called to him, yet again.

But she would lay down any and all pride for Isabella and she'd do it willingly.

"If she were, in fact my child, then we would be family."

"I... I suppose," she said.

"There will need to be photographs of us together, as I would not be a neglectful father."

"No indeed."

"Of course, you know that if Isabella were really my child there would be only one thing for us to do."

"Do I?"

"Yes." He began to pace, like a caged tiger trying to find a weak spot in his cage. And suddenly he stopped, and she had the terrible feeling that the tiger had found what he'd been looking for. "Yes. Of course, there is only one option."

"And that is?"

"You have to marry me."

Continue reading
THE SCANDAL BEHIND THE ITALIAN'S WEDDING
Millie Adams

COMING SOON!

We really hope you enjoyed reading this book. If you're looking for more romance, be sure to head to the shops when new books are available on

Thursday 20th March

To see which titles are coming soon, please visit

millsandboon.co.uk/nextmonth

MILLS & BOON